I0742678

Take Me to Hell

Playing with Demons, Book 1

Sakura Black

Copyright © 2023 by Sakura Black

All rights reserved.

The characters and events portrayed in this book are fictitious. Any similarity to real persons, living or dead, is coincidental and not intended by the author.

No part of this book may be reproduced, or stored in a retrieval system, or transmitted in any form or by any means, electronic, mechanical, photocopying, recording, or otherwise, without express written permission of the publisher or author, except as permitted by U.S. copyright law.

Editor: Lyss Em

Book Cover: Artscandare

Interior Art: Etheric Designs

Contents

Foreword

Thank you for picking up this book.

Just a little word of warning, the book you are about to read contains attempted sexual assault, death of relatives, swearing, violence and steamy scenes. It is intended for mature readers. Head to my author website for the full list of TWs.

I hope you have as much fun reading it as I did writing it!

Chapter 1

Tonight was the night.

Finally.

After years of agonising training, of long hours of study and discipline, of aching fingers and throbbing headaches, of nosebleeds and passing out. It was finally here.

"I can't believe it, Zo," Lyndsey squealed, earthy green eyes wide with excitement. My best friend gripped my shaking hand and squeezed. "We're really going to be initiated! Like *full* coven member status."

I flashed her a smile, trying to stuff my anxiety down as she pulled me along behind her. The carpet of twigs and fallen leaves crackled beneath our feet, accompanying the rich scents of damp soil and sweet wildflowers.

The rest of our coven glided through the enchanting forest, a blend of majestic oaks, elegant beeches, and graceful birches. They followed the luminous path of the full moon, peeking through the entwined branches. We followed in their footsteps, literally and figuratively, as they headed towards our most sacred ritual site.

"Thank fuck. It's not been an easy few weeks since my birthday." My tone came out drier than I'd meant it to, and I offered Lyndsey a grin to soften the stress bleeding through my words.

She squeezed my hand harder. "It's almost over. Now you're the ripe old age of twenty-five like the rest of our initiate group, you can finally stop being a weird hermit in *the library* and come hang out with us all." Her features pinched before she tried to shake it off.

I almost smiled at her affectionate term for my cosy cabin, which was filled with almost as many books as the coven's actual small library. Instead, her brief look of pity had me swallowing back the usual discomfort.

I'd had too much of it over the past decade, let alone the past few weeks of my self-imposed imprisonment. "I can't wait. Just need to avoid the spiked punch until after the ceremony, or I might throw up on Elder Murray's shoes." I chuckled at the mental image, ignoring the unease I always felt whenever I thought of our stern leader.

I'd been with the coven for over a decade, and I could count the number of times I'd seen him smile on one hand.

Lyndsey wrinkled her button nose. "Ew. You can't do that. You'd embarrass our whole intake!"

I smirked, a small part of me relishing the idea of how scandalised my fellow initiates would be, but I'd never do something so reckless. My position in the coven was already on ice so thin I was surprised I hadn't already plummeted to my doom.

Up ahead, warm orange light wove between towering sessile oaks, hugged with an array of pale-green lichens and fluffy liverworts. This deep into the forest, the trees were enormous. They loomed all around me, passing judgement on those who strolled beneath them.

A muted hum burst to life in my mind as I pushed my focus towards the trees, relishing the blossoming connection. A thrill followed in its wake; my affinity powers were finally maturing.

Like most mages, before my twenty-fifth birthday, I'd only been able to perform basic spells. Mostly, I'd just glamoured my lilac eyes blue for my old part-time job in a farm shop outside Quartz Coven territory. Soon, though, I'd be able to tap into my well of magic properly and, after tonight, without fear.

A pang hit me in the chest. I didn't know much about my family's magic except that we were from a line of nature mages. With her animal affinity, my mother had even chosen a familiar to bond with for protection and strength. Though, I guess her grouchy house cat, Onyx, hadn't been much help when she'd needed him the most. After the incident, I'd never even seen him again.

I pushed aside the bitter thoughts before they could resurface. Tonight was a celebration. I wouldn't put a dampener on it by dwelling on the past.

I pressed my thumb into the intricate belladonna design topping my mother's silver ring. The metallic flowers dug into the fleshy pad in a soothing gesture before I spun it around my index finger out of habit.

"So what nature affinity are you hoping to manifest?" Lyndsey asked, but her attention locked firmly elsewhere. She curled a long strand of her moss-green hair around her finger, nibbling on her lower lip.

I followed her gaze.

An unladylike snort escaped me. "Why don't you just ask him out already?" I nudged my shoulder against her arm as we walked, swept forwards with the buzzing crowd.

Fenton skulked through the trees, leading his own gaggle of followers like he was the coven elder himself.

"What? N-No, I couldn't!" Lyndsey shook her head, a blush stealing across her full cheeks. My bestie was catwalk-ready—slim and statuesque, yet her face had kept a youthful curve. She always complained it made her look chubby, but I thought it lessened the harshness of her beauty. She was absolutely stunning.

If only she could see that she was *far* too good for the slimy eel that was Fenton Devon.

I arched a brow. "And why not?"

"He's the coven elder's son," she hissed, voice low as her emerald gaze darted to the other coven members nearby. "Besides, he's so freaking hot. He's out of my league, both physically *and* magically." She sighed, giving Fenton another pining look from her wide doe eyes. "I'm probably going to be blessed with little more than an herbal affinity. I'll be assigned as a glorified farmer, and he's practically magic royalty."

I tried not to take offence at her dismissal of plant mages. In all likelihood, the coven elder would confirm I was one of them too, just with a different specialist subtype from Lyndsey. Like most of her family, my father had a plant affinity, but where they specialised in herbs, his magic had worked best on poisonous plants. They'd all been given roles to tend the coven's valuable flora, just like Lyndsey and I would once we found out what our specific affinities were tonight.

With a frown, I ran my gaze over the supposed "magic royalty" once more.

At six feet, he was above average height for a male in our coven. Like most mages, his eye colour matched his hair, but unlike Lyndsey's earthy green and my light-purple tones, his bronzed hues could easily pass for human.

Fenton had cut his hair in the latest style: short sides and longer on top so he could dramatically run his hand through it and flex his biceps at the same time. I'd seen him use that move on more than one pretty witch over the years. He nailed it every time.

Before he nailed them.

He'd even wear a tight tee that would ride up to show his sexy *V* muscles and the edge of his six-pack abs when he executed said practised manoeuvre.

Tonight he'd dressed up a little more from his usual ripped jeans and band tee ensemble to smart black slacks and a near-see-through dress shirt. I worried for its poor seams. Bulging with lean muscle, the man was in great shape. I'd give Lyndsey that. But other than his steroid-built body and a cheeky smile, he was the worst possible choice as a partner. He'd already left a trail of broken hearts through the witch community, our own coven included.

At twenty-six, he'd only been inducted into the coven as a fully fledged mage for less than a year, but already his mental branch affinity was hot gossip. Like our coven's leader, he was a sin eater—his magic capable of reading your darkest memories and devouring them whole. Rumour said it caused unbearable pain and left a ragged hole in your sanity.

Personally, the idea of losing a few dark memories held a certain allure.

"Lyn, you're powerful in so many ways." I caught her gaze, holding it steady, so she knew I was serious. "Besides, isn't it more useful to grow rare and expensive potion herbs than to occasionally take a bite out of someone's brain? You know how much our coven relies on that income."

Her lips curved slightly, but the longing in her wide eyes didn't budge. I suppressed a sigh. I'd tried, and that was all I could keep doing to support my only real friend. Though, goddesses knew, she was probably getting sick of me repeating the same thing.

"How does it finally feel to be outside?" she asked, quickly changing the subject.

I let it slide. For now.

"Good." I breathed deep, savouring the life all around me—from the rapid buzz of singing crickets to the faint pulse of the ancient oaks, thick and steady, like dripping sap.

I'd barely left my cabin since I'd started maturing into my powers a couple of weeks before my twenty-fifth birthday. Anxiety had sat like a demon on my back, curling wicked claws into my chest and forcing me to carry its weight. Of course, it was incredibly unlikely that the leaking wisps of my affinity magic would attract a hunter's attention, especially on warded coven grounds. I couldn't seem to stuff the paranoia back down into its box though. Instead, I'd distracted myself by re-reading my favourite dark romances—I was a sucker for a devoted bad boy—and scrolling the internet for design inspirations for my next tattoo.

Lyndsey tugged on my hand, hurrying me along even as her eyes softened at whatever she saw on my face. "Are you sure you're OK?"

I swallowed, pushing down the lingering stress and offering a smile. "More than OK. Just counting down the minutes until Elder Murray inducts me into the masking spell."

Most initiates were probably more excited to confirm their magic affinity or find out what job they'd be assigned. What I really craved, though, was the safety that came with being fully initiated. On binding your magic to the communal pool, you were protected by a strong masking spell that drew from the coven's collective power. Afterwards, I'd be able to wander Riverside city freely, knowing my developing magical signature was disguised from anyone trying to track me down. I'd even be able to use my affinity magic outside the coven's territory without fear of discovery.

Lyndsey's soulful green eyes filled with understanding, and she forced a smile right back. "I, for one, am looking forward to getting to access my full powers in a steady stream. Maybe I can be the first mage to successfully brew a love potion." She giggled like it was a joke, but the desperate look she sent Fenton's way sent unease through me.

A few years ago, he'd saved her from a burning building when a house party had raged out of control. She'd had the biggest crush on him ever since.

I didn't blame her. If a handsome man rescued me from a gruesome death, I'd be pretty damn smitten myself. Lately, though, it seemed to have developed into a full-blown obsession, and I wasn't sure what to do to help.

"Stop giving me that look. You're not my mother," Lyndsey said, releasing my hand to flick me on the nose.

I swatted her away with an amused huff. "More like your big sister."

She scoffed. "You're like half my height, Shrimp. Not to mention the youngest in our intake."

I poked my tongue out at the nickname she'd given me when she'd first taken me under her wing as a scrawny, weird teen. "Doesn't mean I can't worry about you. Fenton is bad news."

"You wouldn't understand." She scowled, her temper flaring unusually quick. "He cares about me. It's just not the right time for us yet. You're just jealous because I'm spending time with someone other than you."

Her accusation hit me like a slap.

Before I could recover, she stormed away, lengthening her strides to create a gap between us.

"Lyn!" I called after her, quickening my pace to keep up with her long legs, but she didn't turn back, practically running away from me.

I bit back a sigh, making my way towards the party. Alone. Again.

Chapter 2

Half an hour later, I uncrossed my arms and recrossed them again, leaning back against the sturdy oak with a sigh. Watching other people have fun when you were lurking uncomfortably on the fringes wasn't my idea of a good time. I usually avoided this kind of situation like the plague, but even I wasn't socially awkward enough to skip out on my own initiation celebration.

"Hey, beautiful," a suave, breathy voice whispered in my ear.

I leaped away from the oak sheltering me, heart thudding in my chest as I whirled around.

Fenton flashed me a toothy grin, showcasing his even white teeth. Coven Elder Murray must have paid a pretty penny for them, because I distinctly remembered him having crooked front teeth as a gangly teen.

Up close, the scent of rum and a peppery cologne wafted over me. I couldn't stop my upper lip curling as he forced the overwhelming combination onto me.

"What do you want?" I strived for neutral, but even I could hear the derision in my tone.

I winced internally but refused to simper like others tended to. Enough people already pandered to his ego, and it had only got worse since he'd come into his dangerous affinity power.

"Aw, why you gotta be like that, baby?" he slurred, blinking slowly as his gaze ran down my body.

Everywhere it touched felt like a sticky caress.

Not for the first time, I begrudged our coven's choice of ritual clothing. The guys wore black slacks and a shirt, smart and modern, but they outfitted the women in dresses that seemed just a little too low-cut and short to be appropriate. Especially for an event that bordered on sacred. At least it was long-sleeved, so I didn't have to pretend not to notice the stares. Not many witches got two full tattoo sleeves.

I huffed, crossing my arms over my chest in an effort to dislodge his greedy gaze from my cleavage. "I'm not being like anything. Just minding my own business while I wait for the ceremony to begin."

He leaned in closer, giving me an up-close view of the product shining in his slick bronze hair. I took a step back on instinct. Everything about him set me on edge.

"You're always so cold. Practically frigid." His full lower lip plumped forwards in a pouty expression, but a cruel glint entered his burnished eyes. "All the other lads have been saying how *boring* you are, but I bet you're not boring, are you?" He reached out, tugging on a loose strand of my hair.

My mouth popped open. He'd always been a bit of a prick, but I guessed I'd never realised just how much.

"Are you serious right now?" I jerked my hair from his light grip. The nerve of this guy. "That childish bullshit isn't going to work. Piss off and bother someone else." I waved a hand towards the rest of our coven, talking, drinking and dancing around the bonfire lighting the clearing that we edged.

I wasn't usually so easy to rile up, but something about him just got under my skin, like a splinter I couldn't cut out. For too many months, I'd watched him string my best friend along. He gave her just enough hope to keep her infatuated, even as he slept his way through the rest of our year group of witch initiates. That he'd never tried to flirt with Lyndsey as much as the others made it all so much worse. I'd seen him pay more attention to random strangers on a Friday night at the Witch's Brew, hanging around attractive women like a bad smell.

He blinked. Once. Twice.

As if his brain couldn't quite process that I was rejecting him.

Finally, it sank through his drunken haze. He reared back as if struck. "Who the fuck do you think you are? You should be grateful I'm even talking to you. I'm the best that someone like you could ever hope to get." He narrowed his eyes, rapidly darkening from their golden hue to a murky brown. "No wonder you're hanging out alone at your initiation. Even your own family chose death over being with you."

His words sliced down to my soul, clawing at a wound that just wouldn't heal. I glared back at the spoiled bastard, not giving him the satisfaction of seeing his blow land.

The festering pit of anger in my chest surged before I could stop it. "You're a weak, pathetic dick bag. You know that, right?"

A frisson of unease undercut my knee-jerk bravado. He was the coven elder's son. He could make life even more difficult for me here. Plus, I might not be envious of his mental magic, but that didn't mean I wasn't wary of it.

He smiled. Cold and cruel.

My stomach churned at that look. Time to get the hell out of here.

Flicking my long lilac hair over a shoulder, I strode away, feigning a confidence I didn't feel.

"Come on, Zoella, live a little. Or you might as well have let those hunters kill you too." His mocking voice trailed after me.

My jaw clenched hard enough to hurt, but I refused to turn around. From the corner of my eye, Fenton threw his hands up and trudged in the opposite direction, disappearing between the lichen-dappled trunks. I sent a silent thanks up to the goddesses, breathing out a relieved sigh, when he didn't follow me.

Across the clearing, Lyndsey's eyes narrowed on me. Her gaze darted to her retreating paramour with a pinched expression even as she continued chatting with another tipsy initiate.

My best friend had pointedly avoided me for the past half hour, drinking the spiked punch and joking around with everyone but me. I'd never felt more like an outsider than I did right now. Not even when my family had first joined the coven over a decade ago and the other kids had stared at me with open curiosity. At least then I'd had my parents and older brother to draw strength from. I'd found Lyndsey that first awkward day in my new class, and we'd clicked straightaway.

A heavy feeling tugged at my chest. I still didn't want to join the party, especially after Fenton had tanked my mood even further. Instead, I lingered on the fringes once more, trying to calm my anger. I'd always had a short fuse, but I'd worked hard to control my temper rather than let it control me.

Tonight was already testing that composure, when I'd been so on edge for weeks already. Watching the rest of my coven, Lyndsey included, celebrate the upcoming initiation wasn't helping.

Elder Murray stepped in front of the bonfire, cutting through the chatter with his imposing presence alone. Tall and lean, he was athletic despite nearing his late fifties. Grey hair threaded through the mousy brown at his temples, but his unlined face held an ageless quality. Combined with the wire-rimmed glasses crouched on his nose, it gave him a scholarly appearance. I'd always thought of him as a stern headmaster, but I knew most coven members saw him in a fonder, almost fatherly, light.

He lifted his arms as high as his bushy brows. "Brothers and sisters in magic, it's time!"

Chapter 3

Adrenaline spiked through me at the coven elder's booming declaration.

"Come, initiates. We must first bless you with sacred anchors," he said, beckoning us closer with a crook of his bony finger.

Our teachers had already talked us through how the ceremony would work, with both rituals held tonight. The first involved setting an anchor for the magic, and the second tied it to the coven's collective well of power. It was the latter I'd been desperately looking forward to, since it inducted us into the protective spells.

Palms sweating from the stress, I slunk closer, along with the eight others in my intake emerging from the buzzing crowd. Coven members murmured encouragements as we gathered around the bonfire, our magical community surrounding us like family.

I caught Lyndsey's gaze, chancing a tentative smile despite my frazzled nerves. Her mossy eyes softened, and she stepped around Jacinda, one of the preening initiates, to stand at my side as the nine of us formed a half-moon before our leader.

Some of the tension unlocked in my shoulder blades as we stood together. Today was a big day, and there was nobody alive I'd rather face it with than her, even if we were having another tiff like actual sisters.

The bonfire crackled, creating a soothing backdrop for my eager anticipation. Blazing high behind the coven elder, its warm light cast shadows across the mage's smooth face in an eerie dance.

He scanned the line, and I dropped my gaze before ours could meet, tension spiking through me. I counted the blades of grass, relaxing over his polished Oxford-style dress shoes, instead. His gaze like a heat lamp, I could almost feel it blast over me, and I fought the urge to fidget under the scrutiny.

A quiet exhale sighed past my lips as he finally moved on.

From my periphery, I caught the first in line, Harrel, grinning as Elder Murray stepped up to him. The beaming initiate unbuttoned his shirt part-way to reveal a hairless expanse of tanned skin. With the entire coven's attention on him, my breaths came a little easier. I settled in to watch to the magic unfold.

The elder lifted his palm, a caramel glow lighting his flesh from within. "Tonight you faithful young mages truly become one with your coven. You commit your magic and your life to strengthening this community. We welcome you into our family and our hearts."

His words burrowed into my soul. Excitement lit a fire in my middle as I fidgeted at the end of the line. Elder Murray shoved his hand against Harrel's chest, knocking him back a half-step. Magic fizzled through the air, like the charge after a lightning strike. Harrel hissed in pain but held strong and unyielding before his leader, as was expected of us.

The old mage snatched his hand back with a slight grimace before raising his gaze to the hushed crowd. "With this anchor, we mark the binding of our newest initiates. Let there be no others in their soul but this family."

The coven cheered, applauding and hollering in their shared joy. It lifted my spirits, helping to wipe away the slimy behaviour from Fenton and my usual skittishness in a crowd.

The anchor was my first step to safety, even if it did always make me think of cattle getting branded. Once a coven leader laid their symbol into your flesh, it was a permanent mark of ownership. In theory, the elder who gave it, or another powerful member of the coven, could release you, but it wasn't easy to change covens. My parents had only done so for a quieter life away from the capital, since the politics in their old coven had apparently turned dangerous.

Harrell squared his shoulders, revealing the Quartz Coven anchor in the dead centre of his chest. It formed a rocky cluster of the gemstone namesake, shiny and white like fresh scar tissue. The magic tattoo took on a silvery sheen, seeming to glint with a cold shine.

Elder Murray wasted no time in giving each initiate their anchor, with a flash of tawny light and a crackle of magic that scraped over my skin until I felt raw.

Lyndsey whimpered as he pressed his palm to her chest beside me. This close, I could hear the faint sizzle of his magic on her skin. I squeezed her hand in support, feeling her grip tighten on mine until my bones protested, but I didn't pull back.

My heart pounded as he finally stepped before me. The stern mage looked down his nose at me, a slight curl to his lips. It was so similar in shape to Fenton's that I fought with every ounce of self-control I'd honed not to grimace.

Fixing my gaze to his protruding chin, I tugged on my dress's neckline, just enough to reveal the top of my cleavage.

His salt-and-pepper brows lowered in my periphery. "The mark must be placed in the *centre*, initiate."

I squirmed before mentally scolding myself at how ridiculous I was being. All the female initiates had needed to pull their ritual dresses low enough to reveal their bras.

Quickly yanking mine down, I braced for the pain of his magic. I might be showing the edges of my blackthorn tattoo—barely a few petals and long thorns on show—and more cleavage than I was comfortable with, but this wasn't about him getting an eyeful. It was about finally being a part of the coven. Being connected and welcomed as one of them.

A warm glow brightened his palm once more, biting into the skin between my breasts. I stifled a wince at the vicious sensation, but it quickly faded as Elder Murray dropped his hand.

I couldn't stop staring at the quartz gems, clustered between my breasts like an icy tattoo shimmering in the firelight. I'd left my upper chest bare of ink for this very mark, saving the space for my coven's anchor. My skin felt sensitive there, dry and tight, like a real tattoo after a few days of healing.

Satisfaction buoyed me as I shifted my dress back into place. An ache burrowed deeper beneath my rib cage with every pulsing thud of my heart, but I didn't care about the physical discomfort. This was everything I'd been waiting for.

Elder Murray's attention flitted back to the surrounding coven members. "Once the anchors have settled into their ripening flesh, we will reconvene for my favourite part: divining our initiates' true affinities and tethering them to the coven's magic." His grave voice held weight despite the joyous occasion. "Go. Drink and be merry, for tonight we celebrate the blessings from our goddesses."

The crowd cheered, and I fought not to cringe at the sudden noise, a murmuring chatter sparking up louder than the roaring bonfire.

Elder Murray dropped his stern gaze along the line. "I will announce the start of the final stage"—his gaze darted upwards, locking on the full moon high above like it was speaking to him—"in roughly an hour. Don't get too drunk before we complete this." His dry tone held a measure of exasperation, as if he was remembering a past incident or two.

I beamed at Lyndsey, hardly able to contain my excitement. "We're almost there."

She smiled back. "Only one more hour to go, Shrimp."

My heart warmed; finally, in light of this momentous occasion, our small riff was forgotten. We usually bickered a lot, but lately, Fenton had been a serious point of contention between us.

She grabbed my hand, dragging me to a quiet section of the forest clearing. Worrying her lower lip, she eyed something over my shoulder before her gaze settled on me. "So…" She fixed the hem of her dress before continuing, "What were you and Fenton talking about?"

I bit the insides of my cheeks, battling to keep my frustration in check. "We've just been *anchored*, and that's what you want to discuss?" The words filtered out through clenched teeth.

She threw her manicured hands up with a huff. "I'm only asking. Why are you being so defensive? Did something happen?"

I shifted on my feet, working hard not to snap at her as I braced for how badly she was going to react. "Yes, something happened. He was being a sleazy bastard, coming on to—"

"Zoella," she cut me off. Her rounded cheeks seemed to inflate as her nostrils flared. "He literally saved my life, remember? He's a hero."

I shook my head, unable to believe what I was hearing. I was so done with him getting away with everything. "You need to wake up and stop obsessing over that pig."

"You know what? You're being a real bitch tonight. This is meant to be a celebration." Jaw tight, she fisted her hands in the thick fabric of her black dress. "I'm going to grab a drink. Come find me when you've calmed down."

She stomped off with one last glare, heading towards the wooden table laden with bottles on the far side of the clearing.

My anger spiked at her stubborn faith in Fenton. I wanted to scream. To rant and rave about how he'd tried to come on to me in such an arrogant and disgusting way.

Instead, I drew in a slow breath, letting the faint scents of smoke and sweet wine distract me. I held it for three slow seconds and then exhaled in a controlled stream, letting my frustration rush out along with it as I watched Lyndsey walk away from me again.

I rubbed at my aching chest, yanking my hand back with a hiss as my new anchor flared painfully in response to the scratch of cotton.

With a deep sigh and heavy steps, I picked my way towards where the last part of the ceremony would soon take place: a small glen just out of view from the main clearing.

Wizened oaks ringed the ceremonial site in a perfect circle. My fingertips brushed their rough bark as I passed between the nearest two. Power surged up from my chest to greet them before fading like a shooting star.

Inside their circle, the air felt heavier, as if the sentinel's long years held a weight here. Glowing stars flanked the moon, hung perfectly centred above the hole in the leafy canopy.

It wouldn't be long before everything I'd been waiting for came to fruition. For years, all I'd wanted was to join the coven fully, to be connected to my fellow mages in a real community. A family.

The protection and security were exactly what I needed. I could practise magic without my growing paranoia, and if I was right about my nature mage affinity, I could meaningfully contribute to the coven, tending to the small orchard growing apple trees and blackthorns. I'd expand our stock too, using magic to grow more exotic fruits for us and a few valuable potion ingredients to sell to neighbouring covens.

A sense of peace robbed my anger at Lyndsey's stubborn ignorance and Fenton's vile form of flirting.

In the middle of the space, dramatically spotlighted by the moon, sat a gnarled wooden altar. The top was blackened but worn smooth, almost shiny.

The original tree stump, chosen by the founding Quartz Coven elder decades ago, had been struck by lightning until it cauterised the wood. A blessing from the nature goddess herself, apparently.

Atop it sat the most prized possession of my coven: our grimoire.

Each coven had their own sacred book, used to store the most valuable spells and wisdom from past generations. I'd read a lot of books in my time—hell, my cabin had an entire room where piles of them lined the walls—but this was one book I'd never be able to get my hands on. Not until I'd mastered whatever my affinity magic was and somehow worked my way into the coven elder's inner circle as one of Quartz's most powerful mages.

Worn leather bindings hugged the thick tome, accented by a simple brass lock. Tonight the book sat open, its thin, off-white pages spread wide, exposing its secrets to the night.

I frowned. Even during a ceremony, it was never carelessly left open like that.

A quick glance around showed I was alone. Though, with hints of the buzzing crowd still visible between the trees, it was more an illusion of privacy than anything.

Curiosity tugged me forwards. I peered over the ancient spell book, drawn in like a moth to the moon.

I sucked in a gasp.

Laid before me was a simple spell but one of my kind's most dangerous—how to summon a demon.

1. Cut your palm, pool your blood.

2. Salt the essence.

3. Infuse your power, speak your summons.

The three simple steps burned into my consciousness, like the knowledge could etch itself into my soul.

Below the instructions, a warning waited in a neat scrawl, different from the rest.

Whatever you agree, you'll pay the price.

"Well, that's not ominous," I muttered, leaning closer for a better look despite the frisson of unease skating down my spine.

The following page depicted demons that past coven members had called upon before the magic had been outlawed for safety. There were more castes and names than the ones we'd been warned about in class, but I recognised a few of the types based on their primary food source—blood, sex, or soul.

I wrinkled my nose. You'd have to be incredibly desperate to offer any of those to something as violently evil as a demon.

A twig snapped behind me.

My pulse lurched. I spun, colliding with a hard chest. A throaty laughed filled the night as someone shoved me backwards. The high podium smacked into my side with a hard thud. A hand shot out, clamping over my wrist before I could recover. My bones protested as they squeezed, an ache radiating up my arm.

Hissing at the pain, I glared up at the newcomer.

Fenton's pouty lips stretched into a malicious grin.

Chapter 4

The coven's golden boy looked far too pleased with himself. "Shoulda known I'd find you here, all alone and up to no good," he tutted, voice airy.

"Fenton." I scowled, annoyed I hadn't seen the last of him tonight. "Let go of me."

"Bend over"—the words punched me in the gut—"or I'll tell my father you stole a grimoire key and then I'll tell everyone what a whore you are. That you begged for my cock on your initiation night until I had to shove it down your throat just to shut you up." A sneer twisted his usually charming smile into something menacing. A small brass key peeked from beneath the open collar of his shirt, glinting with an incriminating shine.

Shock held me paralysed. I barely registered that he shouldn't have had one of the grimoire keys.

I sucked in a shaky breath as I tried to process the situation. Surely he wasn't being serious. We'd never got along, him being the prodigy of Quartz and me a barely tolerated burden. Over the years, he'd played too many pranks on me to count, picking on me every chance he got. But this was taking things too far.

I frantically searched his haughty expression for any hint of a joke. Any second now, he'd yell "psyche" and laugh at my expense.

But nothing came.

He just stared me down with an expectant arch winging his brow. A patient creep with his damp palm a shackle around my wrist.

He wasn't joking.

"You're being serious, aren't you?" I swallowed, my throat scraping like sandpaper.

His bronze eyes gleamed in the faint moonlight, oozing confidence with a leering smirk. He might reek of booze, but this wasn't some sloppy, drunken attack.

I recoiled, trying to jerk out of his hold, but he only gripped harder. A mounting horror curdled my gut. "Goddesses... You've done this before, haven't you?" The words shook from my lips. "You bastard," I spat.

A visceral fear zapped me, spurring me into action as I tried to yank my wrist free again, but he thrust his hips, trapping me between his rigid body and the sacred altar. Already, an underwhelming length prodded me in the stomach, and I cringed at the evidence of his sadistic enjoyment.

"Let me go!" I hissed, trying in vain to thrash my way free, breaths coming in uneven bursts.

How could my sweet best friend be mooning over such a rotten creature? My gut roiled at the thought of him doing this to her or someone else. I had to warn her. In fact, I had to tell the entire coven.

Panic overrode logic as I threw my fist towards his face, but he caught my sloppy punch in his much larger hand, gripping it painfully with a mocking scoff.

He rolled his eyes. "Stop being dramatic. I'm not some vile demon. I'll make sure you come too." A cocky smirk curved one side of his pouty lips. "They always do with me."

Yeah, right.

My head snapped aside with a loud ringing in my ear. I blinked, staring out at the party raging deeper in the woods. Pain bloomed across my cheek.

The fucker had hit me.

I worked my jaw, cheek throbbing as I stared blankly up at the cruel bastard. The pain took me right back to another place, another time. Dark memories tried to suffocate me as I fought to stay in the present, a small whimper quaking my throat.

My magic latched onto the nearest trees. The connection thrummed through me like I was a guitar string being plucked on repeat, responding to my chaotic emotions. Vibrating the blood pumping through my veins hard enough to ground me in my current nightmare, rather than a past one.

His hand lunged down my dress, causing my anchor to shriek in pain. Clammy skin met my breast as Fenton shoved into my bra and squeezed. I froze for a stunned moment as he fondled me with a low groan, his grubby fingers poking into my sensitive flesh.

His touch *hurt*, turning bruising as he groped me. But it was the arrogant sneer twisting his handsome features that finally had my rage sparking. My jaw tightened until I thought my teeth might crack. I grabbed for the burning anger, letting it raze my panicked fear to ash.

"You sick fuck!" With a feral hiss, I jerked back harder into the tree stump and slammed my fist into his inner elbow. "Get *off* me!"

He grunted, digging his blunt nails into my chest. The monster loomed over me, pupils dilated wide, as he ground his erection into my front with a grating laugh. "There she is. That angry little bitch who rears her head in training. What's got you so mad all the time, hmm? Did watching poor Mummy and Daddy get tortured break something in you?" His taunting tone pushed more liquid rage through me, ramping up the voltage searing my insides. "The crazy ones are always the best fucks. Now be a good slut and bend over for me. Or I'll make you."

I snapped.

With an enraged snarl, magic burst from my fingertips. Black sparks filled the night like deathly fireflies. Lilac flames raked across Fenton's chest like a set of claws. He yelped, stumbling backwards as he clutched his heart instead of my tits.

I grinned, revelling in the foreign power surging through me in an addictive rush, pulsing deep within my middle.

"Run along now, you festering maggot. Or I'll burn that tiny prick right off you," I hissed, taking a step towards the cowering mage, gaping down at his chest wounds.

Ragged lines singed his otherwise pristine white shirt. They cut blackened scorches across his muscular pecs like I'd tried to gouge his heart out with fire.

"Fucking freak!" he spat, cheeks ruddy. Dead leaves crunched beneath his bulk as he backed away. "No wonder everyone hates you."

Adrenaline pumped through me as hard as the pulse of magic. I bared my teeth in a vicious snarl, ignoring the stab of his words.

He tucked tail and ran.

Wood smoke cloyed my nose, distracting me from the high of watching Fenton's sweat-soaked back retreat through the forest.

Almost in slow motion, I turned.

Glowing purple flames, edged in black, licked up the sacred altar. Flickering ribbons jumped over the smooth timber, tasting the edge of the archaic grimoire despite its protective charms.

"No... No, no, no," I breathed, trying frantically to pull back on the magic I shouldn't even have.

I was going to be a *nature* mage, not a fire elemental. None of this made any sense. I hadn't even matured into my full powers yet. Tonight's ceremony was meant to start its true awakening.

But I couldn't dwell on any of that right now. I had to save the grimoire. My coven would never forgive me if I damaged it, accident or not. I was already a bit of an outcast, a poor orphan liability. This would be disastrous for my place in the coven.

With monumental effort, I closed my eyes and focused inwards.

My magic had always felt primal and untamed, like a pack of wolves or a pounding waterfall. Tonight there was a new sensation alongside the one I was growing used to: a low burning deep in my chest, like the simmering of rage. I reached for the strange heartburn sensation, trying to strangle the flames.

Nothing happened.

The sound of crackling fire burrowed into my ears.

Eyes wide, all I could do was stare in horror.

Lilac flames, haloed in black, writhed around the grimoire's edges. The eerie fire ate away at the protective wards to kiss the fragile parchment beneath.

"Shit."

Chapter 5

I needed help.

Without wasting another second, I sprinted for the bonfire in the distance. For my coven.

Sure, they'd be pissed I'd singed the grimoire, but if there was something I could do to save it, I had to. It was too important to the coven to worry about my already crappy reputation.

"Zo!" a feminine shout rang out. "Hey! I wanna talk to you!"

I skidded to a halt, sucking in a relieved breath at the sight of my best friend, my sister in magic. She glared at me, mossy eyes slitted as she hurried towards me from deeper within the forest rather than the main clearing. A red splotch marred her throat, circular like a hickey, and a flush coloured her usually pale cheeks. I frowned before shoving the question on the tip of my tongue aside in favour of my frantic need to save the coven's sacred tome.

"The grimoire's on fire!" I yelled, running straight for her.

Her lips looked swollen as they formed a shocked *O*. "What did you do?" she gasped.

I bit my lip, trying to rein in the panic clawing at me. "Fenton attacked me. That disgusting maggot groped me and tried to force himself on me." I grimaced at the memory too fresh for me to process. I shoved it down to fester along with my other dark memories.

Her head jerked back as if struck. "He would never!" Her dainty features squeezed into an accusing scowl. "In fact, he literally just told me what *you* did. That you came onto him." Her wide eyes watered, but she blinked the tears back rapidly. "After all the times you'd warned me away from him, and now you go behind my back to steal him from me?"

Pain lanced my chest, and I sucked in a ragged breath. How could she think I'd betray her like that? She was choosing to believe him over me, and that hurt like a knife to the chest. We might not be related by blood, but she was my only real family now. Even if she didn't see it that way.

"He's fucking lying!" I choked back my anguish, voice tight as I rushed the words out. "But it doesn't matter right now. You have to help me put the flames out," I urged, stepping closer.

She instantly stepped back, maintaining the distance between us with a livid glare. "Fine, we'll talk about your betrayal later. Let's get Elder Murray. He'll know what to do."

I grimaced at the idea of telling Fenton's dad that his son had tried to force himself on me, but what choice did I have? I'd only burned Fenton and the grimoire in self-defence.

"Come on." I reached for her hand, but she jerked out of my grip.

Another stab to my chest. Another ignored hurt.

I took off for the main clearing, weaving through the forest with Lyndsey's light footsteps trailing behind me. Bursting between the trees, I spotted the coven elder right beside the bonfire. He nodded slowly, speaking with Yolanda, his second in command, and a new coven member I vaguely recalled as Gregor. Seeing the orange flames beside the group only made the unnatural embers in my chest surge in response. I winced, hoping my weird magic wasn't burning the altar faster now.

"Elder Murray!" I called, racing towards him, waving my arms.

He turned on me with a light frown. "Yes, initiate?"

"The grimoire is on fire!" Panic blurred my words as I heaved for breath.

His bushy salt-and-pepper brows hit his receding hairline before his expression turned thunderous. Without a word, he sprinted towards the sacred glen I'd fled from.

I swerved after him, pumping my legs hard. For a man in his late fifties, he was surprisingly agile. More footsteps pounded the earth behind us as we raced the short distance.

The coven elder raised his hand, outstretched, as he bounded past the oak ring. His palm pulsed with tawny light, dim compared to the haunting purple-black flames filling the glen.

He sucked in a sharp breath. "Goddesses save us."

His glow brightened as he slashed his hand in a vicious arc. The scent of ozone rolled over me in a wave as his magic lashed out.

The crackle of flames ceased with a whoosh, yanking on my power with a painful tearing sensation through my middle. I groaned, clutching at the spot right over the anchor mark. The metaphysical loss felt like he'd ripped something vital out by its roots.

Even as I struggled through the phantom pain, a sense of relief bloomed. The fragile grimoire looked fairly unhurt. Its creamy pages spread innocuously atop the already blackened stump. Sure, the charcoal scorches started a little lower on the altar's rich bark than before, and the parchment looked a little crisp-edged, but overall nothing seemed too damaged.

Lyndsey shifted, taking a step away from me. I shot her a tight smile, and she glared back, lips pressed into a thin line before she looked away. She might be annoyed over for my supposed betrayal, but her proximity still gave me a measure of strength for what I was about to do.

Yolanda and Gregor reached the clearing barely a few paces after us, glancing around in confusion. The older woman's neat plum updo flopped askew with the speed of her assessment. Gregor's wild mane, a distinct sunset orange, blotted Yolanda from view as he took a protective half-step in front of her.

More coven members emerged behind the pair. Their murmuring voices caused my gut to churn harder.

Elder Murray straightened, catching his breath before he lashed an enraged glare in my direction. "What is the meaning of this?" His voice roared through the darkened woods, sending a crow squawking into the night as it fled the oncoming storm.

I watched the inky shape join the night sky with a deep longing.

The feminine sound of a throat clearing snatched my attention. Lyndsey had a strange look on her face as she stepped forwards, gaining the coven elder's attention and resolutely avoiding my gaze in favour of his. An impending sense of doom weighed the moment, pulling taut.

She lifted her curved chin. "It was Zoella's fault. She did this."

Her voice echoed around me, hollowing me out.

Fenton materialised from behind a lichen-coated beech, like a demon summoned. He rested a sun-kissed hand on Lyndsey's narrow shoulder.

"See, I told you." Fenton's breathy tone was hardly audible over the shocked murmurs of the swelling crowd. Malice swirled through his bronze gaze, sliding in my direction. His plump lips curled into an arrogant smirk as he leaned close, whispering in her ear just loud enough for the three of us to hear. "Your *supposed* best friend tried to seduce me and then attacked me when I turned her down. She knows how we feel about each other, yet she betrayed you anyway."

This couldn't be happening. I waited for Lyndsey to question his lies, but it was hurt, not disbelief, that strained her features.

Fenton squared his shoulders, striding forwards until moonlight bathed him in the centre of the glen like a spotlight. A light sheen of sweat plastered his golden-brown locks to his forehead.

The black lines across his chest had since thickened into smears of soot beneath his ruined shirt. The brassy key around his neck from before was nowhere in sight.

He notched his chin, projecting his voice to the crowd. "Lyndsey is right." He pointed an accusing finger at me, plastering on a look of recrimination. "I caught Zoella trying to read forbidden spells from our sacred grimoire. She tried to seduce me so I wouldn't reveal her crime. When I rejected her, she attacked me with twisted magic, lashing out at the grimoire on purpose in an unhinged rage."

"What? No!" I gasped, choking on my own disbelief. "That sick fuck tried to force himself on me!"

"How dare you!" Elder Murray's voice sliced through the forest, cutting through all other sounds. "That is your future coven elder, and you will show him some respect."

More and more figures gathered through the trees, trickling into the glen with horrified gasps as they absorbed the ashy scene. They saw the singed grimoire and the blackened wounds on Fenton's chest and jumped to their own conclusions.

Impotent rage gripped me, strangling the air from my lungs. Condemnation marked every new face. Not a single person looked like they believed me over Fenton and Lyndsey.

And why would they?

I was the traumatised orphan they'd had to tolerate for over a decade. Nothing but a burden on the coven. No matter how hard I worked. Lyndsey was a well-mannered, pretty young witch from a respected family, and Fenton was the coven's future leader.

Elder Murray shook his head with a disgusted tut. "It's clear to me that the tragedy with your family has left you twisted. Rotten inside. You have no place among us." His eyes hardened to stone. "For the safety of us all, I hereby banish you from Quartz Coven." His words were softly spoken, but I felt like he'd roared them in my face.

His hands glowed bronze as his lips moved rapidly, muttering a spell too low for me to hear. Magic fizzed across my skin like static.

My heart thudded dully as time seemed to slow, stretching out the moment where my future shattered before me. My mind struggled to come to terms with what he was saying. Air sawed in and out of my lungs too fast, but it seemed to lack any actual oxygen.

This was a nightmare. It had to be. How could any of this be real? Any moment I was going to wake up in my comfy bed surrounded by the worn beams of my cabin and everything would be OK.

"That's a death sentence," someone gasped from within the crowd.

"Ain't right what happened to her poor family. Anyone would be broken after that," another voice chimed in.

"She's always been a troubled child, but I'd never have expected this from her." A disappointed sigh.

"Fenton is a good man. How could she say those things about him?"

"Cut the rot before it can spread, I say."

Low murmurs wove together as the people I'd considered almost family just stood by and watched my life end.

Unbidden, my gaze swung to my best friend. She wasn't even looking at me. Instead, she stared down at her hand, entwined in Fenton's larger grip, a stark look on her rapidly paling face.

The image blurred as moisture flooded my eyes. With each blink, it overflowed, spilling down my cheeks.

A darkness writhed inside me, begging to lash out at the source of my pain. I swallowed the urge down as I choked back the keening sob climbing my throat.

What was the point in fighting when you had nothing to save?

"Go." Elder Murray thrust his wrinkled hand out, shooing me like the stray dog I'd become. "Never return."

Chapter 6

Rippled bark prickled my palm. It pressed into my skin in tiny lumps and bumps, some digging in sharply, others dull and gentle.

Life pulsed in a steady rhythm beneath the beech tree's thin protective layer. I could feel the flow of sap through the wood, like blood in my veins. Echoes of life pinged all around me as my magic reached out further, caressing the nearby trees of the small forest I'd chosen to hide in for the night.

It was so damn soothing. Even my erratic heart rate steadied. Tears pricked behind my closed eyes. Since my exile five weeks ago, I could use every ounce of calm I could get my grubby little hands on.

An owl hooted, piercing the low chorus of churring insects, before the fluttering of wings signalled its departure.

Exhaustion weighed my limbs, threatening to pull my hand from the thriving tree. I resisted its lazy allure, like I had been for far too many weeks now. I only slept when I couldn't physically keep myself awake any longer. Or on the rare occasion I found somewhere safe.

Though, these days, nowhere was truly safe. Not for me.

The European beech pulsed, taking on an almost aggressive feel through the slippery magic connecting us.

I'd run out of time.

They'd found me.

Again.

I fought back the useless urge to cry, steeling myself for another long night of running and terror and bone-deep fatigue.

Part of me was tempted to just plonk my skinny arse down between the gnarled roots and wait for them to catch me. Maybe death would be preferable to a life on the run. Constantly looking over my shoulder. Never staying in one place. I was already starting to starve. I'd run out of what little money I'd had in my bank account weeks ago, and now I was living on scraps, begging and foraging what I could and stealing what I couldn't.

I'd quickly learned that my nature mage affinity must lie with trees alone, as not a single blackberry bush or strawberry plant had responded to my power. On a good day, my maturing magic would play ball, and I could coax the apple trees to fruit for me, even though it was only just shuffling from winter into spring. Most of the time, my unruly powers just bucked like a wild horse, reckless and out of control, without a coven binding to steady it while it matured.

Even when it worked, it was a risk. Hunters seemed to track me down even faster whenever I caved to the desperate need. Maybe their captive mages were just lurking nearby, waiting for a spike of magic to fizzle through the air.

My stomach churned in a depressing mixture of hunger and fear.

The hunters wouldn't kill me straightaway though. No, I knew in excruciating detail how they'd torture me for information about my coven first.

I was half-tempted to give it to them.

Those miserable bastards had betrayed me and left me for dead, instead of protecting me like they were supposed to. Like they'd promised to. I owed them nothing.

Yet I couldn't quite make myself do it. Every time the temptation struck, the image of Lyndsey right after my family had died—squeezing my hand tight with tears in her big green eyes—would flash into my addled brain. I'd pick my tired body up off the floor and start moving again.

I hated myself for it a little more each time.

She'd chosen to defend that manipulative bastard over me. The thought still stung all these long weeks later. At this point, I was angrier at her for the betrayal than I was at him for trying to assault me.

Lyndsey had finally got her wish too. After my exile, I'd spent several agonising days hiding in the bushes on the edge of Quartz Coven territory like a coward. I'd relentlessly tested the strength of their warding spell, hoping to sneak back in to at least collect my belongings—my *family's* belongings. I hadn't been able to, but the day after my banishment, I'd spotted the pair sneaking off into the woods together, finally hooking up. An image of their lying lips locking together beneath the stars had burned into my retinas, stomping on the already broken pieces of my heart.

It wasn't just the possibility of torture that kept me fleeing though. The hunters would use me for my magic until I burned out. Only *then* would they kill me.

Seemed like a really crappy way to die.

The beech's energy flared again through our hazy connection, warning me of the coming danger, but I was too lost, drowning in my own bitterness to heed it.

Maybe I should just go out in a blaze of glory...throw everything I had at the hunters until there was nothing left.

But they'd make sure to take me alive. They had these twisted hunting dogs known as hell-mutts. The beasts would corner you while the hunters snared you with their ropes or darted you with tranquillizers. Without a coven's masking spell, they could sniff out the magic in your blood and lead their hunters right to you. Rumour said they had bred the beasts from even bigger monsters, somehow dragged from the depths of hell—feral hellhounds with eyes of fire. I stifled a shudder at the thought, a slippery fear curdling in my gut.

I couldn't even join another coven to hide. The Quartz anchor I'd been so excited to receive was still emblazoned in a silvery design on my chest. It was a cruel joke. Elder Murray had left it in place, meaning I couldn't receive another anchor to be inducted into a new coven's protective magic.

I pushed away from the tree, mourning the loss of its steady comfort, but I'd already lingered too long. I cursed myself for getting caught up in my spiralling thoughts. The constant fear, hunger, and exhaustion were making it harder and harder to keep them in an orderly line.

Spindly wisps of magic threaded me to the surrounding forest, but I'd learned quickly that it was easier to commune with nature through direct touch.

I both loved and hated my affinity.

On the one hand, it was the only connection I had left to my family, other than the antique silver ring glinting dully on my index finger. My father had given it to my mother for their first anniversary, the poisonous belladonna a tribute to her beauty as much as her deadly side. Our shared magic made me feel like they were still here, protecting me in spirit, guiding my magic through the instinct they'd passed on to me. On the other hand, it was the very reason I had to run to survive.

With my magic maturing, the hunters had found me quickly. Not one week after my exile, armed men had broken into my hotel room in the dead of night. Whether it was from a hell-mutt scenting me or one of their captured mages feeling me use magic nearby, I didn't know. I'd barely escaped out the window with my life, and only after breaking one woman's nose. I was lucky my brother used to insist on practising his mixed martial arts lessons with me or I'd never have stood a chance.

The hunters had still coated their weapons in my blood though, sealing my fate.

Two days later, they'd caught up to me again in an abandoned warehouse on the far side of the city, confirming my fears.

The hunters' imprisoned mages must have distilled my magic's signature from my blood and infused it into a tracker stone. Made from an unassuming, hollow glass pebble, a tracker stone would warm in proximity to the signature's owner. But the real issue wasn't the game of hot or cold they could play. They could use a map well—a shallow basin of water lined with a crude map. Drop in a tracker stone, and it would give psychics the old fuck you, falling on the rough location of its signature bearer instead.

There was nothing I could do to hide now. Even if I could somehow rid myself of the Quartz anchor and join a new coven, I wasn't sure that would block a tracker stone already infused.

Despite my light running trainers, my footsteps fell heavy as I jogged through the patchy grass, avoiding the main trails as I angled deeper into the woods. If I scaled the wire fence on the far side of the nature park, I could disappear in the city's backstreets. Much harder to track than if I exited through the front gate onto the well-lit roads.

I'd discovered the hard way that I couldn't just hide amongst the masses. Hunters didn't care if people saw them chase me down. Most even wore police uniforms, though I hadn't yet figured out whether it was a cover or their actual jobs.

Stunted ferns brushed my hips as I yomped past. The wind tugged at my hair, whipping lilac strands around my face, even tied back as it was.

Only five weeks after I'd been forced out of my coven, and I was already nearing my limit. Every step was a Herculean effort. My mind was a battlefield of its own as I fought the suffocating hopelessness.

This was no life.

Tears blurred the dark forest as I sucked in a ragged breath, trying to choke down any sound that could give me away.

My family wouldn't have wanted this for me. My fierce mother, who'd sometimes hissed when startled like her feline familiar. My kind father who'd sung eighties rock ballads to his poisonous plants as he tended them. My funny brother, who'd cracked stupid knock-knock jokes just to make me roll my eyes with an affectionate huff before he'd leap at me to practise his newest fight moves.

They'd be heartbroken to see how I'd turned out. A coward on the run. No future. No family. No life.

I gritted my teeth, stuffing down the punishing sense of failure. Forcing the burning ache in my thighs to the back of my mind, I pushed onwards.

"Demon up ahead, heading east!" A voice knifed through the night, stabbing terror through my chest.

Chapter 7

My heart raced despite its heaviness. I willed my body faster, legs pumping as I laboured through the thickening undergrowth.

The tips of my fingers tingled as magic bucked out from my chest in an uncontrolled surge. "Not now," I gritted out, willing it back under control as I ran.

Maybe it was the fear and adrenaline taking charge, but my unruly power had other ideas. Dark tips sharpened my nails, almost blending with the dim night as it sapped a fraction of my waning strength. It wasn't the first time this had happened, but like all my magic, this latest development wasn't something I could control.

Here was hoping I wouldn't need to use my bizarre claws again.

Moonlight bathed me as I reached a gap in the tree cover, seeming to both urge me on and highlight my position. I leaped over a fallen mossy oak and sprinted deeper into the brush, ignoring my disbelief at how nimble I'd become. It was amazing what skills you developed out of desperation. I was borderline athletic now.

Footsteps thudded behind me, followed by an unearthly howl. Fear iced my veins.

They'd brought hell-mutts.

I panted hard as I ran, indecision warring inside me.

"Fuck it," I cursed, barely a breath on the wind.

I reached for my magic, praying to all three of the sister goddesses for a miracle. My connection to the trees surged to life in a mercifully steady flow, vibrating through my bones. I scanned the woods until I found what I was looking for.

A proud oak towered only metres away. Dark gaps lurked between its roots, large enough for me to fit through. Probably.

I raced towards it, dropping to my knees. A thud reverberated through my bones almost as hard as my thrumming connection. Cold mud squished beneath my hands as I crawled forwards, pushing the softer roots and spider-webs aside as the tree swallowed me whole.

An animal must have burrowed in before me, or I'd never have fit, even with the weight I'd lost living rough. I tried to slow my gasping breaths as I curled up in the darkness beneath the great oak. Gripping a solid root in each hand, I focused inwards, following my magic into the tree.

Silently, I begged for help.

I sent frantic mental images of what I needed, but I had no idea if it would even work.

Another keening howl pierced the night. Fear clawed at my throat as I pushed my unpredictable magic harder into the tree. I fed every ounce of my desperation into our connection, praying for salvation.

An ominous creaking echoed all around me. I sucked in a relieved sob, biting my lips to keep quiet. Before my eyes, the roots shifted, barely visible under the scant moonlight. My magic drained at an alarming rate. Black spots obscured my vision. The roots thickened, covering the hole through which I'd entered and stealing my view of the forest beyond.

Darkness became an unbreakable wall around me. I was trapped.

I fought the instinctive panic. The suffocating claustrophobia.

No. I wanted this. I needed this.

"Where the fuck is that sneaky demon?" a gruff male spat, oddly muffled through the root barrier.

Another male grunted. "No sign of the bitch anywhere."

A series of yips and barks had the breath stilling in my lungs. I may be hidden, but I wasn't undetectable. Not to those beasts.

Scratching noises sounded just outside my hiding place. Claws raked the wood and earth right in front of my face. I held my breath. Not daring to even twitch. Hollow barking reverberated through the protective roots. They knew I was in here; they just couldn't get to me.

I hoped.

Something tickled the back of my hand. I bit back a whimper. I'd never feared insects, not really. But if there was a spider crawling across my hand in the pitch black, I *really* didn't want to know.

Another set of too many legs feathered over my neck. I held deathly still, fighting the instinctive urge to brush the unknown creepy-crawlies off me.

"What the fuck are you doing!? That's a tree, you dumb mutt," the second male snarled.

The digging noises ceased with a canine yelp.

A pang hit me in the chest at the thought of any creature being hurt. They weren't natural, but they were still life.

I mentally rolled my eyes at myself.

Now I was feeling sorry for the beasts who would gleefully rend my flesh if they got their slobbery jaws into me.

"Fucking hell. These things are *useless*. Let's get the truck and head back to the entrance. It's got to leave the woods eventually," the first hunter said.

The other male grunted again, and a canine growl sounded.

"Leave it!"

Another pained yelp from the hell-mutt and then the faint thudding of retreating steps.

I waited as silence descended. Long, endless minutes of nothingness.

Darkness creeped in around me—a tangible, smothering weight.

I squeezed the woodsy roots tighter in both hands, fighting back the panic attack looming at the edges of my mind. My magic had drained almost completely, but I needed to get out of here. Now.

I shoved the scant wisps of energy I had left into the roots. Rough beneath my palms, I focused on the abrasive texture of the thicker ones and the fine, almost ticklish, brush of the thinnest strands. Anything to hold back the panic as the last of my magic trickled out of me, leaving me trapped in the dark. Powerless and alone.

My thoughts swirled back to my family. To my brother's terrified lilac eyes, so similar to my own, as the hunters slit his stubbled throat in front of me. The torrid mix of emotions—the fear, the guilt, the pain—hardened my resolve. I would not die entombed in the earth like this, imprisoned by my own magic. Not after all I'd already survived at the hands of those fanatical psychopaths.

I pushed more of my power out, barrelling past whatever limits my body might have, begging the tree to release me back into the night. My head throbbed from channelling too much magic. Wetness dripped from my nose. But I didn't stop. I couldn't.

Rustling leaf litter and creaking groans devoured the heavy silence. Slivers of moonlight pierced the darkness as the tree began to release me, rearranging itself for me once more. Tears pricked my eyes with a desperate sense of relief.

"Thank you." My voice came as a choked whimper.

My legs burned with the need to rush through the widening gaps, but I forced myself to peer out cautiously. Just because it sounded like the hunters and their beasts had left didn't mean they had. I'd already learned the hard way how much hunters loved their traps.

The forest was calm as I scanned each section steadily revealed through the tangle of roots. Only the hoot of a distant owl reached my ears before it quieted. Even the breeze had ceased, giving the forest an eerie stillness.

A strangled sob lodged in my throat as I clawed my way up through the frigid mud giving way beneath my scratched palms, embedding under my too-sharp nails.

The adrenaline holding me together fled, leaving me a shaking, tired mess as I staggered out, gulping down fresh air. The forest swayed around me briefly as I waited for the dizziness to pass, but the fierce ache in my skull only worsened.

I wasn't sure how many more times I could escape them.

Part of me had thought that tonight would be my last. The terrifying thing was that a small voice in the back of my brain had been willing to embrace it.

My stomach chose that moment to protest, aching and gurgling, hollow and clawing, reminding me I hadn't eaten yet today.

Before I could overthink it, I brushed trembling hands down my body, grimacing at my dirty clothes already smeared with mud. Small thumps hit the earth as insects fell before I could freak out too much.

With a shaky breath, I swiped the blood from under my nose and shoved down everything—the hunger gnawing at my middle, the pounding in my skull, the exhaustion dragging on my limbs, the fierce ache behind my sternum. I turned, jogging deeper into the woods.

One thought chased after me as I ran—*I can't go on like this.*

Chapter 8

A crid whisky burned as it slid down my throat. I longed for a smooth scotch or even an American bourbon, but the cheap crap was all I had.

With a grimace, I took another swig, downing the rest of the teensy bottle.

I coughed, thumping on my chest as the liquid went down the wrong hole, searing my airways like I breathed fire.

"Yuck." I ran my tongue over my teeth, feeling the booze's numbing haze set in.

I plonked the little bottle down alongside the others, a neat row of judgement lining up on the stained carpet in front of the humming mini fridge. The cloying scents of must and old cigarette smoke replaced the sharp alcohol, but I was beyond caring.

Pushing unsteadily to my feet, I shuffled over to the flat-pack table I'd dragged to the middle of the room earlier. I avoided looking directly at the objects it held though. I still wasn't quite ready.

I longed for another shot, or two, but with the room's mini-bar empty, I was out of options.

I was also out of time.

Maybe it was paranoia, but I swore I could feel the hunters closing in on the run-down hotel I'd holed up in. I'd spent the last of my cash—the emergency fifty-pound note I'd clung to even when my stomach had rumbled, even when the rain had soaked through to my bones and warmth felt like a distant memory—just to get this crappy room. Chances were I wouldn't be needing more after this, anyway.

Hard to spend money when you were dead.

I took a deep breath, twisted my mother's ring around my finger for luck, then reached for the knife.

The worn wooden handle was smooth against my palm. I gripped it tight, ignoring the trembling in my hand as I brought the blade to my flesh.

"Just fucking do it," I whispered, but everything in me rebelled on instinct.

Or maybe it was logic that held me back.

Indecision waged war inside me as I hovered on the precipice. If I did this, there was no turning back.

An unearthly howl pierced the night. The hauntingly familiar song shoved me over the edge.

My palm stung as I dug the steak knife in. It bit deep into my flesh despite the blunt tip. Blood welled, shockingly bright under the buzzing strip light.

A muffled bang sounded nearby, like a door bouncing off a wall.

"Split up. The tracker is boiling hot. The demon whore is close." A male voice slithered through the paper-thin walls, like he was barely a few doors down the corridor.

I'd requested a first-floor room so I could jump out of the window to escape, but maybe that hadn't been the smartest idea.

My heart thundered, kicking at my ribs as if protesting what I was about to do.

"Forgive me," I muttered, unsure who I was seeking absolution from. Hell, I'd take the blessing from a Teenage Mutant Ninja Turtle right now.

The knife clattered as I dropped it back onto the varnished surface, reaching for the other item I'd stolen earlier tonight.

With another bracing inhale, I upended the salt shaker. White grains hit the blood pooling in my palm, burning my open cut as they melted into me.

I hissed at the sting, trying to wrench my thoughts under control.

A thumping sounded, like a fist against a door. "Open up! Police," a man yelled.

He was already too close, but it wasn't my room he pounded on. Yet.

The alcohol's slight detachment helped dull the sharp edge of fear and let me brush aside the small voice of reason begging me to stop.

I sucked in a deep breath and shut my eyes. Focusing every ounce of my magic and will, I channelled it into a single thought.

"Blood demon, blood demon, blood demon," I whispered over and over. It was the only trade I could stomach. I didn't want to think about the other things a demon could ask for if I called forth the wrong type.

Minutes passed as I continued my low chant.

A door creaked somewhere along the corridor. "What!?"

"Have you seen this woman? She's a dangerous suspect in a criminal investigation," a male demanded.

"Nah, never seen her." A nasal reply.

A door slammed.

"Blood demon, blood demon, blood demon," I continued, ignoring the vice of panic slowly squeezing tighter and tighter as the pounding of a fist got just that little bit closer. The stark raps rivalled the boom of my racing heartbeat.

The stinging pool in my hand warmed. Hotter and hotter until it scalded like boiling water.

My chant cut off in a hiss as I fought to keep the searing blood cupped in my palm.

I gasped as the red liquid seemed to move and sway like a tide pool, unnaturally strong despite my shaking hand throbbing with pain.

The dingy lights flickered overhead.

Fear clawed my insides.

My heated blood spun upward like a vortex, growing until it created a tornado of red. It funnelled from my palm, seeming to suck power from me as it spun back down, hitting the carpet with a wet splatter. The connection snapped, staggering me as magic ricocheted through my chest.

The tornado collapsed in on itself, leaving a gory circle of red.

Inside it lurked a monster.

Chapter 9

I sucked in a sharp lungful.

The figure within the blood circle unfolded, straightening to an unnatural height. I struggled to take in as many details as my frantic mind could.

Tall. Muscular. Slate skin. Fiery hair. Onyx horns. Arrow tail. Glowing red eyes.

Demon.

Instinct reached inside the basal part of my brain and stabbed at my fight-or-flight response until my limbs quaked. I had no clue what type I'd summoned, but a lethal promise saturated the air around him, making it hard to breathe.

That was a good sign though, right?

A strange mix between a nervous giggle and a terrified groan bubbled up my throat. To my horror, it culminated in a high-pitched squeak before I could stop it.

It bounced around the sparse room, echoing back like a death knell.

I cringed, barely resisting the urge to slap my bloodied palm over my face. I'd just summoned an honest-to-goddesses *demon*, and the first thing I did was bleat like terrorised prey? It was going to tear my dumb, tipsy arse to shreds.

Lyndsey would cackle like a stereotypical witch if she found out about this. A pang twinged my chest on the heels of that thought, wiping away my terrified awe. Would I even speak to Lyndsey again, let alone laugh over crazy stories?

Feral anger ravaged the hurt, feeding on my fear until I bared my teeth like an animal.

I squashed the unhinged rage, clearing my throat as if I hadn't just squeaked and snarled like a lunatic.

The demon's lips quirked, eyes devouring me from head to toe before scanning the room.

"Piss off, it's the middle of the night." A gravelly female hacked a cough. "Ain't seen no skinny bitch round here."

My heart kicked as adrenaline flooded me. The woman was lying. I'd seen her when I'd entered my room, hardly an hour ago. She'd grunted a low "hey" before coughing and spluttering as I'd given her a strained smile and darted inside, slamming the door.

Of the room next to hers.

Panic slapped me into action.

"Demon." I glared in what I hoped was an authoritative manner, forcing myself to meet those eerie red eyes. "I have summoned you to offer you a deal—my blood in exchange for your protection. You will receive one non-lethal feeding for a maximum of thirty seconds for every enemy you kill or every time you save my life. So long as I am able to sustain the feed without injury to myself. If it has been too close to a previous feeding, you will wait until my body has recovered enough first. You are not to hurt me in any way and will protect me from all other threats where possible. Do you accept?" The words flowed out in a practised stream.

I'd rehearsed the verbal contract countless times over the past day since the tree root debacle. All the while debating whether this was really any better than capture. Being tied to a demon was dangerous in more ways than one. It wasn't just my life I could lose; if I failed to keep my end of the bargain, what was to stop the monster from dragging me through a portal back to hell with them? A fate that seemed way worse than a little torture and death. At least that had an end in sight. I had no idea what would happen to me if I was taken to their realm, but an eternity of damnation didn't seem ideal. I'd never even heard of a mage coming back after being crazy enough to step through one of the secret portals to their cursed realm.

Maybe this hadn't been such a great idea.

"No, I can't imagine it was." The sound of a deep, velvety voice speaking in near-perfect King's English startled me from my internal panic. "But here we are." He spread his hands wide, showing off wicked, curved claws.

I blinked in shock before mentally berating myself. Either my face had betrayed me or the thought must have escaped my lips. Life on the run meant I'd started talking to myself more than I'd used to, because I was a lonely shrew, apparently losing my mind.

"Um…" I shook myself. I had to get my shit together. "Do you accept my terms?" I repeated, trying to project calm, competent witch vibes.

Another series of bangs preceded more yelling, loud enough that I just *knew* they were only across the corridor.

The demon canted his head aside before a grin bloomed across his animalistic face. "My, my, my, you *are* in quite the predicament, aren't you?"

I scowled, fear and exhaustion loosening the leash I usually kept on my anger. "Coming from the demon trapped in a summoning circle."

At least, I hoped he was.

"And yet it's your life I hold cradled in my claws, little mouse."

As if to punctuate his point, footsteps drew nearer outside my hotel room. They thudded slowly, as if mocking the frantic pounding of my heart.

I bit my tongue, gesturing for him to continue with an impatient wave of my hand.

"I don't want your blood. I'm not that type of demon." His voice was oddly decadent, so deep and rich it resonated through the room. His eerily glowing eyes swept my body again, this time in a more predatory way.

For some bizarre reason, tingles followed in his wake. Almost mimicking the rush of desire. But that couldn't be right. What crazy person would be turned on by evil incarnate?

I needed help. Serious. Mental. Help.

My nails dug into my palms as my fists clenched at my sides. "What do you want?"

He stepped closer, right to the edge of the bloody circle. Seeing him trapped gave me a measure of confidence but not much.

A booming rattled the room's flimsy door as someone pounded their fist against it. "Open up. Police!"

My heart leaped into my throat.

I stared at the demon, desperation squeezing my throat tight as time seemed to stretch between us like used gum.

"Open the door or we will!" the male shouted through the thin wood again.

A wicked grin split the demon's lips, showing fangs as sharp as his claws. "Pleasure for protection."

The door burst open.

What choice did I have?

"Deal!"

Chapter 10

My chest constricted as my left wrist burned with a red glow. The same radiance lit the blood circle, casting a ghoulish underlight across the grinning demon inside. I hissed at the searing bite to my wrist, stumbling backwards into the wall as a burly man in uniform charged into the room.

"There's two!" the fake cop roared, already raising a pistol in one hand and popping off a deafening shot. It narrowly missed the demon, thudding into the wall. In the same breath, the hunter threw a blade towards me.

The demon stepped out of the glowing ring, casually plucking the spinning knife from mid-air. With a cocky wink, he launched it back at its owner. It slammed right between the man's eyes in a sickening thud, sinking through bone with impossible force.

I gaped, shock holding me captive.

The grey beast inhaled deep, ribs flaring as his bare chest expanded wide. Bliss suffused his features. "Ah, the sweet scent of fear and death. Delicious." He shot me an unhinged grin as his tail shot upwards, punching out the ceiling light. Fragments rained down in the gloom. The image of his wicked smile burned itself into my vision like overexposure. Darkness swallowed me.

My heart thrashed in my chest. Terror clamped me in its vicious jaws.

I blinked hard, vision adjusting in time to witness another hunter race inside. He almost tripped over his fallen comrade as he skidded to a halt. More streamed in behind him, silhouetted by the faintly lit corridor. The mass of bodies and impending violence instantly cramped the pitiful hotel room.

Chaos erupted.

A grey blur darted around the room, the demon somehow everywhere at once. Sharp fangs tore out jugulars. Claws disembowelled. Pained howls and shouts followed. Deafening gun fire lit up the dim room in bright flashes. Doors opened down the hall, a mass of humans fleeing the danger even as more hunters, vaguely dressed as police, poured into the tiny room.

The bedside lamp shattered beside me. Porcelain shards sliced into my arm, but it was shock rather than pain that had me crying out. I pressed myself harder into the wall, as if I could distance myself from the violence.

The demon growled, a threatening sound that smothered the dying groans. He moved even faster as he tore another hunter's head off with his bare hands, piling up body parts just inside the doorway. His arrowhead tail stabbed through another man's throat with a sickening squelch. Blood sprayed the mouldy wallpaper like splashes of paint. Its metallic scent coated the back of my throat as I tried to gulp in air, cowering at the back of the room as I witnessed the massacre unfold.

Too late I fought to summon whatever twisted fire magic burned inside me. Useless purple sparks danced around my outstretched fingers, bringing a wave of dizziness. I slumped against the wall, trying to breathe through it.

Within minutes, the last body slid off the demon's claws, crashing to the carpet with a wet splat. Silence entombed us, leaving behind a high-pitched ringing in my ears.

My whole body shook as I surveyed the carnage, trying to make out what was left in the disorienting gloom. Flesh littered the blood-soaked carpet: heads, arms, legs, entrails. Even a hand. A golden wedding band circled its ring finger, glinting at me with accusation. My stomach roiled aggressively as I pressed a trembling hand to my throat.

What have I done?

I swallowed, choking back bile at the thick scents of metallic blood and sour death. The room felt stifling, like a blanket smothered my face, the heavy heat making it hard to take a full breath.

I needed to get *out*. With a shaky gasp, I lurched forwards.

The monster pounced.

I screamed as the horned beast slammed into me, crushing me against the wall before I could escape. The scant air knocked from my lungs in a sudden whoosh. His solid body dwarfed my tiny frame, covering me. Blood-slick skin seared mine, even through my clothes. Heat engulfed my neck as his huge hand gripped my throat, just enough to make breathing a luxury.

Pinned between the hard wall and even harder demon, all I could see was a smooth slate-grey chest, splattered with red.

The demon growled, a low, feral pitch. His deep rumble vibrated from his muscled abdomen into my chest. It rattled through my body and shook all thought from my brain, leaving only an alarming sense of danger. Adrenaline flooded my body until I trembled against the monster.

Curving over me, he leaned down to run his nose along the length of my neck, horns scraping the wallpaper behind my head. All I could do was stare at his bloodied chest, frozen in fear. The scents of smoke and ginger wound around me, strong yet oddly soothing.

A small groan left his lips, vibrating the air just above my skin. I was hyper-aware of the scant distance between his lethal fangs and my throat. It felt like my pulse was trying to leap into his mouth with every hard throb.

He might have been the one to fight a whole mob of hunters, but I was the only one out of breath here.

I swiped my tongue over my lower lip, trying in vain to moisten it. I felt like a little kid again, refusing to look under the bed because of the monster I was convinced lurked beneath. Life had taught me the hard way that monsters were real. It didn't matter whether you looked; they were coming for you regardless.

Slowly, I found the courage to lift my gaze, taking in the rumbling beast caging me in.

Unending blackness stared back, as dark as my nightmares. The unbreakable pools were set deep within a sharply angled face, mired in shadow. I could have sworn his eyes were glowing an eerie blood red when I'd summoned him. Given the circumstances, I wouldn't be surprised if I was losing whatever sanity I might have had.

His upper lip lifted in a snarl, showing long white fangs as he continued to growl.

Any trace of the mocking civility was gone. The act dropped in favour of his true nature: an insatiable beast, drunk on violence and dark need.

The terms of our deal blared through my mind—*pleasure for protection*.

I swallowed back a whimper, throat bobbing against his slicked palm. The movement wrung a warm drop of liquid from his skin to trickle chillingly down my neck—the blood of his other victims.

Shoving down the panic threatening to spiral me out of my mind with fear, I clenched my jaw until I thought it would crack. I needed to stay strong. Take control of the situation. Some people had already fled, but there must be others still inside the building. They were counting on me to contain the monster I'd unleashed before he devoured us all.

Step one: hide the fear and exhaustion causing my body to quake. If I acted like prey, he'd treat me like prey.

Step two: try not to get myself and everyone else in the area murdered in a grisly fashion.

A blueish tongue slid from between his colourless lips. The tip split into a wicked fork like some twisted serpent. I flinched as it swept along my cheek in a warm, wet slide. Impossibly long, it left a faint trail of slick across my skin.

My pulse pounded so loud I could hardly think straight.

"Such a sweet treat," the demon rumbled, the words almost impossible to decipher through the gravelly purr of his voice. "My own sacrificial lamb, already spiced with the blood of my enemies."

My eyes slitted, the heated flames of my anger rising to the insult. I was so damn sick of being sacrificed by people. Of being disposable. Worthless. "Fuck you, demon. I want to renegotiate."

He chuckled, a layered, husky sound like the rattle of a hundred dying breaths.

Given our deal, I didn't think he'd be able to hurt me. For once, I let myself drown in the near-endless pit of rage I tried to smother, desperately clinging to the blind courage it lent me.

I notched my chin further, meeting the monster's depthless gaze head on. "Blood for protection."

He bared long fangs, the sharp points almost enough to make me reconsider my offer. The hard press of his muscular frame had a curious heat pooling low in my body, startling enough to distract me from my anger. Would pleasure be so bad compared to the pain of his lethal bite?

I mentally back-handed myself. What was I thinking? Of course I didn't want all that untamed power unleashed on my sensitive parts. My fragile body would probably break like a twig under the force of his unholy lust. If the hard length against my middle was anything to go by, he'd tear me in half just trying to seat himself inside me.

An involuntary shudder ran through me, along with a dark curiosity I hastily shoved aside.

Clearly, I needed to get laid. But with a nice, tame mage or human. Not evil incarnate.

The beast smirked, gaze carving into me. "No, little mouse. A deal is a deal."

I winced as mental images raced through my mind—a series of violent acts, each more terrifying than the last. What would a monster like him consider *pleasure*?

Deliberately slow, he leaned down, running his nose along my jaw line like an animal, his warm hand tightening a fraction on my throat. The curve of one of his lower horns dragged across my temple. Each cold ridge scraped across my skin like a threat. I stiffened in his hold, breath catching as I fought back another confusing shudder.

"Ah, such delectable fear." He pulled back just enough for his black gaze to bore into my lilac one.

That unhinged grin, which had bloomed right before he'd unleashed his hellish fury, returned. The look of crazed anticipation was forever burned into my memory. Seeing the expression once more set my pulse fluttering like a moth trapped in a jar beneath a full moon.

"But what's this I detect? Surely that's not a delicious hint of arousal?" He gasped mockingly, tutting inches from my face. "How shameful."

My brows furrowed even as I felt a telltale warmth suffuse my cheeks. "Go to hell, you twisted fuck." I fanned my anger, letting it brush aside any embarrassment. "It's rage and revulsion. As an ugly beast, I'm sure you're familiar with both."

I was sure he wasn't. Despite his inhuman features, an insane part of me found him oddly beautiful.

Another layered, smoky chuckle escaped his lips, seeming to drift over my body in a caress. "You tell me to go to hell, yet you're the one who dragged me from its depths. I'm your problem now."

The black abyss of his eyes threatened to swallow me whole.

I hated to admit it, but he was right. I'd been stupid enough to summon a demon, and now I had the responsibility of keeping it in check.

The neat scrawl from the grimoire flashed through my mind—*whatever you agree, you'll pay the price.*

I ruthlessly kept my gaze pinned to his feral face instead of peeking at the carnage he'd splattered through the dingy room.

He'd paid his already.

Now it was time I paid mine. Whether I wanted to or not.

With a deep breath, I steeled myself for the second time tonight.

The thought of what I was about to do was absurd. Too surreal to believe. Maybe I'd never made it out from underneath that oak tree. I was still there, hallucinating this whole insane plan as I slowly suffocated, trapped within the earth.

Neither reality particularly appealed.

At least gripping a demon's dick in my hand was better than welcoming the monster between my thighs.

"Fine." I met his unnerving gaze with a confidence I didn't feel. "Get your little monster out, then." I nodded towards his crotch as much as his hold on my throat allowed.

The demon tipped his horns back and laughed, loosening his grip. Throaty and deep, the sound made something tighten low in my body, even as it triggered another terrified shiver down my spine.

I grimaced, more at my reaction than his, before I knocked his wrist away, finally freeing my neck. "Quit cackling. If you want pleasure, I'll jerk you off. You've not earned more than that. I still got hurt." I lifted my forearm, brandishing the shallow cuts from the lamp's shards like a weapon.

Sure, it was a minor injury at best, and he'd been busy murdering my attackers, but I needed all the bargaining power I could get.

His chuckles simmered down, petering out as he watched me. Mirth brimmed in his dark gaze, giving them an almost silvery shine amid the dim lighting from the corridor.

"You think I want a pathetic hand job to spill my seed onto this putrid floor?" He shook his head, drawing my attention to his huge black horns. One set spiralling down, the other curving up.

I bit my lip, trying to hold in the panic.

He purred, "I said *pleasure*."

Before I could even gasp, he gripped my thighs and shoved me up the wall. My back slid against the wallpaper, tipping me off balance with a startled yelp. On instinct, I gripped his curved horns, cool and textured beneath my hands. A breath hissed through clenched teeth as my cut palm throbbed against the solid onyx.

With a devilish smirk, the demon began to spread my legs. He squeezed my thighs in his huge hands, long fingers encircling them with ease. I fought to keep them closed, whimpering with the effort. He didn't even pretend to notice, his taunting pace unhurried, as his claws dug into my sensitive skin.

"Of course a sheltered little mouse wouldn't know pleasure," he mused, face hovering inches from my covered core. "Have you even been tasted before?" His low rumble mocked me. A velvety tone made for the bedroom.

I fought not to blush at his words. He dipped closer, nostrils flaring as he inhaled deep.

"Of course," I scoffed, strangling his horns harder as I stuffed down any embarrassment I might have felt. Bravado was all I had left. "I doubt your weird lizard tongue would be any better."

Memories of the last guy I'd dated resurfaced to call me a liar. After we'd slept together a few times, where he'd always cajoled me into giving him a blow job before sex, he'd finally decided to "return the favour." He'd alternated between clumsily tonguing at me and asking me to tell him what a sex god he was. Every other minute. Suffice it to say, the whole experience had been more awkward than enjoyable. What had made it worse, though, was that he'd been practising his "skills" on other witches behind my back.

The demon grinned. Slow. Vicious. "Oh, little mouse, I'm going to make you scream."

Chapter 11

F ear and anticipation twined through me.

The demon's slate tail reared over his muscular shoulder, hovering by his cheek like a weapon drawn. I watched in sick fascination as a bone-like talon slid out from the flat arrowhead, like a scorpion's stinger. I sucked in a panicked breath, but exhaustion, and maybe the booze, had me oddly detached.

Was he about to poison me?

Taking surprising care, he drew the sharp point along the seam of my blood-spattered leggings, cutting straight through the

stretchy fabric without touching my delicate skin. With a ripping sound as loud as a gun-shot, the tear gaped wide, my
spread legs splitting the material further.

I swallowed thickly, tasting his smoky ginger fragrance in
the back of my throat. Life on the run didn't give you much
time for laundry. All I'd had left was the cheapest multi-pack
panties I could find. It just so happened that was a skimpy,
neon-pink mesh thong with little cherries stamped all over it.
In the gloom, it was almost offensively bright.

Embarrassment heated my cheeks. For some bizarre reason, my brain chose to focus on that small, inconsequential
detail rather than the precarious situation I'd found myself in. I
side-eyed myself. Did I *want* the demon to like my underwear?

A sinful smirk twitched the demon's lush lips. "Is that a
promise?"

"W-What?" I could barely remember how to speak.

The demon inhaled, a look of dark deviance sculpting his
hard features. "You sure smell sweet like cherries to me."

On instinct, I squirmed against the punishing grip engulf-
ing my thighs, but it was no use.

My frustrated snarl echoed between us, despite the danger
of baiting a hungry demon. "Fuck you. I'm sure anything is
sweet compared to the bitter, raw flesh you normally eat."

"Ooh, greedy little mouse." His eyes flared, the dark orbs
drawing me in. "I can see your pretty pussy already glistening
for me, but you're not nearly soaked enough to take my cock
yet."

His filthy words sent a jolt of lust straight to my core. I almost
choked on my tongue as my brain short-circuited. Nobody had

ever spoken to me like that before. Apparently, some twisted part of me was getting turned on. By a demon.

Covered in blood.

Those tiny bottles must have been bigger than I'd thought, because surely this was a drunken reaction. I'd never felt much for the mages in my coven, or even guys I'd hooked up with at bars. They were nice enough, attractive in a pleasant way, but they'd never set my pulse pounding the way the romance novels I loved always described.

Be careful what you wish for, I supposed. At the sight of the dangerous creature between my thighs, my heart was about to beat its way out of my damn chest.

The bone-white talon spiking from his tail skated along my thigh. Shivers traced behind it, the sharp edge of danger mixing violently with the tingly sensation. I held my breath as it trailed up and over my hip, skirting around the edge of my exposed under-wear. He scraped it higher, along my ribs and over the top of my chest.

I couldn't move, couldn't even breathe as the grey arrow dipped between my breasts, slowly pushing beneath my top and into my bra. The deadly talon was as smooth as his skin and only slightly cooler, like the ridged horns I clung to. It curved inside my bra, oddly flexible as it moulded against my breast. I felt it slide back into his tail, scratching me briefly before only the firm sheath of warm skin pressed against me.

The demon wriggled his silky tail, brushing heat and friction against my nipple. I sucked in a gasp as he repeated the gesture, ignoring the way his eyes locked onto my face with predatory intensity.

"Little mouse..." He groaned, the low noise vibrating the air. "Your delicious scent is driving me wild."

He looked hungry, ravenous, and just a little too high on bloodlust. I closed my eyes, letting my head thunk back against the wall. Surely the image of a blood-spattered demon between their thighs, eager to devour them, would be too much for any witch to bear.

"That's not how this works." He chuckled, his laugh a dark rattle between us. Something warm and wet teased over my inner thigh, causing me to shudder at the taunting sensation before he continued, "You're going to watch as I give you more pleasure than any pathetic human ever could. I want you to know who's shattering your sweet, innocent world."

I glared down at the wicked creature of sin and savagery. There was only so much fear and twisted anticipation a witch could take. "Typical overconfident male. Quit bitching and get on with it, demon."

He tipped his head back and laughed, pulling me forwards like my death grip on his horns was nothing. The deep rumble shook his whole body, rubbing his tail against my aching nipple and digging his claws harder into my inner thighs. The bright pinpricks only added to the confusing sensations sliding through me, and I bit my lip to hold back a gasp.

"Such a demanding creature." His eyes shone silvery in the faint light, lips curved into a sinful smirk. "As you command, *summoner*." He inclined his horns in a mocking nod of acquiescence.

I arched a brow. We both knew I wasn't *exactly* the one in control here.

Before my tired brain could come up with some scathing remark, his forked tongue slid from between his lips once more. In the semi-darkness, it looked a deep blue-grey, and I fought the urge to recoil at how inhuman this beast truly was. As if the ridged horns indenting my palms and the silky arrow in my bra weren't evidence enough.

Some deep, dark part of me was secretly curious too. What had human men really given me except disappointment and betrayal?

I ruthlessly shoved the thought aside. Now wasn't the time to let the crazy out of its cage. The demon may think he had the upper hand here, but I wasn't going to give him the satisfaction of seeing me succumb to his sinful charms.

His tongue laved across my inner thigh, the forked tip teasing in twin points of heated sensation. His soulless black eyes burned into me as he licked closer and closer to my core. An ache started up as he drew nearer, both agonisingly slow and too fast for me to prepare.

I held my breath as his thick tongue hooked under the edge of my lace panties. He traced the crease of my thigh in a warm, wet caress.

I strangled off a groan, barely holding myself back from shifting my hips to draw him straight to my needy core.

Fuck. One little tease and I was half-tempted to throw myself at some unknown beast. I needed to get a grip. But his teasing tongue and the sharp edge of fear and anticipation were quickly unravelling my sanity.

His tail moved once more, slowly brushing his warm, satin-soft skin against my nipple.

"Goddesses," I hissed.

His tongue edged my lower lips in a scant caress.

The demon chuckled, smoky and low, vibrating his tongue against my skin. He repeated the teasing stroke on the other side, slipping beneath the soaked mesh covering.

He angled his face closer and hooked a fang under the transparent material.

The demon paused, black eyes meeting mine as he held my underwear between sharp teeth. A feral glee arrested his features. My whole body tensed.

A loud rip sounded, his fang shredding the flimsy material.

Cool air met my heated core as he exposed me completely. His eyes devoured me as I squirmed beneath his intense focus.

Even in the semi-darkness, I could see how embarrassingly wet I'd become. My lower lips and inner thighs glistened from both his tongue and my own disturbing arousal.

"Beg me to lick your sweet cunt," he whispered his demand against my sensitive flesh, the feather-light caress of his breath ratcheting my need higher.

"Fuck you." I choked on the words, trying to slam my thighs closed. They barely twitched.

Instead, he spread me even wider with a wicked grin, until my knees almost touched the wall. I'd had no idea I was that flexible.

"When I finally throw you to the ground and rut you, little mouse, you'll be begging for every demonic inch. You'll be desperate for my seed in your every hole. Addicted to my rough touch. High on the vicious pleasure only I can give you."

I sucked in a breath at his filthy words and arrogant dominance. They should have made me spitting mad, my mind rebelling at the very idea, but my core clenched in need, begging for someone, anyone, to touch me.

For *him* to touch me.

His grin was borderline cruel. "I knew you'd like it rough. Primal. Dangerous. After all, good little witches don't play with demons."

I bared my teeth, almost wishing for my own pair of fangs.

His tongue swept out in one long lick through my folds before his fork hugged my clit. Hot pleasure lashed through me, sending my hips jerking as I whimpered in need.

He groaned, a look of bliss suffusing his feral features as he dug his claws harder into my skin. "You *do* taste like cherries. Sweet, dark, and oh so ripe for the taking."

"*Demon*," I begged, too far gone from that one taste of bliss. I could hardly think enough to be self-conscious.

He chuckled, peppering my aching core with the tease of his mocking. "You don't even know my name. Look at you, spread wide and gushing wet for an unknown monster. So fucking divine."

Before I could process his words, his tongue lashed out, this time swiping through my wetness in a harder sweep. I moaned, writhing in his hold as he commanded my body. At least one goddess must be watching over me, because he didn't stop there. His forked tongue swirled over my slit, laving through my folds again before returning to my needy bud, demanding more.

His tail wriggled against my nipple before slithering to the other side and repeating the torturous friction. My back arched in a silent plea, pushing my chest into his tail's sinful touch.

"Don't you dare stop, beast," I practically sobbed, feeling his thick tongue circle my entrance in a teasing caress. I gripped his horns tighter as I fought to pull him closer against me.

He responded with a feral growl, vibrating his forked tongue right against my clit as he feasted on my needy flesh, jolting pleasure through my core, richer and deeper.

His fang scraped against me, adding a dangerous thrill. He thrust his thick tongue deep into my entrance. It writhed inside me like a tentacle, the end curling into an even thicker girth, stretching me in a way I'd never felt before.

A keening sound echoed around us, and I distantly realised it was coming from me.

The base of his hot tongue rubbed against my clit, the exact harsh pressure I craved.

It was all too much. The burning stretch and writhing thickness inside me. The demanding press against my clit.

Feral and vicious, the demon snarled intimately against me.

I came undone with a scream.

Pleasure crashed through my body like a tsunami. Waves of bliss flooded my core as my body undulated with the ripples, unable to battle the tide.

Like a starved animal, the demon continued to growl as he feasted, forcing the pleasure on and on until I begged him to stop.

Completely spent, I slumped against the wall, only his unyielding hold on my thighs keeping me from tumbling to the floor.

I panted hard, my body twitching with the aftershocks as I slowly came down from the high. My vision swam, but I could still make out the wicked sight of the blood-spattered demon grinning up at me from between my thighs. Pleasure soaked his lips, dripping obscenely down his chin.

That wicked forked tongue darted out. Impossibly long, the slate-blue length ran across the lower half of his angular face until every last drop disappeared. He hummed in approval, dark eyes alight with hunger, even now.

I swallowed thickly, almost dizzy with the pleasured high thrumming through me.

Maybe I really was hallucinating under a tree after all.

Chapter 12

My world was still spinning when the demon slowly lowered me to the ground.

A tremble had taken my legs captive and wasn't letting go. I casually leaned against the wall for support, feigning nonchalance as I stared up at the wicked demon I'd summoned. A mess of emotions tangled inside me like a knot of thorny vines. Bittersweet ash and ginger smoothed across my senses, trying to drown out everything but him.

Specks of red dotted his high cheek bones, growing into huge smears drying across his broad chest, adding gory colour to the monochrome canvas of his slate skin.

The demon blinked rapidly, as if coming out of a trance. A smug grin stretched his lips as he watched me. "What a *pleasure* it was to make your acquaintance...?" he purred, trailing off at the end in question.

I grimaced, realising I'd just let a stranger eat me out. Not just any stranger, but a *demon*.

"Zoella," I grunted, utterly unimpressed with how my first attempt at summoning a demon had gone.

"Zoella..." He uttered my name as if savouring the feel in his mouth. "A lovely name for a lovely little mouse." His smile seemed sharp, and I didn't just mean the pair of long fangs peeking out. "Call me Rex."

I arched a brow, the sly insult and demanding tone of his voice rubbing me the wrong way. "I'm no palaeontologist, but I don't think T. rexes had forked tongues."

He chuckled, that low rattle that somehow both unnerved and intrigued me. "What a shame for their partners."

A blush crept back up my cheeks as my core clenched with the remembered sensation of his unique tongue against my clit.

The demon had a point.

White seeped in at the corners of his eyes, like smoke rising in the night. It hit the middle and bled, turning the bright-red shade I'd thought I'd seen when I first yanked him from hell and into my own version of it. From one blink to the next, blood-red orbs stared down at me, complete with white sclera like a human's but with the vertical, slit pupils of a beast.

One I'd just let get me off. In a filthy hotel room. Littered with bodies.

As if the thought had summoned it, the stench of meat and death washed over me. Bile threatened to rush up my throat. How had I forgotten all about the carnage he'd wrought in my name?

I gripped the base of my neck, fighting the nausea. "We need to get the fuck out of here."

Sirens wailed in the distance, punctuating that thought. I pushed past the wall of heated muscle and grabbed the fraying backpack I'd stashed under the bed. Despite containing all my worldly possessions, it was painfully light. I shoved the self-pity down and swung it onto my back.

I had no underwear on and a massive hole in my leggings, and I was splattered with blood, but at least my top was long enough that I wouldn't be arrested for indecent exposure. You know, just murder...

Getting changed was a luxury I couldn't afford. So was paying the demon here, yet I'd caved to that insanity.

I gingerly picked my way through the carnage, trying not to look at anything too closely. If I let myself focus on any one detail, the small amount of rubbery steak I'd had in order to get the knife for the summoning ritual would be adding to the mess.

A feeble part of me rebelled, but at each body, I leaned down to search for valuables. If I was going to keep myself *and* a demon fed and watered, I needed money. I pocketed all the cash from the few that held wallets, and stole a gaudy chain from the floor, pointedly ignoring the severed head next to it. I left the wedding ring, still glinting accusingly at me from a pool of red. All this felt wrong, but somehow that felt a lot worse than the rest of my casual grave robbing.

I reached the door in less than a minute, hovering between the bright corridor and dark room. "Are you coming?"

The demon hadn't moved from his position by the back wall. His eerie gaze had tracked my movements through the tiny room though, ghosting like phantom claws across my back.

His focus turned contemplative. A frisson of unease skated down my spine. It was on the tip of my tongue to ask what evil schemes he was concocting, but the sirens were growing louder. As usual, I was out of time.

"Demon. Come on," I snapped.

"As you wish, mistress." He dropped into a sarcastically regal bow before striding towards me, stomping through the gore without care.

That, more than anything, unnerved me. Something about his bare feet squishing into torn flesh and crushing glistening bone, soaking the hem of his trousers in blood, just squicked me out.

Did they not have shoes in hell?

I rolled my eyes, forcing back the useless squeamishness and even more useless curiosity. I hurried down the narrow corridor towards the stairwell. Internally, I cringed for the poor person who had to find the mess we'd left behind, but there was nothing I could do about it. At least I'd checked in with a spelled ID, casting a brief glamour over myself to match. The real police would be after a Mrs Winchester in her early forties with blonde hair and blue eyes. My lilac hair and matching peepers were too noticeable amongst the humans otherwise.

The general human population wasn't aware of demons and mages, and everyone wanted to keep it that way. Even the hunters, given the mass panic would incite a war neither side could win. Not without monumental casualties and world-altering damage. That didn't exactly stop them from kidnapping and murder though. They just had to be careful that nobody got ahold of any *unusual* bodies.

I descended the stairs, a demon on my heels. Quickly shoving out of the disabled fire escape at the bottom, I spilled out onto the cracked pavement of a filthy street. The first rays of dawn peeked between the sprawling, mismatched buildings of Riverside's central business district. It bathed my face in warmth despite the biting chill in the air.

I turned down the main street, joining the other scruffy people shuffling about. A few clutched half-empty bottles, while others curled up, asleep, between overflowing bins and graffitied transformer boxes. None of them looked our way—a blessing from the goddesses, since I'd yet to try casting a glamour on the hulking monster stalking me.

"Your home is so lovely," Rex gushed, his voice taking on a fake high pitch as he easily kept pace with my frantic steps. "I can see why you mages are all so terrified of hell."

I snorted, speed walking along the pavement and yanking the hem of my top down as I tried not to flash anyone. "I'd take a rough neighbourhood over pits of fire and sulphurous smog any day."

He let out a startled laugh. The demon was close enough that I could feel his body heat at my side, unnerving yet strangely reassuring.

"That's what they tell you our realm is?" He tutted with a strange cluck of his tongue. "Your covens are getting desperate. And you younglings more naive. I hate to burst your blissfully ignorant bubble, but hell is just another realm, like Earth, not some afterlife for you naughty boys and girls. We have ancient forests, forbidding peaks, and vast oceans, all teeming with life. Us demons are just like you idiots—self-centred mortals trying to go about our ordinary lives. Sure, hell is a smidge more dangerous given how bloodthirsty some of us are, but at least we don't have an insane cult devoted to genocide."

His verbal jabs had me scowling at the buildings, but what did I care what hell was like? Right now, I was barely surviving Earth.

I ducked into an alley, trying to ignore the grubby welcome of shattered glass and discarded plastic bags highlighting Rex's point. After powering through the narrow space, we popped out into the next street over.

Nobody was in sight, and I thanked the goddesses as I rushed towards the patchy tree line signalling the start of Ramsey Park. Riverside had a lot of issues, but the city was good at keeping large pockets of green space. This was just one of the many public parks I'd sought refuge in over the past weeks on the run.

As soon as we passed the first ash sapling, I breathed a little easier. The trees welcomed me with a small buzz of recognition. Magic surged from my chest, flaring to life a thready connection between me and the park's sentinels.

I allowed myself a single moment to let their strength bolster my tired body and shore up my courage, then I headed deeper into the woods, crunching twigs and crisp leaves with each step. The scent of rich, loamy earth wrapped around me, spiced with the faint musky trace of wood anemone and sweet snowdrops. I caught sight of the small plants, flowering white in dainty patches near a fallen oak that forged a gap in the canopy.

Taking another fortifying breath, I spun to face the demon stalking me. His pace slowed to a halt as he eyed me with open curiosity. If the curl of his upper lip was anything to go by, he wasn't particularly impressed with what he saw.

In the soft light of dawn, he somehow looked more monstrous, not less.

Blood spattered his slate-hued skin—from small flecks across his sharp cheek bones to great smears over his chiselled chest and eight-pack abs. The sheer size of him was almost hard to take in. The demon had to be close to seven feet tall, and that wasn't counting the proud double set of ebony horns rising from his fiery hair. One dark set spiralled in an arc behind his ears like a ram's, and the other curved upwards in an undulating wave like a gazelle's, ending in dagger-like tips.

Broad shoulders tapered down to arms corded with thick muscle. Proportionally, they looked longer than your average human's. Wicked black claws tipped the fingers of his shovel-sized hands.

Low-slung charcoal joggers covered his lower half, clinging to his narrow hips. Even the loose fabric couldn't hide the powerful thigh muscles beneath.

I swallowed, running my gaze back up the painting of violence and lethality.

Glowing eyes burned like hot coals, almost as bright as the red hair that haloed his angular face. It started a deep scarlet at the roots, brightening to a flaming orange towards the ends. A few strands had fallen forwards, the bright tips only just brushing the lethal edge of his square jaw.

I shifted my weight, trying to stand firm before the intimidating devil. "I want to renegotiate."

He lifted an inky brow, the human gesture such a parody on the monster before me. "Haven't we already covered this, little mouse?"

I bared my teeth, letting the pit of rage inside me flare a little hotter. "Blood for protection. I'm sure an abomination like you gets pleasure from such a feed, anyway."

He flinched. The barest flicker of emotion before it was swept away as if it had never existed. If I hadn't been staring him down so intently, I'd have missed it.

A small pang of guilt hit me in the chest before I shoved it aside. Did a killer like him even have feelings?

Cunning slid behind his bright eyes, making me nervous.

"You're right. How about a new deal? For something so much more vital." He inhaled deep, nostrils flaring as his gaze slid to the pulse throbbing in my neck. "If you're so willing to part with that sweet nectar of yours..."

I swallowed, feeling like I was walking right into a spider's web but unable to see the invisible trap lying in wait. "What, exactly, are you offering?"

"Freedom."

Chapter 13

I frowned, trying to suss out the demon's angle.

His full lips, only a few shades darker than his stony skin, curved into a smug smirk. Casually sliding his bloodstained hands into his pockets, he rocked back on his heels. "Surely such a blood-thirsty little mouse wants more than just protection? You may not have been caught by your enemies, but you are a slave to them nonetheless."

Everything about his relaxed posture screamed nonchalant, but I couldn't trust him as far as I could throw him, which was probably not a single inch given the hulking beast was easily twice my body mass. And then some.

His gaze zeroed in on the bag on my back. Its emptiness mocked me, so light it was barely noticeable. He ran his intense stare over the full length of my dishevelled appearance. I felt every inch of dirt coating my skin, but I stifled the urge to brush the peeling flecks of dried blood from my cheek.

Anger sparked in my chest at his judgemental stare. It was *his* fault I was this bloodied. I'd already wasted a few precious minutes to wash off the mud from last night's root-tomb incident before I'd got tipsy and summoned a demon. A decision I regretted, since an extra few minutes of negotiation could have made all the difference.

Clearly, the beast was trying to manipulate me. I hated to admit that it might have been working a teensy, tiny bit.

I crossed my arms with a scowl. "What are you getting at?"

"Blood for blood." He licked his full lips with salacious glee. "I'll sip from that sweet nectar of yours, and in exchange, I'll help you find and destroy the local hunters."

My pulse thudded harder in my ears. Ever since my coven had turned on me, marking me for death, I'd not thought of much beyond surviving another day.

The idea of constantly running, living in fear, was a crushing future. Even with a demon bound to protect me, it wasn't much of a life to look forward to. My family wouldn't want this for me. Hell, *I* didn't want this for me.

A cutting longing mingled with the ever-present bitterness that had taken root in my chest since my coven's betrayal.

But what if the Riverside hunters disappeared? What if I could find their cursed base and kill every monster set on hunting me down to capture me like an animal? I could destroy the tracker stone holding my signature. More than that, I could free their captive mages, saving them and myself at the same time.

When I was just fourteen, hardly a few weeks after moving to Riverside to join Quartz Coven, they'd captured me and my family. I'd only been in their tender care for a matter of days, and it was a nightmare I longed to forget. One my family hadn't survived. This was my chance to help those who hadn't managed to claw their way free. Nobody would be looking for me then.

My mind whirred with the sudden possibilities, chasing the bloodthirsty fantasy.

It would take time before more hunters moved into the area. Weeks, maybe months. I could use that time to prove myself to my old coven. I could show them I was more than some disposable stray. If I honed my violent fire magic, I would be an asset, able to protect them as much as they'd be protecting me by taking me back.

I wasn't sure I could ever forgive their betrayal, but the cold reality was that I *needed* a coven for safety. Being inducted into a coven's masking spell was the only way to stop more hunters from being able to find me now that my magic was maturing. It stopped hell-mutts from picking up the magic in your scent and non-coven mages from feeling your power, unless they were practically on top of you while you used it.

The small patch of skin between my breasts tingled, reminding me of why I only had one terrible option for protection. With the anchor mark branded into my chest, I had to go crawling back to Quartz. I'd never be able to join another coven with the stupid magic tattoo half linking me to them. I bit back the urge to scream in frustration.

At least if I went back to Quartz, I could make sure Fenton was exiled for his crimes instead. If that failed, I'd have to keep an eye on him so nobody else fell victim to his vile ways.

"I can see the wheels turning in that big brain of yours," Rex drawled, red eyes bright with intensity.

Despite his nonchalance, something told me there was more to his proposal than he was letting on. Sure, mage blood was meant to be particularly nutritious for demons, but I couldn't shake the notion that he was after something else.

My eyes narrowed, even as I tried to see the danger in his deal rather than his brutal form. "What's the catch?"

He spread his palms at his sides. Sunlight glinted off his bloodstained claws. "No catch, little mouse. I can scent the sweet power in your blood. Plus, I don't particularly want to be at your beck and call for the rest of your life, despite the perks of payment." His lips twitched into an infuriatingly sarcastic smirk. "I plan to settle down with a beautifully fierce mate one day with tiny, feral offspring nipping at my ankles. Hard to do when I'm constantly up here following a scrappy witch around."

Great. Even the demon had a better five-year plan than I did.

The idea of settling down with a "mate," which I supposed must be their version of partner, and raising a family was so foreign it shocked me out of my train of thought. Who knew the denizens of hell even had families like that?

The demon had a point though. Our deal didn't exactly specify an end date. Would I just keep summoning him anytime I was in danger until one day I failed to call him quick enough?

If it weren't for him, I'd have been captured tonight. But how would our current deal even work long-term?

The breeze kicked up, toying with the loose strands of my lilac hair before I tucked them back behind my ear.

What did I *want* for my future? Other than just to have one...

"Judging by all this"—he waved his curved claws at me—"they've obviously put you through a lot already."

I shot him a flat look. "Wow. Way to kick a witch when she's down, huh?"

He flashed me a shit-eating grin in response, highlighting the model-worthy perfection of his high cheek bones. It was unfair for a creature so evil to look so good, especially while being a dick.

"Revenge would be as sweet as blood, would it not?" he prodded, apparently losing patience with my indecision.

The bastard could wait. I'd already had to rush one magically binding deal.

Revenge for myself would be nice, but what really struck me was the allure of avenging my family. It wasn't something I'd ever thought was in the cards for me.

In the early days, I'd longed for it. Every waking moment was spent obsessing over how to make the hunters pay for the bright lights they'd so cruelly snuffed out. But as my bruises and cuts had healed, I'd realised just how impossible it was for one weak nature mage to take on so many trained killers. Instead, I focused all my energy on burying my dark past rather than weaving it into my future.

"Since I'm not a bloodsucking parasite, I wouldn't know." I brushed a few flecks of dried blood from my palm, all casual-like. As if the idea of revenge, freedom, and safety wasn't an intoxicating cocktail I craved almost as much as my next breath. "What are your terms specifically?"

His arrowhead tail flicked behind him, reminding me of a cat ready to pounce. "Well, little mouse, for my services in hunting down your enemies, this *bloodsucking parasite* will take one small feed a day, up to a minute long. Plus a bonus feed for every injury I sustain in order to heal myself."

My eyes narrowed on the eager demon. "That's an awful lot of blood for one human to give."

I had no idea if that was true, but it sounded like a lot. I'd already fucked up my first round of negotiation with the cunning demon. This time, I wasn't going to be handing out blank cheques.

"So long as there's no toll on the host other than slight fatigue, of course," he amended, inclining his horns in an acquiescent tilt that only made me more suspicious. "If it helps, there are also ways to help boost your blood production and overall health, but we can discuss those if you feel the need." He waved a hand dismissively, but it piqued my curiosity.

What could a demon do to strengthen a witch? If I was about to take on a small army of hunters, I needed all the power I could get.

"So if we forge this new deal, we break the old one?" I asked. It wasn't like I knew how demonic deals actually worked. Would a new one just supersede the old automatically, or did we have to break it first?

He snorted, misinterpreting my question. "Nice try, but the old deal stays. I'm sure you'd rather I catch the next knife thrown your way rather than let it slice through your pretty, pretty face."

I scowled, but the demon had a point. Again. Hard to enjoy freedom if you were dead.

"Hmmm…" I tapped my chin as I pretended to debate my options, but the decision was easy. Did I want a haunted life on the run? Or did I want to gamble a little blood for the chance to carve out a safer future?

The faint breeze fluttered the wisps of my hair that had worked free of my braid. A cuckoo chirped from a nearby branch, drowned out by the honking of a car horn in the distance. I drew in a deep breath, taking in the calming scents of the spring wild-flowers.

"Deal."

A tightness squeezed my chest with a pulse of magic, and a ring of heat circled my right wrist. I glanced down in time to catch a curling red script etch into my pale skin like fresh cuts. The faint pattern hugged my wrist like a glowing tattoo.

Rex nodded towards my raised arm. "The deal's terms sink into your skin. Only a demon can read it."

That explained the odd burning pain I'd felt on my left wrist and weird glow when I'd agreed to our first deal.

Seeing the binding branded across my flesh made everything more real. I barely resisted the urge to scratch at the marks as they slowly faded. Both wrists felt heavy as I dropped my hand back to my side.

Satisfaction radiated from Rex's angular features, giving his predatory face a smug cast. Unease squirmed through me. Perhaps

I'd made another hasty decision. I just hoped I didn't come to regret either demonic deal.

Whatever you agree, you'll pay the price.

The warning from Quartz's grimoire rose in my thoughts unbidden.

I shook off the sense that I'd set something into motion that couldn't be undone. Instead, I squared my shoulders, facing the demon I'd let shackle my wrists with his contracts.

We were bound together now. Might as well get on with things.

"Well...now what?" I asked.

He shrugged. "We find the hunters. And kill them."

My mouth gaped open. "That's it? That's your entire plan?"

I couldn't believe I'd just signed away blood—and other things—to this demon. Maybe it wasn't wise to assume any demon was a useful demon.

He cocked a brow. "What more did you want? A step-by-step breakdown of how I'll punch my claws through a hunter's throat? Maybe I'll sting another with my venom." His pointy tail jabbed forwards over his shoulder in a deadly demonstration. "Is PowerPoint OK?"

I glared at the frustrating beast. "Is there nothing between those horns? *How* are we going to find the hunters?"

He shrugged again, drawing my eye to his broad shoulders. The rising sun caressing him at his back contrasted with the dark grey of his smooth skin.

"We'll ask some locals." The "obviously" was left unspoken, but his flat look practically screamed it.

I swallowed down the urge to conjure a fireball so I could lob it at his stupid, arrogant face. My magic would probably only spark and splutter out, anyway.

I took a deep breath and gestured with a hand, wielding sarcasm instead. "Lead the way, O Wise Hellspawn."

He snorted, the sound making him a fraction less intimidating as he lightly shook his horns. "First, you need to sort that out." He gestured at me with a blasé claw.

I glanced down at myself, taking in the sorry state I'd been reduced to. Both of us looked fresh from a horror movie, not to mention there was a gaping hole in my leggings allowing a rather inappropriate breeze.

A rush of heat lit my cheeks at the memory of *why*.

Chapter 14

"Stop being a prissy little princess." The hulking demon gestured towards the running water. "Get in."

My fists balled at my sides, irritation flaring at his tone. "I will get in. I'm just saying that it's going to be freezing, and you'd better turn around, perv."

After his frankly unnecessary comment about my dishevelled state, Rex had sauntered deeper into the park. His curious arrow tail had beckoned me after him before swaying hypnotically as we'd waded through the thickening underbrush towards a stream he could apparently hear.

Luckily for me, it was still early enough that nobody was likely wandering the woods just yet, but the sun had risen to the point where the air had lost its dewy chill. Still, the gently babbling stream was going to be *fresh*.

A shark-like grin widened Rex's lips. "Worried about me seeing you naked, little mouse? I promise it won't be long until you're begging me to undress you."

The towering demon took a step towards me, his heat reaching out to caress me even from a few paces away. I crossed my arms, standing my ground on the shallow riverbank, shaded beneath the drooping boughs of a sleepy willow. The dark demon, with his flaming red-orange hair and double set of onyx horns, looked so out of place in the tranquil forest scene. I was half-tempted to pinch myself, just to check whether this was even real.

I snorted. "You're delusional. I'd never beg for you to even look at me, let alone touch me."

The gently rushing water created a serene backdrop to the tension mounting between us. We stared each other down, challenging red eyes clashing with my narrowed purple glare.

After a few strained moments, he threw up his hands with a smoky huff. "We're both still covered in blood, and while that's something I'm well used to, we'd probably stick out amongst all the pesky humans."

Before I could open my mouth to snark back, his hands curled into the waistband of his trousers and pushed them down.

I blinked hard, my mind blanking like a slate wiped clean.

Rex stepped out from the pool of dark fabric at his feet.

Muscular thighs framed a monstrous grey length. It hung proud, thick, and fully erect. Bobbing under its own weight, the arrowed tip pointed right at me in what felt like a threat. Or a promise.

Compared to the almost leaden tone of his smooth skin, his cock was an even darker shade, almost blue-tinged like his forked tongue. A thick line of raised texture streaked along the centre from base to pointed head, where a pale lilac bead dribbled from the tip.

Was there anything remotely human about this monster?

My cheeks flamed, echoing the heat that pooled low in my abdomen.

From the corner of my eye, I caught the amused curve of his full lips. "You'll have to open wider than that, little mouse."

Reality smacked me on the back of the head. I closed my mouth with a snick of teeth and, with embarrassing effort, tore my gaze away, turning from the demon to stare at a different kind of trunk. This one significantly less smooth. Maybe just as hard.

"Don't be shy, you're not the first witch to blush at the sight of a demon's...*weapon*." His velvety purr was as devilish as his smirk.

The sound of splashing water saved my poor, exhausted brain from coming up with anything intelligent. Otherwise, I'd have probably blurted out something nonsensical. Or asked for a closer look.

No. Bad witch. Down, girl.

I *really* needed to get laid after this whole debacle was over.

Sunlight sparkled off the clear stream as the demon slowly resurfaced, a monster rising from the deep. His ridged horns pierced the air. The upright set looked even taller as the water weighed his crimson hair. Eerily bright eyes stood in stark contrast to the slate hue of his skin as the demon peered up at me.

Droplets caressed the thick column of his throat as he inched higher. They rejoined the river, almost reluctantly, as they traced over his wide-set shoulders and the top of his muscular pectorals, mixing with the faint pink eddying around him as the river washed away the gore.

He may be a bastard, but some small part of me couldn't help but notice he was a handsome one. Even with all his inhuman features.

"Come on in. The water's probably a little chilly for a witch like you, but I can warm you up." His bright eyes flared with challenge, daring me to join him.

A witch like me, huh?

I was going to get wrinkles with the amount of scowling this demon had me doing.

With a spurt of anger fuelling my motions, I kicked off my muddy trainers and socks, whipped off my long-sleeve, undid my bra, and yanked down my ruined leggings, tossing the clothing in a pile beside my backpack nestled in the grass.

In record time, I was buck-arse naked in nature, like one of those hippy woo-woo witches from the Sage Coven.

A sense of power filled me, but it wasn't the energising pulse of magic. It was unlike anything I'd felt before. I never showed people my body, my skin. Scars criss-crossed my flesh, heaviest along my arms. As soon as I'd turned eighteen, I'd covered them, drowned the reminders of what the hunters had done to me in something beautiful. Nightshade belladonna—my mother and father's favourite—bloomed through the worst of them. But I'd also added others—hemlock, oleander, blackberry, holly, wolfsbane. Foxglove trailed up my spine. Blackthorn wrapped my left ribs, branching around my breast. Silverthorn mirrored it on my right.

Thorns and poisons replaced scars, and I'd become entranced by the poetry of transforming my canvas of pain to one of power. I just didn't show it to anybody. It wasn't for them.

The demon had gone preternaturally still, only highlighting the rushing water as it parted around him. His full lips parted ever so slightly, giving them a sensual pout.

His stare held a tangible weight as his glowing eyes drank me in from head to toe, ink and all. They snagged briefly at my chest, but whether it was my silvery anchor mark or my modest tits he admired, I didn't know.

He looked almost stunned.

It felt good to have someone see me with something other than pity or mild disdain. Even if it was a violent creature from hell. Even if it was probably how he'd react to any naked woman.

With a mental huff at my own pity party, I stepped into the river.

Cold bit at my skin, but I embraced the chill, ducking my head beneath the surface. A weightless sensation cocooned my body. Wisps of pale purple splayed around me as the current tugged my hair. I had the craziest urge to just let go, to let the river take me where it willed. All my problems, my fears, would wash away with me. I could give in and sleep forever. I was so damn tired already. Tired of the running. Of the violence haunting my waking hours and following me into sleep. Of the terror and anxiety strangling my throat a little tighter each day.

My lungs squeezed with the burning need for oxygen, helping me shove away the insanity. The pebbled riverbed dug into my soles as I straightened, breaking the surface with a gasping breath.

The demon lurked barely a few inches away, pulling back a hand like he'd just been reaching for me. He cocked an inky brow. "Hmm, and I thought mermaids had scales, not wands."

I splashed water at him, releasing an embarrassing giggle as it hit him square in the face, causing him to jerk back in surprise like a disciplined puppy.

He swiped a clawed hand down his face, an unamused look flattening his sharp features. "An effective weapon. I can see why you have the hunters running in fright."

"Ooh, what a dry tone for such a soggy demon." I poked my tongue out before turning my back on the sarcastic beast.

Apparently, all my brain could dish out was childish behaviour, but I felt strangely lighter than I had moments before. I didn't want to look too closely at why.

I rubbed at my skin, ignoring the faint raised lines of scar tissue, trying in vain to get clean. Without soap, it wasn't all that effective, but it was better than nothing. I'd settle for not reeking of death.

Unknotting my braid, I let the thick locks tumble into the water and rinsed them as best I could before deciding to leave them loose to dry. I'd always considered myself lucky; my long hair usually behaved itself, even after getting wet. Plus, with the mild temperatures of early spring, there wasn't yet enough heat or humidity to frizz it out of control.

Rex rose to his full height, snagging my attention. I braced for another eyeful, but the river only came up to his waist, giving me an up-close view of his stupidly chiselled abs. All eight of them.

"I'm hungry," he said before waving a hand at me. "Finish up splashing about, little mermaid, while I go fetch us some food."

"Why, thank you for the permission to finish bathing, *Your Majesty*," I said, flashing him a syrupy sweet smile. I hoped it gave the prick diabetes.

He grinned. "Usually, my subjects just call me *Sire*, but I'll admit, the full title has a certain charm coming from your pouty lips."

I was still scowling as I watched him stroll off into the forest. Naked.

Chapter 15

"What in the fiery pits of hell is that?" I balked at the fluffy offerings hanging limp from the demon's claws.

I finished pulling on my last semi-clean top—a stretchy long-sleeve that was both comfortable and dark enough to disguise dirt and bloodstains.

Not ten minutes after leaving me in peace, the demon had returned with what was apparently the promised "food." In the form of dead rabbits.

Each was an adorable tawny shade with an off-white under-belly and a huge puff of fur for a tail.

Rex stepped into his discarded black sweats, still a puddle on the grass from where he'd stripped off before, and pulled them up with his free hand. Somehow, they still looked cleaner than my clothing, despite all the murdering he'd done while wearing them.

The demon raised his brows. "Fooood..." He pointed a claw to the fluffy creatures in his grip as he drew the word out in an insultingly slow drawl.

"You brought me dead bunnies," I hissed. "What am I meant to do with that?"

"Wow. I knew you mages lacked survival instincts, but this really is worse than I'd imagined." He shook his horns, but I caught the faint twitch of his lips before he tipped his head back and opened his jaw impossibly wide.

His fangs looked lethal as they protruded into his gaping maw. With a flick of his wrist, he tossed a single rabbit into the air and caught it in his mouth. His jaws snapped closed with a loud crunch. The demon chewed quickly, pulverising flesh and bone as easily as I'd devour a Victoria sponge cake.

I stared, completely stunned.

He swallowed audibly before flashing me a toothy grin, fangs and all. "It's called *eating*. Or did you need another demonstra-tion?"

I'd only been around the infuriating demon for a few hours, and already I'd been scowling more than I had in the past month. "Thanks, but I can't unhinge my jaw like a fucking snake."

The demon chuckled, that layered, smoky sound so uniquely his. "I'm a demon, remember? Just another '*twisted abomination,*' an '*ugly beast.*'" He parroted my earlier words in a high-pitched, whiny tone that was 100 per cent *not* accurate and then licked his lips with an exaggerated swipe of his forked tongue. "You were right before though; this '*bitter, raw flesh*' isn't anywhere near as sweet as your juices."

Do not *blush. Do* not *blush.*

I held my palm out with a low growl, breezing past his crude remark. I needed him to secure a place back with Quartz; surely I could put up with his bullshit for just a little while longer?

The demon snorted, mischief twinkling in his crimson eyes as he handed over the remaining rabbit. "You're so very welcome, little mouse."

His mocking tone set my teeth on edge, sparking the ever-present embers of anger that lurked in my chest. Already, Rex seemed to have a unique talent for getting under my skin with just a few well-aimed barbs.

I ignored the mouthy demon, steeling myself as I silently thanked the nature goddess for her gifts.

Feigning a confidence I didn't feel, I shut my eyes and reached for the magic humming in my chest. I stoked it to life, willing it to flow down my arms and into my hands.

After a few strained beats with nothing but my rapid puffs of air and the chirping of birds to distract me, the tips of my fin-gers tingled. Relief hit me as my eyes snapped open. My blunt, ordinary nails lengthened into dark claws, like I'd blotted them in ink. They looked sharp enough to rival Rex's, but where his stabbed out several long inches, mine were hardly bigger than the acrylic extensions I'd once got at a spa day with Lyndsey.

Before I could overthink it, I ran a claw along the rabbit's back and dug my fingertips under the thick layers of fur and skin, tugging firmly to reveal the meat beneath. The soft, moist sensation churned my stomach, but on its heels came an empty gurgle as my hunger cheered me on.

If I was going to survive my tormentors, then I'd need to fuel my body and magic. Squeamishness was a luxury living on the run had quickly stripped away, leaving behind a cold, grim creature of pragmatism.

Besides, the poor bunny was already dead. It would be wasteful if I just left it to rot. I'd already been forced to do vicious things over the past few weeks; what was a little more blood under my claws?

I sank my fingers into the lean meat and willed the unnatural flames, smouldering deep inside me, to the surface.

Like most of my wild magic, the lilac flames edged in black were still a mystery. Ever since the whole grimoire-singeing incident, I'd not conjured much more than dark sparks of heat and maybe a few flickers I could stretch to call actual flames. The useless power that had got me kicked out onto my arse was nowhere to be seen when I needed it most. Typical.

If it weren't for the simmering heat I could feel buried in my chest like a rage I couldn't extinguish, then I'd have thought sparkly fingers were all that remained of the cursed ability.

Heat finally bathed my hand. A faint sizzle accented the smell of cooking meat. The aroma was a little too alluring, and the saliva pooling in my mouth had me concerned for my mental health.

For several minutes, I let the hare roast against my searing fingertips. Red slowly faded to a pale pink and finally a whitish hue. With a brief glare at the judgy demon for good measure, I tore off a chunk from the rabbit's side, stuffing the juicy piece into my mouth.

As quick as Rex had, I chewed and forced myself to swallow before I could freak out. I'd never tried rabbit before. My culinary history was like most humans' on the outskirts of a minor city; I bought groceries from local shops and ordered takeout when I was too lazy to cook. Mostly, those local shops were on coven grounds, stocked with produce grown by nature mages.

I'd also got to take home leftover produce from the farm shop where I'd worked, which my thrifty little heart had rejoiced at every time. Every few weeks, I'd still venture into the city to treat myself to the goodies you couldn't just grow with a little magical TLC. Cheesy puffs did *not* grow on trees.

The rabbit meat tasted vaguely like chicken but with an earthier flavour that wasn't bad, just different.

"Poor Thumper," Rex mocked, pressing a hand to his bare chest dramatically. "And you call *me* a beast."

I huffed, stuffing another pale strip into my mouth, chewing with a little too much force.

His gaze alighted on my claws as he flashed me a wicked grin. "Those are cute though. You should definitely unsheathe them next time you need protection. And for the fight before." He winked.

I paused, ignoring the hunger still rumbling my stomach, to shoot him an even more vicious glare.

Far too unconcerned by my impeding wrath, the demon chuckled. I could have sworn I saw faint wisps of smoke leave his wicked lips.

"That's a pretty demonic trait for a witch though," he said, clearly not taking the hint.

I swallowed another bite of my gamey breakfast. It slid down my throat in a thick lump as I waved the demon off with my grease-smeared claws. "I'm a *nature* mage. This is my magic manifesting in animalistic traits. Perfectly normal, actually."

Sure, I'd never heard of another nature mage transforming their features, let alone to borrow the traits of an animal, but it sort of made sense that we could. I mean, my mother had used to hiss like a cat sometimes.

I'd discovered the claw-shifting magic by accident a few weeks back. A hunter had pinned me down behind a grocery store, and my useless fire magic had only sparked enough to singe the bastard's arm hair. I still remembered the acrid scent of burning hair as he'd laughed at me, the cruel glint of excitement lighting his eyes.

A fierce pulse of magic had torn through my chest and rushed down my arms, and before I'd known it, my fingers had sunk part-way into his meaty forearms. The sensation had churned my stomach, but I'd managed to claw his face while he was still in shock, scrambling away. He'd spat curses, sprawled out on the concrete, gripping his face while I'd managed to sprint off into a back alley.

The demon snickered, shaking his horns. "Sure, little mouse, whatever you say."

My hands clenched, claws sinking deeper into the rabbit carcass as I scowled at the infuriating male. Clearly, my face-clawing days weren't over.

Chapter 16

"**W**ill you hold still?" I hissed.

"Your magic feels strange," Rex huffed, crossing his long arms over his chest, causing his pectoral muscles to pop.

I swear the demon had bigger tits than I did. If anyone asked, I wasn't jealous... I'd always subscribed to the belief that anything more than a handful was just a bonus. But maybe that was out of necessity.

I eyed Rex's huge hands, easily twice the size of mine. Not even his meaty pecs could fill those.

This close, bittersweet ginger drugged me with every inhale, trying to entice me to lean in and take a deeper sniff of his unique scent. Maybe even dart my tongue out to see if he tasted as good as he smelled.

Fighting back a blush at the direction of my thoughts, I arched a stern brow at the demon. I kept running my palm over his body, hovering just a few inches from touching.

I'd already muttered the incantation of the basic spell, thanking the magic goddess when I'd felt the familiar rush of power surge within my chest. Apparently my magic was behaving itself today, especially since not thirty minutes ago, I'd roasted myself a breakfast. Luckily for me, a glamour spell wasn't complicated.

Not when you were only trying to hide certain features, anyway. Like his massive horns, devilish tail, wicked claws, and fangs. Oh, and turn his skin from dark slate to a warmer, mahogany hue. To conserve my strength, I only used the incantation for showing the illusion to humans. Other magical beings would see straight through to the monster beneath. Most hunters carried charms made by their captive mages to counter it too, but there wasn't much I could do about that.

The demon scowled, his thick brows slamming low over his burning eyes. "How much longer will this take?"

I gritted my teeth against the urge to shower him in sparks of fire instead, hurrying down the length of his body. I pointedly ignored the heat that bloomed across my cheeks as I skimmed my palm over the bulge at his crotch. Crouching low, I quickly swept his powerful thighs and down his long legs to his bare feet.

The spell worked best if it stuck to all of him. At least, that was the theory. I'd only ever performed this spell on another being in class, and that had been on a mage. Here was hoping it worked the same on demons.

I stood, shaking out my hand to try to dislodge the tingly feeling of channelling the spell. My limbs felt heavier, exhaustion still tugging at me. "There. You're all done."

"Finally," he huffed before pausing. "Thanks." His gratitude fell with an obvious reluctance that had me stifling a snort.

Clearly, manners didn't come easily to the denizen of hell. Shocker.

"So about this highly thought-out master plan of yours...?" I trailed off, waiting for whatever irritating sass he was going to spew next.

He shot me a calculating look, tail flickering behind him. "Why yes, follow me, little mouse. It's a good thing I'm still hungry."

The predatory gleam in his eyes did not give me the warm fuzzies.

Sunlight warmed my back as we finally came to stop after what felt like hours of trekking through the city. Given the sun had barely reached its zenith in the sky, probably just over an hour had passed, full of awkward silence as I glared at Rex's bare back, ignoring the sinuous movement of toned muscle beneath smooth skin and the hypnotic sway of his raised tail, wondering what madness he was leading me into.

I eyed the crumbling brick walls of the Victorian-era building we'd stopped in front of. Chunks of the same dull red littered the gravel, along with a broken wheel cover and too many shards of brown glass, which I'd bet my last pair of clean knickers came from beer bottles. Moss gathered in the dips of the tiled roof, patches having somehow survived on the underside of the modern guttering, giving it the beginnings of a budget living wall.

An ornate wall bracket held a swinging sign above the timber door, proclaiming it Rusty's Pub. Fitting, since an oxidized red edged the vintage iron sign. By contrast, a shiny row of chrome and black leather motorbikes parked outside in a neat line. One grimy window, showcasing off-white net curtains, held a faded placard declaring Rusty's as closed.

I suppressed a grimace as I ran my gaze over Ye Olde Biker Bar one more time. "You're *sure* this is the right place?"

I wasn't sure what to expect when I'd followed Rex out of the woods and back into the hum of the city. I figured any demons hiding on Earth would just be lurking in the shadows of dark alleyways or, of course, the creepiest of places—underground car parks—but I supposed even demons must like to hang out with a casual beer.

Before midday on a Wednesday.

I was a homeless fugitive on the run from a genocidal cult, and even I hadn't resorted to boozing this early. Yet.

Rex waved a clawed hand dismissively. "Of course. I can smell those greedy fuckers from here."

Twisting my mother's silver belladonna ring around my index finger, I eyed the run-down pub again. Wasn't like I had any better ideas.

"Fuck it."

Rex nodded with a look I'd have called approval on anyone else. "That's the spirit, little mouse. Let me do the talking and stay behind me. Unless you want to owe me for protecting you as well as revenge after this."

Pleasure for protection.

An uncomfortable heat bloomed low in my abdomen. Unfortunately, we hadn't broken our original deal when we'd forged the new one, and I didn't need reminding of the...*intimate* consequences.

I rolled my eyes with a snort, trying to cover for the fact I was most definitely blushing. "Yes, *Your Majesty.*"

He regally nodded his horns, and a grin split his full lips. "If things get exciting, remember that most demons are only slightly harder to kill than a mage. Steal one of their weapons and just shoot them in the head or, if you have to, try to saw through as much of their throat as possible with your cute little claws. If you can behead them fully, even better." He eyed up the regular human nails I was currently sporting with a dubious look.

Ignoring the jab at my *impressive*, not cute, claws, I stashed away the valuable information. I huffed, shooting him a flat look like this was all old news to me. In reality, I knew next to nothing about demons and their weaknesses. We'd been taught that they were these all-powerful evil creatures that should be avoided at all costs. They were stronger, faster, and could heal better than even we could, but he'd already let slip that they were mortal. Apparently, even demons needed brains.

Despite how little some of them might be blessed with.

Rex flashed me a chipper grin and strode towards the panelled door, tail twitching in excitement as he called over his shoulder in an imperious tone, "Come, peasant."

A chuckle burst from my lips before I strangled off the traitorous sound, annoyed at how easily I'd been affected by his roguish charm.

This was a business arrangement. We weren't friends. I had no friends.

Ignoring the pang of loss squeezing my chest, I trudged after the demon. Making a quick decision, I stashed my backpack in the wild rosebushes on one side of the building. If I was going to be fighting, I'd rather not have something so easily grabbed by an opponent. My martial arts training was limited to a couple years of basic lessons from my brother over a decade ago. I'd been a gangly, uncoordinated teen, and he'd refrained from ever actually hitting me, but at least I could throw a half-decent punch.

Rex slammed his palm into the peeling door, smashing it to pieces with a loud crash. I gaped at the destruction, momentarily stunned.

Voices yelled. Furniture screeched.

I caught the edge of Rex's unhinged grin as he stepped through the broken door frame. "Ooh, a boozy brunch, my favourite!"

His tail shot out to the side. A gurgling scream followed.

The sound penetrated my shock. I scrambled to enter behind Rex, preparing myself for the fight he was practically giddy to start.

Rex inhaled deep and roared, a primal sound that jarred my muscles, locking them up tight with an instinctive fear. My brain sharpened with the need for fight or flight.

It took a single second to process the scene we'd stumbled into. A small crowd of grizzled men spread throughout the room, clad in cliché leather jackets and varying shades of battered denim. Most clustered before a long bar along the back, overturned stools scattered at their booted feet. Shock plastered a few faces, but aggression painted more.

Beside Rex, a man on his knees rapidly turned an alarming shade of purple, one beefy hand clamped around the tail pressed to his neck. The demon whipped his tail back, revealing his blood-coated stinger tipping the devilish arrow. Rex's victim collapsed forwards, a silvery blade clattering to the floor beside him.

"Slade!" A rotund bartender planted his palms on the wooden surface, concern lacing his anguished yell. "Fuck. Kill the demon prick!" He pointed frantically at Rex, as if there were any other assailant killing patrons.

The bikers lurched into action, drawing knives and pistols in a flurry of movement.

I dived aside, landing hard on the sticky floorboards behind a snooker table just as gun fire boomed through the space. My heart hammered as I reached for my fire.

A smoky chuckle floated over the chaos. Eerily loud and full of violent glee.

Screams and groans layered the air, accompanied by wet squelches and hard thuds in a violent symphony.

Lilac-and-black sparks danced between my fingers.

Here goes nothing.

I peeked over the green felt. A biker charged towards me, pistol raised. With a rush of power, I threw my hand forwards. A flaming sphere shot towards the man, colliding with his shoulder. He shrieked, batting at the ghostly fire as he slammed into a nearby table in panic before going down in a heap.

Burning flesh soured the air, along with the metallic tang of blood and other fluids. My stomach heaved at the thick stench, but I clenched my jaw and tried to stay alert.

The bikers attacked Rex, shooting the grey shadow bouncing around the room. He was just as impossibly nimble as when I'd summoned him. His claws flashed as he leaped through beams of sunlight, cutting down a man almost as tall as him.

He grabbed another victim: a heavily scarred male brandishing two comically large bowie-knives. Knocking the blades aside, Rex darted close and buried his fangs in the man's neck. Bliss lit the demon's features as his throat worked. Cradling him close like a lover, Rex spun them, using his victim like a shield. Bullets thudded in the dying man, shaking his body.

Only three men remained standing, and they fired in chaotic waves, shouting obscenities while Rex forced them to watch another comrade die. The demon sidestepped their reckless pot-shots as he continued his feast, unfazed.

A shadow dropped over me, and I rolled aside on reflex. Metal flashed in my periphery.

"Stay still, bitch!" a gruff male snarled.

A beefy man loomed over me as I scrambled back from his next thrust, adrenaline striking through me. The knife stopped inches from my throat. I lunged for my magic, willing the flames into being. Lilac-and-black sparks swallowed my hands as I threw them upwards.

Nothing happened.

The biker howled with a grating laugh, chins multiplying as he snarled down at me, scurrying back on my arse. "The fuck is them sparkles gonna do?"

Before I could wrangle my power, a limp body flew into him. The pair went down in a tangle of limbs. I blinked, recognising the pale face of the scarred man Rex had drained as the body sprawled over my gruff attacker.

"That's at least one debt of protection." A low purr in my ear had me jolting.

Crouching low, Rex leaned around me, slashing the trapped biker's inner thigh with his claws. The man screamed as Rex severed vital arteries, writhing beneath the dead weight of his friend.

Had Rex just *thrown* a man from across the pub?

Chips of wood rained down as a shot hit the pool table, sheltering us.

"Quit hiding, fucking cowards!" a male yelled.

I twisted to face the demon curved protectively around me.

Lips twitching, Rex held up a single claw doused in red. "I'll just be a minute." The black abyss had returned to his eyes, but silvery flecks sparkled in the darkness.

Of course the demon was having fun in a bloodbath.

He turned and leaped clear over the pool table. Screams followed.

I risked another peek over the felt. Rex slashed out a final throat, dropping the human to the floor in a loud tumble, shattering a wooden barstool.

For the second time, in as many hours as I'd known him, red painted Rex's grey skin as he stood amid a grisly display of body parts. His depthless gaze hunted me, the predatory intensity giving me shivers.

This was his true nature. His demonic need for violence.

"What is it, little mouse? Are you afraid of me now?" He smirked, showing off a sharp fang on one side. "Or are you more afraid of what you owe me?"

Yes. I wanted to scream it and sprint out of the building, tainted with fresh blood and bowels, and never look back.

But more than that, I wanted to live. And that meant working with the demon.

Hiding the tremble in my hands, I stood, flicking my lilac braid back over my shoulder and ignoring the magic-induced ache building within my skull. "What? Another boring romp?" I covered my mouth with a palm, feigning a loud yawn.

His wicked smirk told me he saw right through my bravado and found it as cute as my claws apparently were.

"Was the killing spree really necessary? I thought we'd come here to get information." I pointedly eyed the dead biker at his feet, ignoring how my stomach hardened at the gore. "Not particularly chatty now, are they?"

Rex chuckled, his tone dry. "Don't get your pretty cherry panties in a twist, little mouse. They may not be hunters, but these evil henchmen deserved death. They're people traffickers, amongst other things... Besides, I let them call for backup. Their dick-swinging bosses should be here aaaaany second."

Before I could process his snark, or his accusations, the distant rumble of engines reached my ears. As if his words summoned them, the thunder of motorbikes reverberated through the open door as a flood of black and chrome parked up. The throaty engines died down with a splutter, chased by the thumping of boots on gravel.

A feral roar tore apart the silence.

Chapter 17

I tensed, fear clamping my muscles.

Five male demons, clad in similar leather-and-denim ensembles as the dead bikers, strode into the pub. They fanned out, partially eclipsing the sunlight that streamed through the net curtains.

They eyed the room in strained silence, and I took my chance to assess them right back.

The three on the left wore identical menacing expressions on their flat faces similar enough that they could have been brothers.

They were tall and lean, with too-long arms that gave them a creepy vibe. Compared to Rex's threatening double set, their short horns were almost cute, like cartoon devils'. Each had pin-straight navy hair that perfectly complemented their lavender skin. Stubby tails drooped behind them, fleshy and thick.

The other two demons were built stout, with shadowy skin and swirling tattoos. They moved eerily across their flesh like living smoke. I'd heard of their kind: the shadow-walkers.

We'd been taught that they fed on souls and if we ever encountered one, we should run for our lives while praying to the goddesses for salvation.

Both shadow-walkers watched me with an interest that made my palms sweat. More so than being confronted by a pack of hell-mutts. At least those monsters would only devour my flesh.

"Rexar...," the male in the centre snarled, beady eyes casually surveying the chaos of blood and bodies. His horns looked slightly longer than the rest of his lavender brethren's, and he radiated an entitled air of authority. His upper lip lifted in obvious disgust as he glared at Rex, yet something in the tense lines of his body seemed on edge. "What the fuck are you doing in my territory?"

Rex grinned, lips stretching manically wide. "Zatar, a pleasure as always. I've come to ask a few questions. Answer them and I'll let you live."

His threat was delivered so jovially I almost missed it, too caught up watching the demons eyeing me like their next meal.

I scanned the five demons, taking in their powerful forms, from their muscular limbs to their sharp horns, claws, and fangs. Compared to the newcomers, Rex was vastly outnumbered. Despite his immense size, and the constant danger he emanated, he looked almost vulnerable.

My heart pounded in my chest. I might question our chances against five aggressive demons, but Rex seemed completely at ease.

Zatar laughed, chest shaking with a hearty guffaw, but it sounded forced. "The *Outcast King* thinks he can take on the Five with nothing more than one of his feeble pet witches?" He shook his head, but his eyes remained pinned to Rex, alert and ready. "This is why all mutts should be put down."

Shock had my brows shooting up even as fear skated down my spine. I'd thought Rex had been joking about having *subjects*. Had I summoned a genuine demon king? How was that even possible with my weak, unruly magic? I may not know how summoning actually worked, but surely a more powerful being couldn't be wrenched from their own kingdom so easily.

"Scoff all you want. You think I can't scent that delectable fear wafting off you?" Rex bared his fangs, raised tail swaying hypnotically over his shoulder like a snake about to strike. "It'll spice your blood so sweetly."

I had to admit—he posed a menacing sight, his muscular body covered in gore with his wicked fangs on display.

Zatar hesitated, but beside him, his reedy possible-brother bristled with a low hiss. "Mongrel scum," he spat. "It'll be your polluted blood spilled today. I wouldn't drink that vile filth if I were dying of thirst." His gaze swung to me, and I froze under his lecherous glare. "Your witch, on the other hand, looks delicious indeed." His fat, forked tongue swiped over his thin lips like a writhing slug. "She'll fetch a good price once we've had our fun."

Revulsion squeezed my guts, heaving and pitching my stomach as my mind helpfully conjured vivid images of the threat he implied. Whatever happened here, I did *not* want to end up in his clutches.

Maybe following a demon into a dingy biker bar hadn't been such a good idea.

Rex snorted, unfazed by the possibility of my impending doom. "That vicious witch will roast your wiener quicker than you can say 'sausage sizzle.'" He waved his claws, flicking blood dismissively. "Enough foreplay. Where are the Riverside hunters?"

Zatar's gaze cut to the shadow-walker on the far side, who still watched me with unsettling intensity, before snapping back to Rex with a sneer. "Why would we tell you anything, mutt?"

I guess we at least knew who to question.

"Last chance." Rex shrugged, curved claws splaying at his sides. "I've been waiting eagerly for my opportunity to end your flesh trade here, but I'll let you return to hell, alive, if you tell me what I want to know."

Zatar snarled. "Kill him."

The demons exploded into action.

Rex whooped loudly, grinning manically wide as he beckoned the charging males closer.

The nearest lavender demon barrelled towards me instead, swiping out with wicked claws inches from my face. Displaced air brushed my cheek as I dodged backwards just in time.

With a yell, I swiped out, whipping purple flames across his chest. Flesh burned, stinging my nose as four singed lines appeared through the demon's leather jacket.

The demon flinched, hissing out a breath before charging me with an enraged snarl. My back hit the wall as I scrambled away, eyes wide. I reached for my power again, but my fingers sparkled uselessly.

I had no time to think, only react.

I dropped to the floor. My fingers throbbed as claws burst from their tips with a pulse of magic. An ache built in my mouth, but I ignored the odd sensation, already lashing out as the demon slammed into the bricks above my head. My fingers sank easily through denim into his meaty thigh as I took a page from Rex's book, cutting vital arteries before I dived through the beast's legs.

With a yelp, his tail slapped the side of my head hard enough to make my ear ring. He spun to track me even as he stumbled, injured leg buckling beneath his weight.

A grunt sounded right behind me before something clattered to the floor. I risked a glance over my shoulder. Paces away, sinful black eyes met mine. Rex shielded me with his enormous body. Something slammed into his back, knocking him forwards a step. A silvery blade jutted through his upper chest, skewering him clean through, the navy-soaked tip pointing out at me from his flesh.

I sucked in a gasp—his blood was *blue*.

With impossible flexibility, he reached his long arm behind him and yanked the blade from his back, launching it towards me in one smooth motion. I froze, but the knife sailed past my face, hitting something behind me with a dull thud.

The lavender demon collapsed, grasping the blade in his neck.

"That's two," Rex purred, hungry gaze devouring me despite the blood pouring down his chest.

"It's more revenge than protection," I muttered, fighting a blush at the implication of his words.

He was already darting towards the others, a stream of blue escaping the open wound in his back.

I twisted towards the lavender demon Rex had killed for me, yanking the blade free in a spray of arterial blood. The weight of the warm handle helped to ground me as I ran past the snooker table to confront the remaining demons. Only Zatar and a shadow-walker remained, both locked in a vicious battle with Rex.

Rex was a shadowed blur, moving with impossible speed and skill, dodging blows and dealing his own in rapid succession.

"Tell me what I need to know, and the fun stops." His voice came out level, like they were casually discussing the weather, despite the deadly dance amongst the trio.

"Get fucked, hybrid abomination," Zatar hissed, trying to cling to some of that menacing authority he'd first radiated. The blood dripping into his eyes from a nasty gash on his forehead ruined the effect. "You should have stayed hiding in the woods. Once we kill you, I'm going to burn down the hovels you've built and cut down the rest of your pathetic kind."

I grasped for my magic, pleading with it to manifest its haunting flames. Sparks danced uselessly around my bloodied hands. Frustration clawed through me as I watched helplessly from the sidelines, head pounding as much as my heart.

Injured and alone, Rex fought the remaining demons.

I gripped the knife tighter in my palm. I was a witch barely out of basic magic training. What did I know about battling demons? I'd been learning spells and rituals, only going through some very basic self-defence and fitness training. Nothing that prepared me for this life of violence I'd been thrust into.

Rex roared, stepping forwards into the claws arcing towards him. Zatar sliced into Rex's side, but Rex gripped the shorter male's head in his hand. He yanked aside and buried his fangs in Zatar's throat, tearing the flesh wide open with a ragged bite.

His tail struck in a coordinated attack, piercing the shadow-walker's chest as the demon pounced. Yellow eyes rolled back. His shadowy form dropped, convulsing on the floor as foam bubbled from his mouth. In seconds, he stilled.

Rex gripped Zatar's leather vest, holding him upright while his victim bled out.

Zatar gurgled, head lolling. Somehow, he still glared at Rex, choking out words almost too faint to hear: "Y-You're still...hybrid s-scum."

Rex watched his victim with hard onyx eyes, unmoved by the dying man's words. He released the body, letting it fall to the floor like discarded trash.

As he stood in profile, sunlight bathed his granite form, setting his ombre hair aflame. With a ragged breath, he turned towards me, flat expression unreadable.

I sucked in a gasp at the sight of him.

Navy blood wept from the gaping hole in his upper chest. His side was drenched, even more dark liquid leaking from the ragged gashes. White bone gleamed wetly beneath.

"Zoella," he grunted, the word almost too gravelly to understand.

The demon took a single step towards me.

He listed aside, falling into a table with a great crash as the wood shattered beneath his weight.

Chapter 18

"**F**uck!" Too late, I lurched to help.

Panic clawed through me as I knelt beside Rex, ignoring the warm liquid soaking my knees through the thin material of my leggings.

"Rex!" His name came out as a strangled squeak. I frantically searched his slackened features for any signs of life. "Come on, you royal prick. *Wake up.*"

Guilt gnawed at me. If he hadn't taken that knife to the back for me, he wouldn't be in such rough shape. He might infuriate me, but I didn't want to see him hurt.

Inky lashes fluttered before peeling back to reveal blood-red eyes, slit pupils dilated into wide ovals. A frown scrunched his features. "Did you just squeak again, my little mouse?"

I scowled at the collapsed heap of demon, but relief swam through me. If he was giving me sass, he was probably OK.

"You must be hearing things." I sniffed, ignoring the nagging urge to ask if he was OK. "Probably hit that fat head of yours too hard."

Mirth danced in his glowing eyes, but his grey complexion looked paler than usual, an almost ashen shade rather than a dark slate. "Were you worried about little old me, witch?"

I huffed, not trusting myself to speak. Who knew what crazy confessions might spill out?

Taking a deep breath, I shoved my nerves aside and yanked my sleeve up. A colourless wolfsbane tattoo curved around my wrist, and I thrust it into his face. It was my fault he was hurt. "Here, you've earned it."

Demons needed to feed to regain their strength, right? The coven teachers had told us that demons healed incredibly fast, but the ragged wounds across Rex's upper body gushed blood. Every time I glanced at them, a panicky feeling scratched inside my middle. I wasn't sure I had enough blood in me to replace all he was losing.

Rex's eyes pierced mine, holding me captive with a near-feral intensity, as if he was waiting for me to yank it away again and yell "psyche!"

I held my arm steady, meeting his challenging stare head on.

Whatever you agree, you'll pay the price.

I wouldn't balk at the agreement I'd made. Rex had tried to get the information I needed. He'd taken a knife to the back for me. The least I could do was bleed a little for him too.

His ashen lips parted, revealing sharp fangs. I waited for the predator to strike, balling my fist to stop the slight tremor.

Pain spiked up my forearm as he bit down, quick as a viper. I hissed but held steady, pressing my skin against his lips. Heat bloomed from his fangs in twin points, spreading outwards until it felt like I'd dunked my arm into a bath. The pleasant sensation stole the pain but also spread another kind of warmth.

Heat spooled through my body, heading south. My core clenched as an unexpected need wound through me. I squirmed, pressing my thighs together in an effort to dispel the sensation. The need for *more.*

Rex groaned against my skin, sending shivers through me. Every pull at my wrist throbbed right to my clit in a sensual echo.

"Rex," I groaned. "W-What's happening?" A needy whine vibrated my chest.

Rex growled, releasing his hold on my flesh. With one last lick, his horns clunked back to the floorboards.

Like I'd drugged him, his pupils had dilated until the black pools were barely ringed with red.

He shuddered on the floor, forked tongue swiping across his plump lower lip to catch the few remaining drops. "So fucking delicious, almost as sweet as your arousal on my lips."

What little blood I had left rushed to my cheeks. I squirmed. Need pulsed through me at the reminder of how good his wicked tongue had felt between my thighs.

The offer was there, gleaming in his hungry gaze.

If I wanted, I could straddle his face. Here and now. Let him devour me until I shattered.

I hated to admit it, but the demon had given me more pleasure with his inhumanly forked tongue than any guy before him.

I blinked sharply, coming back to my senses.

No. I'd already given in to his wicked spell once. I wasn't getting pleasured surrounded by so much violence. Not again.

I grimaced, surveying the carnage around us. "Let's go."

Rex grinned, not offended in the slightest by my brusque tone. "After you, little mouse."

I huffed. "And I did *not* squeak."

His infuriating smile only widened.

Without giving him a chance to reply, I put a healthy amount of space between us as I subtly inspected my wrist. Only faint twin punctures marked my flesh neatly between a gap in the clustered wolfsbane hoods. Somehow, the wounds had already nearly healed.

Making my way around the room, I pocketed cash, knives, guns, anything useful I could find on the humans and demons. At least there was one pragmatic, but morally grey, upside to this whole debacle.

"So much for talking to *the locals*, huh?" I said, eyeing Rex as he climbed unsteadily to his feet.

He grunted, stumbling a step before reaching down with a trembling hand to search the fallen shadow-walker at his feet.

Concern squirmed through my chest. Rex's skin was still a pale hue, and his wounds had barely closed, trickles of navy liquid still seeping down his bare chest.

Guilt at what Rex had suffered on my behalf had me pausing, fisting the bills in my hand. "Are you OK?"

He moistened his lower lip, an oddly nervous gesture for the usually confident demon. Avoiding my gaze, he stared down at his victim. "I'm fine."

His words rang false, and I quirked a brow in response. "If you need more blood, just say."

He hesitated, seeming to weigh his words carefully. With a terse gesture at his wounded side, he said, "I still need to feed."

I frowned. "That's what I'm offering..."

He was already shaking his head, the fiery strands of his hair swaying around his spiralling horns. "Not blood."

My left wrist felt heavy with the weight of our original deal, inscribed beneath my flesh. *Pleasure for protection.*

"Oh," I breathed, trying to control my heart rate as it sat up and took notice.

Wicked need, already simmering from his bite, surged straight to my core. A small part of me craved more of his sinful touch and the bliss he'd seemed eager to give me.

The larger, logical part of me knew this was nothing but a business transaction. A deal to get what we both needed. For hell's sake, my pleasure was his *food*. Nothing more.

I straightened, clearing my throat. "Fine. But not here."

I waved a hand towards the back exit and made a beeline for the door. My nape prickled with awareness as Rex stalked behind me. Escaping outside, I gulped fresh air, savouring it despite the stale scents of motor oil and weed mixed in. Anything was better than the thick stench of death.

The sun had crested the buildings in the distance, peering down at the city sprawled beneath.

Rusty's Pub had a fenced-in backyard like some suburban house. Overgrown grass ran riot, almost swallowing the paving stones and hiding oxidised car parts dotted at random intervals across the lawn.

"Zo..." Rex trailed off, voice oddly serious. It was the first time he'd used the shortened version of my name, and an unusual sense of familiarity accompanied it.

I paused but couldn't seem to face him.

He cleared his throat. "You don't have to do this, little mouse... I can find someone else."

Little mouse.

He'd been calling me that since I'd summoned him. But I wasn't some meek creature, cowering away from the big, bad wolf. I'd accepted the deal, and I'd be damned if I broke it now. Maybe literally.

I wasn't sure if he was trying to con me into breaking our deal. Maybe he really could drag me back to hell, or do something equally sinister, if I did. Either way, I was sick of being underestimated. Being the victim.

I pivoted on my heel, our gazes clashing.

Indignation, and something dark and needy I didn't want to examine, flashed through me. "You think I can't handle it?" I planted a hand on my hip. "Come here. Let's get this over with."

For a loaded beat, his fiery eyes searched mine. What he was looking for, I had no clue.

My eyes narrowed on the blood-soaked male. "Lost your nerve, demon?"

He huffed through his nose in an animalistic snort, stomping closer. "Fine, but don't come crying to me when you're a shuddering mess, high on demonic pleasure and begging for more."

I snickered at the sheer absurdity of his arrogance. Plucking his wrist, too aware of how his warm skin felt against mine, I tugged him around the corner of the bar. The garden felt too exposed, but being sandwiched between the shoddy fence and crumbling brick wall around the building's flank gave us a modicum of privacy. Even though I felt like I was in some dingy alley instead.

Before I could overthink it, I shoved Rex against the bricks, ignoring the alluring way his firm abs tensed beneath my palms. Anticipation lit blood-red eyes. A secret part of me relished his eagerness.

"And just what are you planning to do with me, little mouse?" A taunting smirk tipped up one side of his full lips.

Lips that had been pressed to my skin moments ago. My wrist throbbed with the remembered sensation, not exactly as unpleasant as I'd have liked it to be. The thought of how sensual his daily feeds might be was a problem I'd have to deal with later though.

Rex's bright gaze flared with a mocking challenge as I stared up at him for a long moment.

My hackles were well and truly raised.

If he thought he was the only one who could take power from pleasure, he had another thing coming. I may not draw strength from it the demonic way, but I knew seduction was its own kind of magic.

And this time, I was the one in control.
I raised my chin.
And dropped to my knees.

<h1 style="text-align:center">Chapter 19</h1>

Rex's lips parted. Blackness swallowed his red gaze in an instant. "Zoella...," he breathed, voice tight with strain.

The way he said my name...like a curse and a prayer wrapped into one.

I couldn't help the grin that stretched my lips. "Yes, demon?" I purred, running my short claws over his thigh, feeling the muscles twitch beneath the soft fabric of his trousers.

Some unknown seductress had taken hold of me. Maybe I was possessed by a succubus. Either way, the feeling of being in control was a drug I could quickly become hooked on. I may be operating out of desperation, but that didn't mean I couldn't enjoy it a little.

This close, his unique, bittersweet ginger scent invaded my senses, threatening to make my mouth water.

Rex wet his lips. "Are you sure about this?"

I bared my teeth, feeling as animalistic as he looked. "Shut your mouth. And let me open mine."

Maybe snarling up at a demon I was trying to give head to wasn't a great strategy, but he acquiesced with a tilt of his horns, armed with a sly grin.

I reached for his trousers, slowly drawing down the elastic waistband. His cock sprung free, a huge grey length bobbing heavily before me. Compared to his lead-grey skin, his cock was a slightly darker shade, a colder hue despite the warmth radiating from him.

A pale bead of mauve dribbled from the pointed tip. The head was an almost bulbous version of the arrow shape crowning his tail. The blunt point seeped more fluid as I watched the pale-purple liquid dribbling down the side.

Both the topside and underside of his curved manhood had thick lines of flexible bristles, each only an inch or so long. I'd thought they were a textured strip, or maybe a trick of the light, before. With a frown, I stroked a fingertip cautiously over one of the short spines. It writhed under my touch. I yanked my hand away with a gasp, eyes shooting up to judge Rex's reaction.

He smirked down at me, seeming amused but not uncomfortable as his demonic black eyes tried to hold me captive.

I reached back for the curious bristles, letting them sway and brush against my fingertip. They tickled my skin, moving like a sea anemone in a tide.

Rex groaned, his hips jerking.

I bit my lip, stroking my finger along the full length of bristles, earning another low rumble from the demon. How would they feel brushing in and out of me? The added sensations had me more than a little curious.

When I'd caught an eyeful in the forest, I'd hardly noticed anything but how inhuman his *weapon* had looked. Now I realised I was strangely intrigued by all those odd features.

"Fuck, Zoella. The way you look at my cock. Like you're wondering how I taste," Rex growled, his pitch low with hunger.

I smirked up at him, feeling my lips plump. "That's because I am."

Without warning, I leaned forwards and licked the stray drop. A burst of flavour hit my tongue—a sweet yet earthy taste, reminding me vaguely of blueberries.

I groaned, the unique flavour ratcheting up my need. It tingled lightly on my tongue, and my body warmed, coming alive.

"Fuck, little mouse," he groaned. His claws curled into the brick at his sides with a loud scrape, crumbling flecks of red falling to the paving stones. "Do that again."

I obeyed, running my tongue more fully across his pointed tip, earning myself another shuddering groan from the demon and a tantalising hit of blueberry.

I stroked my claws over his hips, following the lines of his muscles down to his groin. My hands circled the base of his hot length. I groaned as I squeezed him, feeling that throbbing firmness against my palms. He was so wide at the base that I couldn't even touch the tips of my claws together. His length was just as impressive, easily as long as my forearm, probably longer. I stroked along one side, avoiding the curious bristles, fingertips caressing in a feather-light touch with just the barest hint of threat from my ink-dipped talons.

I took a moment to thank the goddesses that he'd only feasted on my core in payment before. There was no way that monster would fit inside me.

A smoky chuckle rattled above me. "Don't worry, little mouse, I'll make it fit. You'll love every fucking second."

I raised a brow, shooting Rex a sceptical look as I wondered if I'd said that thought aloud.

"You're so fucking beautiful, little mouse." Rex's claws gouged harder into the wall, as if he was struggling to hold himself back from forcing my jaw open and thrusting down my throat.

The thought drowned me in a heady thrill, only heightened by the unexpected sweetness of his words making me blush. Wetness had already gathered between my thighs, only becoming more obvious as I squeezed them together in an attempt to ease some of the building ache.

Black eyes bored into mine. "Open those lips for me, my pretty witch."

With a smug smirk, I heeded his command once more, parting oh so slowly.

"That hint of defiance, even as you obey me, is sexy as fuck," he growled. His hand shot out, fingers twisting in my hair as he gripped the back of my head. Claws pricked my brow as his large hand engulfed my skull with ease.

I gasped, lips parting wider.

He seized the opportunity. With a thrust, the pointed tip of his cock slid between my lips.

Blueberries coated my tongue as more of his tingly sweetness filled my mouth. I lapped at the source of the strangely addictive taste, feeling my body respond to his flavour with a savage ache pulsing low.

"Yes, that's it, little mouse." Rex's eyes glittered with dark intensity. "Take what you want. What you need."

His wicked encouragement spurred me on. I sucked on the arrowed head of his cock, groaning as more fluid filled my mouth. Hot need burned through me.

As if he could sense my growing abandon, he fed me more of his heated length. Those inhuman bristles tickled my lips, but the rest of him was silky smooth as he slid inside, inch by inch.

I opened wider for him, jaw aching at the forced stretch, but I couldn't bring myself to stop. When I was not even halfway down his length, he hit the back of my throat. I gagged, wrenching off him with a hacking cough.

Rex chuckled, that alluring, low sound like he was exhaling smoke with every amused huff. "Poor little mouse, is your demon's cock too much for you?" he cooed, stroking a claw along my cheek, a tender caress laced with danger.

Something warm pushed into the waistband of my leggings. I jolted at the sudden intrusion, but his claws tightened on my cheek, keeping my eyes on his face.

From my periphery I could just make out Rex's thick tail, curled around his leg to bury itself between us.

I raised my brows, earning a devious smirk in return. His wicked arrow wriggled into my panties to slip against my slit. I gasped, nerves lighting up at the smooth, heated surface stroking against my sensitive parts.

A moan escaped my lips as I melted under his sinful touch. The desperate noise pierced the haze of pleasure wrapping around me. I fought to regain some composure. Damn him, I was the one meant to be in control here.

I pointedly eyed the weeping length just inches from my lips. "That thing couldn't fill up a shot glass."

The beast hummed in amusement, but the flat of his tail glided along my pussy harder in retaliation, sending a bolt of pleasure through my core.

His fangs caught the sunlight as he grinned down at me. My wrist pulsed with the memory of his delicious bite.

Cold seeped into my aching knees, but I couldn't care less, my body burning for more.

"Ooh, feisty little mouse," he tutted. "But I can feel just how wet and needy you are for me. How this sweet cunt is desperate for me to fill it."

I felt his arrow, hidden beneath my clothes, turn. The soft tip ran between my lower lips before circling my entrance with a torturous slowness.

I swallowed another moan, fighting back the drugging need beckoning me to lose myself in him. Even on my knees, I wasn't here to submit. Not this time.

With a snarl, I wrapped my palms around his base and slid him into my mouth. Right down to where my hands gripped him.

Rex growled, a purely demonic sound that had a thrill of power humming through me. He stroked me harder in turn before lightly dipping the thick head of his tail inside me, teasing the desperate ache of emptiness. I groaned, feeling my throat vibrate around him, earning me another feral snarl of approval.

I peered up at the demon from under my lashes, keeping him as deep as I could take him as I tried to swallow him to the back of my throat. Black eyes burned into me as he kept a feral watch on my face.

His tail moved up to my clit, circling wetly.

I moaned again before working his length in earnest. His bristles stroked my lips as I moved, adding another sensation into the mix. His tail moved faster, harder, rubbing at me until I was wild with the swelling pleasure.

I sucked him harder, using both my hands to squeeze and pump the thick base of his cock as my mouth struggled to cover the rest. Each swipe of my tongue against his tip as I pulled back for breath rewarded me with more delicious, salty, sweet berry flavour.

"Fuck, little mouse. Feels so fucking good," he groaned, claws pressing into my scalp as he fisted my hair, encouraging me faster, deeper.

I'd never felt so damn sexy in my life.

His hips began to thrust a little, jerking his tail against me quicker as he accelerated the rhythm of our pleasure. I rushed towards that delicious peak, teetering on the edge of bliss as the demon worked me while I gave just as good as I got.

"Make me come, witch," he snarled, tightening his grip in my hair as he thrust deep. "Drink down every drop of my seed."

I strangled his hard length and braced to take everything he had to give.

His tail vibrated, pressing hard against my clit. He roared his pleasure, a ferocious sound that tightened my body yet triggered my own orgasm. I shattered with a moan, struggling to swallow the hot liquid gushing down my throat in a tingling surge. The combination was dizzying as I writhed on the floor before him, holding on to his length for support while his blueberry taste choked me.

Unable to swallow any more, I reared back, and he didn't fight me. Heated liquid overflowed my mouth, soaking my chin as he spurted the last thick ropes against my lips, cock kicking in my hands.

Heat radiated from my middle as more of Rex's essence slid down my throat, a sensation unlike anything I'd felt before. I swallowed the final traces, licking the rest of his addictive taste from my swollen lips with a low groan. My whole body felt languid, blissed out as I came down from the giddy high of pleasure. Power pulsed inside my chest, settling in the place where I always felt my magic.

Rex gently tugged on my hair, tilting my face up to his. He slid his tail from my panties, bringing the arrow up to his plush lips. His forked tongue slid out, running obscenely along his glistening skin. I groaned, gaze latched onto the erotic sight of the demon tasting my pleasure from his flesh.

I shuddered, my need for him reigniting in an instant. A dark smirk curved his glistening lips before he finally loosened his grip, stroking his palm along the back of my head like he was petting me instead.

I'd never admit to it, but the sensation was so soothing I wanted to purr.

Warm hands shackled my biceps as he hauled me up. My legs threatened to buckle, but he held me close in his unyielding grip.

"That was quite the show." His low tone had roughened, doing things to me that should be impossible after the pleasure he'd already flooded me with.

His thumb came up, swiping a stray drop of liquid from the edge of my lip. I fought the blush that heated my cheeks. I must look like a complete mess. He pushed his digit between my swollen lips, and I groaned as I savoured the last of his sweet blueberry taste, careful not to cut myself on the sharpness of his claw.

He pulled back with a shudder of his own. A thrill ran through me at the evidence of my effect on him. Far too much pride surged through me for any good, sane witch.

Maybe I'd been corrupted by a demon. Or maybe I'd always been a bit of a deviant. Either way, as I stared up into Rex's inhuman black eyes with the aftershocks of bliss still singing through my veins, I couldn't make myself care. Not one bit.

Somehow, this wicked beast made me feel alive. It was terrifying.

Chapter 20

When I was confident my legs wouldn't buckle, I stepped from the demon's embrace. Fresh air rushed into the space between us, cooling my fevered skin.

I waited to be hit by a shameful regret—I'd literally gone around the back of a biker bar, got down on my knees, and given a demon a blowjob—but the feeling was suspiciously absent.

It wasn't something your average witch did on the daily. At least, not any sensible, well-to-do coven witches I knew. But, if I was being honest with myself, I'd never exactly been one of those.

Maybe I was allowed to have a little fun where I could get it. If the past few weeks had taught me anything, it was how unpredictable, and short, life could be. A lesson I hadn't really needed reminding of.

So what if I might have enjoyed myself? Just the teensiest, tiniest bit.

Though, I'd never admit it to the demon watching me, his handsome face carefully arranged into its usual cocky smirk. I met his challenging stare head on, arching a brow in silent question.

"What? No tears of regret? How about another snarky insult?" Rex drawled, breaking the silence before it could stretch into full-blown morning-after awkwardness. His eyes drained of their predatory darkness, leaving behind the slightly less inhuman version—a blood-red shade slashed through with a vertical pupil. "Go on, call me an *ugly beast* again. You know you want to."

I huffed, trying to cover the surprised laugh that burst free, narrowing my gaze on the vexing demon. "I'm not always the raging witch you seem to think."

He hummed, shrugging one broad shoulder. "Shame."

A buzzing I hadn't noticed lessened, distracting me from my building exasperation. Like an energy had been dancing through my veins beneath the blissful haze of pleasure. The magic in my chest swelled and roiled, eager to be used. I frowned, pressing a hand between my breasts, flinching slightly at the tingle from my cursed anchor mark, even through my top.

"It's not just demons who benefit." Rex's voice startled me from my internal analysis. "Certain demons have power in their seed."

"They *what*?" I gasped, instantly wincing at the high-pitched noise that bounced back at me off the brick wall. I'd never heard even a rumour of such a thing. "How does magekind not already know about this?"

My cheeks blazed on the heels of my question. The taste of blueberries lingered on my tongue. Perhaps not many of my kind were as willing to get down and dirty with a demon.

A laugh boomed from Rex, rumbling his barrel chest. "Oh, little witchling, your uptight coven elders definitely know." He waved his bloodstained claws dismissively. "They just don't enjoy sharing knowledge or power. I can't imagine they're telling all the horny young initiates about how to summon a pleasure demon and boost their magic with us."

I frowned, something Zatar had said clicking into place. "So you're a pleasure demon? But you're also a hybrid? What other type are you? And are you an actual *king*?" The flow of questions tumbled out of my mouth as I thought about how little I knew. About demons. About hell. About Rex.

Or was that *Rexar*?

The demon stiffened. "I am descended from two lineages, yes." The flat press of his lips told me that was not a line of questioning he wanted to indulge, but I needed to know what I'd got myself into. And maybe a small part of me was curious about Rex himself.

"You're one of the blood types as well, then?" I ventured, trying to puzzle it through. He had to be. Otherwise, he shouldn't have shown up when I'd called out for a blood demon, right? My eyes narrowed on the tricky demon. "But you said you weren't. Back when I summoned you."

He bared his fangs, more snarl than smile. "I lied."

Well, that was about all I'd get from him on that touchy subject. For now.

I stuffed back the urge to keep prodding until the answer spilled out. Instead, I ran my gaze over his body, trying to ignore the way the sight of his lean eight-pack abs had me wanting to caress them with a purr. Beneath the navy of his blood, the skin had knitted itself back together.

I nodded towards the small white scar where the hole in his upper chest had been. "Will the scar heal too?"

He glanced down, as if only just remembering he'd been injured. "It should disappear in a few more minutes. The power of your pleasure is as fierce as you, little mouse."

His tone sounded sincere, but I couldn't help but wonder if he was mocking me. Again.

A strained silence descended as he watched me with a casual ease and I blatantly avoided his gaze like an awkward squirrel by staring at his closed wound.

After a long minute, I cleared my throat. We weren't here for this. I'd summoned him to save my life, and he'd offered to secure my freedom.

"Right, well, that was a bust, huh?" I scrounged up the courage to look at his handsome face.

He grimaced. "I was planning to take one of those vile maggots alive, but with the poison that coward Zatar had laced his knife with..." He paused, taking a deep inhale. "I couldn't defend myself without taking them down," he admitted, words heavy with an unexpected self-recrimination.

I frowned, something in me softening at his admission. "I'm not blaming you. You took that blade for me. Thank you. I mean it."

He nodded stiffly, glancing away as if he was uncomfortable with my gratitude. "The deal..." He trailed off.

Right. He'd only been keeping up his end of our bargain. Both of them. And I'd paid him back his due.

A business transaction. That was all this was. He was my hired muscle. I was his battery pack.

Unease twisted through me at the callous thought, but I shoved it down deep, stashing it alongside all the other useless feelings I had no time for.

"What now?" I asked, cutting off anything else he might have said.

Relief eased his features before he tilted his horns, seeming to consider my words. "We need another way of locating the hunters."

"Why don't we question one?" I asked.

He pursed his lips. "That's the most logical next step, but even if we find one, most of those zealous idiots are pretty impervious to interrogation. They activate some kind of suicide charm or poison before you can do too much damage." He flashed his fangs, as if remembering some violence he'd unleashed before.

A nervous energy streaked through me. I knew exactly how to get a hunter *and* make them talk. I just didn't particularly like the idea.

"I know a basic truth spell that almost puts you in a trance, plus..." My teeth worried at my lower lip. Since it was tender from my recent activities, I released it in a hurry. "I'll act as bait."

Rex's dark brows slammed low. "Absolutely not."

Mine shot up in retaliation. "I'm sorry. Did you think I was asking permission?"

He growled, muscular chest reverberating with the deep noise. "I'm here to protect you. We're not throwing you into the hellhound's jaws."

"You protect me to get fed." I crossed my arms, short claws digging into my biceps. "But you also agreed to help me get free of these evil pricks."

He scowled. "What good is freedom if you're dead?"

I huffed, throwing my hands up. "Do you have a better idea?"

His scowl deepened, but he remained silent.

"That's what I thought. Now, *Your Majesty*, we try things my way." I flashed him a sarcastic grin.

He hissed, sounding aggressively feline as his tail whipped behind him. A smug hit of victory thrilled through me. I'd won this round, at least.

"Fine," he snarled, pointing a claw at my face. "But first you need to rest, and then we need to discuss the problem of your magic."

Self-consciousness twined with embarrassment, but I lifted my chin stubbornly. "What problem? It's fine."

He arched an imperious brow. "You almost died while trying to impersonate a sparkler. I can help you."

I shot him a sceptical look. "A demon is going to teach me to control magic?"

He smirked before the levity dropped from his face like a stone. "You're not the only witch I know."

The cryptic statement seemed laced with something like guilt. A bolt of jealousy hit me, catching me off guard. I mentally slapped myself. As if I was getting jealous because a demon I'd known for less than twenty-four hours had mentioned he *knew* another witch. What was wrong with me?

And really, was I in any position to turn down help? Even if it was from an unusual source.

"Fine, O Wise Demon, teach me about human magic," I snarked.

"Keep being a brat. See where it gets you." His voice was silky with threat, but heat flashed in his eyes, daring me to push him further.

I bit my lip, trying to hold in the sensual provocation that demanded release. We'd literally just got off together. I didn't need to rekindle any more madness. Not when so much was on the line. Like my life.

Clearing my throat, I gestured for him to follow as I trudged towards the side gate. "Come on, T. rex, we've got enough grave-robbing cash for a hotel, and for once, I'm feeling generous."

He followed me out to the front of the building, and I searched the bush where I'd stashed my backpack. Quickly pulling it on with a sigh of relief, I turned towards Riverside's crooked spire. The gothic cathedral was taller than most of the city's buildings and marked its centre.

"Wait up." With a smirk, Rex held up a claw. "I'll just be one second, little mouse."

I arched a brow, watching his tail swish as he disappeared back into Rusty's through the broken front door. I crossed my arms with a huff. "What could he possibly have forgotten inside?"

Glass shattered in a series of great crashes one after another, followed by a whooshing sound I was becoming intimately familiar with.

With a bright grin, Rex skipped back out into the sunshine, arms flung wide as he spun around like the hills were alive with the sound of music.

Windows shattered behind him as he pranced, flames roaring and crackling as Rusty's Pub became a fiery hell of Rex's making.

All I could do was gape at the manically grinning demon.

I'd bound myself to a fucking psychopath.

Chapter 21

Sunshine blared through the windows, mocking the exhaustion that dragged on my limbs.

I hadn't slept in over twenty-four hours, running mostly on fear and adrenaline. Even before that, for weeks I'd been surviving on a few broken hours snatched here and there.

Despite the boost from Rex's...essence...I was reaching my limit.

I swayed as I dumped my backpack on the carpeted floor beside the bed. The only bed. I'd made the pragmatic, if uncomfortable, decision to only pay for a room with one. I didn't know how long we'd need to make the cash we'd appropriated last. And I, for one, would take food over sleeping distance from the demon any day. I wasn't too keen on sending Rex to murder more bunnies for us.

A small part of me wasn't against the idea of snuggling up with the sinfully hot demon either.

I slapped down that annoying inner voice. It grew with every passing hour I spent in Rex's presence. The demon was a bad influence. Who'd have thunk it?

I mentally rolled my eyes at myself.

Rex searched the small room like a hunter might be hiding behind the TV cabinet. Deciding to leave him to it, I grabbed the cleanest set of clothing from my bag and headed into the bathroom. With a toilet, chipped sink, and off-white shower-bath combo, the cupboard-sized room was just about functional. It also wasn't too grimy, which was as much as a broke outcast witch could hope for.

I caught sight of myself in the mirror above the sink, stifling a wince.

My long lilac hair was barely contained by the braid I'd put it in before we'd hit the bar. Pale-purple wisps framed my face in a wild mane. The intense shade matched my eyes, in stark contrast to my lightly tanned skin. Dark bags smudged beneath, imitating the faint bruises I could feel littering my arms beneath my top. A few cuts peppered my exposed collarbones, but most had now closed, thanks to speedy mage healing.

Still, the number of pale scars was growing, and I wasn't sure that would end anytime soon. At least once all this was done, I could get a few more tattoos to cover them. I wouldn't even have to worry about whether my clothing would hide them from my uptight coven. I'd already burned to ashes the nice, obedient witch image I'd tried so desperately to project.

My angular jawline and cheek bones looked even sharper than before, and I grimaced at the reminder of how much weight I'd lost living on the run. I was a gaunt, haunted thing. My full lips twisted with the expression, revealing a slight sharpness to my canine teeth.

I frowned, leaning closer to the mirror as I lifted my upper lip higher.

"Huh. Well, that's not fucking weird," I murmured, prodding the tip of one tooth with a finger. The point bit into my flesh with a sting, causing a vibrant drop of red to bead.

They were by no means actual fangs like Rex's, but they were a touch too long and sharp to be human.

The overall effect gave me a feral visage. I looked like a stray beast.

I *was* a stray beast.

I couldn't deal with this right now. My magic was manifesting some weird changes, and I was questioning just how much of this was normal. I'd never met another mage with diddly fangs or retractable claws.

Not for the first time, I wished my family were still alive. If he were here, my father would push his wire-rimmed glasses higher up the crooked bridge of his nose and dive right into a lecture on magic theory.

I sucked down the pained whine that tried to claw its way up my throat. Before I could lose myself to the unending well of grief and rage simmering like a pit of hell-fire in my chest, I turned from my reflection, shoving my useless feelings and unanswered questions back down.

I used the facilities, then stared longingly at the bathtub. With a sigh, I turned on the shower instead, letting the water heat before stripping off, unbraiding my hair, and climbing into the tub. I ignored the silvery gemstones scarring my chest. Just catching the edge in my periphery was enough to stab anger and hurt through me.

I burned to ink over it with something beautiful, to reclaim my skin. As soon as they'd cast me out, I'd gone straight to the tattoo studio, but I'd never made it inside. I couldn't spare the money. Thank the goddesses, because I needed to get back into Quartz, and they wouldn't stand for anything covering up their sacred anchor.

My legs wobbled a little, but I rushed through a shower, using the free mini toiletries in a nook within the tiled wall. They even had a lime-scented conditioner, and I squeezed the entire bottle onto my damp hair, relishing the small luxury. Rex's fiery hair looked soft enough already. I needed this.

The urge to stay under the warm spray was strong. I could just curl up in the tub and sleep for a week. But then I'd be murdered by hunters while I slept. Or at the very least, Rex would wake me up after a murder spree for his...*payment.*

The thought warmed me more than the hot water, my body feeling tight and needy at the very idea of waking to the feral demon ready to pleasure me.

Would it be so bad?

I hated to admit it, but the infuriatingly hot demon was already growing on me. Like a weed. He was strangely protective, more so than I'd expected for someone just doing it to get paid. His humour kept catching me off guard too, somehow breaking through the dark cloud that had been hanging over me. I hadn't scowled or smiled this much in weeks. Probably longer if I was being honest with myself. Maybe it was the loneliness talking, or the crazy, but a small part of me was grateful for his presence for more than just his ability to dismember genocidal lunatics.

I was such a sap.

With a mental shake, I turned off the faucet and climbed out. Drying myself off in record time, I pulled on my last set of clean underwear before dressing in the same leggings, but with a semi-clean baggy T-shirt at least. Long-sleeved, out of habit. I made a vague attempt at towel drying my hair before giving up. Wet hair was the least of my problems.

I stalked back into the main room, a cloud of steam following me out.

Rex prowled the middle like he'd been pacing, a picture of sculpted violence with his chest bare of anything except blood. He stilled, features easing a fraction as he caught sight of me. "There you are."

I frowned. Was he...worried about me?

The thought churned my stomach even as it spread warmth through my chest. Nobody had worried about me in a long time. Except Lyndsey. And she'd clearly not cared about me much in the end.

My throat felt tight as I offered a closed-lipped smile. "Any monsters under the bed?"

He smirked, full lips curving up on one side. "Not under, but I'll get in with you if you'd like."

I chuckled, the tightness loosening at his flirty humour. He was nothing like I'd expected. Were all demons as irreverent yet charming? As violent yet protective? As sinful yet sweet?

Just looking at him made my head spin. Too many questions, too many contradictions. I'd shared my blood, my body, with almost a complete stranger.

"Tell me more about yourself," I blurted, immediately wishing I could take the words back. What was I doing? This was business. Nothing more.

Yet every time I tried to remind myself of that fact, it seemed a little less true.

Rex frowned, carved features scrunching as he canted his horns aside. "What do you want to know?" An edge of caution laced his tone, as if he expected some kind of trick.

Hmm, where to start? So many questions vied for attention. It was hard to pick one.

"Are you really a king?"

He straightened to his full, near-seven-feet height, raising his proud horns so regally that they might as well be a crown. "Why yes, *peasant*, I am." He sniffed before flashing me a cheeky grin. "Can't you tell?"

"Of course, Your Majesty." Stifling an embarrassing giggle, I dropped into my best impression of a curtsy, like they described in all the Regency romance novels I loved. "My humblest of apologies," I said, dialling my common British accent up to tea-with-the-queen fancy.

He chuckled, his smoky, almost-coughing sound that warmed me from the inside. "What else did you want to know?"

I hesitated, knowing my next question would break the light mood, but I needed to understand what was going on. "If you're a king in hell...then why are you here? Why did you turn up when I cast that summoning spell?"

His blood-red eyes hardened before he glanced out of the window at the bustling city beyond. A part of me mourned the loss of his mirth. The room felt colder without it, despite the mild spring breeze blowing through the open window.

An almost inaudible sigh left him as he watched the people scurrying about the streets below. "You're not the only one after the hunters." His tone was measured, as if he'd chosen his words carefully.

"OK," I said, looking back at our interactions so far with the new lens of motive. "So you knew when I performed the summoning spell I was being targeted by hunters?"

How could he know that though?

I frowned as even more questions popped up. What powers did demons possess that us mages had no clue about? What other secrets was this demon hiding?

Rex shook his head, the slight movement enough to send his long hair swaying about his curling horns. "Nothing like that. I needed to get to the surface, and summoning is the quickest way." He shrugged, still avoiding my gaze. "I could sense what area the call was coming from in this realm. Being summoned by you was a lucky coincidence, I suppose."

For some inexplicable reason, his words cut me, sliding between my ribs like blades.

"Right. You're here for your own purposes. Of course you are. Us working together is just a convenience more than anything." The words felt sharp as they tumbled from my lips.

Why was I being such a sap about this? I'd known what this was from the beginning. We were using each other. So what if he set my pulse pounding or made me feel safe? Like maybe I was worth protecting?

He twisted back with a slight frown. "Zoella... It's not like that."

I held myself stiff, trying to stuff down any silly emotions that threatened to bubble up. "What is it like, then?"

Goddesses, I sounded like a clingy ex-girlfriend, but I couldn't seem to stop myself.

His lips parted, some indecipherable look crossing his handsome face.

"Right. That's what I thought," I said, throat tight.

His fists clenched at his sides until a drop of navy squeezed from one hand, falling to the worn carpet. "Tell me, witch, why did you summon me?" Despite his obvious frustration, his tone came out soft.

His question caught me off guard, but I quickly raised a brow. "Do you kill hunter squads in random hotel rooms that often?"

His lips twitched as he shook his horns. "Why do you need protection from hunters in the first place? Where's your coven?"

My heart clenched so violently I thought I might be having a heart attack. The anchor on my chest tingled mockingly. Every feeling I'd tried to stuff down into the dark began rattling in their cage. "I was exiled," I said, the words jagged, scraping against my throat like broken glass.

He took a step closer, a frown scrunching his features. "Why? What could a fledgling witch like you have possibly done that was so terrible?"

I knew he wasn't trying to insult me, but his words scratched at something hidden within. Some wound I wasn't fully aware I carried. The world saw me as an innocent, placid woman. They expected me to behave. To smile and nod. To be a good girl and do as I was told. Fenton certainly had when he'd told me to bend over. So had the rest of my old coven. Even Lyndsey.

But despite how hard I'd pretended, maybe I didn't want to obey.

I bared my teeth at Rex. "I tried to set the coven leader's son on fire and burned their precious grimoire."

A smile crept across Rex's lips, transforming into a vicious grin. "Good."

For a moment, I wasn't sure I'd heard him right. "What do you mean, '*good*'?" I did my best impression of his low, smoky voice.

He chuckled, and I could have sworn a small wisp actually left his pouty lips. "If you burned some entitled fuckwit, he must have deserved it."

Tears flooded my eyes.

I barely knew this demon. Yet he was the only person to actually believe me, and he'd not even heard the full story. Embarrassment followed the tear that overflowed, running down my cheek.

Rex was there in a blur, wiping away the stray drop of weakness with his thumb as he cupped my cheek. His warm touch was soothing, even with the sharp claw edging my vision. Bittersweet ginger and smoke wrapped around me.

Glowing eyes bored into mine, cradling me in their intensity. "Don't cry, little mouse. I'll kill him for you. Free of charge," he murmured, offering me a sad smile.

"Not if I kill him first," I said, voice warbling slightly.

"There she is," he purred, "my fierce witch."

His lips descended at the same time as I leaned up on tiptoes. I moaned the second his lips touched mine, their softness contrasted by his demanding kiss. His forked tongue traced the seam of my lips, and I opened for him, desperate for more. He swept inside, plundering my mouth with a wicked intensity I'd never known I craved.

The sinful demon growled into my mouth, his curious tongue tangling with mine. The world narrowed down to the feel of Rex. His dizzying kiss, his heated body pressed against mine, his palms cradling my cheeks, his wicked tail curving around my waist, holding me close.

With a groan, he finally pulled away. I gasped in a deep breath, somehow forgetting that my poor mortal body needed oxygen. The whitewashed room swayed behind my dark demon.

"Get some sleep, Zoella." His forehead rested against mine, spiral horns framing both our faces. "I'll keep you safe. I promise."

Chapter 22

“**W**hat in the name of fluffy bunnies are you doing?” I hissed, fighting back a grin. I reached out, snatching the clothes hanger from Rex's grip.

The white foot of the unnecessarily fluffy bunny onesie flung out wide. It smacked into a middle-aged woman perusing a nearby table of folded jumpers.

“I'm so sorry.” I cringed, offering an apologetic wince.

She huffed, shooting me a glare before raking her gaze over Rex with unabashed interest.

I was half-tempted to whack her with the bunny onesie again.

He grinned at me, completely oblivious to the number of stares glued to his unholy hotness. Glamour only went so far. If I looked at him while connecting to the well of power in my chest, I could see the image the humans did. My magic might hide his demonic features, but the bastard was still inhumanly good-looking. It did nothing about the high, angled cheek bones; square jaw; straight nose; full lips; thick, fiery hair; broad shoulders; chiselled abs.

Sauntering around a department store topless was just asking for trouble.

I was half-surprised nobody had asked him to leave for the sake of public decency, but then again, who would tell such a lethal, yet stunning, male to put a top on or get out?

Thankfully, it was mostly empty, given the shop had only opened ten minutes ago.

Not long after waking, I'd decided a shopping trip was in order. Rex couldn't traipse around the city half-naked without drawing attention, and I was out of clean clothes. And food.

Riverside wasn't a big city, but it was large enough to have several shopping centres with everything from sprawling department stores to boutique tearooms. This store was only a few streets over from our hotel, making it the perfect stop after we'd checked out. Or after Ms McCleary had checked out, since I'd been spelling my ID to help avoid detection by the hunters. Not that it had helped me all that much so far.

"You said I needed clothing," Rex pointed out, nodding his horns at the ridiculous outfit I was clutching in a death grip. His bright eyes gleamed with mirth.

I shook the garment at him. "You are *not* parading around the city dressed as a giant rabbit."

"Why not?" Those full lips, which I knew intimately now, plumped sinfully in a mock pout. "I know your tastes. Maybe you'll eat me again if I wear it."

He winked.

My mouth popped open, cheeks blazing. The nosy woman swung her gaze to me with a dramatic gasp, one hand pressed to the base of her throat like she was clutching imaginary pearls.

I snorted at her shocked expression. "Oh, close your mouth already. Don't pretend you wouldn't too." I waved a hand at Rex. "He's delicious."

Her mouth shut with an audible snick. Cheeks reddening enough to match mine, she promptly hurried off between the racks of clothing with a final harrumph.

Rex tipped his horns back and laughed, deep and loud. The sound warmed me from the inside, and I had to bite the inside of my cheek to stop myself from grinning like a lunatic. He was always attractive, but I was quickly coming to realise that the sight of him in the throes of mirth was my favourite.

I mentally rolled my eyes at myself. One kiss and I'd apparently lost all sense. I liked watching a demon laugh? What was wrong with me?

His chuckles petered out, the smoky sound accompanied by a few faint wisps from his lips. Lips I'd not stopped thinking about since I'd woken this morning to a stroke of his claws along the side of my face. I'd blinked awake with a shiver, immediately feeling my body respond to his sensual threat. Before I could do something foolish, like drag the demon into bed with me, he'd smirked as if he could read my thoughts and told me we needed to get moving.

Having a demon watch you sleep should have been straight up terrifying, but waking up to his huge grey form looming over me was comforting. The hunters would have to go through all that barely leashed violence to get to me.

Besides, last night had shifted things between us.

A few times this morning, I'd caught him looking at me strangely. The intensity caused butterflies to hold an underground rave in my stomach.

His red gaze almost glowed as he flashed me a teasing smirk. "Who knew such a little mouse could be such a wicked witch?"

I fought another smile. My cheeks were starting to ache at this point. "Oh, hush, you. I will not be judged by uptight strangers eye-fucking you in public."

He quirked a dark brow, pouty lips twitching as he purred, "Jealous, little mouse?"

My cheeks flamed. "What? N-No," I rushed out.

Oh yeah, real convincing.

I wanted to slap some sense into myself but apparently couldn't spare the brain cells.

His lips curled upwards until he flashed fang in an almost secretive smile. "That's OK, I like it."

Stepping close, he hooked his warm palm around the back of my head, smoothing through my locks. Smoke and ginger twined around me before his tail followed suit, cuddling my waist in a heated band. He brought his lips to mine, curling his fingers in my hair. His kiss was fevered, hungry. He claimed my mouth, forked tongue coaxing my own to give as good as I got.

The world dropped away, leaving only him as he devoured me whole. I forgot about the fluffy outfit trapped between our bodies. I forgot about the department store filled with what must be shocked onlookers. I forgot about the hunters chasing me down. I forgot about the deals binding us.

After a dizzying eternity, he broke the kiss, forked tongue flicking out to give my sensitive lower lip one last tease. My breath heaved as I drifted back down to Earth.

"Wow. I should have *totally* filmed that." A round of giggling followed, snapping me from Rex's intoxicating spell.

A gaggle of young women armoured in matching yoga pants laughed nearby, fanning themselves dramatically.

"Yaaas, you get it, girl!" one of them cheered, giving me a saucy wink.

I blushed even harder. Ducking my head, I shoved the fluffy outfit onto the closest rack, grabbed Rex's hand, and dragged him deeper into the men's clothing section.

He chuckled, letting me pull him along without a fight. "I'd say I'm sorry, but I couldn't lie to you like that. I already care about you too much."

I peeked over my shoulder, catching him staring at me with that weird intensity again even as he flashed me a heart-stopping grin. Heat spread through my chest at the sight.

Nobody had told me they cared about me. Not in a long time. And they'd certainly not shown it. Too many emotions surged through me, vying for attention, from a warm giddiness at his light-hearted flirting to a nagging certainty that he was just going to leave once we'd finished using each other. How did he make me feel so many things at once?

I felt like I'd been strapped into a rollercoaster with no way off. Exhilarating yet terrifying.

My teeth sunk into my lower lip as I wrestled with myself to meet his intense gaze. "I...care about you too."

I cringed at how ridiculous I sounded, but my embarrassment was quickly soothed by his answering grin. He was genuinely going to give some poor, unsuspecting passer-by a heart attack. Even I wasn't in the clear.

Rex could be so charming for such a bloodthirsty demon.

I pulled him towards the men's T-shirt section, turned my attention to a table of folded tops laid out before us. "Got any preference? Maybe something to inspire more fear in our enemies than a fluffy bunny costume?" I asked, tone dry.

He waved a dismissive hand. "I don't care much for fashion, little mouse. In my kingdom, people are in all kinds of clothing, from leather tunics they've skinned and tanned themselves to couture gowns and designer suits bought from this realm."

I still couldn't shake the image of pits of hell-fire and tortured souls, so hearing that some of his demons wasted money on high fashion piqued my curiosity.

"What's it like?" I asked. "Your kingdom?"

He shrugged. "It's not too different from a human village. Except my kingdom is on the edge of an ancient forest, almost merging into it. Since most other kingdoms shunned me when I tried to build a quiet life for myself on the edge of the Bloodwood, I had to build from whatever materials I could gather myself. I started from nothing, using my bare hands to rip trees out from the ground for timber or smash rocks together to create usable blades to craft with. A few people heard about me living in peace out there and joined me." He rubbed the back of his neck in a move that stretched his eight-pack abs, snagging my gaze. "I never set out to build a kingdom; others just sort of found me."

A frown scrunched my brows. "Why would the other kingdoms shun you?" The sneering faces of those demons at Rusty's Pub swam through my brain, making my jaw clench. "Because you're a hybrid?"

He stiffened, hardly noticeable except for the tightening around his eyes. "Yes." He spread his claws at his sides, lips a mocking curl. "The Hybrid King, they call me. Or the Outcast King when they think I can't hear. I accept all the unwanted hybrids and give them a home. A sanctuary where they're not hurt for merely existing. For being born different."

Unbidden, moisture filled my eyes. Rex looked defensive, as if he expected me to dismiss him too. To reject him for being a hybrid and for defending others like him.

I reached out, taking his warm hand and squeezing it. "I think what you're doing is brave." My voice came out small, awe softening my tone. "Your people are lucky to have such a fierce protector."

His gaze dipped. "I couldn't protect them all." The confession fell heavily from his lips, so at odds with the shop's cheery brightness. "That's why I'm here, after the hunters."

My heart ached at the look of devastation on his handsome face. This was the real Rex. The one who cared deeply for his people. If you'd have told me a few days ago that demons could care about anything except power and violence, I'd have laughed so hard I peed a little. But the things my coven had taught me about demons wasn't matching up with the reality of Rex.

I squeezed his hand even harder. "But you're trying to save them. Risking your life by making deals with random witches so you can rescue your people." More of the mystery that was Rex unravelled. His desperation to be summoned here and his insistence on going after the hunters made sense now. "Sounds like it's more than anyone else would have done for them."

Determination hardened his features. "I'll never stop fighting for my people."

"I know." My heart hurt looking at him. He was a protector, through and through.

A hint of his usual mischief warmed his expression, thawing the icy chill of his fear and guilt. "And that's why I need a mate just as fierce."

I quirked a brow, a streak of something sharp running through me with unexpected viciousness. "Mate?" The word fell between us harsher than I'd meant it to.

He grinned, eyes brimming with some intensity I couldn't define. "Oh yes, little mouse. We demons call our chosen life partners 'mates.' Like a human marriage, we propose and hold a binding ceremony to celebrate the union, but we don't break our vows. When I commit to forever, I mean it."

My heart thudded in my chest as I tried to soak up his words. His intent.

Was he trying to tell me that this *thing* between us was only temporary? That he was waiting for his forever demon? Or was he telling me he'd already found them? Did he already have a mate in mind back home? But if that was true, why would he have kissed me? Why would we have done...*intimate* things together? Was it just a food thing for him and therefore didn't count?

My head spun with questions, but embarrassment, pride, and maybe a hint of fear meant I had zero intention of voicing them.

Unsure what to say, I dropped my gaze and swiped up an XXL tee from the stack, strangling the soft cotton like it had stolen my last slice of Bakewell tart. "Black like my soul, it is," I joked, awkwardly trying to defuse the strange intensity writhing between us.

Even distracted as I was, I'd picked up the cheapest top on the display. Pragmatism struck again. He was only going to get it drenched in blood.

Rex's eyes continued to burn into me. He picked up a few more tops without looking away. "I know darkness, little mouse, and your soul is as beautiful as you are."

I swallowed thickly, a small part of me crying out to just woman up and ask him about whatever was going on between us. But the cowardly part of me pasted on a brittle smile and hurried off towards the women's department instead.

A glance over my shoulder revealed my dark demon tracking my every movement. He looked like a predator. His prey locked firmly in sight.

Without much thought, I quickly picked out clothes for myself—drab, discounted exercise gear in the form of long-sleeved technical tees and stretchy leggings. Because, let's face it, everything I bought would also get covered in blood, and my days of running for my life weren't over yet. When I finally got back to the safety of Quartz, I was going to treat myself to some elaborate full-length dress that was impossible to even walk in.

I'd picked this store because it had already been cheap before the new season sale, knowing I'd need to fork out some of our limited cash on both Rex's clothing and mine. I'd never been one to spend frivolously—learning to budget your own finances from the age of fourteen would do that to you—but my frugal instincts had ratcheted up since becoming unemployed and homeless.

I sighed, hauling the bargain clothing with me as I hurried to the underwear section next. Thankfully, Rex was nowhere to be seen.

If picking out clothes for him had been strangely intense, lingerie shopping with the dark king would be a whole new level of awkward.

"Don't worry, little mouse, I've already got this covered." A familiar purr in my ear had me spinning with a startled squeak.

Rex loomed behind me, regal horns almost blotting out the light. His wicked grin showcased pearly fangs, and my gaze dipped to his full lips.

My heart raced in my chest, a mix of adrenaline and anticipation surging through me at his sudden closeness.

The sinful demon lifted a hand. From his claws dangled white lace panties, bright-red cherries printed across them like the pair he'd destroyed.

My cheeks flamed as I snatched them from his grip, adding them to the pile of clothing in my arms, too embarrassed to even check the price tag.

He chuckled, so deep and smoky that I could have sworn actual wisps rose between his lips.

Chapter 23

Purple flames smashed into the tree stump with a whoosh.

"Fuck yeah!" I whooped, victory surging through me despite the drain on my magic.

"Such a fiery witch," Rex drawled. "You sure you're not part demon?"

I poked my tongue out at him, already turning back the overturned ash tree stump, now crackling with my lilac fire glinting black at the edges.

I ignored the little niggle of doubt that wormed its way in. A whole branch of elemental mages had an affinity for controlling fire, but I'd never heard of any with an unusual colour before.

Taking a deep breath, I felt for the connection between myself and the magic fire. With a jerk of my hand, I extinguished the flames. My face ached with how manically I was grinning.

After our morning shop, which included grabbing a bunch of protein bars and snacks on our way out and Rex *finally* putting on a T-shirt—even though the XXL top was tight enough to have been painted onto his sinfully muscular torso—we'd discussed the best way to move forward with our hunter destruction agenda.

Rex had demanded we take the time for him to train me before doing anything else, and I'd grudgingly agreed to try it. I couldn't get any *worse* at magic, after all.

I'd ungraciously chowed down my late breakfast protein bar while I'd led him to a sprawling deer park not ten minutes east of the shopping centre. It had a small woods set along the back, thick enough that it wasn't easy to see through, and with my connection to nature, the trees would hopefully warn me if someone was straying too close. We'd stalked amongst the mixture of ash, chestnut, and oak trees until Rex had declared this clearing suitable for our needs.

I'd insisted he take his daily feed before I could lose my nerve. He'd quickly sipped from my wrist while I'd tried valiantly to ignore the heat squirming through me. He must have fed for ten seconds tops, but I'd let the suspicious behaviour slide.

While I'd reeled from the sensations buzzing through me, he'd jogged off and quickly returned, hefting a huge tree stump on his muscular shoulder with envious ease, and Magic 101 had commenced.

Calling on the well of power in my chest, I willed it into my hand in another fiery wave. Lilac-and-black flames burst to life. A sparrow swooped overhead, distracting me for a beat, and it was enough that my flames flickered out before I refocused.

Nothing happened for a long few moments as I wrestled my bucking magic, trying to work with its wildness rather than fighting it. Slowly, I coaxed the power back into a smooth flow rather than the erratic peaks and dips it preferred.

Given it had only been a matter of months since my twenty-fifth birthday, my affinity magic was still maturing. During what I liked to call *magical puberty*, the power spikes would be at their worst, probably for the next few months, maybe even years. Especially without a coven binding to help steady the awakening.

Triumph bloomed as my flames reignited with a quiet crackling, emitting a purple glow across my sleeve. My limbs felt heavy from channelling and trying to control the power, but I was too excited to care.

Ever since I'd first hit Fenton with this strange power, I'd had so little control over it. Within a few infuriating hours, Rex had guided me on how to centre myself and accept the different facets of my magic. That everything, from my connection to nature and ability to cast spells to the dark fire and retractable claws, was all a part of the same well of power within me. That it just travelled down different streams of magic as I pulled on it.

I'd never thought of it that way before. But my magic was just energy produced by my body. It was my mind that directed how it manifested.

In the coven, we'd been told that once our powers began maturing from our twenty-fifth birthday, we *needed* the coven's binding spell at our initiation ceremony to control our magic. The coven elder would inform us of our specific affinity using a sacred divination ritual, and we would finally join the coven's communal pool of magic through our anchors, which would smooth out our power spikes as well as contribute our energy to the coven's joint strength. Looking back, it sort of felt like a pyramid scheme but for magic.

After that, we'd need the experienced mages from our specific branches of magic to teach us the strict discipline, gestures, or words needed for channelling those affinity powers.

If life had been kinder, my father would have taught me about my budding connection to trees. An old fire elemental, Mr Dubois, would have probably taught me how to wield my odd purple flames. I had no clue who would have worked with me on the claw thing, but at least I'd have had a pool of experienced mages to ask for help and guidance. I should have had a magic family, my coven, around me to help figure out the weird changes I was going through.

Instead, under a demon's tutelage, I was doing everything the wrong way. Yet it seemed to be working.

I'd never felt more like a rogue mage.

"So tell me again how a demon knows so much about human magic?" I quirked a brow at Rex, who stood not even a few paces away from the target. He had way too much faith in my aim.

The demon shrugged, broad shoulders lifting, but the gesture was a little too casual. "Like I said, I know another outcast witch. She was having issues controlling her magic, and I helped her work through them. It was mostly trial and error, but we got there in the end," he said, an almost wistful quality to his voice.

Vines of jealousy tried to take root, but I ripped those questing fuckers out before they could find fertile ground. So we'd kissed. Twice. That wasn't exactly a committed relationship.

For all I knew, he could already be mated with kids. He'd never said he *hadn't* already found this "fierce mate" he'd mentioned before.

I ignored the toxic churning in my stomach. I was in way over my head. In more ways than one.

So what else was new?

I gave him a tight smile. That was right. Nothing odd here. Just one side witch totally unfazed to be discussing his main witch. "Makes sense."

Who was this other witch he spoke of? Today he seemed to think of her with longing fondness, but last time, there'd been a hint of guilt. Was he feeling guilty for whatever was happening between us? Was he longing to get back to hell to see this other woman? Was she his chosen mate?

All I had were questions. I still wasn't sure I wanted to face the answers to any of them. Not enough to actually open my mouth and spit out the words, anyway. Apparently, I was a coward.

Somehow, despite what I'd love to believe were impeccable acting skills, Rex took in my expression with a light frown creasing his dark brows. "You know... You're one of the most powerful mages I've met," he said, misreading my social ineptness.

I cleared my throat, shifting on my feet as I fought to act like a capable, functioning adult who wasn't suddenly overcome with emotion. My whole life I'd felt weak. Useless. I couldn't save my family, and now I could hardly survive this world on my own. "I... I am?"

He canted his horns aside, a look of bafflement splaying his handsome features. "You have strong offensive magic, and those overgrown toothpicks are basically an early warning system." He waved his claws at a slender chestnut sapling nearby. "With the right training, you'd be powerful enough to protect yourself from the hunters."

His words burrowed into my brain, seeding a fantasy I could hardly let myself hope for.

In the next breath, reality crashed down. Hard.

I was still an untrained witch with maturing magic. If my chaotic power dipped while I was under attack, I was done for. I needed more time. More training.

But maybe I only needed to go crawling back to my traitorous old coven for a few years before I could strike out on my own. The idea was intoxicating.

Yanking on my magic store, I channelled the flow into the fiery feel of my dark magic. Lilac flames engulfed my hand before I threw them towards the charred stump. It sailed over the short target, hitting a juvenile ash with a roaring crackle. The entire thing was swallowed up in seconds.

I winced, quickly recalling the magic that fed the burning. My connection to nature sharpened into focus on instinct. I felt the damage I'd done to the living tree, grimacing at the wailing feel vibrating down the bond I'd created. Feeding magic into the connection, I felt the ash sap my strength. The darkened bark peeled away, leaving fresh grey-hued roughness beneath, newly grown with magic.

I sighed in relief despite a magic-induced headache throbbing between my temples. Having healed nothing before, I was surprised it had actually worked. Guilt lingered regardless. It might not feel pain the way animals did, but I'd hurt an innocent tree minding its own damn business.

Rex flashed me a wry smile, brushing back a few red-orange strands that had fallen across his chiselled face. "Should I get some marshmallows for the next one?"

I snorted. "Knowing you, you'd probably return with more dead bunnies to swallow whole."

He smirked, tail twitching over his shoulder. "I do eat regular food, you know."

My mouth popped open.

"Demons eat the same food as you humans. Our more acquired tastes strengthen us, hence why I'm faster and stronger after taking blood or pleasure, but we aren't actually the feral beasts you seem to think." He grinned his lethal smile, charming and vicious in equal measure. "You should have seen how prissy and uptight you were when you summoned me. It was just too fun to mess with you. I couldn't resist."

I scowled, stomping a foot like some petulant child. "You prick! You made me roast a poor bunny with my magic and rip shreds off its carcass like a rabid animal. We could have got takeout!"

A deep chuckle rumbled his chest, letting out more of those smoky wisps I swore were real. "I know. It was hilarious." He bent slightly with the force of his laughter, clawed hand to his flat stomach. "Your horrified face."

My scowl melted at his infectious mirth. "I guess I probably did look pretty funny."

He straightened, laughter petering out into an almost growling sound as he pinned me with his glowing stare. "Still the most beautiful creature I'd ever seen though."

I sucked in a breath, struck by the unexpected compliment. A witch could quickly become addicted to the demon's devilishly sweet words. Being around him was like a shot of whisky: sharp and invigorating yet smoothly intoxicating.

Ignoring the way he made my cheeks heat, I glanced away, calling another fistful of flame.

Chapter 24

Chilled air gusted through the open zip of my jacket, cooling my heated skin. Footsteps bounced off the brick walls as I wandered along the dimly lit alley. Sadly, the sound belonged to me.

For over an hour, I'd traipsed through the abandoned streets of Iron Heights, an industrial section in East Riverside, hoping my enemies would find me. This part of Riverside was empty at night, most of the city's residents smart enough to be tucked away safely in their homes. Not that Iron Heights was a slum. We'd picked somewhere quiet on purpose—fewer prying eyes and innocent bystanders.

Hopefully, I was an even more juicy bait as a result.

How things had changed. Just days ago, I'd have been terrified to be out at night, exposed and alone, where the hunters could kidnap me with ease.

Now I was impatient for them to catch up to me.

My nerves jangled as I fought to keep my pace slow and casual. So far, I'd only been confronted by a regular human mugger brandishing a switch blade. I'd been preparing to lash out with a whip of flame, when Rex had materialised behind him, as if from the shadows themselves, pulling the thug back into the darkness with him as he'd buried his fangs into the man's neck, eyes as black as a starless night. Rex had drained my would-be attacker, palm muffling the man's panicked screams as he'd watched me with a predatory intensity. As if I was the one he'd been feeding on.

I'd left him to his easy meal, a confusing mix of heat and fear curling through me, heading off alone once more.

The weight of a pistol I'd commandeered yesterday dug into the small of my back. A constant reminder of the danger I was in. Hopefully, I wouldn't need the weapon, especially as I didn't know how to use it beyond point-and-shoot. I'd sheathed a knife at my hip too, though that seemed even less useful, since I'd probably just cut myself by accident.

After practising magic all day, Rex and I had collected the ingredients for a truth spell—sage leaves, oak bark, and sloe berries—ready for us to launch into the next step of our master plan to destroy the Riverside hunters. We'd still argued about it the whole way back to our latest hotel though. Rex had campaigned to spend a few more days honing my powers and resting while we moved around the city, staying a step ahead of the hunters chasing me.

But I was done running.

I'd already learned to form a steady stream of fire, throwing fireballs or lashing out with flames like a whip. By the afternoon, I'd hardly needed to focus before summoning the power into my hands.

Sure, the flow could be spotty, and if something distracted me, it flickered out, but it was astonishing what I'd achieved today.

That would have to be enough. At least for this first step. Once we'd located the hunters' main compound, where I was sure they'd keep the tracker stone holding my magic signature, we could scope it out. See if we needed more firepower, literally, before metaphorically storming the castle.

Either way, time wasn't on our side. I was all too aware that the hunters must have at least one imprisoned mage to create the trackers. I knew from experience how every hour in the hunters' care only brought more agony. I relived it in my nightmares: vague flashes of pain and terror, the screams of my family.

The sooner we found them, the sooner we could end the cruelty.

It wasn't my only concern—the local hunters could only lose so many brainwashed goons before they appealed to their neighbouring factions for backup. I didn't want to think about how dangerous it would be to fight the combined power of several groups at once.

With Rex bound to protect me, I could end up getting him killed right alongside me.

My chest tightened at the thought, strangling my lungs until I almost tripped over my own feet. In the brief time I'd known him, I'd come to care for the wicked demon. More than I should. And he was so fiercely protective I wasn't sure he'd leave me to face the danger alone, even if I told him to.

It was a heady thought. When everyone else had abandoned me, finding someone who might be strong enough to fight to stay with me, and care enough to do so, was a terrifying fantasy.

But once we destroyed the hunters, and I rejoined my old coven, my revenge would be fulfilled. I wouldn't need protection any longer. I wouldn't need Rex.

Pace slowing, I rubbed a hand over my chest, trying to ease the ache in my heart.

When our deals were done, would we just part ways forever? Just a casual wave goodbye as he strolled back through a portal, never to be seen again?

I sighed, breath misting the night air as I walked. Already it was hard to imagine life without the chaotic demon's presence. He was a violent splash of colour disrupting my monochrome days.

I took a sharp right onto a wider street, lined with closed storefronts, a resigned sadness weighing my steps. A single street-light buzzed faintly as I crossed the road, deliberately stepping under it like a spotlight.

My life in Quartz had been drab. Every day the same. I'd woken up alone, in the cabin my family had only lived in for a few weeks, before attending classes with the rest of my initiate group, learning both human academics and basic magic.

I'd always felt out of place. I'd tried my hardest to blend in meekly, never wanting to draw attention to myself or cause problems. I knew it was only the coven's goodwill and sympathy that had kept me there. I hadn't contributed anything. When my family had died, there'd been barely enough money saved in their accounts for me to get by for a year, paying my bills and buying cheap food and necessities.

I'd got a job as soon as I could glamour my lilac eyes to blue. At only sixteen, I'd been young enough that I didn't yet have detectable levels for the hunters to track. I'd worked evenings and weekends for a quiet farm shop only a few miles south of Quartz territory. I'd strolled there and back through woods and wheat fields each day.

I'd been devastated when I'd been forced to quit, months before my twenty-fifth birthday. After all they'd done for me, though, I couldn't put anyone from the farming collective at risk. Hunters didn't aim to hurt humans, but they weren't careful with "sympathisers." Though my employers didn't have a clue I was a witch.

I cut down another alleyway, crunching small shards of glass beneath my running shoes. The wind tugged at my pale-purple hair. I quickly brushed it back from my face as I thought about my future, the small, niggling worries I tried to ignore now screaming in my face.

When I went crawling back to Quartz, what would my life even look like? Would I just go back to learning magic? Be assigned a position tending the coven's orchards? Keep building my ro-mance book collection, getting lost in the escapism so I wouldn't wonder what might have been with a certain captivating demon?

Would Lyndsey and I repair our relationship? Or would I just avoid her for the rest of my life? The coven wasn't *that* big. Quartz might be the largest in the East of England, but their numbers only just crested the hundred mark.

Was Lyndsey still loved up with that scumbag Fenton? A cosy, happy couple laughing about my demise? About what a freak I was with my weird purple fire and pathetic sob story?

Was my only friend glad she'd kicked me out of her life?

My throat closed off as useless tears pricked the backs of my eyes. Now wasn't the time for an emotional breakdown—I was literally waiting to be attacked—but I supposed you could only push down your feelings for so long until they broke free of their cage.

My best friend's betrayal still stung all these weeks later. But it wasn't just her I was angry at. Did *anyone* from Quartz even think about me now? Did they care if I was still alive?

My head tipped back as I tried to swallow past the emotion clogging my throat. Thick grey clouds obscured most of the stars. A few gaps revealed a thin sliver of the moon amongst their ominous swaths. The pavement was still damp from an earlier downpour, and another spring shower was probably headed our way.

If I went back to Quartz, it wasn't just Lyndsey and the coven I'd have to confront.

Rage burned in my middle, pumping liquid heat through my veins enough to combat the slight chill in the night air. My fingertips tingled as my inky claws shifted out, pricking my palms as I balled my fists.

I remembered the feel of a clammy hand squeezing my breast hard enough to hurt. The scent of spiced cologne and rum. The shock of a sickening demand.

I was so mad I could hardly breathe.

What kind of world allowed twisted bastards like Fenton to take what they wanted without consequences? I felt sick and so, so angry. Angry at him for doing that, angry that others had let him, and angry at myself for letting him get away with it.

Had he tried to force himself on anyone else since?

I grimaced, teeth sinking into my tongue as I fought to keep my pace steady through the quiet street instead of stomping around in a rage.

Even though I'd tried to tell everyone what he'd done, and was magically barred from coven land, I'd never be able to forgive myself if Fenton attacked another. As soon as I got back to Quartz, I'd prove his crimes and put a stop to his sick behaviour.

And if that failed, maybe I could ask Rex to kidnap and intimidate the weasel until he vowed not to touch another unwilling woman. Though knowing my dark demon, Fenton wouldn't make it out alive.

I mentally slapped myself. Rex wasn't *my* anything. Even after those dizzying kisses. If anything, he might already be involved with someone else, pining to get back to her after his business with the Riverside hunters was done. I might be left reeling once he went back to hell, but he might not.

At least he'd be safe though. Not caught up in taking poisoned knives through the back meant for me.

And I'd be right back to where I'd started. Alone and trapped in a coven that didn't care about me, feeling like an outcast even as I wormed my way back in. After all I'd been through, I wasn't sure I could just slot back into the shell of a person I'd been. It would be like trying to shove a square peg back into a round hole. I wasn't the same meek witch I'd tried so desperately to be growing up. I was something a little more feral now, and deep down, I knew Rex was playing a part in that.

He didn't make me feel like I was a burden, like I was unwanted or useless. He protected me, but he also helped me protect myself. He encouraged my fierce side, poked and prodded at me until I stopped hiding and started snarling back.

Lost in thought, I had no idea how long had passed with no sign of the hunters. I was half-tempted to call out to Rex and give up for the evening. The ghostly sensation of insects crawling across my skin while trapped beneath the roots of a great oak slunk through my memory. Nothing but cold soil and darkness surrounding me as a hell-mutt had scratched at my hiding place, trying to dig me out.

I shuddered, the night air taking on a chill. I never wanted to be in that position again. And that meant baiting a hunter so Rex and I could question them.

The sour tang of rotting trash, overflowing a bin on the sidewalk, had me scrunching my nose. Releasing the pent-up breath, I exhaled my worries right along with it. Being distracted was a great way to end up in a hell-mutt's slobbery jaws.

I headed left down the side of a darkened factory, trailing along its edge as I scanned the night. A glint caught my eye, something shiny flashing briefly across the next junction. I frowned, crossing to get a closer look.

Burning pain shot up my arm as something yanked on my wrist.

Chapter 25

I staggered into the side of a dumpster. Pain bloomed through my shoulder on impact, but an agony spiking my chest eclipsed the physical sensation.

I hissed at a shadowed figure lurking behind the trash, stumbling back on instinct, but something at my wrist jerked me to a halt.

A reedy man, dressed in a full suit like some ridiculous mobster, emerged from behind the metallic bin. He grinned with a fierce joy as he stepped into the light. A metal chain wrapped around his hands, attached to a cuff on my wrist.

I bared my teeth, already summoning my fire magic. Panic froze my movements. Someone had slid bulletproof glass over my well of power. I could sense it, almost picture the roiling mass inside me, but I was smashing into a barrier, unable to reach my magic.

"What have you done?" I gasped, yanking on the chain. I'd heard of magic-blocking bindings before, but I'd hoped never to experience their effects.

He held firm, barely pulled forwards with my frantic tugs.

A grin split his thin lips. "The prettiest packages always hold the wickedest sins," he whispered, lips returning to their eerie smile. "I'm going to enjoy breaking you, demon."

Ice slid down my spine. I pushed at the invisible barrier, ramming it over and over, but my magic was out of reach. I couldn't even call on my claws.

Doing this the old-fashioned way, then.

I lurched up, pulling on the chain as I smashed my fist into the unbalanced hunter's face, kicking back to add momentum. It was a move my brother had been obsessed with when we were teens. He'd seen a superman punch on some ridiculous TV show, and we'd practised it on his punching bag for hours afterwards.

The hunter's head snapped back with a satisfying crunch, spraying blood from his nose. A deep ache radiated through my hand, but I couldn't care less.

"Not if I break you first," I snarled, following up with a vicious kick towards his middle.

He dodged back, slamming into the wall behind him with a grunt.

Slow clapping sounded behind me. "Six out of ten for technique. Ten out of ten for corny one liners."

I tensed, but the deep, velvety voice soothed my fears.

Since when was a demon sneaking up behind you *comforting*?

"Are you going to help? Or just watch me play tug of war?" I bit out, keeping my eyes on the glaring hunter holding my chain.

His free hand dived behind his back.

I lurched forwards, body slamming him into the bricks as I scrambled to get to what must be a weapon before he could. Cold metal filled my hand as I wrenched a small pistol from his hold. Victory thrilled through me as I stepped back, cocking the gun with one hand like I'd seen them do in the movies. It was only then I remembered I had one of my own I could have pulled this whole time.

If I weren't busy threatening a man, I'd have slapped myself. Clearly, more training was needed before I starred in any action flicks.

The hunter's narrowed eyes darted between the barrel aimed steadily at his face and the hulking demon I knew lurked behind me. His prominent Adam's apple bobbed as he swallowed, but to his credit, he didn't back down. "Fuck you, demon whore." His voice came out nasal from his broken nose, and I bit my lip to hold back a laugh.

Rex had no such restraint, his smoky chuckle slithering through the hushed night. "In your twisted dreams, I'm sure, but you'll never lay so much as a finger on her."

He stepped up next to me. Warmth seeped through my shoulder even with the small gap between us.

Lightning quick, his tail darted out. The pearly stinger sank into the man's wrist, just below the gleaming links still binding me to him.

He jerked back, releasing his grip on the chain with a metallic clatter as he scratched at the swollen punctures on his wrist. "W-What the fuck was that?" he screeched.

Warm fingers, wet with blood, slid beneath the handcuff circling my wrist. With a sharp yank, Rex snapped the metal hinge like it was a KitKat. Magic flooded me. I gasped at the sudden rush, clutching at my chest where I felt it swell. The relief was immediate. I hadn't realised how much I'd grown to rely on my powers until they'd left me.

I looked up just in time to watch the hunter slump to the concrete in a heap, eyes rolling back in his skull.

Lowering the gun, I clicked on the safety and shoved it into my pocket before twisting to Rex with an arched brow. "You seem to have a bad habit or murdering everyone. I thought we needed one alive for questioning?"

An innocent smile stretched his lips, so at odds with his feral features bathed in the faint moonlight. Shadows pooled in the hollows of his cheeks, giving his face a fiercer cast, as sharp as his gleaming fangs on proud display. "I only gave him a *tiny* dose of venom. Should knock him out for a few hours." His deadly tail flicked playfully behind his head as he tapped his chin with a bloodied claw. "I wonder what we could do to occupy ourselves in the meantime?"

His eyes glinted a solid black, in what I'd come to think of as his hunting mode. Even with all the darkness, they looked hungry enough that I swallowed nervously, dropping my gaze.

I gasped, finally getting a good look at the rest of him. Blood spattered across his neck, down his arms, drenching his long fingers and curved claws. No doubt even more soaked his tight black-on-black tee and trousers.

His tail circled my waist, yanking me against his firm body. We collided hard, instantly overwhelming me in the best way, as his bittersweet scent made my mouth water in anticipation.

I bit my lip at the solid length pressing against my stomach. Heat flooded me, rivalling the warmth of his muscular frame. A single claw pressed under my chin, pricking my skin in lingering threat as he lifted my face towards his.

He dipped down to meet me, only highlighting the extreme size difference between us. Everything about Rex was huge. His presence alone overwhelmed me, like he took up more than his fair share of oxygen in the deserted street.

"What do you say, little mouse? Any ideas, hmm?" He spoke so close to my lips that I felt the air vibrate against them.

"I..." My mouth felt dry, all the moisture having fled south. "What if there're more hunters?"

He quirked a dark brow, voice dropping even lower. "Where do you think all this blood is from?"

Right. Stupid question. Of course he'd already killed the rest of this hunter's team. They might be brainwashed lunatics, but they were smart enough to never hunt alone. I knew Rex wouldn't have left me to fight by myself for that long unless he was already mid-murder.

"You don't get a blowjob in every alley." I licked my lips, so close to tasting him barely an inch away. They felt fuller somehow, as if remembering the plump tenderness after I'd pleasured him outside Rusty's.

He chuckled, little wisps of smoke tickling my sensitive lips. Or maybe that was just his faint exhale. "A demon can dream." He flashed me a lopsided grin that had my racing heart stalling.

"And just what do wicked demons like you dream of?" My voice came out husky, and I gave myself a mental pat on the butt for a sexy job well done.

"You." His forked tongue flicked out, viper-quick, to whisper over my lips in a teasing swipe that had me shivering in anticipation. The black abyss of his eyes bored into me. "Only you, little mouse."

Chapter 26

My dark demon slammed his lips against mine. Hard and demanding, he kissed me with a dizzying passion. With all the ferocity I'd come to expect from him in the short time I'd known him.

He pulled back, just enough to murmur against my aching lips, "I'm going to take you against the wall now, little mouse. And you're going to scream for me."

I jolted against him, his words shocking a bolt of pure lust through me. Was I really going to let a demon fuck me in public?

In an alleyway in the dead of night? Right next to a hunter he'd knocked out, while he was still covered in blood? I supposed, with Rex, he was covered in blood more often than not.

Before I could process what was happening, he spun me away from him, shoving me up against the solid bricks. My palms slapped against the rough surface as my face collided with the back of his warm hand. He slipped it out quickly, leaving my cheek pressed to the cold wall instead.

My chest heaved, faintly scraping my nipples against the brick even through my clothes. I was already panting. What did that say about me?

A desperate sense of anticipation stretched out every second as I waited for his next move.

Claws pricked my neck as Rex gripped my nape roughly. His other hand snaked under my top, pulling the gun from the small of my back and the knife sheathed at my hip. I didn't see where he put them, but I didn't need weapons right now. Not when I had all that barely leashed violence behind me.

Heat engulfed my back as he pressed against me in full, sharply contrasting the chill seeping into my front. The electrifying scents of smoke and ginger wrapped around me, only ratcheting up my desire as a hard length prodded the middle of my back in sensual threat. I already knew how impressively well endowed he was, and I couldn't deny a part of me had been obsessing about how those strange, flexible bristles might feel inside me.

"Rex," I groaned, squirming against his immoveable hold.

Even I couldn't tell if I was trying to get away or even closer.

"Yes, witch?" Rex purred in my ear, his forked tongue flicking out to trace the shell. "Tell your demon what you need. Your wish is my command."

I could hear the smirk in his voice, but with my cheek against the bricks, I could only see the edge of one dark spiralling horn and an even darker eye in my periphery.

I snorted. "Is it? You've not been a particularly obedient demon so far."

He chuckled, rich and deep. "Maybe you've tamed me, little mouse. Maybe I'm a whole new demon. Just for you."

I didn't want a new demon. I wanted Rex. With his fiery eyes and smoky chuckle, with his irreverent humour and violent tendencies, with his hidden, caring side and unfounded belief in me.

"Rex." His name sounded like a plea on my lips. I had no clue what I was begging for.

But my body knew.

On instinct, my back arched, pushing my hips against him, but with the height difference, my arse rubbed against his muscular thighs rather than the hard length I craved.

"You want to get fucked, little witch?" His voice was a harsh growl. "You want me to take you like the monster I am? Is that what makes your greedy pussy gush, hmm? The thought of being used for pleasure in this filthy alley?"

I couldn't help the faint moan slipping from my lips. His words shouldn't affect me this much.

"Can you feel the blood of your enemies coating me? I killed them for you, and I loved every second. Their fear was almost as sweet as your pleasure on my tongue." Rex ran his nose along my jaw, the cool ridges of his horn brushing against my cheek, sending a shiver through me. "I can scent your arousal, like ripe cherries just begging for me to take a bite. Fucking divine."

His hand tightened on my nape, and my body locked up on instinct.

Claws slid against my skin as he pushed my leggings and underwear down my hips, exposing my wet heat to the cool air. I was breathing too hard, my ragged panting filling the quiet night.

Rex stepped back, his too-long arm pinning me with ease. My body mourned the loss of his solid heat.

"Such a pretty pink pussy, already weeping in need for me." Rex growled, curling one set of claws into my hip, hard enough to pinch but not to cut. He angled my pelvis back, dragging me down the wall and exposing me even further.

Something slid through my folds, and I cried out at the sudden pleasure.

A firm heat pushed into my entrance, stretching me with a delicious burn. I sucked in a gasp as I caught sight of the grey length of his sinuous tail disappearing between us. I could feel the arrowed head smooth in and out, sending shivers of pleasure through me.

"Yes, that's it, little mouse, cry for me," he purred.

I whimpered louder at his encouragement, pushing back into his tail as much as his fierce grip on my neck and hip allowed.

His tail yanked out of me with a harsh suddenness. I felt empty. Wet and needy. Too desperate to think, to worry about how anyone could stumble upon us in this darkened side street.

"Rex," I whined. "Please."

"Yes, sweet, innocent witch, beg for your pleasure." Rex's voice was a harsh snarl in my ear as he leaned close. His forked tongue trailed along my jaw in a wet caress, causing shivers to bloom in his wake. "I'm going to fuck this needy pussy now and fill you with my seed until it overflows, gushing hot cum down your thighs."

I moaned, his wicked words hitting me like a drug. A desperate need sang through my veins. I wanted every filthy ounce of pleasure he could give me.

"Please," I groaned, widening my stance for him. "I need you, Rex."

He chuckled, smoky and sinful. "That's it, open that pussy for me. *My* pussy."

Something pointy yet blunt lodged against my entrance, too wide to be his tail.

I sucked in a breath.

Rex thrust into me. Hot and hard, his solid cock overwhelmed me with a burning stretch that was too much and yet not enough all at the same time.

I cried out at the fullness. At the dizzying pressure inside me.

Rex growled at my back, feral and animalistic. "So tight and wet. This sweet cunt was made for me. You were made for me."

His bristles rubbed against my inner walls even as he held perfectly still, buried deep. The flexible thorns at my entrance tickled my lower lips. Somehow, a few swayed against my clit too. I saw stars for a moment, eclipsing the red bricks and dark night.

"Wh-What is that?" I gasped, fighting my body's instinctive need to squirm on his monstrous length. The stretch stung as my channel fought to adjust to the invasion.

Rex placed a small kiss to the base of my neck, just below his hand collaring me. "My thorns can stretch to give you all the friction you crave." His voice was low, an almost indecipherable growl.

As if to demonstrate his point, more thin, soft bristles stroked my aching clit in a teasing, wet caress. They massaged the needy bundle of nerves a fraction harder, and I jerked against him, pushing his cock even deeper with a moan. I could hardly think straight.

"Rex," I whined, "so fucking good. More. Please."

His clawed hand left my hip, and I yelped as Rex ripped my top and bra, yanking the material down to my waist, exposing my heavy breasts. His strong tail wrapped around my waist like a snake, warm and smooth against my skin. The arrowhead, still moist from my own arousal, stretched up to rub at each of my nipples in turn, winding me tighter with more desperate need.

Sharp fangs nipped my bare shoulder, and I gasped at the distracting sting. Rex groaned as he lapped at the wound he'd made. "Your blood is divine, little mouse. You taste like winter berries and sin, like pure power."

I pushed back in silent need, claiming another thick inch of the demon impaling me. Now that I'd had a few moments to adjust to his immense size, the burning ceded to devastating bliss. The hot weight of him, so deep inside me, was enough to have me nearing my peak already. With his wicked thorns, I was about one thrust away from coming undone.

He drew back, achingly slow, until just the pointed head of him remained inside me. Without warning, he snapped forwards in a ruthless thrust. I screamed, pleasure shooting through me in a harsh wave. But he didn't stop there. Pulling back again, he plunged in to the hilt with a feral snarl.

The beast snapped.

He unleashed all that ruthless fury on my pliable body, pounding into me from behind. He snarled in my ear, tightening his grip on my neck and hip, his tail squeezing my waist, as he forced me harder onto his length, dragging me back from the wall to suspend me in mid-air as he rutted into me like the monster he was. My own claws curled into his muscular forearms for support, the only thing I could hold on to.

I couldn't think. I could barely breathe with his firm grip on my neck. All I could do was feel. A slave to his dark need. Pleasure spiking through my core in dizzying bursts.

"So." He thrust deep. "Fucking." Another ruthless thrust. "Good." Thrust.

He growled and snapped his fangs as he jerked me up and down on his length like I was a weightless doll. I was completely trapped, ecstasy smashing through me in waves with every wicked thrust. His thorns rubbed me, inside and out, his heavy balls slapping against my clit with every pounding thrust of his cock. They smashed his thorns hard against me, shocking pleasure through my sensitive nerves in bright flashes of bliss.

Mewling sounds spilled from my lips, the only thing I could do as Rex slaked his thirst for pleasure on my body. My moans bounced off the walls, echoing around us with the rhythmic slap of flesh on flesh.

He snarled in my ear, "Come for your demon. Now."

I shattered. Nothing but shards of ecstasy as my body splintered apart with pleasure. The world ceased to exist as I writhed on

Rex's hard length, my core clamping around him as I obeyed his wicked command.

Rex thrust. Once. Twice. To the hilt.

He roared, the sound deafening. His cock kicked hard inside me, flooding me with wet heat.

The tingling feel of his power-rich essence filling me was too much. Another wave of bliss washed over me, dragging me under the tide as I drowned once more, screaming my pleasure to the night.

Liquid squelched, soaking my thighs with a light fizz against my skin as my clamping pussy forced his seed to overflow despite the fat girth practically plugging me full.

Rex groaned, breathing as hard as I was. His breaths peppered my shoulder blade before he pressed a chaste kiss to my skin in a surprisingly sweet gesture. Compared to the rough way he'd used my body, it was almost painfully gentle.

My body twitched with the aftershocks, and my brain had posted a "back in ten minutes" sign.

The demon unwound his hand from my nape. I sagged forwards, but his tail hugged my waist tighter, holding me up. Along with his claws on my hip and his cock lodged deep, he held me in place with ease. I was a puddle of blissed-out jelly. If he weren't keeping me upright, I'd have already collapsed.

Rex pulled out slowly, a gush of liquid flowing in his wake to splatter on the concrete. I bit my lip, feeling thoroughly scandalised by what we'd done.

What I'd let a demon do to me. In public.

He released my hip, leaving small pinpricks of throbbing sensation from where his claws had pierced me. Using his tail, he turned me to face him. Bloodstained claws cupped my cheek, a mixture of warm comfort and lethal danger, as he stared down at me.

Something unreadable filled his black eyes as he drank me in. "You're perfect, Zoella. Utterly fucking perfect."

My tongue felt too thick in my mouth, but I managed to pry my lips apart enough to utter a small noise somewhere between sceptical dismissal and grudging thanks.

A smile curved his full lips, transforming his serious expression into heart-stopping, handsome charm. It struck me then, just how beautiful this monster was. With his high cheek bones, angular eyes, and chiselled square jaw, most statues must be weeping in envy.

"I suppose we'd better get that prick tied up so you can perform your *other* magic," Rex mused. His endless eyes never left mine, almost glittering with intensity.

Through the haze of bliss and power singing through me, buzzing in my chest, I realised I'd completely forgotten the unconscious hunter in a heap by my feet. Right where my clothing was bunched around my ankles. Right where pale-lavender liquid had splashed across the man's shoulder.

A fierce blush seared my cheeks.

Rex had an unfortunate talent for making me forget everything but him.

Chapter 27

An eerie grin split Rex's lips. He lifted his hand and brought it down in a blur, slapping the hunter's pale cheek hard enough to rock the plastic chair we'd strapped him to.

The man groaned, his too-flat features scrunching as Rex delivered another rude awakening, this time with the back of his hand. The smack bounced off the wallpapered walls of our latest hotel room: another bland, boxy room with hardly enough space at the end of the bed to perform a decent interrogation.

After Rex had corrupted my soul with wicked pleasure in public, the demon had slung the unconscious hunter over his shoulder like a bag of potatoes, and we'd hoofed it back to the hotel we'd checked into this morning. Or maybe that was now *yesterday* morning, given the alarm clock on the bedside table displayed "02:03" in its angry glow.

With nobody manning the plywood reception counter, we'd managed to slip through the lobby and up the three floors without seeing another soul. A gift from the goddesses, since I'd been forced to tie the remains of my ruined top around my chest and Rex had been covered in blood, carrying a limp body. Even in this part of town, some eyebrows would have been raised.

The hunter's skin was clammy as I gripped his bony shoulder. Rex had ripped the reedy man's suit jacket and dress shirt off when he'd started tying him up, claiming he'd be less likely to squirm free with the tape sticking to his skin. I suspected the real reason was an evil joy at the idea of ripping the duct tape from the man's hairy arms afterwards.

I gripped the prickling bundle of herbs in my left hand, taking a deep breath. Beneath the scent of stale cigarettes and citrus cleaning product, which all cheap hotel rooms seemed to have, the soothing combination of sage leaves, oak bark, and sloe berries greeted me.

"*Essentia veritatis liberabit vos,*" I chanted low, barely a whisper of sound.

A tingling wave of magic coursed from the well in my chest, down my left side, and into my hand. Magic heated the small bundle of plant matter before it dissolved into a chalky ash, clenched in my fist. A familiar buzz of power ricocheted back my up arm, seeming to vibrate the very air around me, lifting the fine hairs on my nape. An arc of magic connected the warm ash in my left hand to the male gripped in my right.

He stirred with another low groan as if he could feel the magic digging into him, eyes fluttering open as he worked his jaw. No doubt from the ache Rex had just instilled with his hard slaps. Wrists, waist, and ankles secured to the chair with an obscene amount of duct tape, only his head had free movement.

His wan complexion paled further as he struggled in his bindings. The hunter glared at Rex, leaning over him, before spreading that hate to me.

"Scared?" Rex purred, eyes alight with a hunger that had his slit pupils dilating wide.

My magic pulsed again, sapping a little of the power high Rex had given me.

The hunter shook his head, jaw clenched, but after a strained second, his mouth opened. "Y-Yesss." The word came out strangled, but my magic had him in a vice he couldn't break. Not without any of his own power, and Rex and I had both taken the time to search him for charms while he'd been unconscious.

The ash in my palm warmed pleasantly.

I nodded at Rex, signalling the spell was working. As far as I knew. It was all textbook theory for me until today.

"Of course you are." Rex patted the man's cheek in a patronising gesture. "You've been caught by the very creatures you hunt, torture, and put down like rabid dogs. Many of my people are still searching for their missing mates. I am not a very forgiving dog."

The pulse in the hunter's neck throbbed at an alarming speed.

"Woof." Rex gnashed his fangs aggressively, inches from the man's face.

The man jerked in his bindings, panting in fear. His skin had turned almost as grey as Rex's. My magic might hold him in a sort of trance, in theory, but that didn't stop him from feeling every emotion running through him. From what I could gather, the spell only slowed physical reactions.

I had to hide a wry smirk at Rex's antics. The psycho demon was enjoying himself far too much.

I made a "get on with it" gesture with my left fist, careful not to release the spell's ashes as I tried to focus on the magic thread linking me to our captive. I wasn't sure how long I could hold it, even with the swelling of energy from Rex's *donation*.

Said donation still seeped from my core into my already soaked panties. Thankfully, most of its uniquely sinful tingling had faded. Or I'd never have been able to focus enough to perform the spell. I fought the urge to rub my thighs together to help ease some of the aching wetness. Given how sore I was, a part of me was thankful for the strangely soothing liquid.

A pleasure demon had magical sperm. Who knew?

Rex flashed me a smug grin, taking a deep inhale that had his nostrils flaring in a distinctly predatory way. Surely he couldn't scent me over the terrified feast just under his nose. Right?

His forked tongue swiped across his lower lip, as if he was remembering my taste. A blush stole across my cheeks.

Ugh, what was wrong with me? Rex had me hooked on his decadent touch. I guessed that was what I got for getting hot and heavy with the devil.

Giving myself a mental slap, I refocused on the mission: survival.

Clearing my throat, I shot a pointed look at the quivering hunter. Rex shook himself, both sets of black horns glinting with the new angle under the weak, artificial light.

The demon flashed fangs at his prey. "Where are Riverside's hunters based?"

The human parted his thin lips, but no sound came out. A choking noise spluttered up from his throat. My magic bucked, shaking the man and draining me at an alarming rate. I swayed, grip tightening on the hunter to hold me steady.

Rex frowned, a look of concern twisting his features as his gaze jumped from the man to me.

I had no idea what was happening, but the hunter clearly wasn't spitting out any information, let alone the truth.

"Why isn't he answering?" Rex asked, raising his claws as if he could fight whatever problem I was having with the spell.

Magic tugged at my chest, but the drain eased up to a steady level.

"C-Can't," the man spluttered, gasping for breath as if he'd just been strangled. "Spell."

"Truth." I grimaced, feeling the ashes respond warmly at the man's words.

Rex growled, dragging his claws along the man's neck, just hard enough to leave lines of red in his wake without drawing blood. "Oh? What can you tell us about the hunters' whereabouts?" His voice turned silky, loaded with so much threat that it shot down my spine.

Tension bolted through the hunter's thin frame like he'd been electrocuted. He thrashed in the flimsy chair, and I struggled to keep my skin against his. Breaking contact would break the spell. I hissed, digging my claws harder into his shoulder to keep us locked together.

He sagged, head lolling back as all the fight drained from him in a rush. "There's a drop tonight with a regular dealer. Old Town Docks. Two a.m."

I frowned, opening my mouth, but Rex beat me to it.

"A drop of what?" he snarled, blood-red eyes glowing with a rage I'd not yet seen from him.

Something in me shied back from that feral look. Why did this question seem almost more important than their base's location?

My magic tugged again, but the flow of energy arcing through me from the ash and into the man felt sluggish, like a stream of syrup rather than water. A warning throbbed in my skull as I reached my limit.

"I-I...don't know," the man whined, "something about magic weapons. Maybe abominati—"

Rex roared, cutting the hunter off as black flooded his eyes in a vicious sea of hate. Before I could blink, his claws punched into the man's chest, yanking out a throbbing mass of wet flesh.

I gagged, the metallic tang of raw meat nauseatingly strong.

Rex clenched his fist, popping blood all over us as he crushed the man's beating heart. The flow of magic snapped with a lash of power, causing me to wince at the strike deep in my chest.

Rex growled, a feral vibration that echoed through the silent room.

"I'm not sure who you're threatening," I rasped, feeling a shocked daze settle in at the gory scene. "He's already dead."

Chapter 28

Rex blinked rapidly, like he was coming back to his senses. He stared down at the red mass in his claws.

For one crazy moment, I thought he was going to take a bite. Nausea churned my stomach as I watched him, afraid to so much as twitch. My heart thudded in a sluggish rhythm. I knew he was a literal demon, but if I had to watch him consume raw flesh, I *would* throw up on him.

With a grunt, he dropped the fleshy handful into the man's lap, adding to the blood already streaming down the man's stomach. A hole gaped in his chest, lined by gleaming shards of bone.

I swallowed, finally managing to unclamp my hand from the still-warm body. My mini claws squelched a little as they slid from his wiry shoulder muscle. Bile hit the back of my throat, and I clenched my jaw to hold it back.

When I'd wrangled my squeamishness back under control, I blew out a slow, controlled breath.

I eyed Rex with budding unease. He stared down his victim, an unreadable expression flattening his angular features.

For a moment there, I'd let myself forget about his demonic nature. I'd let his sweet words and sweeter touch lull me into a false sense of security. Violence was an integral part of him. As natural as breathing. He might feed on pleasure, but he also fed on blood.

Could I really trust the demon king?

I already knew the answer.

I couldn't trust anyone.

"What? Never seen someone rip out a heart before?" Rex drawled, wriggling his blood-drenched fingers at me with a slight smirk.

His unexpected teasing burst the swelling tension that had filled the small room.

I quirked a brow, lips twitching. "Unsurprisingly, no. Why? Is kidnapping and heart ripping on your usual Thursday night agenda?"

He chuckled, disappearing into the room's darkened en suite before re-emerging with a fluffy towel. He wiped his claws off on the pristine cloth, staining it a garish red. "I'm usually busy running a kingdom, actually. Since most of my subjects are hybrids, of all types, many are borderline nocturnal. On a Thursday, I hold a sort of late-night open office. That way, they can come see me without an appointment and bring up anything that's concerning them."

The image of a demon like Rex, brimming with primal lethality, in an *office* was jarring. Did he wear a tailored suit like some billionaire CEO too?

"You have an office?" My head tilted aside. Gleefully distracted, I jumped down the conversational rabbit hole in favour of dealing with the gory scene lurking before me.

Rex paused, gripping the bloodied towel as he shot me a puzzled frown. "Yes." He said slowly, "Did you think I worked in some supervillain's evil lair? Perhaps built into a volcano? Please tell me you at least pictured identical henchmen and a trapdoor that dropped unsuspecting victims into a pit of flesh-eating monsters."

I snorted out an unattractive giggle, waving him off. "I've sort of avoided thinking about all that."

His frown deepened until intense lines appeared between his brows like crevices in a cliff face. The silence thickened as he watched me, almost as if he was internally debating something. His expression hardened, only adding to the rocky effect. "We should talk about the future," he said, cultured voice even.

I nodded, realising we were wasting time nattering on like gal pals when we should plan what to do with the meagre information we'd obtained. "You're right," I said. His expression softened, something like relief smoothing his handsome features. "I think we should go check out this drop," I continued before glancing at the clock, eyes bugging at its aggressive declaration. "Goddesses, it's already five a.m. We need to find somewhere else to sleep before we raid that exchange, because a dead body isn't exactly a relaxing addition to the décor."

I glanced around the run-down suite, noting the fading rose-print wallpaper now held a few extra touches of red. The brown carpet hadn't been winning any points to begin with, but now it was completely ruined by the dark stain spreading out from under the chair holding a cooling body in the only free space.

The narrow flat-pack dresser in the corner, where I'd stashed my half-empty backpack, and the low queen-sized bed hadn't survived the ordeal unscathed either, more flecks of blood decorating them. I finished my quick sweep of the room, landing back on the towering slate-grey demon. His tail's raised arrowhead was visible over one muscular shoulder like usual but flicking from side to side like a twitchy cat's.

His frown was back.

Rex's gaze dropped as he ran a hand between his horns, brushing through his fiery hair. Burning red eyes met mine, their intensity making me squirm. "I'm talking about *us*."

I stilled, my throat suddenly feeling like I'd swallowed a spoonful of peanut butter. I barely managed to unglue my tongue enough to croak out words. "What do you mean?"

He drew in a sharp breath, briefly luring my gaze to his wide chest, speckled with blood. "This"—he gestured a tinted claw between us—"is more than just pleasure for me."

The admission fell like a splattered heart between us, shocking me to my core. Sure, I could admit I was starting to care for Rex more than was healthy, but I'd never expected him to develop any kind of feelings for me. I was the unwanted witch outcast. He was a stunning yet terrifying demon king.

Maybe I was getting ahead of myself.

"More?" I asked, carefully folding away any ridiculous seeds of hope trying to sprout. Even if he was saying what I thought he was, I was in no position to be thinking about romance. My life was on the line. Yet a small, stupid part of me couldn't help but wonder what a future with Rex in it would look like.

What if he stayed?

One corner of his pouty lips twitched into a wry smile. "Maybe they don't have this concept in your realm, but I want more than just pleasure and power. More than the perfection of your tempting body, your intoxicating blood. I want your heart. Your soul."

The fleshy mass of the hunter's crushed heart loomed in my periphery. My own squeezed in a sympathetic panic.

"I..." My voice trailed off into silence, but internally I was screaming and running around like a headless chicken.

At my hesitation, his features arranged into an impenetrable mask.

There was no denying he was out of my league—gorgeous royalty, with endless muscles and charm. He was infuriating enough to bring out the sass in me, and then he revelled in the fiercer side I usually buried. He dived horns first into the darkness with me and lightened every moment until I could smirk in the face of danger right alongside him. His crazed violence somehow made me feel safe rather than afraid, and he sparked a passionate hunger in me I'd never felt before.

Yet my heart was as battered as the dead hunter's beside us. I'd barely survived the loss of my family, both physically and emotionally. Lyndsey and the rest of Quartz Coven had only shredded the scraps I'd sewn back together over the last decade.

I didn't think I'd survive another hurt like that. How could I trust someone not to betray me again?

Let alone a violent demon I'd known for a mere few days.

My mind spun with the conflicting thoughts, my pulse racing like a pack of hell-mutts chased me.

Things were good between us. Confusing but exhilarating. We shared pleasure, and I gave him blood. In exchange, he protected me, and we worked towards destroying the monsters hunting me, for both my reasons and his, so he could go back to his life in hell where I wouldn't be selfishly throwing him into constant danger. There was a clear end date to whatever *this* was.

I didn't know what to make of the idea that he wanted more, but a secret part of me was crying out to grab onto the chance at something real and never let go. But what if I let him in and he didn't like what he found?

"...It's only been a few days," I finished lamely, cringing at how pathetic that sounded, but my brain power was being used on the questions flitting through my mind at rapid fire speed.

Could I really date a demon? How would that work? Would we be exclusive? Was he seeing someone else too? Would he expect me to hop through a portal and visit him in hell? Would we just go out to a restaurant like the humans and have a normal date night? Maybe snuggle up on the sofa and watch a movie?

His gaze remained steady, but behind his glowing eyes, a depth of emotion churned.

The intensity cut through some of my internal panic.

He nodded slowly, keeping his voice a soft rumble, like he was trying not to spook a wild animal. "Think it over, little mouse. I'm not usually a patient predator, but I can try for prey as sweet as you."

He leaned down and hauled up the body of the hunter, heart and all, chucking it onto his shoulder. He strode past me, dripping more blood onto the carpet. I watched with stunned silence echoing through my brain.

His tail curved up, the arrow's flat stroking over my exposed collarbone above my long-sleeve's low neckline as he sauntered away from the room's exit. A shiver worked down my spine as faint tingles spread from where his warm skin had caressed mine.

"Stay here, Zoella. I'll be back soon." He casually shoved the window open with one hand and shrugged the corpse out of it.

I winced at the wet splat. Hopefully, nobody was awake to watch a dead man fall several stories out of a window. At least this room faced the hotel's small courtyard rather than the street.

My brows shot up as Rex ducked through the sill, flashing me a devilish wink before launching himself out after the body.

Without his consuming presence, my thoughts churned louder, one screaming above the rest. Could I trust the demon with my heart?

Chapter 29

"You're a skittish little mouse now," Rex murmured, gaze scanning the nearby quiet warehouses and gently bobbing ships visible between them on the waterfront.

Unease slid down my spine as I fought to stop fidgeting with the belladonna ring on my finger and lie still in the wake of his almost question. My gaze darted to the demon stretched out, prone, beside me, hugging low to the top of the rusted shipping container.

As usual, he was only in a comfy pair of trousers, this time from the human realm. Earlier, I'd watched in fascination as he'd poked a hole in them for his tail. Apparently, he must be allergic to tops, because he hadn't bothered to pull a shirt on despite the brisk night air. I was sort of mad I'd wasted money on getting him more than one top, but at least I now had spares that were long enough to serve as dresses for me in a pinch. I was surprised he'd even put shoes on this time, since he hadn't seemed in a rush to get any.

A light rain misted us, dewing small beads against the ridges of his black horns. Even in the faint light from the various lamps spread throughout the docks, Rex's every demonic feature was eye-catching. Like he'd been made to draw attention, despite the slate grey of his skin.

I swallowed, unsure how to answer. Since he'd declared his intention to hunt my heart as much as the rest of me the night before, things had shifted between us again. I was going to get whiplash with the way things were constantly changing, but I'd regained a sense of self-preservation and, I supposed in the process, sought some kind of distance between us. To say letting Rex feed from my wrist this afternoon was awkward would be a hellhound-sized understatement. I both wanted him and wanted to get away from him, in almost equal measure.

"I'm not scared you'll hurt me." I moistened my lower lip with a quick swipe, unsure how to voice the confused jumble of emotions that still left me reeling.

He paused, and the very air around him seemed to still too. The demon turned his face slowly, onyx eyes swirling with intensity as they finally met mine.

"I would rather snap off my own horns."

His low tone rolled over me in a dark wave, sending shivers along my spine. This close, his endless eyes swirled like an ocean of night, ready to drown me.

Before I could put my churning thoughts into words, he pointed off to one side. "There. Looks like at least four hunters." He paused, eyes narrowing dangerously. "With cages."

Saved from having to tease out my own thorny emotions, I followed the line of his claw, squinting into the semi-darkness. Movement snagged my gaze along a corridor of stacked shipping containers, roughly a football field away. I finally saw what Rex had: two men pulling a long, mechanised trolley stacked with boxy cargo half-hidden beneath a dark sheet. The material didn't reach all the way to the bottom, revealing the base of silvery cages. They reminded me of the kind you'd keep a large dog in but twice as sturdy-looking. Things moved behind the thick bars, but from this distance, I couldn't make out what as they moved through patches of darkness. Behind the cargo, two more men followed, rifles held loosely at their sides.

My brows shot up. The hunters who'd tracked me down repeatedly didn't usually carry such obvious weapons. They mostly loaded up with pistols and an array of blades. I assumed because I tried to hide amongst the general population, but it could be budget cuts for all I knew.

"Those sick fucks," Rex snarled. A grating sounded as his claws tore into the corrugated metal beneath him.

I winced as the sound shrieked through the quiet night.

"Rex." My voice came out tight. "We wait, remember? Follow them back to their base to get the location, then come back with reinforcements, right?"

That was the loose plan we'd come up with this afternoon, after debating options for what had felt like hours. Since I'd refused to go to sleep in a crime scene, we'd switched hotels after Rex had returned from disposing of the dead hunter. I hadn't asked what he'd done with the body. I wasn't sure I wanted to know. Either way, we were *not* getting our deposit back.

Being the Hybrid King apparently had its perks though, and those included calling on some of his closest generals to help take down the hunters. From what I could gather, they were already on their way to the portal nearest to his kingdom, but it was a long and perilous journey, since it wasn't technically in his territory but part of the kingdom that bordered his. Apparently, Rex wasn't on borrow-a-cup-of-sugar terms with his neighbours.

Hence why he'd jumped at the chance to be summoned. Rex was light on the details though, as usual, but apparently I could summon a specific demon if I focused on their name, their essence, or any connection to them I had. Since Rex was their king, he had a bond with them I could use to help focus my summoning call.

We'd have already summoned them if Rex hadn't dug his heels in, insisting I needed to recover after the truth spell, just in case things went wrong tonight and I needed my fire to defend myself. His overprotective side had come out in full force, but even that hadn't been enough to melt the icy walls I could feel were going up.

Rex's hard jaw ticked, eyes locked on his prey in the distance. Menace radiated off him in almost tangible waves. Were some of his people in those cages?

Trepidation shot through me at his brooding silence. "The *plan*," I hissed, but he was already jumping to his feet.

"New plan." He flashed me a reckless smirk and stepped off the container's edge, some of his usual charm joining the murdering psycho vibe.

Rex plummeted to the ground, hitting the concrete with hardly a whisper of sound despite his considerable weight. I gripped the edge of the cool metal, contemplating the eight-foot drop. Rex disappeared into the shadows, hunting his prey through the run-down shipyard. And I didn't blame him. If anything, I was impressed. Rex would put himself in extreme danger to save his people. Elder Murray hadn't even sent out a search party when my family and I had disappeared.

I cursed under my breath but swung my legs over the edge backwards, letting my arms extend fully as metal scraped at my running clothes. Even though things were awkward between us right now, I couldn't let Rex face this alone. If some of his people were being captured by hunters, I had to help free them.

With a deep breath, I let go.

My trainers hit the ground with a thud as I bent my knees to lessen the impact, stumbling aside as my ankle twinged.

Straightening with a huff, I sent a silent prayer to the goddesses that at least Quartz had made us run an assault course a few times a month "to prepare our bodies for the physical toll of spellcasting."

Rex was nowhere to be seen as I shook my ankle out and jogged in the direction he'd taken off, easing between the rows of battered shipping containers and empty buildings, trying to stick close to the walls for cover.

A scream pierced the night.

Gun fire echoed in a rapid retort.

"Rex," I breathed, flying into a mad sprint.

My heart thudded against my ribs as I called to my inner fire, summoning the magic in my chest to pool as light-and-dark flames in my palms. The bright-purple fire tingled as it flickered and swayed, sparking black at its edges.

I burst past the last container and into chaos.

Rex slashed at an armed hunter, cutting his throat before ripping away his rifle to throw into another male's face. More hunters emerged from the far building, shouting as they sped towards Rex.

Feral snarls spilled from the cages. The material covering them slipped, revealing the beasts inside.

Hellhounds.

Silky fur, as black as night, wrapped their enormous forms, accented with shocking splashes of colour. Unlike the mutts the hunter's had bred, pure hellhounds had a fire inside them you could glimpse through their eyes. Built sleek and powerful, they held a lethal beauty.

Lilac eyes burned into me, eerily familiar. The caged hellhound at the front of the stack didn't snarl or howl. He just stared right at me, bright eyes searing. My chest burned more the longer our eyes met.

"Zo!"

I jerked around as a hunter fired.

Grey eclipsed my world, a hard body slamming me to the ground. Pain radiated through my back as Rex landed on top of me with a grunt. He pushed up, leaping away in a single beat, roaring at the enemy.

Rex had just saved my life. Again. I needed to get my head in the game. Before it was too late.

I rolled to my feet, launching a ball of flames at the closest hunter as I ran towards her. It hit the woman in her shoulder, spinning her with the force. She screeched as my flames ate through her jacket. Frantically shrugging the material off, she swung her pistol around. But I was already throwing my next set of flames. They smashed into her outstretched hand. With a yelp, the gun clattered to the concrete as she shook her flaming limb. Quickly dropping, she rolled on the ground, but my fire still grew until it engulfed her in purple-black flames.

Already scanning for my next target, I swallowed down the horror as the stench of burning flesh hit me.

"Kill the witch!" a breathy voice demanded.

My brain short-circuited. I *knew* that voice.

Half-hidden behind another mechanical trolley, loaded with covered cages, a familiar bronze-haired male waved a pistol in my direction.

Fenton's chiselled features had gone slack, tanned skin turning ashen. Like he'd seen a ghost.

I supposed to him, I was one.

But the bastard was going to join me in hell. I'd make sure of it.

Chapter 30

Something feral dug its claws into me, carving out all emotion. Except rage.

A deep, burning rage.

My throat vibrated as a growl spilled from me in an uncontrollable stream. I threw a fistful of lilac fire at a hunter sprinting towards me. He screamed, going down in a tumble of limbs and fire, falling into the stacked cages Fenton hid beside. As the hunter bounced off the trolley, the material covering stuck to him, wrapping him like a flaming burrito as he hit the ground. A shock of colourful beings were trapped inside the cages, but before I could process the sight, another male leaped over his fallen comrade towards me.

Fenton clutched a fat envelope to his chest. If that thing wasn't stuffed full of cash, I'd get a tattoo of his face on my arse. He jumped up, racing in the opposite direction.

Dodging past the hunter before he could grab me, I charged after the traitor.

This time, it wasn't just me he'd wronged but the demons and all of magekind.

That weasel wasn't here as a captive; that was for sure.

My feet pounded the concrete, adding to the cacophony of chaos Rex stirred up behind me. Screams and grunts of pain, the sickening wet squelch of limbs being torn apart, the solid thuds of broken bodies hitting the ground. And amongst it all, the sharp rap of gun fire, ratcheting up my heart rate. I prayed a bullet wasn't heading for the back of my skull as I pumped my legs harder, racing through the shipyard.

Fenton darted out of sight, disappearing through the aisles of rusted shipping containers stacked tall like a metallic maze.

Something smashed into the back of my shoulder, sending me sprawling forwards. I slammed into the concrete, scraping my palms as I managed to catch myself on instinct, face inches from the ground. A scream tore from my lips as my shoulder lit up with agony.

I clamped my mouth closed, sucking back the scream as I struggled to scramble behind a stack of wooden pallets. A feral whine sounded from the cages in the distance, but I couldn't focus on anything except trying to breathe through the pain.

A ragged hole sat just below my left collarbone, oozing red through my dark top.

I'd been shot.

My brain got stuck on that single thought. I gritted my teeth against the pain, watching in sick fascination as blood continued to seep from the wound, every breath agony as it tugged and stretched at my flesh.

"Zo!" Rex's voice roared. "Run!"

I peeked around the wooden pallets, heart pounding. Several figures raced towards me, brandishing pistols and knives. A grey blur bore down on them, but he was too far away.

With a sharp inhale, I staggered upright, clutching my injured arm to my middle.

The hunters opened fire as I ran, weaving erratically. My shoulder jarred with every step, sending a fresh throb of agony, but I shoved it aside in favour of survival. Making a hasty decision, I darted through a small gap between the nearest shipping containers, weaving back on myself down the next row to crouch one container closer to the action.

I summoned a ball of fire in my palm.

A figure sprinted past my hiding spot. I launched my magic. He cried out as it smashed into his back, stumbling him. The next hunter tried to stop, but he ploughed straight into the flaming male. I whipped lilac ribbons of fire across a third figure as he joined them. He screamed, following his comrades down in a flaming heap.

But more hunters raced into view, passing the edge of the container. They stopped short, spinning to lift their rifles as they spotted me leaning against the wall of metal at my back. Pain and exertion had sapped my strength until I could barely keep flickers of purple fire in my palm. I didn't have another fireball in me.

I bared my fangs, bracing for pain. For the end.

Rex loomed behind the hunters like a dark god. He tore clean through one man's neck, separating head from shoulders, while his tail slammed another forwards, stinger flashing in the light.

One of the hunters swung his rifle towards Rex. I lurched forwards, raking claws of spluttering fire across the hunter's back before he could pull the trigger, sending him to his knees with a yelp. I leaned around him, quickly tearing his throat in a heated slash of pure desperation.

The remaining male swiped his blade across Rex's chest while he was occupied. The demon hissed before smacking the blade from the man's outstretched hand. He snarled, darting in to bury his fangs in the man's throat. Rex tore free in a spray of lifeblood, dropping his victim with a wet squelch.

The messy slash bled navy across his bare chest, but more than one injury already peppered his hulking frame.

Hard black eyes swept me from head to toe. A snarl curled his upper lip when he ran past the wound in my shoulder. As if his attention brought it to life, it flared bright with pain. Fighting for my life had dulled it temporarily. Now it was back with a vengeance.

I hissed out a breath, trying to swallow back the whine that clawed up my throat.

"The others?" I choked out through gritted teeth.

Rex's eyes never left my shoulder. "Dead. Apart from the one you were chasing."

Fenton.

Frustration and betrayal cut through me all over again, enough to rival the pain in my shoulder.

"We need to do something about your wound." Rex tipped his horns to the ragged hole in my upper chest.

I nodded, the pain making it hard to concentrate. "I need a handful of common haircap moss and several strips of bark from a silver birch."

Thank the goddesses I'd paid attention to Lyndsey with her knowledge of herbs and their magical properties. I'd learned the incantation for activating a general healing poultice in class, but it was only used for minor injuries.

Nobody had taught me how to heal a gun-shot wound.

Rex eyed me sceptically. "Some bits of plant will fix this?"

I went to shrug, but pain shot through my left shoulder, halting the movement with a ragged exhale. Mages healed quicker than humans, but even with the poultice, it wouldn't be enough. "It's the best I've got. I'm a nature witch, not a healer."

Hard black eyes softened, showing the swelling concern as he eyed the blood running down my front, seemingly unfazed by the navy running down his. I was trying my best to ignore the warm liquid I could feel flowing over my chest, down my side.

"You need real help." Rex's voice came out harsh, worry bleeding through his tone. "We can take you to one of those human hospitals." He stepped forwards as if to haul me into his arms and run off with me.

"No. We'll be sitting ducks, and a fight in the hospital will get innocents killed. Plus, we need to free those captives," I gritted out.

Rex frowned. I could tell he'd forgotten all about the beings caged on those mechanised trolleys. Even after he'd ditched our plan in favour of rescuing them. Barks, snarls, and shouts for help still reached us from where we'd left them behind in the middle of the shipyard.

"I don't give a fuck about them," he snarled. "We're getting you a healer."

Something in my chest warmed, even as the pain made it hard to focus. "Healers are extremely rare, and I don't know any outside the covens. I'm guessing you don't either." I waited for him to contradict me, but he narrowed his black-abyss eyes. I narrowed my lilac ones right back. "The longer we argue, the longer I bleed."

"Fine. The bullet went clean through. We stop the bleed now." Silver flashed in his gaze like the glint of a blade.

"How?" I spoke through bared teeth, pain and blood loss already making me woozy.

He grimaced, gesturing at my hands. "With fire."

My claws clenched with the rush of anxiety. But he had a point. I didn't know how long it would take before I bled out. "Okay," I whispered, trying to steel myself, to be brave in the face of pain and danger like Rex always was.

Warm palms engulfed my right hand on the opposite side of my wounded shoulder. Eyes hard, Rex met my gaze, unflinching. "I've got you. Light up for me, little mouse."

I nodded, pushing my remaining energy up from my chest and into my hand. Small flickers of purple and black engulfed my fingertips.

"You're going to have to will it to burn you," Rex said, voice strained. "It's your magic. It's not designed to hurt you."

I swallowed, feeling the fear but focusing on Rex's deep voice, so familiar now. His solid presence helped me push through the pain and hesitation. Before I could overthink things, I willed the flames hotter, willed it to heal me with its heat.

"Three...two—" Rex shoved my fingers against the bullet's exit wound.

I screamed, feeling my shoulder burn so hot it was almost an icy pain. He pulled away my hand, now extinguished, leading it over my shoulder to the back. The angle was strained, but he held me gently yet firm.

"Again," he snarled, tone hard and eyes wild.

"No." The whimper escaped my lips, but I fed my flames once more.

He didn't hesitate, pushing my fingers into the back wound.

Another scream wrenched from my throat, ending in a strangling groan as agony lit up my world. I was braced, more aware of the pain this time, but it was over in a flash as he pulled my hand away.

His palm smoothed over my hair, my cheek, as he murmured sweet nothings, cradling me against him. "You did good, my brave, fierce witch. You're okay. It's over now. I've got you."

I let my forehead thunk against his chest, breathing hard as I tried to ride out the searing in my upper back and collarbone while Rex comforted me. Swallowing down the whimpers that had already slipped free, I let myself breathe in the scent of Rex. Heady and sinful, he smelled like ash and ginger. The smoky-sweet combination was enough to distract from the undertone of metallic blood and burning flesh I was becoming sickeningly familiar with.

Claws smoothed across my skull, soothing me when they should have inspired fear. "I've got you, little mouse," he whispered, body rigid with tension. "We'll make them pay for every drop of blood they took from you."

A small chuckle left my lips. "Pretty sure you already killed them all."

Except one.

Chapter 31

I followed Rex towards the cages. His tail swayed behind his bare back as he walked, raised high so the blood-dipped arrow waved from side to side behind his head. No doubt ready to stab anyone he felt deserved it.

My shoulder ached in a constant throbbing pain. Less now my flesh was cauterised, but the skin around the wounds burned fiercely. It wasn't something I'd ever thought I'd need to do.

If it hadn't been for Rex, gently forcing my burning fingers into the bullet holes, I wasn't sure I'd have been able to stomach it.

The moon had swelled from last night's sliver to a thicker crescent. The flood lights, dotted throughout the old shipyard, outshone its faint glow. Though, towering security lights hadn't exactly kept anyone in this mess safe. Metallic blood and foul gore were thick in the air, combining with the salty breeze and tang of rust.

Rex and I rounded the final shipping container stack, entering the sizeable gap before the next rows began.

Cages rattled as clawed fingers poked through silvery bars, a flood of voices speaking all at once. Bodies littered the concrete: severed limbs, wet entrails, and pools of red everywhere I looked.

Rex had been busy.

We passed a pile of bones, charred black. My demon wasn't the only violent one here.

Revulsion shivered through my whole body, but I couldn't summon any regret. Those hunters had been trying to hurt Rex and me, not to mention whatever cruelty they'd inflicted on their captives.

I wasn't sure how exactly, but Fenton had played a hand in their capture. Why else would he be here? There was no way that envelope he'd clutched held anything but cash.

"Outcast King! Witch!" a high-pitched whine pierced the others. "Please, help us!"

A masculine voice grumbled from a back cage, "About time a hybrid was useful."

Rex's shoulders lifted in a slight hunch, and my steps faltered. He quickly eased the tension from his body without breaking stride, reaching the first trolley of cages in a few unhurried strides.

A hush fell across the cages. Even the hellhounds stacked on the other trolley quieted at Rex's formidable presence. I ignored the same hound with the odd lilac eyes that kept staring at me and met Rex's black gaze instead. He flashed me a reassuring smirk. No hint of emotion at the caged demon's callousness.

By unspoken agreement, we searched the nearby bodies. Apparently, I was becoming a pro at this, even with one arm throbbing painfully. My fingers closed around a metal ring inside the cargo pants pocket of one of Rex's dismembered victims. I refused the morbid curiosity asking me to look for his missing head or arm.

"Got it." I lifted the set of keys with a metallic jangle.

Rex grunted, holding out his hand. I obliged, clumsily chucking over my stolen prize, which of course he caught with one-handed ease.

He eyed the cages before speaking in a harsh language I didn't recognise. Curiosity dug its claws into me, but I held my tongue. It would make sense that not all demons could speak my language. He was probably asking for information on where they were being held or taken to. Maybe even checking if they were OK.

Heads shook, and a few voices responded with similar guttural sounds before silence fell.

Rex sighed before he quickly began unlocking cages, starting from the top after a few tries from the different keys on the loop. Either we'd lucked out and found a skeleton key, or each cage had the same lock on it.

"Nobody knows where the base is?" I asked, throat tight. Now that my adrenaline was fading, pain and exhaustion were taking over. Not to mention the mother of all magic-induced headaches.

Rex shook his horns, quickly freeing each demon. Most staggered from their cages, hurrying off without so much as a backwards glance to acknowledge their merciful saviour.

I had to bite my tongue with each ungrateful demon freed but even more so as the rude male who'd insulted Rex was released. He stretched, joints popping as he climbed from the shiny cage. Under the harsh light of the nearby floodlight, the demon looked like some kind of orc from the movies. His grey skin was only a shade lighter than Rex's but heavily wrinkled and craggy compared to Rex's smooth, if bloodied, perfection. His face had an almost pug-like squish about it, only worsened by the sneer scrunching up his features.

"I remember you as a squealing babe," he growled, doing his best to look down his flat nose at Rex despite the king being at least a foot taller. "Your mare should have put you down herself. A coward's errand, leaving you alive for the Bloodwood."

I waited for Rex to tear the demon limb from limb, like one of the hunters littering the concrete. Instead, he just stood there, features hard but unmoved.

"*Coward's errand*? Are you fucking serious?" The words burst free, the headache pounding in my skull destroying any caution I should have had about going up against a terrifying, unknown demon. "Rex, claw this crusty Uruk-hai before I do."

Rex turned his intense stare on me. A small twitch of his lips softened the deadly image of my bloodstained monster. "Such a flirt, little mouse. I long ago stopped wasting my time on entitled purebloods though." The black of his eyes bled to his glowing red shade. "Your weakness is showing, old man. I can smell your fear."

The grizzled demon scoffed, but he leaned back, an almost unconscious shift at the aura of dark lethality radiating from Rex. He'd never looked more like a king, with his fiery ombre hair in a blazing corona around his imperious face and sharp horns crowning his head. He bared his fangs in wicked threat even as his muscular body held a relaxed, almost lazy, ease.

"Run along now, before I decide to take payment in blood," he drawled with all the smug aloofness of a predator sure of their prey's easy demise.

"You'll always be hybrid scum." The orc spat on the concrete, inches from Rex's shoes.

Rex arched a brow, patiently waiting.

The other demon stomped off with a huff, disappearing between the abandoned storage buildings.

I eyed Rex, but he seemed unfazed by the demon's scorn. Outwardly, at least. He quickly freed the remaining few, who were all too happy to scurry off with the briefest thank you.

Rex watched the last demon run after the others, towards the city and I supposed wherever they called home. I had no idea whether they lived in this realm or hell, but I guessed I didn't really know much about demons, despite the magical connection between their kind and mine.

"Well, seems you're more polite than the average demon. Who knew?" I chuckled, but even I could hear the strain in the sound.

The burning pain through my shoulder and the throb in my skull were having a knock-down, drag-out fight for my attention.

Rex flashed me a wry smile, thawing his stony expression. "You'd think they were the ones raised in the wilderness."

An odd sort of anguish squeezed my chest. "So it's true...what that wrinkly old prune said? Your mother just left you in the woods as a child?"

Rex's glowing eyes tightened a fraction. "Hybrids are often killed before birth, or right after." He shrugged, as if it were no big deal. "My mother raised me for a few years before it was too much for her. The pressure from her family and clan, I presume. So she left me in the Bloodwood when I was four years old."

The ache in my chest worsened with every word he spoke. I rubbed the spot, feeling the odd mix of sympathy and rage welling up. "How did you survive? A four-year-old all alone in the woods? In *hell*?"

He cocked a dark brow. "Hell isn't all pits of flames and tortured souls; it's a world just as beautiful as this one. Vast and varied. Full of life and wonder."

I frowned. Nobody had ever described hell to me before I'd met Rex. If anything, the coven teachers had hinted it was all fire and brimstone and evil from the humans' biblical depictions. Had I learned anything true? Was I some brainwashed cult victim and I *still* didn't even know it? I was going to have a serious talk with the coven instructors when I returned.

It was my turn to arch a brow. "And yet I still wouldn't leave a toddler in the woods here either."

He grinned, baring his lethal fangs. "I was raised by beasts."

My other brow joined the first.

Had I even heard him right?

He nodded towards the cages stacked on the other trolley. "Hellhounds, to be exact."

Chapter 32

My jaw hung open like a gaping fish.

Somehow, Rex continued to surprise me at every turn.

I snapped my mouth closed with a snick. The noise reminded me of the mini fangs I was resolutely ignoring I even had. Surely Rex was joking. Right?

The towering slate-grey demon drank in my expression with a grin.

"So you were raised by wolves? Like literally?" I asked, just to double-check I wasn't hearing things.

"Yes, little mouse." He smirked. "Does it scare you? I might be more beast than demon. Even my kind gives me a wide berth."

Maybe a little. What did it say about me that I'd been secretly enjoying the company of a demon that even other demons were afraid of? But this was *Rex*. Funny and protective and so vibrantly alive. I was like a moth drawn to the inferno that was him.

I looked pointedly in the direction the freed demons had run. "Oh, I hadn't noticed."

"Come on, little mouse, open the cages. Or are you scared of those pups too?" he drawled, stepping close and eating up any crazy ideas of personal space. "I already promised I'd keep you safe. They won't hurt you." He lifted his hand, gently caressing the edge of my sealed bullet wound, his eyes filling with unexpected rage. "I won't fail you again."

I swallowed back the swell of emotion at his declaration. If it weren't for the weight of our bargains etched into my wrists, just below the surface, I'd almost have believed the fantasy he was offering.

A small part of me yearned for it, so much so that I had to check the urge to lean into the shelter of his strength.

I stepped back instead, instantly chilled by the loss of his warmth.

The hunters could have called in backup before Rex killed them all. Or that maggot Fenton could be fetching more hunters. I needed to get out of here, not swoon into a demon's embrace. I also needed rest. My shoulder chose that moment to throb harder, as if in agreement.

I swiped the keys in Rex's hand with my good arm, quickly striding over to the first caged hound.

I glared right into its eerie golden eyes. A multitude of shades flickered and swayed like flames of molten metal within. They matched the golden hue of his wide-set muzzle.

Animals had always responded well to me, especially dogs. Maybe as a part of being a nature mage, I had a slight connection, but it was nowhere near what I'd seen my mother do. She'd basically talked to animals like they were her friends. We'd had the same robin visit us every Christmas to share oat cookies with us as we opened our presents, and every time we visited the lake on Quartz territory, the same three terrapins would wait on a huge, flat rock to greet her. All I could do was talk at the two sheepdogs who'd walk me to and from the farm shop I'd used to work at each day. I didn't think the cute collies had ever understood a word, but it had been nice having the company.

Hellhounds were basically just big dogs, right?

Lifting the key, I hesitated near the lock. "Don't bite me, OK?"

My depleted magic gave a pulse, almost like a sense of recognition, but it only spiked my headache. I wasn't convinced, but I had the strangest suspicion that I could connect to the beast. I frowned, wondering just what that connection would look like. I hadn't managed to bond with animals or plants in the way I had with trees.

Shaking off my curiosity, I took a deep breath and twisted the key in the lock. The demonic beast burst forwards, smashing open the gate as I leaped back with a yelp. The hound barked once at me and bolted off into the night like a streak of black and gold.

The other hellhounds barked and yipped in canine excitement like your average dog. Except these flashed vicious fangs in their maws and keen intelligence in their colourful, glowing eyes.

"You didn't want to say goodbye to your uncle?" I aimed a wry smile at Rex, trying to lighten the tension.

He chuckled in that smoky caress I was quickly becoming addicted to, waving a hand at the remaining few cages. "Once you free my cousins, we'll have a big family reunion, I'm sure."

The smile on my lips stayed, despite the exhaustion and pain dragging on me. I quickly worked through the remaining cages. Each hound burst free dramatically, setting my erratic pulse racing, but none of them so much as growled or snapped their jaws in threat. A few of the beasts even sniffed Rex's hand before running off.

Until there was only one remaining.

The hound I'd been avoiding. The quiet one with flaming purple eyes nagging at my brain with an unsettling sense of familiarity.

I swallowed thickly, my throat suddenly too dry.

"What's wrong?" Rex asked, his claws trailing along my arm as he pressed close to my uninjured side.

How could I put into words the strange feeling thrumming through me? Like an awareness of the beast but different from any connection I'd formed to nature before. Thicker, somehow, yet frayed and broken. It was unnerving as hell.

"His eyes are the same bewitching purple as yours," Rex murmured, awe softening his usual gruff tone. "What does it mean?"

Steeling my nerves, I looked up at the final beast. "I... I don't know."

The hound just stared, those eyes burning with a fire in every stunning shade of pale purple.

My hand shook as I raised it to the lock. The key squeaked as I twisted it, pulling it free as I cringed into Rex's solid warmth behind me, waiting for the giant hound to burst free like the others had.

Instead, he raised his dark nose with an impertinent sniff before nudging open the door. It clanged as the gate swung into the rest of the metal.

He leaped from the cage, claws clicking ominously against the concrete. I tensed, but he merely sat back on his haunches, regarding me in the heavy silence.

I stared right back.

The tips of his perky triangular ears came up to eye-level, but with the sleek muscle cording his frame, the hellhound was easily double my size. His paws were as big as dinner plates, his fangs longer than my fingers. There was no question he was a formidable creature, even amongst hellhounds. Most of the others I'd freed only came up to chest height. This one was closer to Rex's size.

A purple scruff hugged his chest in an almost heart shape, tapering along his belly. Darker than the glowing shade of his flame-filled eyes, it matched the short fur on the side of his right ear and the "sock" pattern on his front, left paw. The rest of him was as black as a starless night.

That disorienting sense of déjà vu hit me all over again.

I *knew* this creature.

But how?

The hellhound lurched forwards with a whine. I felt Rex tense behind me, his arms banding my waist, ready to yank me aside, but the hound only pushed his massive head against my raised palm.

The second my hands sank through his sleek fur, a memory rolled over me.

"It's OK, sweetheart. Everything's going to be OK." My mother smiled at me despite the tears running freely down her face.

I bit my tongue hard enough to taste copper pennies. None of this was OK.

My mother's tears mixed with the bloody trails from her split cheek and brow. Bruises already purpled her swelling eye, the mottled pattern only growing every time I'd got to see her.

"Everything will *be OK. You just need to tell us where your London coven is. Or we'll kill you in front of your daughter. If you're good, we'll kill her first so she doesn't need to watch another parent die," the cruel man spoke calmly, like he was presenting logical and easy options as he pushed his thick-rimmed glasses up his straight nose.*

Tall and reedy, the male reminded me more of a librarian than the burly hunters who'd kidnapped us. Somehow, he seemed more dangerous than the enormous males who'd knocked us out with ease.

A whimper escaped my mother as she glanced towards the empty chair to my right. I couldn't look away from her though, terrified every second would be her last. Or mine. She jerked against her bindings again, anger sparking in her violet eyes.

I followed her lead, struggling uselessly against my restraints. My shoulders ached fiercely from how tightly they'd tied my wrists behind my back, over the chair, and blood seeped down my arms as some of the half-healed cuts reopened.

"*What about you, little demon?*" the man sneered, his brown eyes swimming with a vicious hate that had me freezing. "*If you tell me where your coven is, I'll let you and your mother go free. You already let your brother and father die. Are you going to fail your mother too?*"

The urge to spill our secrets choked me. But he wouldn't let us go. We all knew how hunters operated. To them, we were demon scum and only deserved torture and death. He would kill us whether we told him or not. I couldn't let him kill all those other families too. The coven elder had just had an adorable baby named Lilibeth with sea-foam hair. My family had moved away over a week ago for a quieter life out of the capital, but that didn't mean I no longer cared what happened to my old coven.

A keening sound left my lips, and the world swam. Pain bloomed across the side of my face in a delayed burst. The man had back-handed me.

"*No!*" my mother screeched, "*Please, stop it. I'll tell you, and then you can keep her alive. She's special. She has powerful magic. She can already perform amazing tracking and summoning spells,*" my mother begged, her voice frantic.

"*Mother, no,*" I whined. Why would she lie? I had no magic. Not yet, anyway. And why would she betray the coven we had lived with for years?

My heart slowed to a sluggish thud, like all the panicked racing over the past days of torture and constant terror had exhausted it to the point where it wanted to give up.

She sat taller, squaring her shoulders despite the cuts and bruises littering her body. "*Our old coven is in the north-east corner of Kingswood.*"

I gasped. That wasn't where we'd lived. "W-What are you doing?"

My mother's purple eyes, only a few shades darker than my own, locked onto me. "I love you, sweetheart. Never forget who you ar—"

Her head snapped aside with a bang, blood and brains exploding out the side. Her body collapsed in the chair, dripping thick red globs onto the floor.

A ringing sounded in my ears. My mother's violet gaze dulled.

I screamed, a broken sound filled with anguish tearing from my very soul. Something swelled deep in my chest, rising to meet my pain. A fizzing rush exploded outwards in a harsh burst, so strong it hurt.

The man holding the pistol swung it towards me with a victorious grin.

The buzzing wave crashed from me into something outside the room. Heat lashed from that point to my chest in a line of fire.

A howl joined my pained keening. A blur of black and purple smashed through the small window in the door, crashing straight into the wiry man. A dog ravaged the man's arm. The gun clattered to the floor, skidding to a halt at my feet.

The man screamed, punching the small dog even as it clawed its hind legs into his stomach, tearing the flesh through his fancy shirt. The animal snarled, shaking its head before clamping huge jaws around the man's throat and tearing it free. Blood sprayed, the man gurgling in his death throes.

The dog—a puppy, really—growled at the dead body before turning on me.

Lilac eyes bored into me with a feral intensity. Something flowed between us in that burning stare.

He gave a small woof before rushing over. I tensed for more pain, but the beast clawed at my rope bindings, ripping them free. The moment they fell away from my skin, I sagged forwards, struggling to hold myself upright as my hands tingled in a painful rush.

The puppy bounded back around, and my fingers brushed against his furred side.

Fire burned through my hand and straight up into my chest. I groaned at the odd heat, overwhelming every other sense, for a strangled breath.

"Run!" a gravelly voice yelled in my head as the dog growled again.

I blinked. Had I heard the puppy talking? I looked him over, noting the strange purple on one paw and triangular ear before I sucked in a breath. Cuts littered his small body. He'd just killed a hunter, yet he barely came up to my knees.

I must be hallucinating.

I wished I was. The sight of my mother, crumpled in the chair, had a keening denial rising in my throat. I staggered across to her, choking on a sob as I brushed her bright hair back from her bruised face, ignoring the steady dripping from the side of her skull. With a whimper, I gently closed her eyes. My hands shook as I eased the silver ring from her still-warm finger, the only part of my parents I could take with me. The flower design dug into my palm as I gripped it tight.

With a stuttering breath, I pressed my closed fist to my pounding skull. Ignoring all the other cuts and aches across my body, I reached for the man's dropped gun.

I had to get out of here.

Soft fur brushed against my hand. I stared down at the puppy, bright-purple flames burning in its eyes.

The innocent girl I'd been died that day. I left her down there with the remains of her family as I ran towards the door, a vicious puppy at my heels.

Chapter 33

A whimper left my lips in the wake of dark memories, hitting me with agonising force.

"Zoella? Are you OK?" Rex's velvety tone welcomed me back into the present.

I blinked hard, still gazing into those flaming lilac eyes.

Was this the puppy who had helped me escape all those years ago? I'd suppressed the memories of that day so hard I could barely remember what happened. I knew I'd escaped by shooting several hunters, but I'd thought they'd shot the puppy dead as we were fleeing their bunker.

I'd also had no idea he was an actual *hellhound*.

"They've had you this whole time?" Guilt strangled me with the weight of over a decade of his suffering.

"Yes." A low, gravelly tone bounced around inside my skull as the hellhound gave a short bark.

The shock of hearing his voice in my head gave way to guilt. His admission hit me like a blow. What had they done to him over those long years of captivity?

My hand shook as I raised it to the hound's face, almost level with mine. I held still, letting him stretch forwards to sniff me. Pale scars slashed across his black nose, disappearing into the short fur of his muzzle.

He canted his head, and I took the invitation to stroke along his neck. His dark fur was smooth and so incredibly soft for such a terrifying creature.

"I'm sorry..." My throat closed off, halting my apology at that pathetic attempt.

"What am I missing?" Rex's voice was laced with concern, one of his warm palms rubbing along my spine in a comforting stroke.

The hound looked over my shoulder and barked. My mind supplied the translation. "Bonded."

I sucked in a gasp as everything suddenly made sense. "Holy goddesses... He's my *familiar*."

Rex stilled at my back. He stepped up beside me so he could look from the hound to me before he snagged my gaze. He raised a dark brow. "You're a witch bonded to a hellhound? Is that even possible?"

I shrugged, feeling self-conscious. What did it say about me that my chosen familiar was a vicious hound from hell?

"Apparently so." I swiped my tongue across my lower lip. "I guess the fire and claws make a bit more sense now."

The hound yipped, bouncing his huge front paws. The second they hit the concrete, lilac flames swallowed them, imitating my fire exactly. Black lowlights even glinted through the rich purple hues.

I arched a brow at the almost playful beast. "Show-off."

He gave a doggy impression of a grin, his wicked fangs giving him a menacing edge.

Rex chuckled, his familiar smoky rattle oddly comforting. "I guess he'll be coming with us, then? We'd better get you out of here. You need to rest before we go on another hunter killing spree."

"We weren't meant to be on this one." I arched a brow at Rex, who didn't even have the good grace to look bashful. I blew out a breath, giving the hound another stroke. Despite the throbbing wound in my shoulder and vicious headache, I couldn't find it in me to regret his hasty change of plan. What would have happened to all those hellhounds and demons if Rex hadn't run horns first into danger?

I shook my head. "Come on, let's get somewhere safe."

The hound yipped again in agreement, and Rex led us towards the edge of the shipyard.

"So what's his name?" Rex asked.

I eyed the hound as he trotted casually alongside us. He swung his massive head towards Rex, giving a small woof, sounding almost smug if that was possible. "Alpha."

I snorted, sensing his near-cocky joy at the declaration as I translated for Rex.

The demon's pouty lips twitched up at the corners in his usual infuriating smirk, and I knew he was about to bait the hound. "Ironic. I like it."

Alpha bared his fangs as he prowled beside us, but I could tell he wasn't actually about to attack. I hoped.

"So I guess he isn't your cousin after all?" I asked, flashing Rex a cheeky smirk to defuse any tension. "Or is he your leader now, *Your Majesty*?"

Alpha chuffed, shaking his head as he stuck close to my side.

"I believe we have a vacancy for royal slipper fetcher." Rex bared his fangs in the same feral grin as Alpha.

I was starting to see the familial resemblance.

The sun had already risen by the time we'd made the twenty-minute trudge back to the chain hotel. The king-size bed called to me like a siren, promising me comfort and safety. I knew from experience how plush the mattress was, how soft those cloud-like pillows were, how snuggly and warm the snow-white duvet was.

A smoky chuckle wrapped around me. "I wish you'd look at me with that much longing," Rex said, stepping up beside me as I fantasised about all the things I wanted to do with that bed.

Even better if Rex was in it with me.

I slapped down the saucy thoughts before Rex could read them on my face, or in my pheromones somehow, using his crazy demon senses.

"Maybe if you gave me more than dead bodies, I would." I snorted, trying to cover my embarrassment.

Rex flashed me a smirk, as if he could see past my distraction. "You specifically called me up from hell to give you dead bodies." He flexed a bicep dramatically, straining blood-spattered grey skin over striated muscle. "I know you damsels in distress love a show of violent prowess."

I rolled my eyes with a huff of laughter, flipping him my middle finger.

"There she is," Rex purred, low and sinful, "my fierce witch."

I shot him a glare, but it lacked the heat of any real anger. Other heat, however...

Alpha bumped against my arm, his smooth fur rubbing against my skin as he barked. "You don't need that runt. I will protect you. Always."

My heart swelled with unexpected emotion as I met his fiery purple gaze. "Thank you." I scratched the back of his purple ear, grateful my short claws were back to regular human nails.

I'd never had anyone other than myself to protect me. It was strange but nice knowing there were two others looking out for me. One might be doing it partially because of a magical contract, but it was still nice.

"What did he say?" Rex asked, an edge of admiration widening his red eyes.

I smirked, knowing Rex was going to scowl at Alpha for this. "He called you a runt."

As predicted, Rex's handsome features twisted as he glared at the hellhound. "I'm still bigger than you, pup."

Alpha chuffed, his smooth tail wagging behind him as he jerked his muzzle towards Rex's face. "Tiny fangs though."

I giggled, enjoying their back and forth. Rex swung his fiery gaze my way, raising a brow in question.

I cleared my throat, trying to hide my smile. "He said you have tiny fangs."

A growl rumbled from Rex's wide chest, spilling through the corporate-style room.

Alpha stepped his purple paw forwards, returning the menacing growl, but even I could tell neither of them meant it.

Rex arched a brow at the hound, unfazed by the intimidating sight. His gaze pinned my familiar, but his words were directed at me. "Can we send your puppy out on guard duty or something?" Rex pointed a bloodstained claw at me. "You need to rest, little mouse."

I eyed the bed once more, feeling my chest wound throb harder as if to remind me it was still there. It already felt more tolerable, but in truth, it had barely started to heal. Mages healed quicker than your average human, but it was still nowhere near as fast as a demon.

Another scar for me to add to the collection, I supposed.

I swallowed down the guilt that hit me as I eyed the small pink lines on Alpha's nose and the faint gaps in his coat where scar tissue partially hid beneath his fur. I wasn't the only one with evidence of the hunter's cruelty etched into my skin.

Determination burned through me as I let myself think through all the hunters had done. To my family. To Alpha. To other mages, demons, hellhounds. To me.

I still wanted to destroy the tracker stone holding my signature, giving me time to return to Quartz Coven so I could stop selfishly putting Rex in danger, but something more drove me to destroy the hunters of Riverside.

Seeing so many beings caged and abused sickened me. There were more innocents trapped at the hunters' base. I had to get them out.

I'd been lucky enough to escape all those years ago, which I now realised was only because I, by some miracle, had managed to bond with Alpha at such a young age. But while I'd broken free, others had been left behind to suffer.

I'd selfishly tried to forget the whole ordeal, like it had never existed, when I should have been trying to convince the coven to go find the place and shut it down. Maybe if the entire coven had stood together, we could have ended Riverside's hunter infestation.

Hell, we could have summoned an army of demons to fight with us.

I bit my lip, already knowing it was useless to think that way. The coven would never have stuck their necks out for demons and hellhounds. Elder Murray hadn't even tried to rescue my family when we'd been caught.

My heart hurt with the weight of all that injustice and, underlying it all, the guilt I knew would never leave me.

"You're right." I drew in a deep breath. "I need to heal before we try to find those bastards again."

Alpha tilted his head aside in question, black ear flopping forwards slightly before popping back upright. He gave a quick series of barks. "You're going after them?"

I nodded, regarding him carefully as my mind whirred. "Do you know where they held you?"

Alpha shook his head, taking a step back with a growl. "Don't want to go there." His voice in my head held the pained edge of fear. He barked, sharp and harsh. "They can't have you."

My heart ached for him, for the frantic fear widening his huge eyes. "Alpha," I breathed, reaching out to stroke along the tense line of his neck. "It's OK. We're not going in unprepared. We're going to scope it out first, then we'll bring backup and a real plan. I promise they won't take either of us again, OK?"

"What do you mean, '*again*'?" Rex's tone was deceptively soft, silky with the threat of violence.

Tension stilted my movement, making my slow strokes along Alpha's neck turn jerky. It hadn't occurred to me to tell Rex about my horrific few days in the hunters' clutches as a young teen.

I couldn't look at him, drowning in the raw agony of revisiting the memories now so fresh once more. "They captured me and my family, over ten years ago." I choked out the words, trying to get it over with. Rip the Band-Aid off.

I felt more than saw him still in my periphery. My hand ran harder through the soft fur along Alpha's neck, probably comforting me more than him at this point.

"Then I've been killing them too quick." Rex's dark tone was roughened yet steady. "...Your family?"

I shook my head, fighting back the moisture blurring the ferocious sight of my canine familiar, of his blocky head and sleek muzzle. His intelligent, flaming eyes.

Rex exhaled heavily. "I'm sorry. I know what it's like to lose loved ones. Violently."

I twisted to face Rex, scrounging up the courage to meet his piercing gaze, but no words came to my lips. Tension bracketed his mouth, the weight of so much responsibility seeming to press on him. He'd never looked more like a king.

I gave him a small, useless nod, my heart breaking for all three of us.

Alpha gave a low whine. "Don't go back there."

I swallowed, feeling the weight of the last few months—the last years, even—settle heavily across my shoulders. "I have to. Will you help us?"

Alpha looked away before meeting my gaze once more with a faint growl and jerk of his tapered muzzle. "For you."

I breathed a sigh of relief despite the guilt plaguing me at the thought of making him go back to where he'd been tormented for so long. "Thank you." I twisted my fingers in his thick fur, taking comfort in the warm strength he radiated, offering what I could in return.

How had I survived this long without the strange bond between us? The warm connection flowed from my chest to Alpha's. I could have sworn the thick bond was almost visible, like a beam of light ghosting through the air. It felt like I'd been living with one arm tied behind my back, and I was finally whole in a way I hadn't realised existed.

"Alpha can lead us to the hunter compound," I said, glancing at Rex to gauge his reaction.

He looked straight at the hound, dipping his chin in thanks. "I will keep both of you safe."

Alpha yipped, biting at the air in Rex's direction. "All right, enough sappy stuff. I wasn't let outside often, so I'm keen to explore. I'll check for threats so Tiny Fangs here doesn't get scared." He chuffed in a doggy chuckle, jerking his muzzle towards Rex before staring at me intently, blinking once with a small woof of sound. "Zoella—heal. Rest."

"I will," I said, deciding not to translate that one for Rex as I gave my familiar one last stroke before stepping back.

He turned with a swish of his tail, catching the door's lever with his paw as he pulled it open and wandered out with surprising ease. Especially for an oversize wolf who'd lived most of his life as a captive.

I *really* hoped the neighbours just thought he was a massive Doberman with spray paint on.

Chapter 34

I stepped out of the bathroom, luxuriating in the feeling of being clean. I'd had to wash blood off so often since I'd summoned Rex that I was starting to become used to the constant swirl of pink down the drain. My shoulder still throbbed, and numerous cuts and bruises littered my body, only half-covered by my tattoos. I'd had to avoid getting the gun-shot wound wet in the shower, because the burns still stung despite it beginning to heal.

At least my magic-induced headache had lessened with every relaxing minute under the spray. Even if my brain wouldn't stop whirling with all the thoughts bouncing around it—could I really take on the hunters and win? If I managed to destroy the tracker stone holding my signature, would Quartz ever take me back? Could I prove Fenton's crimes? What would happen between Rex and me? How much longer could I ignore the inconvenient feelings he churned up?

All I had were questions without answers, swirling around my mind on a loop.

This time, I'd insisted Rex shower first. Some wild part of me had been tempted to join him. I mean, after he'd protected me at the shipyard, our deal meant I owed him pleasure, right? But before I could work up the courage to slip into the bathroom, he was already sauntering out with a towel slung low around his hips and a charming smile lighting his feral features.

Worried he could read the lusty indecision on my expression, I'd hurried past him into the bathroom. In my flustered haste, I'd forgotten a change of clothes. Now we were both in nothing but towels, and my inner hussy was just a little too giddy about it.

Rex lazed on the bed, one hand propped under his head, that tiny towel barely covering his hips and the beast I knew lurked beneath. The fiery tips of his hair brushed the white bedding, like he was dripping ribbons of flame. The demon was large enough to dwarf even the king-sized bed, his feet hanging over the edge almost comically.

His body was a masterpiece of defined muscle beneath silky slate skin. My gaze lingered over the dips and valleys across his chest and eight-pack abs. I had the wildest urge to trace them with my tongue.

"See something you like?" Rex's low tone rumbled through my fantasies.

I stilled part-way to the bed he'd sprawled out on like a horizontal throne. How could I have missed that royal arrogance to start with?

Heat stole across my cheeks, but I studiously ignored the sensation, willing the blush away. "Yeah. That bed looks super comfy."

He smirked, all masculine confidence, hungry eyes devouring me right back. "What are they?" he asked, nodding his horns towards one of my arms.

I followed his gaze to my skin wrapped in black ink. "They're thorned or poisonous plants," I murmured, lost in the memories they represented.

"Fitting," he murmured, eyes burning into me with a loaded intensity. "Beautiful yet deadly."

His compliment warmed me from the inside even as my throat thickened with emotion. Lyndsey had always thought they were a little too morbid. She'd always said I should have gone for something prettier, like lilacs to match my hair.

I cleared my throat, looking away.

"Why do you always cover them up?" His voice deepened, a velvety, soft rumble.

"I guess it's just a habit." I shrugged, suddenly feeling self-conscious. "Not a lot of witches get tattoos in my coven. It's kinda frowned upon, like the only mark on your flesh should be your coven anchor." I gestured to the silvery crystals scarring the middle of my chest.

He raised a brow. "Well, that's dumb."

A laugh spilled from my lips, helping to lift the intensity settling into the room with us.

His magma eyes glowed as he watched me. "Come here, little mouse."

I froze, sensing the trap he was laying. My eyes narrowed as I wondered what his game was.

Rex chuckled, his broad chest shaking the bed. Small wisps of grey floated from between his lips. "Don't look so suspicious. I only eat bad guys. Or naughty witches." He winked.

I'd never been more aware of how naked I was beneath a towel.

I tried to scowl, but my lips twitched with the hints of a smile instead. "Or poor defenceless bunnies."

He grinned. "If I remember rightly, you ate one too."

I grimaced at the memory of me cooking flesh with my fire magic and tearing off chunks with my hellhound-inspired claws. "You've turned me positively savage."

He pressed a clawed hand to his heart. "Such a shame," he drawled, tone dripping false devastation.

My lips twitched harder as I fought back that damn smile. Even amid the dumpster fire that was my life, Rex somehow had an uncanny ability to bring out a lighter side of me. That and my dark, violent one. Probably in equal measure.

Rex pushed up to sitting, beckoning me with a single claw. "Come on, little mouse, don't be shy. Let me pleasure you. Let me give you my seed." He eyed the damaged spot just below my collarbone, a heavy look of guilt weighing on his features. "It's the only way I can help you heal."

The closed bullet wound throbbed in remembered agony. It still felt tender and raw, twinging every time I moved my arm. I bit my lower lip, a confusing muddle of emotions causing me to hesitate. Was he only offering out of some twisted sense of duty? Was this another form of protection? Or did he really care about me?

His glowing gaze held mine steadily, as if he could feel me wavering. "We have a deal, remember?" Rex murmured, waiting patiently on the bed for his prey to realise it was already caught. A little too willingly.

We had more than one agreement in place. The reminder helped me push back some of the crazy that tried to seep in. Rex and I had a complicated situation already without adding feelings or rogue ab licking to the mix.

"Do you need blood?" I asked, taking a cautious step closer to the bed looming in the middle of the room.

Rex licked his lips, growling suggestively. "Only once you're healed. What kind of potential *ma*—" He coughed. "—protector would I be if I took from you now?"

"Hmm..." My eyes narrowed suspiciously at whatever he'd been about to say. I tapped my chin as if in thought. "The demonic kind?"

In a grey blur, Rex leaped from the bed, landing an inch in front of me with nimble ease. He hooked a claw under my chin, tilting my face up to his.

Deep red eyes swirled with desire. But also something more, something so unfamiliar it took me a long moment to decipher the look.

Caring.

Genuine, caring affection.

I swallowed thickly, feeling my own emotions scramble more the longer he held my gaze. I didn't know what to think, to *feel*, any more. How was he able to tie me in so many knots and yet cut through all the noise until it felt like there was just him and me?

"Rex." His name left my lips in a plea.

He bent down, swallowing the height difference to press a chaste kiss to my lips before pulling back just enough to catch my eye. Fierce hunger contrasted the stiff control he used to hold himself in check, body taut like a bowstring.

I swayed into the scant space between us, his desire calling to my own. The bittersweet scents of smoke and ginger wrapped around me, luring me in.

His eyes blackened, fiery red bleeding to a starless night. "Little mouse... I could have lost you tonight. My fire in a world of darkness. I *need* you," Rex whispered against my lips, his words a feather-light caress. "I have ever since you squeaked in fear with one breath, then bared your fangs in a defiant rage the next. My beautiful, fierce witch."

The way he spoke about me, like losing me was some unthinkable horror. When everybody else had been so eager to throw me away, the idea of being precious to someone like Rex was intoxicating. He was a force of nature, powerful and confident and so goddesses-damned stubborn it drove me crazy, but if he didn't want to be here, saying these things, nothing in this world or his could make him.

I held perfectly still. Mentally, I leaned over the edge of a cliff, staring down into the rocky abyss ready to swallow me whole.

As if I'd summoned the devil himself, a slow smile spread across Rex's lips. Wicked. Seductive.

Victorious.

In my mind, I flung my arms wide and tipped forwards. The lurking darkness surged up to meet me. Covering me. Filling me. Possessing me.

Until I couldn't breathe through the assault, yet somehow it felt like I'd never breathed until this moment.

A low growl lifted the hairs on my nape.

I dug my nails into the hard flesh of his upper back, unaware I'd even wrapped my arms around him. Wetness graced my fingertips. "Take me to hell."

Rex licked his vicious fangs. "I thought you'd never ask."

His mouth descended, but instead of soft lips, this time, I was met with sharp teeth. His fangs punched into my lower lip. I hissed at the sting, but his tongue laved across the blooming wound. He groaned, lapping at the fresh blood of my throbbing lip.

His dark need pulsed around me, an almost tangible aura of smoke and sin. He sucked my lip into his mouth before claiming my lips in a feral kiss that devoured all thought from my brain.

The room spun in a dizzying swirl. My back hit the bed, its soft covers a stark contrast to the solid heat of my demon as he pinned me without breaking the kiss, the orange tips of his fiery hair brushing my cheek.

He swallowed my gasp as he settled between my thighs. Even through the towel covering me, I could feel just how hard and ready he was. He pressed his firm length against my aching core, still tender from his rough attentions back in the alley.

But I didn't care.

I was drowning, and he was oxygen. Precious and sweet and vital.

My sharp nails dug into his back even harder. I relished the feel of heated skin beneath my hands.

He ground his hips against me, giving me a tease of that friction I craved. I groaned into his mouth, his wicked forked tongue toying with mine as he dominated the kiss.

"So fucking beautiful," he murmured against my lips, breaking the kiss. "And all mine."

I sucked in a ragged lungful, feeling dizzy with my need for breath just as much as my need for him.

"Please, Rex," I begged, angling my hips to cradle his thick shaft as best I could between my thighs.

"Anything for you, little mouse." He pulled back, nipping my lip. "But I need you to tell me now if you don't want this. If you don't want *me*. If you're not ready." He eyed my exposed shoulder, and I followed his gaze to the pink flesh. The small mess of burns was only about two inches wide, but it looked like someone had held a flame to wax. "I don't think I can control myself. The *urges*. Not this time." His voice had dropped to a low octave, closer to growling than speech.

Didn't he understand?

"I don't want control." I licked my lips, back arching in need on the bed. "I want every demonic inch of you, Rex. Wild. Untamed. Fierce."

Like a rabid dog snapping his leash, Rex snarled, fangs gnashing inches from my face as he shredded the pillows above my head with his claws. Desire and fear swallowed me in a rush. The feral sound echoed in my ears.

His black eyes swirled with a silvery sheen.

I curled my claws into his back, lunging up to nip his exposed throat with my sharper teeth, narrowly avoiding hitting his spiralling horn. I tasted blood, metallic yet smoky, sweet and all *him*.

With a moan, I gave myself over to the feral hunger lurking inside me too.

Chapter 35

Rex growled as I lapped at the bloody wound I'd made. My body lit up with desire, need taking me hostage.

He arched back, hands banding around my biceps and stealing my bloody prize but giving me an uninterrupted view of his muscular chest and eight-pack abs. Of the power his body held.

My gaze dipped, lodging on his hard grey length. As big as my forearm and ridged with those wicked, flexible thorns, it pointed up at me as it rested between my thighs. Only the fluffy white towel around me separated us. Rex had lost his somewhere along the way, and I couldn't find an ounce of remorse over it.

Lavender liquid seeped from his flared tip, making a mess of the material covering my stomach. I groaned at the erotic sight, wanting to feel all his hot seed dripping onto my bare skin instead.

Rex snarled, yanking on my attention.

His face was a thing of feral beauty. A shiver of fear ran down my spine. He looked unhinged. His black eyes devoured me with a predatory hunger. It was still Rex, but right now, he looked as demonic as I'd expected when I'd first summoned him.

He bared his lethal fangs as his tail arced around him. The arrow darted towards me, wriggling under the edge of the towel, somehow valiantly holding on to my body. It shoved the material apart, unwrapping me like a gift. My golden skin and dark floral tattoos contrasted with the smooth grey perfection of Rex's body, but it looked so right having his inhuman tone against me.

His hot length finally pressed against my needy core. Thick. Heavy. So much pressure against my lower lips. So much heat. My wetness slicked his soft thorns, prickling me in the best way.

I *needed* to feel those intriguing, almost tentacle-like bristles stroke across my lower lips. I tried to roll my pelvis up, but the demon snarled, pressing his cock harder against me, pinning me in place with his formidable size and weight.

His seed continued to drip, this time splashing onto my stomach in hot, sinful drops, tingling lightly against my skin.

My chest heaved as I struggled to catch my breath. Anticipation was a living beast inside me, as feral as my dark demon.

"Mine," he growled.

His tail reared back, the bony talon sliding free. It glinted ominously.

Then it struck.

I screamed as the tip sank into the top of my left breast, then right. The sting was immediate, twin wounds throbbing in time with my pounding heart. Heat quickly replaced the faint bite of pain, so warm it was like I'd dunked my chest into a bath, the sensation like his fanged bite but on steroids.

"Rex." I groaned, my core pulsing as the heat in my breasts began to tingle, to ache in the best kind of way. "What the fuck?"

His lips peeled back, more a baring of fangs than a smile. "Mine," he said again, this time with more force. Like a demand.

I nodded slowly. Despite the lick of fear at his untamed wildness, I trusted him not to hurt me.

The stinger slid away, and his tail curved downwards, swiping through the warm liquid at my stomach. His tail glistening pale mauve, he caressed my breast with the silky arrow.

My back arched as the warm venom reacted in a tingling rush, like he was dousing me in champagne, tiny bubbles tickling my flesh. The arrow drew back and landed with a faint slap against my nipple. I screamed, seeing stars as a line of heated sensation arced from my breast down to my clit.

Rex chuckled, little wisps of smoke escaping his plush lips.

He repeated the gesture on the other side, earning another pleasured groan rumbling my throat.

"Rex," I panted, dizzy with pleasure as every breath quaked the sensual poison in my breasts. "Please. I need you. All of you."

He drew his cock through my folds in a slick glide. I felt every soft thorn brush against me in a teasing stroke.

"Yes, little mouse. You're mine to pleasure. Mine to take. To own." His eyes flared with enough heat to rival the poison flushing my chest. "Your sweet cunt is already weeping for my cock, for my seed."

His words, combined with the achingly slow glide between my thighs and the tingling in my breasts as his tail teased me, had me thrashing on the bed, half out of my mind with need. His hands stayed locked around my arms, pinning me with ease.

He pulled back, and I whined at the loss of his thickness against my core. On his knees between my spread thighs, he was a monstrous sight. Every line of his slate-grey body hard and unyielding. His thick cock was big enough that I'd be convinced it wouldn't fit, except he'd already proved just how good he could feel stretching me to my limits.

His hand released me in favour of gripping his length. He squeezed it in his huge fist, from base to tip. Pale-lavender liquid flowed from the pointed head, splashing against my pussy. Every hot drop hit me with a bolt of heightened pleasure. I couldn't help but moan as I watched him touch himself. His dark eyes ran across my body and face in a ravenous sweep. He growled, pumping himself faster.

"Rex," I whined. "More. *Please*."

My pleas landed on deaf ears as he continued to stroke himself. His tail moved from my tingling nipples down the valley of my breasts, stroking over my slicked stomach to tease across my inner thighs.

I snarled, need driving me crazy as he teased me, denying me what I craved almost more than my next breath.

He bared his fangs right back. His tail lifted and came down between us with a firm slap against my clit. Pleasure slammed through me like a lightning bolt, bringing my upper chest off the bed as my body bowed.

He repeated the move, the wet slap against my pussy a lewd sound puncturing his low growl. I thrashed at the harsh pleasure, a keening sound slipping from my lips.

He stroked himself faster, a ferocious pace that I craved. His tail disappeared from view, running along my lower lips. I felt him nudge at my entrance.

My legs opened wider of their own accord, begging him to enter me.

The warm arrow slid inside me, thick and flexible. He wriggled it in deeper, quivering inside me like a vibrator.

Rex gnashed his fangs, continuing to stroke himself as he pleasured me at the same time.

He released my arm, huge hand encircling the hawthorn tattoo hugging my thigh as he forced me to open wider for him. I groaned as claws pricked my skin, the edge of danger sending me racing towards my peak as he tail-fucked me with ruthless determination.

"My sweet little mouse..." His words were low and guttural, barely audible above his snarling growl. "I'm going to drown your needy pussy in my seed. Scream for me."

His cock jerked in his hold, thick ropes of lavender splashing against my entrance. So hot it was almost too much. Jets of cum lashed my pussy. He roared, quaking the bed with the force of his release. His tail thrust in and out of me, vibrating at the same time.

Cum spurted against my clit, the pressure and heat shoving me over the edge.

I screamed for him, pleasure exploding through me as I came apart.

More liquid lavished my needy bud, an almost never-ending stream that forced my orgasm even higher, waves of bliss arcing through me.

I writhed at the overwhelming pleasure. More hot liquid hit my breasts, the tingling surging, drawing another groan from my lips.

The jets hit my lips, my chin, my neck, my stomach, my thighs. Everywhere. In a faint imitation of his venom, it tingled in a light fizz against my skin.

"Rex," I groaned, body twitching with the aftershocks of the intense orgasm, causing liquid to slide between my lips. Blueberries coated my tongue. I hummed at the sweet taste of the sinful demon, unable to resist licking my lips to swipe up another heady drop.

I peeled my eyes open, relishing the sight of him leaning over me, eclipsing the world with his powerful bulk.

His eyes were pitch black as he squeezed my breast in his hand, rubbing his release into my skin. I was wet all over, a hot layer of slick covering me like the softest silk.

He snarled, eyes running across my naked body in blatant need. I shuddered, reduced to a boneless puddle of tingling bliss.

"I'm not nearly done with you yet, little mouse." He bared his fangs in a wicked grin.

Chapter 36

My head swam as I tried to process his words with the drugging sweetness of his earthy blueberry taste tingling on my tongue.

Between us, his grey cock hung heavy, the short thorns along the top and underside swaying and dancing, like they were celebrating his announcement.

"You look so fucking good. Covered in my seed like the greedy witch you are. This little pussy open and ready for me." He popped his tail free, leaving me empty and wanting even as bliss sang through my veins.

Tauntingly slow, he brought the wet arrow up to his lips. His forked tongue slid out, laving across the flat side as he tasted me off his skin. The erotic sight had heat sparking through me all over again, despite the tremors still shaking my body underneath him.

"My tail feels good in other places too," he growled.

As if to demonstrate, he stroked his arrow through my folds. I arched at the caress against my sensitised flesh, trying to wriggle away from his questing tail.

He grinned, hand squeezing my breast, sending a burn of heat and pleasure through my chest as he held me down. I felt something tickle against my back entrance. I jolted, eyes widening.

Nobody had ever touched me there before.

Rex watched my face as he stroked harder against me, the wet tip of his arrow pushing lightly at the tight ring. I forced myself to relax as he pressed further. The stretch was strange. Not bad, just different.

I felt the tip curve, like he was folding the arrow in on itself, making it narrower but just as long.

Anticipation cut through the hazy post-orgasm bliss. I bit my lip, holding perfectly still.

The wet head pushed firmer, edging into me slowly.

"Rex." His name was a plea on my lips, but I didn't know what I was begging him for.

His thumb found my clit, lightly teasing the sensitive bundle of nerves. Twin pools of black, framed by inky lashes, held me captive.

I gasped as his tail head slipped in fully, past the virgin ring of muscle. The burning stretch held a pleasurable warmth, a new sensation that changed the angle of bliss.

"Such a good girl," he cooed, stroking his hand across my clit in a wet glide that had me clenching against the thickness of his tail inside me. "My beautiful, fierce little mouse." His other palm stroked down my side, spreading his thick cum across my skin as he petted me. "All mine to protect, to cherish, to claim."

I groaned as his claws scraped my breast, still heated from the inside with whatever venom he'd given me.

I felt his cock nudge at my entrance. I gasped as he pushed the pointed head inside me.

The burn rivalled that of his poison as I struggled to adjust to his immense size. I whined, the stretch almost too much for my tender flesh even with the flood of endorphins running through my veins.

"Shh, little mouse. This pussy was made for my cock. You will take it, and you'll fucking love it." His low growl rolled through me, his possessive hunger as fierce as my own. "I've waited my whole life for you."

Something about his intensity struck me, seeming to weigh the moment.

Dark eyes held mine, boring down to my soul and laying claim. "I choose you, Zoella. Now and always."

His sweet words warmed my chest until I felt like I'd burst, but I could hardly focus on the sensation as he pushed in another inch, making me writhe.

"Do you want this?" he asked, a vulnerability creeping through the feral visage. "Do you accept me?"

I bit my lip, trying to think through the delicious sensations assaulting my body. I was high on pleasure, and I only had him to blame. How could I not crave more of this? Of him? My sweet monster.

"Yes," I breathed, feeling an embarrassing burn start up behind my eyes as I rapidly tried to blink back the moisture before it could gather. "Rex, I want you. I want everything you have to give and more."

He swooped down, lips crashing against mine in a feral kiss. My head swam as his forked tongue tangled with mine, dizzying and drugging as he took my mouth. His wicked thorns tickled my flesh, stroking through my folds and seeking out my aching clit. They stroked and teased, heightening every sensation as the burn gave way to bliss.

Our kiss ended as he nipped lightly at my lower lip, making my head spin even more.

"Ah, sweet little mouse." He grinned, as wide as I'd ever seen, dark eyes alight. "My perfect mate. You're ready."

It was all the warning I got.

He thrust in, filling me to the brim. His pointed tip nudged my cervix, the monster bottoming out inside me. I groaned, stuffed full.

I'd never felt so complete. So overwhelmingly, blissfully full.

Pleasure transformed his feral features into a look of unadulterated joy. An endless hunger waited in the abyss as he captured me with his demonic eyes.

"Rex, please," I whined, panting hard as pleasure scrabbled my brain.

He snapped with a roar.

He drew out and slammed back in. The power of his thrust lifted me off the bed, the move jostling his tail, still curiously plugged inside me.

I screamed at the lash of pleasure, the fierce bliss. He set a punishing pace, feral and unhinged. My dark demon gripped my throat, squeezing lightly as he held me still for his pleasure. He rutted into me like a rabid animal.

The force of his passion had my head lolling, only held steady by his grip on my neck. He pounded into me, snarling and growling. My breasts bounced with every rough thrust, triggering wave after wave of those poisoned tingles.

His tail began to jiggle, vibrating inside me as he continued to fuck me. His thorns found my clit and lavished me with their delicious attention.

"Rex, Rex, Rex." His name fell from my lips in an almost unintelligible chant.

"Mine!" he roared, slamming me full. "Come. Now."

I detonated for him.

I screamed and writhed, my pussy clenching around the hard invasion as waves of pleasure smashed me against the rocks, breaking me apart.

Blackness edged my vision as I came undone, lost to the intense bliss.

The fullness inside me swelled. His hard length kicked deep. I could feel every hot lash of cum. The pressure was too much. I whined and mewled, claws scrabbling against the hand at my throat, drawing blood.

"Too much," I groaned as his cum gushed out of me with rhythmic squelches as he rocked back and forth inside me with every fierce clamp from my spasming core.

Lips pressed to mine, swallowing my pleas as Rex held himself still inside me. He devoured my mouth, only adding to the dizzying sensations making the world blur with pleasure.

"It's OK, little mouse. Let my seed fill you up and overflow. If you thought this was a lot, wait until our first mating frenzy." He chuckled, smoky exhales tickling my swollen lips. "This is just a warm-up. You'll be drowning in cum and ecstasy for days on end."

Chapter 37

His words penetrated my pleasured haze, and I frowned as my brain tried to catch up.

Rex chuckled, smoky and rich. The decadent sound wrapped around me, trying to lull me into a comforted bliss.

"My cute little mouse, don't look so concerned. I'm not going to breed you just yet. It's too soon; even I know that. Though, I can't say your sweet cunt isn't tempting me to." He shook his head with a sly tilt to his shadowed lips, the red-orange ombre of his hair swaying around both sets of onyx horns. "The panic on your face, my beautiful mate."

"*Mate*?" I squeaked, the shrill bleat piercing the intimate cocoon he'd forged.

The memory of his honeyed whispers during sex came back to me. He'd been talking about *claiming me as his mate*, and I'd been too immersed in the moment's passion to really absorb his words. Or maybe a small part of me had known, and I'd let emotion overrule logic. I shoved aside the troubling thought.

He thrust his hips, sinking his cock deeper through the silky liquid he'd filled me with, tingling against my inner walls. A low groan rumbled his barrel chest, and I cried out at the spike of pleasure through my overstimulated pussy. He'd softened only slightly inside me, still almost double the size of any man I'd ever been with.

Rex grinned down at me, pure adoration softening his inhuman features. Nobody had ever looked at me that way before. His angular eyes bled back from their dark abyss to the red glow, slit pupils dilated into wide ellipses.

"Yes, *mate*," he agreed. "I was planning to ask you in a more human way, but...the urges." His smile turned almost sheepish—if any part of this demon could ever be compared to prey like that. "I claimed you the demon way, at the height of passion." Warmth suffused his expression, tipping his lips up as his gaze brightened further.

A ringing sounded in my ears. All I could do was stare up at the demon who'd sent me tumbling like he'd pulled the rug out from under me.

Shock must have stamped across my face.

Rex cleared his throat, giving me a softer smile. "I'll admit, I wasn't expecting to develop such a strong connection so fast either, not when you first summoned me and squeaked like a startled little mouse. But now I know; you're as fierce as the sun and as beautiful as the moon. You make me laugh like a lunatic and challenge me endlessly. There is nobody else like you, in this realm or the next. Any male would be lucky to have you, and I'm the luckiest fool of them all." He stroked a claw along my cheek, eyes blazing with sincerity. "I *choose* you, Zoella."

He looked happier than I'd ever seen him. Sweet. Gentle. Caring.

Lowering onto his side, he eased out of me, unleashing a torrent of sticky heat as his seed gushed over my thighs, soaking the bed beneath me. I gasped at the overwhelming sensation, but the churn of emotions kept me focused on the conversation rather than the idea of clean-up or going another round.

His horns hit the pillow beside me, strong arm pulling me onto my side with him so he could keep the most intense eye contact. His tail stroked up and down my leg in a soothing caress.

"I know we've not talked a lot about the future." A hint of something vulnerable entered his bright eyes. His words lowered to a breathy whisper. "But...will you choose me too?"

A storm of emotions overwhelmed me, anxiety and uncertainty quickening my heart as I fought to keep my voice steady. "Rex... What are you asking?"

His tail stilled against my leg, red eyes burning like hot coals. "Zoella, I want you to be my mate." His words were slow, measured. "Once we finish our business with the hunters here, come home with me. You'll be safe in my kingdom, and we can be together. As a bonded couple. Say yes, little mouse."

The hope in his eyes was mirrored in my soul. I wanted to be with him, to be happy together in our own little world. But caution and panic stabbed through the swelling joy, an almost physical sensation knifing into my heart.

"Rex," I wheezed, a tightness banding my chest. "I can't just move to *hell*. Once we deal with the hunters, it's only a temporary fix for me. I have to rejoin my old coven if I want to survive."

One side of his lip curled in disgust, revealing a sharp fang. "To the people who threw you away? If you're so safe with them, how did the hunters take you and your family all those years ago?"

A frown struck me. "I... I don't know." For some odd reason, I'd never thought about how safe I truly was at Quartz.

Rex's eyes were hard, glinting like rubies. "You're safer in hell. With me."

Tears filled my eyes as I struggled to express myself. "I can't just bet my life on us," I said, voice shaking. "What if you change your mind? We've only known each other for a matter of *days*; what do I really know about you and your life in hell? And besides, you're a demon, and I'm a witch."

His expression darkened, but I couldn't stop the fears spilling from my lips.

"If I moved to hell, and we broke up, I'd be back to square one—running for my life with no one to protect me," I choked out. "It's not that I don't want to be with you—"

"Zoella." He cupped my face, cutting me off mid-ramble. His warm body crowded even closer on the bed until our chests were only a breath apart. "If, for whatever reason, you wanted to end things between us, I would never exile you and just throw you to the hellhounds. Surely you know me better than that?" he said, his voice low and urgent. "My feelings for you are real. Mating isn't a bond to be taken lightly, and I know it's fast, but you're worth the risk. What can I do to convince you to trust me? To take a chance on us too?"

I wanted to fall into his embrace and say yes. I wanted to kiss him until I couldn't breathe. To get lost in him until the real world fell away.

But I couldn't.

Life had taught me the hard way not to trust anyone to stick around. He might have the best intentions now, but what about next week? Next month? Next year?

It wasn't just my heart that was on the line.

"I can't, Rex." The tears spilled over, running down my face to seep into the pillow beneath. "I want to, but I can't."

His hand withdrew, a chill rushing over my cheek in its absence, as his expression blanked. "You mean you won't. You're choosing to go back to the people who've betrayed you over taking a chance on us. On me." The mask slipped for a brief second, features crumpling to reveal the anguish inside, before he smoothed his imperious façade.

My throat closed off at his visible pain. "We can still be together though."

He arched a brow. "You think your coven will let a demon waltz around their territory?"

"They might..." The protest died on my tongue.

Of course they wouldn't. They'd see him as a threat. As a vile monster, seconds from tearing them apart to feast on their blood and flesh. If I couldn't even convince them of *my* innocence, what chance did I have to convince them of his?

"I could summon you in the evenings..."

He scoffed, pushing up to sitting. The thick blanket pooled at his waist, revealing his bare chest heaving in anger. "At your beck and call like a pet? Meeting in secret so nobody finds out?" He shook his horns, a deep pain reflecting in his fiery eyes. "I've been the dirty secret for too many demonesses before. I promised myself I'd never let someone do that to me again, not even you, little mouse."

I followed him upright, clutching the soft duvet to my chest as more tears blurred my vision. Emotions snared and tangled like thorny briars in my middle. "So that's it? I either move to hell with you as lifelong mates or we just part ways?"

He shrugged, jaw clenching as he looked away, fixing his gaze out the window. "I want all of you, little mouse. Forever. And I won't settle for anything less than a real partnership." A deep exhale deflated his broad chest. "We're both worth more than that."

He slid from the bed, every movement stiff and deliberate as he picked up his trousers from the floor, smoothly pulling them on. His expression closed down. Flat and lifeless, he avoided looking at me.

How had we gone from the highest of pleasured highs to this?

Rex strode for the door without a word, yanking it open.

I clutched the duvet tight to my chest. "Rex, don't go." Desperation choked my voice. "I need you."

He stiffened further, if that was possible, like he was one sharp word away from shattering. The bunching of his shoulders only highlighted their powerful breadth. Even wounded like this, he brimmed with lethal promise. He always did.

He twisted to face me, gripping the door knob until it gave a metallic whine. "For protection and a little fun?" A self-deprecating smile hooked his lips, the slight movement so at odds with his violent hold on the brass. "I thought this time would be different."

I shook my head, opening my mouth to deny his words, but he ducked out without looking back, shutting the door behind him with a sharp crack.

The frame splintered with the force.

My heart cracked in my chest.

Silence descended.

My lip trembled. A sob climbed up my throat.

I finally let it out.

Chapter 38

"And then he just left," I whispered, reaching up to stroke my fingers through the soft fur along the hellhound's back.

Grass tickled my arm with each movement as I lay beside Alpha. My shoulder barely twinged with the motion. The bullet wound had almost fully healed. Rex hadn't been lying when he'd said the magic boost would help. I'd even had enough to put a decent glamour on Alpha without feeling the strain. So now, at least to the humans, he looked like an oversize Dobermann–Great Dane cross.

The ground's chill had long since seeped into my back, icing me through as I sprawled amongst the leafy blades. I sighed, staring up at the darkened clouds rolling across the dulled sky. It was probably about to rain, but I couldn't summon the energy to get up and find shelter.

Even now, several days later, my throat closed off with the emotion choking me. The mess with Rex had been playing on my mind since the situation had blown up in my face. After he'd stormed out, I'd not seen or heard from him once.

And a small part of me argued I was right not to jump into anything serious with him. He promised to protect me, to help me secure my freedom, yet here I was, moping around without the demon who'd claimed to care for me. Could I really trust him?

He'd left knowing I at least had Alpha at my side though. Maybe he thought we could handle one or two stray hunters if they cropped up. Especially given the Riverside chapter couldn't have that many brainwashed goons left. Rex had cut through their numbers pretty fast in the last week or so.

Another voice chimed in that he had feelings too, and maybe he was hurting as much as I was. Given his past, how so many of his kind had treated him, could I blame him for taking rejection badly? It stabbed right in the festering wound I knew he carried. How could he not? He'd been rejected by his own kind constantly. His own mother had abandoned him. His past partners had tried to hide him like a dirty secret. Then the person he wanted to mate with had tried to do the same and then turned him down when he'd refused?

My chest tightened as I thought about how I'd probably made him feel. Having been discarded like trash by my own people recently, I could relate.

But I didn't think I was wrong either. I couldn't just leave my world and traipse into his, a completely unknown realm to me, hoping Rex would never dump me. A broken heart would be bad enough, but my very survival was at stake here too. Could I bet my life on Rex actually wanting me enough to stay?

Once I destroyed the tracker stone, I had a small window of time to get myself back into Quartz. If I went to hell with Rex and he eventually cast me aside, I'd either have to live in his kingdom as his barely tolerated, rejected ex-lover, if he even let me, or return here. I'd have to constantly fight for my life while *still* trying to convince Quartz to take me back. Especially with the stupid anchor mark on my chest that prevented me from joining any other coven.

And now I had Alpha to think about too. We were bonded, and I knew he'd never leave my side, like my mother and her grumpy cat familiar. I couldn't put him at risk of being recaptured. He'd suffered enough. We both had.

My feelings were a confusing jumble inside me. I swung constantly between running as far from Rex as I could in emotional self-preservation and running into his arms and begging him to never let go.

I was a mess.

I eyed my wrist, the long-sleeve having bunched up enough to reveal a band of tanned, smooth skin inked with wolfsbane flowers drooping heavily from a long stem I knew curved around my forearm.

Beneath, I swore I could feel the weight of the deal I'd made with Rex. The thought of summoning him had occurred to me, tempting me on an almost hourly basis. I'd even started carrying a salt shaker in my pocket, but every time I unleashed my tiny claws and held them to my palm, I balked.

If Rex wanted to hear me out, to see me, he would have found me by now. Hell, I could still see the whitewashed hotel on the far side of the small park I'd chosen to haunt for the day. It rose a few stories above the other bland commercial buildings around it. I hadn't exactly gone far.

But he didn't want to see me. And I didn't blame him. Either he'd get physically stabbed by my enemies or I'd emotionally stab him in the heart again.

At this point, who wasn't better off without me in their life?

Alpha yipped, nose nudging at my forearm. The shock of cold and damp broke me from yet another spiral. "You've already told me this. Many times. You're being a wimp. Just summon Tiny Fangs already. Or don't. Either way, we need to infiltrate the hunters' base and destroy the tracker stone."

I snorted, shooting him a mock glare. "Easy as that, huh? Aren't you meant to be an emotional support dog or something?"

He bared his lethal fangs, lurking inside his great maw like a forest. "I'm a *familiar*. We keep our bonded mage safe and share our power with the ungrateful dolt."

I arched a brow, fighting back the twitching of my lips. "In exchange for belly rubs?"

He snorted, a surprisingly human sound from the giant beast. "A side benefit of my duties, I suppose."

I giggled, but a weight still crushed my chest. It hadn't shifted since Rex had stormed out the door, never to return.

I'd moped about in the hotel for the day before Alpha had convinced me to get a grip and leave. It wasn't safe for me to stay in one place too long, even with the hunters likely in a panicked disarray after Rex's impromptu murder spree at the old docks.

Now that I'd had time to think after that reckless night, I was more determined than ever to stop the hunters and their cruelty. I just didn't know how to go about it without Rex's help. If Alpha took me to the Riverside base, they'd easily recapture us into their tender, loving care. I'd been practising with my magic every day, but I wasn't exactly a one-witch army.

I'd debated summoning a random demon again, but every time I thought about it, my stomach churned. Rex might not even care, but for me, it would feel like a betrayal.

So many beings had suffered for that cult's brainwashed fanaticism though, my familiar included. I couldn't give up. I just needed to figure out a viable way forward.

Plus, Fenton the Betrayer was still out there somewhere, probably cackling with his fat envelope of blood money like Scrooge McDuck.

The thought had me scowling up at the gloomy sky. If anyone deserved to be suffering right now, it was that slimy maggot.

I pressed the pad of my thumb into the metallic flower on my finger, trying to draw strength from my mother's ring, the one possession I had left to tie me to my family. I wondered what had happened to the rest of my family's belongings. Were they gathering dust inside the rickety log cabin I'd lived in on Quartz territory? Or had Lyndsey ransacked the place and ditched the rest?

I bet she was enjoying her life as a fully inducted coven witch, tending to her potion herbs and humming tunelessly, completely unaware of the snake in her bed. The entire coven was probably in danger and didn't even know it.

An idea bloomed through my mind. Sure, it wasn't my best, but it was better than moping around and waiting to be kidnapped and tortured.

I bolted up to sitting, a few twigs raining from my wild lilac mane.

Alpha barked, his furred muzzle swinging around to follow my gaze. "What is it? Squirrel?"

I chuckled, shooting him an amused look. "No, you crazy hound. Better. Revenge."

Alpha bared his long fangs in a vicious canine grin.

I scratched him behind his purple ear, feeling the thrill of purpose lighten my limbs. "I'm going to make the bastard responsible for all my problems pay. And, in the process, I'm going to save the coven and get my life back."

I ignored the tiny voice in the back of mind that screamed, *What life?* Instead, I climbed to my feet, brushing grass off my jeans.

Swinging my pack onto my shoulders, I took off towards Riverside's north-eastern forests. With Alpha on my heels, I headed for the only home I knew, determination crystallising with every step.

Chapter 39

A rustling disturbed the steady cadence of the forest.

Rough bark pressed into my palms as I gripped the thick branch supporting me. Anticipation tightened my muscles as I prepared to jump.

A faint breeze swayed the oak's leaves around me, almost like it was waving me goodbye or wishing me luck. My connection to the sturdy tree was a steady, pulsing beat. In truth, like everyone except Alpha, it couldn't care less about me.

But that was OK because I wasn't sure how much I cared for oaks after my stint almost buried alive under one's roots. It felt like a lifetime ago, but in reality, a little over a week had passed. So much had changed in such a short time.

I blew out a breath as I eyed the invisible barrier to Quartz territory. The warding spell lurked only a few metres away. It threaded between two young birches and a patch of scented wood anemone before extending outwards to circle the whole hidden settlement. I'd expected to feel a sense of longing for the forest I'd once called home, but only a resigned disappointment remained.

Would I really change anything?

If Lyndsey hadn't betrayed me, I'd have never met the wicked demon who turned me inside out. Who set my blood on fire and made me feel alive. Who brought out the vicious side of me until I forgot even the notion of being a victim. Who kissed me like I was the air he needed to breathe. Who made me feel safe. Cherished. Seen.

My fists clenched at my sides, hard enough to sting as my short claws dug into my palms.

It didn't matter. If I never made it back into Quartz, either I had to move to hell or keep putting Rex in danger here on Earth with our deals.

A tuneless humming followed the whispering of bushes and snapping of twigs.

Mossy green curls bounced through the shrubs before me, right on time. Every Tuesday at dusk, Lyndsey collected her potion herbs on this route. Luckily for me, it strayed right to the boundary of Quartz Coven's ward spell.

A faint green glowed from her fingertips as she stroked along a wilting sage bush. It swelled, the white-kissed leaves unfurling, perking up at her magical touch.

"There you go," Lyndsey cooed. "Just needed a little TLC, huh? Don't worry, Auntie Lyn-Lyn has got you."

A smile twitched my lips. That was the kind, caring person I'd thought I knew.

Not the one who'd betrayed me for a crush. Got me exiled in shame. Practically handed me back over to the hunters on a silver platter. Something she knew I feared more than anything in this world. Most mages did.

If the carefree humming and healthy glow to her skin was anything to go by, she hadn't exactly lost sleep over it.

Tight bands squeezed my chest at the reminder of all I'd lost. Yet now, faced with my emotional turmoil for Rex, the sting of Lyndsey's betrayal had dulled slightly. It still hurt, losing someone I'd considered a sister, but now that I thought about it, had anything really bound us together other than time? I was a book-obsessed, tattooed introvert, and she was a prim and proper social butterfly. I still cared for her, despite everything, but if we'd met under different circumstances, I wasn't sure we'd have been friends.

Either way, she was the only person who might hear me out. She might be open to listening to my side of things and take the warning to the rest of the coven on my behalf. Really, Fenton had betrayed her too. The sweet girl I'd grown up with would be horrified if she knew she was dating a shady criminal.

Taking a deep breath, I twisted my mother's ring around my finger once for courage, then pushed off the branch. I plummeted several metres, landing quietly in a crouch, paces from my ex-bestie. Ever since I'd reconnected with Alpha, my body had felt stronger, more agile. Not to mention the ease at which I could call upon the sharpening of my nails into inky claws and the haunting fire that simmered in my chest, just begging to be used.

I straightened, clearing my throat to get her attention.

Lyndsey spun, yelping as she caught sight of me, one hand clutching the base of her throat, the other cradling a wicker basket in front of her like a shield.

Familiar doe eyes rounded as her jaw slackened. "Z-Zo? Is that you?"

I quirked a brow, irritated by her wide-eyed innocence. Of course she was shocked to see me; she'd sentenced me to death. "No, it's the fucking Easter Bunny."

Seeing her beautifully made-up face and perfectly styled moss-green hair had anger simmering in the unrelenting pit in my chest. I'd been reduced to sleeping on the streets and burning grown men to death just to see the next sunrise. Yet here she was, glammed up for a stroll in the woods, not a care in the world.

Lyndsey rolled her eyes, adjusting her grip on the basket filled with greenery as she recovered from her initial surprise. "Same old Shrimp, huh?"

The familiar nickname sent a pang of longing through me. Her lack of emotional reaction at my sudden appearance quickly devoured the brief hit of nostalgia though.

"I'm not here to reminisce." I smoothed my expression, trying to rein in my emotions. I was here for a reason, and I couldn't get sidetracked by my burning need for retribution. "I have a warning."

Her glossed lips twitched as sweeping brows hit her hairline. "Are you threatening me?"

Clearly, she didn't think I was all that dangerous.

But she had no idea what I'd been through. How much blood soaked my hands. Because of her.

The thought of how close we'd used to be seemed impossible now. Even back then, had she ever really known me? Cared for me? Or had I just seen what I wanted to?

I'd needed someone to latch onto after my entire world was ripped away at the tender age of fourteen. When the hunters had murdered my family. In front of me. After days of tortured abuse. Even being separated from my familiar must have traumatised me, though I'd been too naive to realise what had happened.

I'd used Lyndsey as a crutch for so long. Too long.

Really, it wasn't fair to either of us.

I blew out a breath, my heart aching for the broken little girl I'd been and for the bubbly one I'd put all that pressure on to help put me back together.

All the self-righteous rage left me in a rush, leaving me hollow. I shrugged, the exhaustion from weeks of fighting for survival weighing on my shoulders. "No. It's a warning for the entire coven. I need you to pass on a message for me. It's about Fenton."

Lyndsey's entire demeanour changed.

She took a step forwards, almost crossing the ward, as she bristled in outrage. "Save it, bitch. I don't have to listen to more of your vicious lies and spiteful jealousy. Leave now or I'll call the coven elder." Her pretty features twisted into an ugly snarl. "Why can't you just leave me alone? Be happy for me. I'm in love with a wonderful, powerful mage. He's a good man. Everyone just needs to back off and stop trying to stir shit in our relationship."

It sounded like she was trying to convince herself more than me. And that I maybe wasn't the only one casting doubts against her dear Fenton.

"At least hear me out." I balled my fists, willing myself not to snap and go off on a rant that would only fall on deaf ears. "Fenton is working with the hunters. I've seen it with my own eyes. You need to warn the rest of the coven, or at least look into it yourself. They could all be in danger. If anything, we should work together to stop the hunters and rescue all their captives."

She paused, creases appearing between her brows. "Even for you, that's a new low." She shook her head with enough force to jiggle the woven basket looped over her elbow.

My eye twitched as I fought to keep my tone even. "I was telling the truth before, and I'm telling the truth now." I shifted forwards, trying to contain my frustration. "He tried to assault me at the initiation ceremony, and I saw him getting paid off by the hunters down at the old docks four days ago. Where was he that night, huh?"

She opened her mouth, something like doubt entering her expressive eyes. "I... He..."

Hope surged within me like a spring. I took a cautious step closer, raising my hands like I was approaching a wounded animal. "Where was he last Friday, Lyn?"

She lifted her chin. "He was with me." The words fell harshly between us.

"Did you see an envelope of cash on him? Bloodstains on his clothes?" I asked. It was a long shot, but it was worth a go. Maybe he'd gone crawling into bed with her to help lick his wounds after betraying our kind.

I still wasn't sure what the hunters were paying him for exactly, but it couldn't be anything good. Those cult fanatics thought of us as demons too, even though we were basically just humans with benefits. It would take a pretty juicy bait for them to take whatever Fenton was selling over Fenton himself.

Lyndsey shook her head, features pinched. "This is ridiculous. Fenton would never betray us. Betray *me*." She pinned me with a vicious glare, and I knew I'd blown my one shot to warn the coven of Fenton's crimes. To get back into their good graces so I could rejoin them once I'd destroyed the tracker stone or, in a best-case scenario, secured their help with the attack. "So what if he's making a little extra on the side from selling filthy rogues and those evil beasts he summons?"

I felt like I'd been shot.

She *knew*.

She already knew.

Fenton was selling covenless mages and summoned demons to the hunters. Selling *people*. And she didn't care.

I struggled to process the depth of their combined depravity.

Her hands balled at her sides, sending her basket tumbling to the ground. "Leave. Now. For old times' sake, I don't want to see you hurt, but I will call Elder Murray. You're not welcome here."

I couldn't help it; I saw red.

Anger burned through the shock of emotional agony.

A harsh scoff fell from my lips. "You don't want to see me hurt? That's rich from the girl who chose her twisted obsession over her best friend." Rage scorched my insides, adding fire to my words. "You betrayed me. You knew I'd be found by hunters, tortured and killed, and you did it anyway. For what? Some weasel dick? I hope he's the best fuck of your miserable life."

Tears filled her eyes, but she notched her chin. "Fuck you, Zoella. You were never my best friend. Just some charity case I hung out with because I felt sorry for you. Family is who you choose, and I don't choose you. I never did."

"What am I doing?" I shook my head, disgusted with myself for ever having believed this plan could work. "You're as messed up as he is."

Anaemic green light swallowed her hands. The sage leaves around her grew, gaining an almost sharp edge as they pointed towards me. Her face became a mask of violent intent.

Shock struck me like lightning. All I could do was stare as Lyndsey primed her magic for the attack.

Self-absorbed, callous cruelty, I could believe, but I'd never thought she was capable of actual violence.

The idea of returning to my old life crumbled to ash, piling up around me and burying me. Coating my throat and choking me.

This whole time, I'd been fighting to give myself a chance to convince my old coven they'd made a mistake in abandoning me. I'd foolishly thought that if I could get them to take me back, everything could go back to the way it had been. That I could be safe amongst their sheltered ranks. But would I be any safer with them than on the run? At best, the coven was blissfully ignorant of their future leader's corruption. At worst, more than just he and Lyndsey were in on it.

I'd been going about my situation all wrong.

I shouldn't have been focusing on how to get back to my hollow existence within Quartz. I should have been carving out a real life.

The past few weeks had been terrifying. I'd had to fight for each new day, for food, for warmth, for survival, for joy. But I'd never felt so alive. I'd rather battle hunters for the rest of my days than go back to being the ghost that haunted Quartz.

Life was for *living*.

And there was one person who ignited a fire in my soul like nothing else.

I cocked a brow at the bristling witch. "You're going to cut me with a bush now?" I chuckled, smoky and low in a poor imitation of Rex. "You have no idea what I've gone through. What I'm capable of now."

Rich lilac flames burst from my palms, hot enough to wilt the surrounding foliage. My nails lengthened into ink-tipped claws. I flashed my sharp canines in a wicked grin.

I felt positively demonic.

Lyndsey gasped, youthful features slackening in fear. She stumbled back, hiding behind the coven's protective barrier and almost tripping over her discarded basket in her haste. "Y-You're a monster!"

I leaped forwards with inhuman speed. "Boo!"

She screamed, a high-pitched wail of terror as she tucked tail and ran. Her white sundress tangled around her legs, tripping her mid-stride. She slid forwards in the dirt before scrambling back up in a mad dash.

My ex sister in magic disappeared between the sun-dappled trunks, running like her life depended on it. The pale-purple flames in my periphery died out right alongside my childish triumph, leaving me cold and empty.

Coming here had been a mistake.

Lyndsey would never see reason. Fenton had her shackled by his charm and eating up his every manipulation. Judging by the resounding support at my dramatic exile, nobody else from Quartz would believe me either. Not without undisputable proof. Even then, I wasn't convinced they wouldn't just bury their heads in the sand.

Betrayal and failure raked at my insides in slow, painful, slashes.

Once again, I was covenless and alone. No family. No friends.

But was that really true?

I could hear the quiet padding of Alpha's steady gait several metres away. He'd stayed out of sight, obeying my request to let me handle this alone, as much as I could tell he'd wanted to protest.

But it wasn't just my familiar.

Somewhere out there was a crazy male who set my pulse racing, and I wasn't going to let fear stop me from exploring what could have been. It was time I started living.

Chapter 40

Sweat slicked my palms. I wiped the clammy sensation off on my leggings with a grimace.

"Come on, Zo, get your shit together," I muttered, mentally stabbing at the butterflies organising a coup in my stomach.

I'd never been good with the sappy stuff, but if I wanted to be with someone as fully as Rex deserved, I had to expose the vulnerable, squishy parts of myself. I just hoped he didn't smash whatever was left of my broken heart.

With a deep, calming breath, I tilted my face up to the moon, framed by the white boughs of haunting silver beech trees. The pale orb was almost full, hardly a sliver missing. The night sky, filled with stars, only reminded me of Rex's endless eyes when they flashed with the silvery specks I'd come to recognise as high emotion.

Shifting my claws, I slashed a dark tip across my palm. Pain bit instantly, and I hissed out a breath. Blood welled until a shallow lake of red was hemmed in by the pale skin in my cupped hand.

Swiping the salt shaker from my waistband, I upended it before I could lose my nerve. White grains melted into the warm liquid, adding to the sting assaulting my open cut.

"Rex," I whispered. His name whipped away in the breeze. "Rex, Rex, Rex."

I chanted, slow and steady, focusing on my intent to summon, just like the grimoire had said, but this time feeling for the threads connecting us. Our deals weighed my wrists, giving my focus an anchor. Rex and I had a connection, at least in magical terms. I hoped there was *something* else between us too, but I wasn't sure if I'd damaged whatever bond might have formed before it could fully grow.

"Rex, Rex, Rex," I continued, fighting down the turmoil of emotions and willing the spark of magic in my chest to ignite.

Quicker than before, the pool of blood in my hand drew heat, flaring hotter with every strained second until it felt like I'd set it aflame. It roiled and swayed like a churning tide trapped in a puddle.

My chant cut off in a hiss as I fought to keep my hand steady through the searing burn.

Anticipation twined with terror as my magic swelled, emanating from my chest to pulse through my body.

The heated liquid surged up, swirling and growing until it created a bloodied tornado, almost grazing the branches above. It funnelled from my hand, devouring my magic as it spun downwards, hitting the grass with a wet splat. The connection to my hand cut abruptly, staggering me as my energy drained in a rush.

The vortex collapsed in on itself, leaving a gory circle.

A familiar grey demon snarled within.

My heart thundered, constricting at the sight of him. I'd missed my feral demon. Apparently, even a few days apart was too much.

I was such a sap.

While I'd been moping around and pining after him, he'd apparently had enough carefree time to cut his fiery hair, of all things. I had the completely inappropriate thought to ask if he'd just gone through a nasty break-up, but either I was the bad break-up or I wasn't. Either answer would hurt.

Now his red-orange ombre waves only just caressed his lower spiralling horns, the fiery strands curling around his lightly pointed ears.

I frowned even as my gaze greedily drank in every inch of him. How hadn't I noticed he had pointed ears until now?

I still had so much to discover about the mysterious demon. The thought that I might have lost the chance to do so punched me right in the chest, knocking the air from my lungs.

"Rex." My voice came out small, desperate.

He spun, claws raised and tail primed with his bony stinger unsheathed. His black gaze skipped right over me, scanning the dim forest.

He canted his onyx horns aside, as if straining to hear something.

Deep lines creased his brow. "Where are they?" His voice was flat, his gaze aimed everywhere but at me.

I swallowed, feeling the sting of rejection at his refusal to even look at me. "Who?"

His eyes finally snapped to mine, narrowing dangerously. "Your sacrifices."

I bit my lip. Of course he'd assumed I was only calling because I was in trouble. "It's just us. And Alpha patrolling the area." I gestured off to the side, where the forest thickened beyond the small clearing I'd chosen.

"Then why have you summoned me?" His detached tone knifed through me.

I cleared my throat. Maybe I'd made a mistake in calling him like this, but we'd not exactly exchanged numbers.

He looked ferocious. Powerful and feral, just like when I'd first summoned him over a week ago. If anything, his shorter hair only sharpened the hard cut of his angular features.

Had it really been only a week? I felt like I'd known him for years.

Now the sight of his inhuman features made my heart pound for different reasons. He was beautiful. Every sharp point and rough edge.

"Rex, I…" Words failed me as a bolt of adrenaline spiked through me. I'd had several hours to work myself up to this since I'd left Quartz territory, and still I was a terrified mess.

He raised a brow, ever the patient predator.

If I wanted a future with Rex in it, I had to be as willing to put myself out there as he'd been.

I cleared my throat, trying again. "I'm not going back to my old coven." The words spilled out in a nervous rush. "I don't ever want to hide you away or make you feel like less, because you're perfect, Rex, and anyone would be lucky to have you in their life."

My throat tried to close off with the emotions surging through me. I meant every damn word.

His harsh features softened, hope glimmering in the dark depths of his unwavering gaze.

"I'm not going to let fear dictate my life any more. If I run away with you to hell, I'll never know if a part of me was driven by self-preservation. I need time to explore this connection. We can date here on Earth, and I'll come visit you in hell."

"And the murderous cult baying for your sweet blood?" he asked, tone wry.

"Fuck the hunters," I growled, feeling a determination solidify in my chest. "I'm going to fight for my future, and I want you to be in it."

His features flattened slightly, defensively neutral. He remained silent, a stony sentinel in the pale forest.

I ploughed on. "But I don't want you to bleed for it. Rex, I care about you." Lifting my wrists, I held them towards him. "We have to end these deals, or how can we know what's real between us?"

He flinched. Such a slight movement, yet he might as well have been struck. "I already know my feelings are real."

My hands dropped back to my sides. Seeing his pain only made my heart ache more. "You hardly know me, Rex. What's my favourite colour? What am I allergic to? Goddesses, what's my last damn name?"

A muscle feathered along his sharp jaw. "I may not know all the details, but I know *who* you are. I know your soul, Zoella." His inhuman eyes bored down to my core. "You're a walking contradiction. You're beautiful yet almost as monstrous as I am. You're gentle and kind yet fierce and protective. You make me laugh and growl. You make me feel warm when you look at me like I mean something to you. You ice my veins when you throw yourself into danger. Nobody has ever made me feel as much in my entire lifetime as you have in a single week. I know enough to know you're the mate I've been waiting for, whether you like red or blue. And I want to spend the rest of my days learning every facet of your being."

His chest heaved, words falling with so much weight every sentence felt like a blow to my heart.

"I... What if you don't like what you learn?" My hands found each other, twisting and squeezing despite the sting of my cut palm, as I tried to get my words out. "I need time for you to get to know me, to prove to me that this connection between us isn't some star-crossed affair. What if we only burn so bright because we're destined to fade?"

Tears swam across my vision with the thought. I was so goddesses-damned terrified.

And now we'd circled back to a similar argument as before. I wanted to go bash my head against a tree trunk because I wasn't sure which of us was right. All I knew was that I wanted to take things slow, to get to know each other and prove our relationship was strong and real. I never wanted to be abandoned by someone I loved again. I wasn't sure I could survive it, not from him.

But the reckless demon wanted to dive right into the deep end. Wasn't he scared to drown?

"What if we last a lifetime?" His eyes captivated me, as endless as the night sky. "You're what I want, Zoella. Body, heart, and soul."

"Then let's end our deals. Give this a chance to grow without the pressure," I pleaded, taking a single step closer to the summoning circle that held him. "Let's try things my way, at least to start with."

He tipped his horns back like he was imploring the stars above. His pulse throbbed the column of his throat as he sought whatever wisdom, or patience, they could offer him.

After a heavy moment, he looked back at me, seeming to come to a decision.

"For you, little mouse." He drew a deep breath, flaring his ribs wide before releasing it in a controlled stream. "I want all of you, but I'm so damn hooked on you I don't think I could stay away even if you did run back to that twisted coven of yours. Watching you from afar these past few days has been agony enough," he whispered, his confession trailing off to be snatched by the night.

His words eased some of the weight that had settled in my soul. I rubbed at my chest, feeling the strange ache lift. Had he never really left me?

A small, tentative smile curved my lips as a fledging hope took flight. Despite the evening's chill, my body warmed, like the sun had replaced the full moon. I hadn't been sure we could work things out, and it almost felt too good to be true. Like at any moment, he was going to laugh in my face and walk away instead.

Every instinct I had screamed at me to keep my guard up, to protect my heart and stop plummeting towards the L zone with this wicked demon. But for a chance at happiness, I needed to let him in. I wanted him to see the real me and still choose to stay.

And that started with breaking the magic that bound us together. I bit my lip, praying I wasn't about to make a mistake that could cost me my life.

Chapter 41

"So, um… How do we actually break these deals?" I asked, holding my wrists out. My long-sleeve running top covered them up, but I swore I could see a faint red glow through the material.

Rex's inky brows shot to his horns. "You don't know?" He shook his head, fiery locks swaying. "You made a deal with a *demon* without knowing how to end it?" His tone implied just what he thought about that.

I scowled, irritation sparking enough to cover my embarrassment. "Oh, I'm sorry." My tone dripped sarcasm. "I guess I must have missed that detail in the two seconds I had to read my coven's grimoire before I was almost assaulted and set it on fire."

He stilled. The deadly kind of still that only a predator could tame.

Darkness flooded his eyes. Oh so carefully, he parted his lips, drawing out a single word. "Assaulted?"

I sucked in a breath, only just realising I'd never actually told him *why* I'd attacked Fenton. I hadn't needed to. Rex had believed in me regardless.

"Who?" he roared, wrath shaking the surrounding trees.

I flinched at the boom of sound, but despite his rage, I knew he'd never hurt me. Anxiety choked me at the thought of Rex trying to storm coven grounds to get at Fenton. Even he couldn't take on that many mages and win. "It doesn't matter."

He stepped clear of the summoning circle—something I hadn't thought possible—devouring the space between us in a blink. His claws curled into my shoulders, pinching my flesh. The forest swayed as he lightly shook me.

"Tell me and I'll rip their entrails out. Suck the marrow from their bones while they watch. A mage can survive the removal of quite a few broken bones before they succumb to the delicious agony," he snarled, long fangs flashing in the moonlight.

I shuddered at the vivid image he painted, but a part of me wanted to curl into a ball and sob. Nobody had ever defended me like that. Nobody had actually *cared* about me since my family had been murdered. Not my supposed best friend. Not my coven.

Black eyes narrowed as he waited, until his inky lashes barely showed the lurking abyss beneath.

"Rex..." I trailed off, trying to puzzle out the right words to say. "That was the past. I'm trying to create a new future." I swallowed, squaring my shoulders despite the prickling threat of his claws against them. "And I don't want to see you hurt for it. How do we break them?"

His black eyes bored into me for a long moment. Square jaw clenched, he finally looked away. "Swipe my blood, freely given, across the contract inscribed in your flesh. Connect to your magic, will the binding to break, and it shall."

There was a justice to the demon-summoner contracts. If you needed mage blood to summon a demon and make a deal, then it made sense you'd need theirs to break it.

"Let's do it." I peeled back my sleeve, revealing the black-berry branches entwining my wrist. Their thorns covered my scars, and the delicate flowers bloomed where once bruises had marred my flesh.

The reminder of all I'd been through only crystallised my determination. I never wanted to be at the mercy of the hunters again, but I also wanted these deals gone so I could be with Rex as an equal, not a master summoning their monster. He was more than a weapon to me, and I never wanted him to take another blade or bullet meant for my flesh.

Rex slashed his forearm without hesitation, opening a large gash bleeding a dark navy, like ink. He plucked my offered wrist, dripping warm blood over it. The heated drops hit my skin with a faint tingle.

I closed my eyes, seeking the weight of our first deal at my wrist, where his fresh blood ran across my skin. I reached for my magic, sending it down my arm and into the circle of power that hosted the contract we'd made.

"Break, break, break...," I whispered, feeling the strands of my magic pluck at the strange weight. Like cutting an elastic band, the deal snapped, lashing me with energy.

I sucked in a breath, meeting Rex's gaze as he winced from the backlash, jaw clenching tight enough to highlight the hard angle. His eyes had burned back to their glowing red, slashed through with vertical pupils.

He swapped his grip on my arm, stroking his thumb along my skin. I pulled back my sleeve, revealing my wolfsbane tattoo and the buried script of our final deal.

Trepidation bit at me. This connection was the last thing truly binding us together. From here on out, it would only be feelings and loyalty. I didn't exactly have a great history with either.

More fiery blood splashed against my skin before I could overthink this. I repeated the focused will on my other wrist, braced for the whip of power settling back inside me.

Rex's gaze met mine, swimming with some unknown depths. "Zoella, I want you to know I'm not going to let anything happen to you, deals or not."

I swallowed, overcome with a weird mix of relief and doubt. I desperately wanted to cling to his words, but I'd come to realise I needed actions to make me truly believe.

A ferocious snarl filled the night, but Rex's lips remained pressed into a firm line.

I spun, heart jumping into my throat as I prepared for hunters to come bursting from between the silvery trees. Instead, a colourful array of demons barrelled from between the trunks, snarling and growling.

Alpha leaped overhead, clearing several sets of horns to land squarely between the newcomers and me. A hair-raising growl rumbled from the hellhound, warning clear.

A towering demon skidded to a halt before Alpha's snapping jaws, leathery wings flaring wide. His mouth gaped open as his head whipped between Rex and me with an almost comically bewildered expression.

He jabbed a clawed thumb in my direction. "That's *not* your witch. Where's Eve?"

Chapter 42

Who's Eve?

The question slammed around my skull, demanding attention despite several more lethal demons striding out from between the white trees, rapid breaths misting the night air.

"Why thank you, Coran, for your oh-so-insightful observation," Rex drawled. "Yes, it wasn't Eve who summoned me like we'd hoped."

Claws raked into my stomach, hollowing me out.

Like he'd hoped? He wanted to hear from her, not me.

Rex waved his claws at me in a sweeping gesture. "This is Zoella, the one I *had* the deals with." His eyes scanned the rest of the demons as they emerged, a concerned intensity carving his features. "Did you find it?"

Coran nodded, horns gouging the air, trying to edge around Alpha without success as the hellhound growled in warning at the navy demon.

"Yes." Coran sounded almost pained. "Briar and Killian followed the rest of the instructions while we tracked you, just in case it was her."

As if on cue, two more demons ran into view, even more out of breath than the others.

Rex nodded, a look of grim determination hardening his features, but I was still reeling. Questions and confusion bounced around my brain. A sinking feeling weighed my gut.

"We go. Now." He turned to face me. "Zoella, take Alpha and go back to your room at the Crown Hotel. We've found the hunter base. I'll come back for you after, but I have to go. Eve needs me."

I felt like I'd been exiled all over again. Everyone kept shooing me away like the inconvenient stray I was. Someone else needed him, and he couldn't get rid of me fast enough.

Of course. How could I have not realised it sooner?

Eve must be the mystery witch he'd mentioned so many times before. The one he'd helped discover her magic.

Rex was here, searching for her. That was the true reason he was after the hunters.

And now he needed to leave me. For her.

Pain coiled inside my chest like barbed wire. It felt ten times worse than when Lyndsey had chosen Fenton over me. I felt like a fool. Rex and I were just about to start a genuine relationship. I'd put my faith in him and released him from our deals. Yet he was already running off into the night after some other woman.

They always left. A snide voice in the back of my mind screamed, *I told you so*. Logically, I understood his urgency to leave—someone he cared about was in danger—but that didn't stop my chest from caving in. Insidious doubts latched onto my thoughts like parasites.

Was Eve his *mate*? Why had he said he'd chosen me? Did demons mate with more than one person? Or was he just screwing with my head? He was a *demon*, after all. What if he'd been lying this whole time? A master manipulator, pulling my puppet strings for fun?

This Eve must be very important to him if he'd go through the risk of getting himself summoned by a stranger, ripped away from his kingdom, his realm, just to look for her. Especially when, as a king, he must have people to do that for him. Like the scrappy band of demons who'd barrelled through the forest like demonic linebackers.

Everything he'd done since I'd taken him from his home had been for her, hadn't it? Making those deals, protecting me, going after the hunters.

Another realisation hit me like a slap. *He* was the one who'd convinced me to go after the hunters, not the other way around.

I was a means to an end. A convenient, maybe even fun, way for him to get what he really wanted.

Her.

He stepped closer, and I backed up on instinct like a wounded animal.

A frown creased his features with hurt. "Zoella..." He reached a hand out, but I dodged back again, heart pounding. His jaw clenched. "I won't be long. I'm going to destroy those bastards, and then you'll be safe, little mouse."

But I hardly heard his words. All the doubts and fears I'd tried my hardest to bury deep surged up like toxic sludge, choking me with my own anxiety.

Of course he didn't really want me. How stupid of me to think that someone might actually choose me for once and mean it, despite his pretty promises. He was just another person choosing someone else over me. Just like Lyndsey and my entire coven had.

It was too much. The bitterly familiar agony of betrayal suffocated me. My lungs refused to inflate as I stared at the grey demon who'd turned my world upside-down.

For a moment there, I'd let myself believe Rex was different, but everyone betrayed you in the end.

I drowned in the emotional pain for one beat, two. Then I carefully folded it away.

I took every hurt and betrayal, and I stuffed it deep down into the dark box inside where I kept all the ugliness I couldn't deal with. Sure, it was getting pretty damn full, but now wasn't the time to worry about that.

Rex turned to leave, tail swishing and tense lines etching his frame. The other demons followed suit, disappearing through the trees at a run.

"Wait!" I called out, voice echoing through the woods.

Rex paused, glancing over his broad shoulder, features pinched.

"I'm coming with you." The words were out of my mouth before I'd had a chance to really think about them, or the fact that I'd left most of my stolen weapons back at the hotel. I'd only strapped on two pistols and a knife before we'd left, since I was *still* more likely to hurt myself than anyone else with them.

I needed to find that tracker stone and destroy it. Rex and his merry men weren't there for me. If they slaughtered every hunter in Riverside and freed every captured demon and mage, that could still leave my magic signature lying around for the next group of hunters to find once they got around to searching the rubble.

Alpha barked at me, still bristling with tension as he watched the newcomers leave. "We."

I nodded, grateful for his support as I corrected myself. "We're coming with you."

Rex's eyes darkened from magma red to cold, coal black. "No."

I flattened my lips into a single line, imploring the goddesses for patience. "I wasn't asking."

He stared me down for a long few seconds, despite the urgency clearly riding the demonic group.

"Boss," one of the winged males, with feathers like an angel's, uttered in low demand. His white claws balled into fists at his sides, showing off the flex of his muscles beneath taut purple skin.

Rex stared down at me, ignoring the other demon. His eyes bled back to red, a sigh leaving his lying lips. "It's not safe, little mouse. I know you have a better hold on your magic. I've watched you practise, but it's not enough."

I ignored the stab of hurt at his dismissal of my abilities. I was a damn strong witch, familiar-bonded to a hellhound of all creatures, and I'd been training with my magic non-stop since he'd left. Even with his apparent stalking, I doubted he knew how far I'd come.

Not that it mattered. This was my best chance to buy my and Alpha's safety, at least for a little while. I'd be damned if I was going to let this chance pass me by.

I arched a brow, tone droll. "You're wasting time, demon. Alpha can lead me there without us even following you."

My faithful hellhound barked, underscoring my point.

Rex looked away, nostrils flaring, before he seemed to wrangle his temper back under control. "Fine." He pointed a pearly claw at my face. "But don't you dare get shot again, witch."

I bared my short fangs, relishing the fierceness my bond to Alpha gave me. "I'll just have to find a demon willing to give me another power boost, then." It was petty, but I couldn't stop the venom spitting from my lips. I eyed a random demon, noting striking ruby skin and curving tusks. "Maybe my favourite colour is red after all."

Like flipping a switch, Rex's eyes flooded black. He flung his arms wide and roared at the poor bewildered demon in question.

On instinct, I backed up.

Colour blurred across my vision as several others jumped on Rex, hauling him back. Alpha bumped into my side, moving me further from Rex as he braced to defend me. I gripped his fur for support, heart pounding.

I'd never seen Rex lose control like this.

The king fought to get closer to the ruby male, snarling and snapping his tail like a whip.

The huge, tusked demon edged backwards, palms raised in surrender. Strange tentacles curled against his back as he tried in vain to disappear behind a pale sapling.

A demon with impressive antlers wrestled with Rex's venomous tail. The talkative navy one yanked back on Rex's vertical horns. The angelic demon gripped one of Rex's arms while a furred male held back the other.

Dark eyes locked back onto me, devouring me like prey as Rex growled, more beast than man. Yet I didn't feel the rush of fear that a sane person would. If anything, a niggle of guilt wormed its way in, that I'd resorted to such juvenile behaviour.

The angel-winged demon hauled back and slammed his fist into Rex's cheek. The king's head whipped aside with a loud crack, breaking our intense eye contact.

I gasped into the sudden silence, concern slicing through me before I mentally berated myself for being a sap. My lip curled as I stuffed down my concern. He'd not been concerned about me when he'd manipulated me into a deal to help him find someone else.

My jaw clenched as anger spiked through me.

"Thanks, Kill," Rex grunted, looking steadily at the hellish angel. "Let's go before we waste any more time." His magma gaze jumped to me, promising a punishment that had shivers racing down my spine for all the wrong reasons. "We'll talk about whatever the fuck this was later, little mouse."

I managed not to flip him off. Just.

Chapter 43

Tail swishing, Rex loped between the birch and oak trees, heading south. As a group, we took off after him, Alpha and I drawing up the rear.

I eyed the other demons, who I assumed must be the generals that old King Rex had mentioned summoning for backup before.

They stared over their shoulders, or wings, right back at me as we ran. Until now, Rex and the demons from Rusty's Pub were the only ones I'd seen. Like Rex, these males were tall and muscular, topless and clad only in those soft-looking black joggers. Clearly, tops were some kind of taboo in hell. That or every male demon loved showing off their ridiculously toned abs.

Each demon varied in their inhuman traits; some had horns and tails, while others had wings and arm spikes. The ruby one I'd accidentally sicked Rex on even had great, big, curving tusks and a set of fleshy tentacles flaring from his back. Blues, purples, reds, greys. They were all a mismatch of colours, from their skin, fur, and scales to their hair and eyes. Most had interesting patterns across their flesh: stripes, speckles, scales, fur. Without a closer look, I couldn't make out what was natural or just a tattoo.

The angelic demon fluttered his feathered wings as he ran, but I had no idea whether that was in agitation or nervousness or just that he had twitchy wings.

My feet pounded the earth as I followed the group beneath the canopy of leaves and stars. Twigs and foliage crunched beneath my trainers, but the others hardly made a single sound. And I'd thought I was the forest witch here.

The slimmest general, a male with pine-green skin and curious patterns of white running through the rich shade, twisted around to run backwards. He regarded me with a frown, indenting his graceful features. Proud antlers branched from his short brown hair, adding to his lean height.

I quirked a brow, stuffing down the awkwardness at being stared at like an animal in a zoo.

He inclined his head with a faint smirk. "I'm Briar," he began. "One of Rex's generals, and—when he's not being a saggy horn—his friend." The fit demon wasn't even slightly out of breath, despite the pace Rex set. He spoke with a casual ease, dodging trees backwards like he'd been born in this very forest. "It's nice to meet you, Zoella. Rex has spoken *very* highly of you." He winked like we were in on some inside joke.

Rex shot a glare back at Briar but kept running in stony silence.

I suppressed the urge to roll my eyes at the cagey king, giving Briar a wry smile instead. "Oh yeah, grouchy T. rex up there sure likes to run his mouth." I couldn't help the slight snarl that had me baring fangs in Rex's direction.

His voice slithered through the woods in a decadent threat, the demon not bothering to turn around this time. "Keep sassing me, little mouse. We'll see how brave you are when I get you alone later."

My cheeks warmed at the sensual undertone.

Ugh. Keep it together.

I cleared my throat, choosing not to dignify that with a response.

"This is Alpha." I nodded to the majestic beast bounding sinuously at my side. His flaming eyes had locked onto Rex like he could sense my anger at the demon.

Briar gave us both a welcoming smile before gesturing a claw at the rest of our demonic pack, nimbly darting out of the way of a robust ash. "Since our leader is playing the brooding king, I'll introduce you to the remaining, *more boring*, generals of the Hybrid Kingdom."

A low growl spilled from Rex's full lips.

Briar ignored his king, and the flat looks from his peers, waving a hand to the finned demon to my left. "Our fishy friend here is Tarek," he said before gesturing towards the purple demon with stunning feathered wings and tattoos of raptor birds in flight along his neck and back. The one who'd sucker punched Rex. "Pretty-boy over there is Killian."

The demon in question smirked at Briar before he half turned to me with an almost lazy curiosity.

Briar swept a hand towards a furred demon with perky wolf-like ears next. "The moody one is Night," he continued.

Night narrowed his eyes at Briar, lightly pumping his thickly toned arms as he ran. He stared at me with open distrust, golden eyes glowing in the darkness.

Briar nodded his horns at the last demon, the one with tentacles and tusks. "And the meathead you apparently have a crush on is Grell," he said, mirth bubbling through his smooth tone. "Poor choice, by the way." He lifted his hand beside his mouth. "I hear he's a selfish lover," he stage whispered.

I fought off another blush as my childish behaviour came back to bite me on the arse.

Grell snorted, tossing his curved tusks in what seemed like a playful gesture as he ran, steps a little more lumbering than the others'. "Oh, go shed your horns, Bri. You're just bitter that I racked up more kills than you at the portal."

Briar flashed me a knowing grin, showing off sharp fangs. He bounded towards Grell with a pirouette leap thing, graceful enough to shame a gazelle. "Ah, my sweet, delusional brother-in-arms, we both know you cheated."

"Using tentacles is not cheating. That's like saying you can't use that chandelier on your head to fight," Grell huffed.

"Yeah, but I heard you agree to use the same appendages as poor peasanty four-limb over there." Armed with a dark smirk,

Killian fluttered his feathers, drawing my eye to the huge wings arching elegantly from his back.

Coran chuckled. "Eve would have all your hides for that. You know how much she hates it when you lot bicker."

Her name stabbed through me, scratching at the fresh wound. I looked away, catching sight of Killian's furious features. His aggressively chiselled jaw popped with enough tension to flutter the wing tattoos on his throat.

"We'll get her back, brother." Night clapped a furred hand on Killian's shoulder, neither breaking stride as we raced for *her*.

Shame washed over me in the next breath. Here I was, drowning in bitterness, when a woman's life was on the line. I was angry at Rex. Confused. Hurt. But I would do what I could to help rescue his captive witch, even if for a moment I'd craved what she had.

Someone who cared.

Time seemed to stretch as anticipation wound through me. Every pounding step took me closer to danger but also freedom.

Rex slowed his pace, letting us catch up as we passed the last rows of silver birches, spilling onto the narrow access road beyond the public park.

We briefly hit the main street before Rex led us down a narrower side road. Street lamps highlighted the demons' every inhuman feature like a spotlight, and I couldn't help but cringe. None of the generals wore a glamour, as far as I could tell, so even stealing through the quiet night was a risk. I had enough problems without being the witch associated with outing demonkind.

Thankfully, Rex took an even more abandoned path, cutting through a gap between two closed shops, forcing the group into a single line. Tarek dropped back so he could run behind me. It seemed oddly protective, even if it had the hairs on my nape rising as a lethal stranger chased me through a dark alley.

We wound through the city, and before long, my legs began to ache, lungs burning with exertion. I knew Rex wasn't running anywhere near the speed he was capable of, but I was still flagging. I'd spent a lot of time resting over the last few days, conserving my strength. The most I'd done was practise magic and run with Alpha through various nature parks.

I looked at my familiar, effortlessly racing beside me. "Are we going the right way?"

He yipped, then growled low. "Yes. Unfortunately."

I flashed him a grateful smile, trying not to let my weakness show. "How much further?"

A demon up ahead snorted, but I couldn't tell who the mocking noise came from.

Alpha bared his teeth at Grell's fleshy tentacles, telling me which prick was on my shit list. My familiar gave a low woof. "We're close."

His steady presence at my side was my only comfort as we continued running, helping me ignore the churning in my gut every time I looked at Rex. Even the sight of his muscular back as he sped through the city was enough to both piss me off and claw my shredded heart.

Just a little longer.

Streets turned to a gravel path as we ran down a side road edging a small farm and what looked like abandoned factories.

Rex slowed, ducking into a thick copse of sycamores. The generals, Alpha, and I quickly fell in line, gathering behind him.

Air sawed in and out of my lungs as I struggled to catch my breath, fighting the urge to collapse onto the hard mud.

"We're almost there." Rex's voice was low, barely audible over my embarrassingly loud panting. "Tarek, approach from the river. Kill, Coran, take to the skies and eliminate their roof patrols. The three of you will then enter together through the front doors. Briar, Night, Grell, and I will approach through the tree cover and enter via the rear doors on your signal."

I raised a brow, but Rex pointedly ignored me.

"Right, well, since I don't have scales or wings, I guess I'm in the forest crew," I muttered.

Kill's lips twitched, despite the tension popping the chords in his neck. "Yes, witch. I doubt Rex could stand letting you out of his sight."

Rex cut his obsidian gaze to the tattooed general, but Killian seemed unfazed by the ire of his king.

I frowned, pretending I wasn't gasping for air after near sprinting for what must have been close to half an hour. "What's that supposed to mean?"

The purple demon flashed me a cryptic smirk.

Chapter 44

I drew in a measured breath, trying to squash my nerves. Loamy earth sank under my trainers as I shifted on the spot. Even from this distance, a metallic tang accented the scents of rotting food and pollution. It overpowered the faint woodsy smell of bark as I crouched beside a narrow sycamore on the ridge.

Beyond the tree line, boxy factories and warehouses, dark and empty, spread before us. City lights glittered in the distance, peeking between the monstrous structures. A murky grey river sliced down the far side.

The hunter compound lurked on the edge of a run-down industrial estate. Our tense group coiled within the paltry cover of trees, set a good hundred metres back from our sprawling brick target.

A part of me expected the sight to trigger a torrent of memories, but the ordinary building behind the barbed wire fencing only looked vaguely familiar.

I twirled my mother's ring around my index finger, trying to ignore the dread sitting in my stomach like a boulder. The compound was the only illuminated structure on the estate. A handful of security lights blazed outside, but high-set windows spilled more light from within.

Pairs of hunters, dressed in an array of black-on-black clothing and bristling with rifles, patrolled the area in slow sweeps. Alert and ready, they swivelled their heads constantly to scan the area. I counted only three sets total, which seemed a little light to me, given the size of their local chapter was probably closer to a hundred. Rex had single-handedly cut a bloody path through their numbers in the past week though.

How long did it take to brainwash new recruits?

Rex pressed on through the heavy silence, leading us to the rear of the building. I crept through the trees behind him until I could see the back entrance across the half-empty car park. A corrugated roller shutter, big enough for a lorry to drive through, seemed like the best option for entry given the size of Rex and his generals. Only two hunters waited in front, like nightclub bouncers but white-knuckling rifles.

"When Coran and Kill dispatch the fence patrol, we go," Rex murmured, religiously scanning the base.

Alpha pressed close to my side, knocking my shoulder into the rough bark. A fine tremor shook his frame, and my already battered heart squeezed painfully in my chest. What horrors had he suffered behind those unassuming brick walls?

I ran my fingers through the soft fur along the back of his head, smoothing down his spine. "You don't have to go back in there." I kept my voice pitched low, but I knew the demons crouched around us could hear.

Alpha swung his face around, fiery purple gaze alight. He growled low, an almost whine tailing the rumble. "I'm not leaving you. Not again."

My fingers tangled in his fur. Guilt writhed through the lilac flames of his eyes.

My throat clogged with emotion as I shoved back the dark memories that threatened to surface. "Don't. It wasn't your fault. I was the one who left *you*, and I can never atone for that, but I'll keep trying for the rest of our lives. Please, stay outside."

He whined quietly, a soft canine sound. "Your freedom is my freedom. We stick together."

A small smile twitched my lips. I might have lost everything, but I'd gained my familiar, a piece of me I'd never known was missing. "Always."

I leaned up, pressing my forehead to his. Warm and reassuring, the bond between us thrummed steadily, just below my sternum.

A low snort sounded from the other side of the tree. I leaned forwards, glaring at the tentacled brute who was more tusks than brains. Of all the generals I could have randomly picked to fake interest in, I'd chosen the right one. At least now his boss was visibly, yet irrationally, mad at him.

"Snort at us again and I'll burn your little piggy nose off," I hissed, staying as quiet as I could.

Grell bared his fangs at me, an interesting onyx black compared to the bright white of his curved tusks. "You're talking to a *hellhound*. That's kinda nuts."

"He's my familiar, and he's a better conversationalist than you." Shooting him a last glare, I refocused on the compound instead of his almost comically raised brows.

From the corner of my eye, I could have sworn I saw Rex's lips twitch, but the expression was gone the moment I turned. Crouched on the other side of Alpha, he hunkered down, half-hidden behind the next tree over. Like the others, his wide bulk was too large for the stunted sycamores to hide completely. With the cover of darkness and his shaded skin, he blended in better than his generals though.

A screech of metal pierced the night. The roller door lifted, spilling harsh light onto the cracked tarmac, haloing two figures inside. The guards hesitated in their circuit of the fence but continued onwards, disappearing around the far corner.

Like a shard of the night itself, Coran dropped from the sky behind the hunters. He ripped a guard's throat out while Killian landed stealthily behind the other to bury his fangs in the man's neck.

"Now." Rex's voice was steady and low, as if he hadn't just unleashed madness.

Chapter 45

R ex sprinted down the short slope to the rear car park. He tore at the wire fence as if it was tissue paper, leaving a gap big enough for the rest of his burly generals to sprint through behind him. Rex weaved between vehicles, the rest of his demons fanning out, mimicking his stealthy speed.

They were already halfway to the entrance.

"Shit." Straightening, I lurched into action with nowhere near as much grace. My trainers slid through the mud as I half fell down the grassy incline, stumbling as I hit the uneven tarmac to duck through the gaping fence. Momentum dragged me forwards, and I managed to get my feet under me rather than face-plant.

Alpha trotted at my side, ears flattened to his skull.

A roar sounded up ahead, hidden by the scattered cars. Screams filled the night before the harsh bang of gun fire reverberated through me. My shoulder throbbed with the ghost of pain at the reminder, but I shoved the fear aside, sprinting across the car park with pounding steps. My heart raced me there. I drew both pistols, and within seconds, I reached the last car, stumbling into the aftermath of the demons' ambush.

Rex slashed a hunter clean in half, spraying me with blood as he roared, loud enough to cover the sound of the body thumping to the tarmac. I slid to a stop before I could trip over the detached torso. Bile hit the back of my throat, but I clenched my jaw, forcing it down. Adrenaline and fear only made me queasier as I spun, weapons raised. I scanned for a target of my own, but Rex and his demons had made short work of the patrols, leaving only chunks scattered across the lot.

I tried to slow my rapid breathing before I did something stupid, like panic in the midst of a battle.

Rex chuckled, emitting wisps of smoke with an unhinged mirth. The familiar sound broke through my spiral, strangely comforting. If the biggest predator I knew was laughing, then all his enemies were about to die. Just another weeknight slaughter. Everything would be OK.

"The door's that way, little mouse." Flicking red, Rex pointed a claw at the entrance. Briar was already ducking through, his branching antlers grazing the half-lowered shutter. "Run along now so I have another warm body to chase." He bared his bloodied fangs. Combined with his solid black eyes, he looked utterly monstrous.

A wicked thrill shot through me at the thought of him chasing me down. I mentally slapped myself. We were literally on a mission to go save his other woman. He'd used me. Betrayed me. Just like everyone else.

If only I could convince my dumb heart to stop squeezing at the sight of him.

I bared my own fangs, feeling my connection to Alpha heat my chest as I drew on his feral strength. "Go to hell."

I sprinted past the traitor. Alpha's fur brushed my hand with each pump of my arms as he kept pace.

Rex's cackle reached after me, drawing closer.

And I was supposed to be the witch here.

Grey blurred past me as Rex launched himself inside the building ahead of me. His torso twisted, dodging aside as gun fire boomed through the space. A metallic ding sounded as a bullet found its home in the doorframe to his right.

The crazy bastard only laughed harder. "You'll have to do better than that!"

With a snarl, Rex darted forwards and slashed at a hunter trying frantically to shove a new magazine into his rifle.

I stepped into the warehouse, assaulted by piercing screams, bangs, and crashes. The scent of blood and gore was thick on the air. I backed up to the edge, heart in my throat. Alpha pressed into my side, a quiet sentinel as I took a moment to assess.

The generals darted around the enormous open space, wreaking violent havoc. Tarek slashed his claws through a hunter's soft middle before his spined elbow fins slammed into another attacker's throat. Briar charged a group of hunters firing rapidly at him before he gouged them with his antlers, knocking them aside like bowling pins. Night tore out the throat of a man in a lab coat with a howl. Grell slammed an armoured male into the wall with his tentacles. Killian dropped from the ceiling to snatch a reloading hunter up into the air, sinking his fangs into his struggling victim. The extent of the gory scene stunned me for a dangerous second.

Then my eyes latched onto the real horror.

Haggard mages were chained along one wall. They were bloodied and emaciated, torn clothing hanging in tatters from their thin frames. Every inch of them was bruised or cut, with swollen lips and eyes, chunks of hair missing.

I gagged, stomach roiling violently.

It was the fate I'd narrowly avoided as a teen.

I sucked in a gasp as I spotted a familiar mage. Sunset-orange hair wasn't common, even amongst mages. Gregor had joined our coven only a few weeks before my exile. How had he fallen into the hunters' clutches?

Tarek ran to the captives, getting to work on their bindings.

In the middle of the room, a shadow-walker and a grey spiked demon I didn't recognise clung to the bars of an enormous circular cage. Somehow, they were even more battered than the mages. Colourful blood smeared across the platform base. Chairs sat askew around the edge, like the hunters had been watching them like animals in a zoo.

Rex's dark gaze caught mine, and he jerked his horns at the cage I'd been staring at.

Right. Time to make myself useful.

I sprinted to the enormous structure, eyeing the thick lock on the door. It looked stronger than even the chains holding the mages. "How do I get you out?" I called to the two males trapped inside.

"That fuckwit had a key." The spiky demon grunted, pointing towards a bloodied heap near my feet.

Ignoring the squishy wetness of his tactical clothing, I holstered my pistols and rummaged through his pockets. Finding the key, I quickly unlocked the bloodied cage.

The demons rushed out. The quiet shadow-walker limped off, heading for the door at the back. I didn't blame him; blood coated his midnight skin, and his arm hung at an unnatural angle. He was in no condition to stick around this war zone. I prayed to the goddesses he made it out OK.

The other demon stalked in the opposite direction. Charcoal skin contrasted with pearlescent spikes along his shoulders and spine. The same shiny spikes burst from the heart-shaped tip of his tail as he whipped it into a groaning hunter trying to crawl past him. It smashed into the man's face with a sickening slap.

"Wait!" I called. "The exit is that way." I pointed to the shutter behind us.

He eyed me over a spiked shoulder, pushing forward despite the injuries giving him a slight limp. "I have a certain hunter to retrieve first," he rumbled. "She can't escape me through something as mundane as death."

I shivered at the darkness in his low tone, but before I could try to convince him to get to safety, Alpha slammed into me, knocking me aside.

A pained howl pierced the din. I hit the ground, air exploding from my lungs.

Winded, I gulped a panicked breath, scrambling back.

Alpha snarled, clamping a skinny man in his jaws, shaking him viciously. Red seeped from my familiar's dark fur, dripping across the concrete. My ribs throbbed, like I could feel Alpha's wound even though I could hardly see it.

Rage burned through my shock.

Whipping the stolen pistol up, I fired at a hunter sneaking up behind my distracted familiar until the weapon clicked to empty.

Not a single round hit its mark.

"How is that so fucking easy in the movies!?" I snarled, throwing the gun at the male instead.

The scarred hunter winced as the metal connected with his shoulder, but he flashed me an arrogant smirk and swiftly raised a long blade, swinging at Alpha.

I called on my magic instead. Flames exploded from my hands, the light purple blazing in my periphery as I sliced out.

The man screamed as my fire whipped across his face, spinning him around. It spread quickly, swallowing his face and strangling his pained whimpers.

"Downstairs!" Rex roared, yanking on my attention.

At the far edge of the warehouse, the hulking charcoal demon limped down a half-hidden staircase. A few generals raced after him before the king himself followed. His gaze met mine before he disappeared, running over me in a quick sweep.

Tarek snapped the final mage's shackles, like the sturdy metal links were only paper clips. He, too, ran for the stairs, leaving me and Alpha, a final hunter in his jaws.

Alpha spat out the meaty torso and barked. "Come on. The tracker stone must be down there. We can't risk any of the rats grabbing a load and escaping out a back door."

"Go, stupid mutts. Attack!" a distant voice yelled.

Feral snarls flooded the cavernous space.

Alpha threw his head back and howled. A hair-raising sound that struck fear into my chest even though I knew he'd never hurt me. Lilac flames lit up his paws with a whoosh, flickering eerily off his silky fur.

Claws scrabbled across the concrete as huge black beasts spilled inside through the shutter.

The hell-mutts had been unleashed.

Chapter 46

Several beasts paused as the ferocious roar from Alpha reverberated through the cavernous warehouse.

"Attack them!" a robust male snarled. "Useless fucking runts." He lumbered inside behind them, a metallic whip cracking across one of the more hesitant hell-mutts. Blood poured down the poor beast's side, but the animal didn't even cry out.

Everything in me rebelled at the cruelty. Vengeance sang through my veins as I snarled, throwing flames before I could even process what was happening. It hit the hunter smack-bang in the crotch. He screamed, dropping his whip and going down in a tumble of lilac fire.

A few of the hell-mutts growled in my direction but didn't try to stop the demise of their handler. Instead, most of the beasts darted forwards to snap their jaws threateningly at Alpha. Some held back, pacing the edges of the fight, tails between their legs, looking confused more than anything.

Alpha dodged a set of lethal fangs and launched forwards, his sleek body at odds with the boxy muscle of the hell-mutts. He was larger than all of them, yet his slimmer build made him look twice as fast.

His jaws clamped around the scruff of a smaller beast before he jerked the creature aside, throwing it into another one leaping for him. The mammoth creatures collided in mid-air, whining and snarling as they hit the ground with a meaty thwack.

Alpha swung his head towards me with a bark. "Go! I've got these pups."

I tried to protest, but he was already lunging towards another beast with a ferocious growl, raking flaming claws through the air.

"You'd better not die!" I yelled, trying to shove down the fear and guilt gnawing on me as I ran for the staircase.

I descended into a darkened corridor sprayed with blood. Each door hung askew, as if something had smashed them open. Screams and snarls echoed through the long hallway, coming from the far end.

A memory superimposed across my sight. Recognition made my head swim as I staggered through the hallway. A whimper escaped my lips as I passed a battered door roughly a third of the way down, a cracked glass window inset at head height.

I *knew* I'd once been trapped behind it. Where my family had died. Cut and beaten in front of me before our captors had slit their throats. I'd watched my brother bleed out, choking on his own blood, strapped to a chair. Then my father. Before they'd shot my mother.

Their screams bounced around my skull.

Fragments of violence sliced into my mind in quick succession. Each painful memory a stab to my sanity. A small keening echoed around me as the images assaulted me in a sickening rush I couldn't fight.

I crashed into the wall, the weight of memories dragging me down. Battering me. Ghosts from the past pulling me towards them.

A familiar roar cut through the violent haze, making my heart squeeze for a different reason.

Rex.

I gritted my teeth through the onslaught. Taking a deep breath as I struggled my way back to the present.

What had happened to my family, to me, was horrific. No matter how hard I tried, I could never forget it.

The hunters had destroyed my past.

But they couldn't have my future.

"I'm sorry," I whispered, seeing the faces of my family in my mind, as I pushed shakily up from the wall. "I couldn't save you. I love you all so much."

I sent a silent prayer up to the goddesses for strength and staggered towards the sounds of violent agony.

I should have been searching each room for the tracker stones, but the thought of Rex hurt, or worse, dragged me down the corridor.

A door banged open, flying off its final hinge to shatter against the far wall. Lilac and black swallowed my hands in an instant, my heart racing as I slid to a halt. A familiar spiked demon limped into the corridor, cradling a woman in a lab coat in his arms, bridal-style.

"Sin, you vile beast, put me down!" She thrashed and screamed, knocking her clear-rimmed glasses askew, but he just grinned viciously down at her without stopping.

"Thanks for the rescue," he grunted as he barrelled past me. "Sorry I couldn't stick around for all the fun!" he called over a spined shoulder.

She was clearly a hunter, if the lab coat was anything to go by, but a small niggle of guilt wormed through me, like maybe I should have tried to stop him. They disappeared up the staircase before I could act on the crazy impulse.

I shook off the weird sympathy, running the rest of the hall-way. Only splinters remained from the end door. I stepped over the debris, cautiously joining the colourful crowd in a daze. Demons and hunters were everywhere, battling in pockets throughout the large room. It looked like some kind of prison, with cages lining the walls, filled with shouting demons.

Rage burned through me at the sight of so many more captives. Gritting my teeth, I launched a fireball, feeling the strain on my magic as a painful twinge in my chest. Lilac smashed into a hunter's back, but he'd already fired. Grell snarled as the bullet slammed into his torso.

My heart panged as the ruby demon fell to his knees, tentacles clutching at his side where the bullet had caught him. Coran grabbed his fallen comrade, dragging him off to the side as he pressed his hands to the wound, eyes widening in panic.

Cheered on by the caged demons, Rex's other generals scuffled with the last hunters. The bastards were already dead, as far as I was concerned.

I blew out a terrified sigh. It was almost over.

All I had to do was find the tracker stone and I was free.

"Let me through or I'll fucking kill the bitch!" a breathy voice snarled over the dying din.

My heart pounded as I stilled. I *knew* that voice.

Fenton held a pistol to a young woman's head as he dragged her in through a door set between two empty cells.

"Uncle!" the woman cried out, tears running down her cheeks. "I'm sorry, I-I should never have left with him."

Every demon in the room froze. The last hunter fell with a wet thump, loud in the aching silence.

Bruises and blood covered a slim waif. She couldn't have been older than eighteen. A faint aura of magic radiated from her, but a short set of black horns poked up through her crimson hair.

"Impossible," I breathed.

"Eve." Rex stepped forwards with a pained look on his blood-smeared face. "It's OK. Everything's going to be OK."

Realisation slammed into me.

Eve wasn't his lover. She was his niece. A young hybrid demon-witch, trapped in the hunter's clutches.

Trapped in *Fenton's* clutches.

"That's the piece of shit she was dating," Killian hissed, wings flaring at his back.

"More fucking trouble than you were worth, you useless slut," Fenton snarled, yanking on his hostage's loose curls with a vicious tug that had her crying out. "Should have doubled the price. Lousy fuck too."

Rex snarled, a vicious growl rumbling his chest, tension making his muscles pop beneath his blood-spattered skin.

Killian looked unhinged in his rage, eyes too wide. "You'll know pain like never before," he promised, voice silky with threat.

"You're all so fucking stupid, I love it," Fenton sneered, digging his gun harder into the witchling's skull, causing her to wince. "I'm a sin eater. I can end this bitch even without the spelled gun. A single bite of my magic and she's brain dead." He swung the gun across the semi-circle of demons as they tried in vain to sneak closer. His eyes narrowed on Rex as he paused, aiming right at the bristling grey demon. "I've seen you before."

His gaze swept through the wider room, zeroing in on me. His jaw hardened, a dark rage entering his soulless bronze eyes.

A smile split my lips, as vicious as the hate roiling inside me, seeping into my veins like poison. Like power. I gave him a tinkling wave. "Oh, hello, Fenton dear. Fancy seeing you here. Again."

I strolled towards him, feeling like a predator as I stepped over the corpses of my enemies.

We'd won.

And yet that one innocent witchling was trapped in a nightmare. As soon as Fenton made it to safety, he'd kill her. Put a bullet in her brain and dump her lifeless body.

Large eyes, the same bloodied shade as Rex's, met mine, terror evident in their glassy sheen. Purple already circled one of her wide orbs, ugly evidence of what she'd already suffered at the hands of Fenton and the hunters.

I couldn't let her face any more.

I might not have clawed my way out of here in one piece, but she could still go home to her family. She clearly had people who cared about her. Her whole life ahead of her. One in Rex's kingdom. I already knew the sort of leader he was. The sort of person he was. He'd never betray her. He'd never cast her out to suffer. To die. Alone.

She would grow up safe and cherished.

She would have a real future.

What did I have?

"Take me." The words were out of my mouth before I was aware I'd made a conscious decision.

"No!" Rex snarled, whirling to face me instead. Fear contorted his features.

I couldn't look at him.

I cleared my throat, the thickness of my emotions trying to choke me. "Leave her here and take me instead," I repeated.

Fenton cocked a sculpted brow. "Any why would I do that? A hostage is a hostage." He shook the witchling until she released another pained whimper, pulling the generals in my periphery up short.

Fenton glared at them in clear warning as he stepped towards the exit, keeping just out of reach of the captives trying to strike out through the bars. The witchling favoured one side as she limped along in front, nothing but a damaged shield to him.

Rex was too far away to do anything but watch.

I licked my lips, nerves jangling inside me. But a burning need to save the battered woman was stronger than any fear for myself. "I'm the only one who knows who you really are. What happens when you leave here without me? I'll lead all these bloodthirsty demons straight to your coven's territory." I stepped in time with the pair, angling between him and the only exit. "You can't afford *not* to take me with you."

One way or another, he was going to have to go through me to get out.

His handsome face was a mask of contempt. "Or I could just shoot you now and still have this bitch." He shook the witchling once more, but she must have braced for it, because no sound escaped her split lips.

I forced a smirk. "You think you can shoot me and get that pistol back to her head before one of these demons is already wearing your blood? You've seen how quick they move."

"Zoella, no," Rex pleaded, the agonised sound tearing something inside me. "Don't do this. We'll find another way." I ignored his imploring black gaze, unable to let myself sink into the safety he was trying to offer.

Fenton snarled like a rabid animal backed into a corner. "Fine. Come here."

I didn't hesitate, closing the gap as Fenton met me part-way, gun still pressed against Eve's red curls. I raised my hands, showing I was unarmed, as he released his grip on her hair to yank mine painfully instead. I swallowed back the hiss of pain that rose in my throat. He spun me, pressing my back to his front.

With a vicious kick to Eve's back, he sent her sprawling over the downed body of a poor demon missing half his face. Killian leaped forwards in a purple blur, pulling her up to safety and shielding her with his powerful frame.

I blew out a breath. She was safe.

My gaze found Rex at the far side of the room.

Anguish sculpted his features. "Little mouse... What have you done?"

Chapter 47

I swallowed, ignoring the burning in my scalp as Fenton tugged my hair tight, trapping me against his front. The edges of his magic raked against my mind in warning, like he'd reached beneath my skull.

I shuddered at the phantom pain, trying to remain calm despite the heavy thud of my battered heart smashing into my rib cage.

Fenton edged us towards the door. Rex moved with us, chest rattling with a feral growl.

Blunt metal dug into my temple as Fenton shoved the gun harder into me. It was an almost-welcome distraction from his insipid magic, despite the weird static energy crackling from the weapon. "Move again and I'll splatter her pretty face all over the fucking floor."

"It's okay." I held up a hand, urging Rex back. "I'm sorry. For everything. I..."

Fenton scoffed, the sound booming in my ear loud enough to make me wince. "You actually care for that beast? Did you spread your legs for an animal, Zo? I always knew you were a freak, but that is some sick shit."

Shame coloured my cheeks for a hot moment before anger replaced it. "Get fucked, you limp weasel. Rex is better than you in every way. He's perfect." My gaze bored into my demon's dark eyes.

There were so many things I should have said and done. I should never have let fear stop me from flinging my arms wide and embracing Rex with everything I had. I'd been convinced that taking things slow was the way to protect myself and see whether I could really trust Rex. But I should have listened to my heart and risked it all for happiness. For him.

Now I wasn't going to get the chance, but I wanted him to know I meant it. He *was* perfect, no matter what he'd been told by others in the past.

A loud snort echoed in my ear. "You're as stupid as these cash cows. My dad was right to get rid of your whole weak family. Nothing but hunter fodder."

Air turned to lead in my lungs. "You sold us out," I breathed, barely a whisper of sound wheezing past my lips at his sickening revelation. "That's how they knew exactly when and where to find us outside the coven wards..."

Fenton laughed, a deranged sound grating against my tightly wound nerves. "My family are the shepherds protecting the sheep. You think Quartz just runs itself? We did what was needed to keep the hunters off our back and the coven afloat. Not that you'd understand; the weak never do."

My head swam at the implications. I stiffened in his grip, struggling to take a full breath as he slowly dragged me closer to the exit. "But...you let me live. When I made it back...why?"

"I can't believe you managed to escape in the first place," he scoffed. "Personally, I wanted to bring you right back here, but the other sheep would have been suspicious. You didn't leave the damn territory for a year, and by then, you were too integrated. An unmatured mage isn't worth much anyway. If you ask me, the old man waited too long to finally get rid of you." He kicked the arm of a dead hunter as we shuffled past. "Though, these dumb fucks couldn't even grab you when we pointed them right at you."

Rage burned me up from the inside until I was a wildfire of anger. My whole family had been brutally murdered, and for what? An easy pay cheque? A tenuous agreement with our kind's sworn enemy?

I stilled, ignoring the vicious tug on my hair. "Your corrupt father is just as sick as you." Venom dripped from my tone.

"So dramatic. So stupid. You should have just bent over when I told you to," he hissed in my ear.

I saw the second Rex realised just who held me in his clutches.

His pained expression morphed into one of blinding fury. His jaws opened impossibly wide as he roared, tendons popping in stark relief along his neck.

Fenton swore, jolting at my back before his gun swung into my vision.

Boom. Boom. Boom.

Deafening blasts of gun fire exploded right by my face. My ears rang, pain spiking into my skull with each shot.

I screamed, the agonised sob wrenched forth as I struggled to process what I was seeing.

Navy bloomed across Rex's chest, right over his heart as the spelled bullets slammed into him. He might have survived regular shots, but these were *magic*.

Rex staggered, clutching his chest, but his infinite eyes calmly met mine, lips mouthing a single word. "Now."

Terror for Rex had me reaching for every ounce of fire I had left inside me, summoned from the depths of my soul.

Power flooded me.

Bright flames lit up the world, cocooning me in a wall of lilac and black. A shriek echoed behind me, piercing the fierce roaring of my magic.

I screamed back as claws raked into my brain, trying to tear apart my memories. Scrambling my thoughts. I clutched my head, feeling Fenton's grip on my hair give. I threw every ounce of rage I had into fuelling the fire that swallowed our bodies, relishing the sight of it working up to his face.

He snarled at me, frantically trying to slap out the flames burning his flesh while lashing out with his magic in painful whips. "Takin' you with me, bitch!"

Black spots swam through the purple across my vision. Agony bit through my skull, like phantom snakes striking my brain. I staggered, struggling to keep my feet under me, to keep my magic flowing despite the pain.

Fenton dropped to the ground, rolling amongst the blood. But my fire was magic. Oxygen didn't feed it. I did.

I bared my fangs with a snarl, fighting the pain shredding my focus, the exhaustion heaving my limbs. But I'd burned through too much magic earlier. My lilac fire dimmed, revealing sickening charred patches of Fenton's once golden skin.

No. He can't win. Not after all he's done.

My father singing to his plants. My mother meowing at her familiar. My brother laughing at his own jokes.

Thoughts of my family fuelled me as I unleashed the rage I'd kept buried for so long, pouring every ounce of pain and loss into strengthening my magic. For them. For Rex. For Alpha.

For me.

I lifted my inky claws, lurching onto Fenton's writhing form, flames swallowing us both.

With a final scream, I slashed.

His throat gave beneath my fingers in a hot spray.

Honeyed eyes dulled, reflecting the lilac flames dying down around us.

I staggered to my feet as the pressure in my skull let up, leaving a dizzying vertigo in its wake. A headache throbbed in time with my racing pulse, my mouth stuffed with cotton.

I turned my back on the past, facing my future.

The world swayed.

My grey demon staggered closer, almost tripping on a downed hunter. Pain etched into his features. Midnight blood ran freely from three ragged holes in his upper chest.

"Rex," I whined, but the ringing in my ears drowned out my voice.

I blinked, and the world stuttered.

Rex appeared above me, his powerful arms holding me at an odd angle, a ceiling light haloing his fiery hair and dark horns.

I frowned. Had I blacked out? Or was I dead?

"Little mouse," he whispered, black eyes swimming with emotion.

Warm liquid seeped into my top. I must be alive, because heaven wouldn't have my demon bleeding all over me. Or maybe I was finally in hell.

"Rex," I breathed, relishing the feel of his heat encasing me. I was tired. So damn tired.

I reached up, cupping his cheek. My pale skin looked almost peachy next to his ashen hue. He was warm, and real, and safe.

"I thought I'd lost you there." He swallowed thickly, a crazed panic creasing his features. "I'm sorry for being a stubborn bastard. Of course you'd want to start things slow. I shouldn't have pressured you so much to be as ready to commit as I was." He held my gaze, unwavering. "Little mouse... Can you ever forgive me?"

I shook my head, quickly blurting out the words as I watched his face fall. "No, Rex. I mean, *yes*. But I'm the one that should be sorry. I was too scared to listen to what my heart was telling me, and then I panicked and thought maybe you were just using me...and maybe you were seeing someone else." The rambling thoughts spilled out, and I blushed, feeling ridiculous all over again.

"Have I made it a secret?" His dark brow winged into its questioning arch. "How much I crave every drop of your pleasure? Of your blood? Your essence? You." I couldn't look away from the dark intensity of his gaze. "There is no one else in all the realms for me."

"I..." My lips parted and emptied all the thoughts from my already scrambled brain. I cleared my throat, struggling to re-grip my tumultuous emotions. The memory of how much it had hurt when I'd thought he'd betrayed me had me hesitating, even now. "You're a demon. You're always hungry for more."

His black eyes hardened, the unending abyss crystalising to obsidian. "You know me better than that. When have I ever taken what was not freely given, little mouse? What was not already mine?"

I opened my mouth again, but he cut me off.

"When I first worshipped your sweet cunt?"

His dark words sent a bolt of heat through me, despite the exhaustion dragging on me. I sucked in a sharp breath, but he wasn't done.

"When I first tasted the nectar in your veins? Or when you first moaned my name when I joined us as one?" His words were a growl, promising a lethal pleasure I wasn't sure I'd survive. "I still have nightmares of that single delicious moan. How you breathed my name like a prayer, like I was both sin and salvation and you were ready to throw yourself to my mercy."

"Nightmares?" For some reason, the word struck me.

His lips twitched in a knowing smirk. "Oh yes. The dark things I do to you after that needy moan couldn't possibly be something so innocent as dreams."

My teeth bit into my lower lip to hold back the breathless sound that tried to escape me. I swallowed, trying hard to keep the composure my dark demon seemed determined to steal.

"What? Nothing to say now? I thought my little mouse liked to squeak," he taunted, running a claw along my cheek as he held me up tenderly despite his ragged wounds.

"You know, a cornered mouse will go for the eyes," I murmured, staring into the abyss waiting hungrily for me. "What a shame that would be. A *blind*, ugly beast."

He grinned, a slow stretching of his full lips to show off his vicious fangs. "So fierce. So beautiful," he whispered, eyes glowing with darkness. "So brave."

My breath hitched. Not just at his words. But at the emotion churning behind his inhuman eyes. He was the only person to have ever seen my fire, and where others wanted to contain it, he encouraged it.

Every time he pissed me off, poked and prodded at me, he was feeding the flames within me, not trying to smother them like everyone else.

He cupped my cheek. "You are my fire in a world of darkness. Burn us both, my vicious witch."

Tears pricked the backs of my eyes. Someone was finally seeing me, darkness and all. Yet he wasn't running away or trying to change me. He was asking for more. For every broken, jagged part of me.

How could I have ever doubted the connection between us? Doubted him? Rex was everything I'd never known I needed. And more.

"Say you'll be mine, Zoella. My one and only, for the rest of my days." His voice roughened, hope and something darker swirling through his gaze. "We can call it whatever you like, but I can't lose you."

So what if being mates was new and scary? I trusted Rex to catch me if I fell.

He cradled me closer to his chest, sheltering me with his warmth.

I had already fallen.

"I'd be honoured to be your mate, Rex," I whispered. "I love you."

Joy like I'd never seen it lit Rex's features, bringing startling warmth to his shadowed face.

"And I you, little mouse. My mate. Forever."

His lips claimed mine, slow and sweet. My mind spun as his kiss scrambled all thought. There was nothing but him.

And that was all I needed.

Chapter 48

A throat clearing drew me out from the haze of love and lust. Rex pulled back from the drugging kiss, eyes locked on mine.

"Yes?" he asked, voice raspy like he'd just woken up.

Heat coloured my cheeks as the sound of metal screeching and murmuring voices penetrated. Almost all the captive demons had been released from their cages by Rex's generals, clearly having found the right keys while Rex and I had been...distracted.

"Uncle... You've been shot with spelled bullets..." An unsteady voice rolled between us, snapping my gaze down to the ragged wounds in Rex's chest.

I gasped, feeling a wave of guilt crash over me. "Oh my goddesses, we need to get you healed, not make out!"

His lips stretched into a lazy smile. "Worth it."

I scowled up at him, warning saturating my tone. "Rex."

He flashed fang in a toothy grin before standing us upright fully. I swayed slightly, my body screaming at me as my mind swam. Beneath the magic-induced headache, a light fogginess clouded my thoughts—no doubt an aftereffect from Fenton's vicious affinity. If I hadn't been a mage myself, I'd have been dead already. Thankfully, we held a slight resistance to most types of magic. Plus, being set on fire was a great distraction.

Still, I'd probably lost more than a few memories. Something I wasn't sure how to handle. It wasn't like I knew what he'd taken from me. It was just gone.

I shoved the worrying thought aside in favour of running my gaze over Rex's chest. Navy liquid still flowed from the three holes, right over his heart.

"You can heal this, right?" I asked, voice tightening.

Rex pursed his lips, glancing down as if only just noticing the open wounds. "Pah, a measly little chest wound?" He waved his claws, but my blood chilled at the near miss. If Fenton had aimed for his head, I'd have lost him. "The spelled bullets will slow things, but thankfully, it's not the first time I've been shot with them. This particular magic acts like a poison, but you can develop tolerance with exposure."

I frowned, only adding pressure to my already intense headache. "Who's been dosing you up with magical poison?"

"Um... That would be me..." A low feminine voice tentatively invaded our little bubble, and I belatedly realised it was the same one that had first interrupted us.

I smiled sheepishly as I turned to face the woman beside us. Rex had a way of devouring my attention.

My gaze was immediately drawn to the curious horns topping her head. They were smaller than any of the demons' I'd met so far, almost dainty in comparison. Stunning blood-red hair matched the intense shade of her large eyes, in true mage style, and both shone with a glossy sheen. Bruises littered her pale skin, and she held herself stiffly, but she looked defiant rather than broken.

I swallowed hard, feeling so dumb at how wrong I'd got the situation. I'd let paranoia and fear mess things up in my head, and it had almost cost me everything.

Rex squeezed me closer into his side, his warmth helping erase some of my awkwardness. "Eve, this is Zoella—my mate."

Eve's split lips stayed in their brittle line, but her bruised eyes widened a fraction.

"Zoella, this is the ungrateful succubus-witch runt I took in a few years back," he said, grinning at us both.

The demon-witch's fragile countenance cracked with Rex's teasing jab, revealing a genuine smile complete with a mischievous curve. A raspy huff fell from her split lips. "You're lucky you found me, old man. Think about how dull your kingdom would have been without me."

"I couldn't agree more." His bright smile dimmed a fraction as his expression turned earnest. "I'm glad you're safe, kid."

"Ugh, stop." She inspected her chipped red claws, as short as mine were, but her irreverent tone wavered slightly. "You're so emotional in your old age. It's embarrassing."

Rex snorted, muttering something in a demonic language under his breath that sounded suspiciously like swearing.

Eve ignored him and turned her attention to me in full, swallowing hard. "What you did..." She trailed off. "I can't thank you enough." Unshed tears swam in her eyes, causing my heart to ache.

I reached out, taking her icy hand and giving it a squeeze. "We witches have to stick together." I winked, trying to lighten the suffocating weight in the room. She had a lot to process after what she'd been through, and I couldn't help but want to lighten that crushing darkness, even if only temporarily.

Her smile turned knowing. "I think you're going to make a great queen."

I startled at her words, gaze snapping to Rex.

The wicked demon beamed, looking wholly unconcerned by the claim. "I couldn't agree more."

My mouth opened. Then closed. Then opened again.

Killian appeared behind Eve, staring down at her with a heavy mix of emotions. He dragged his gaze up to Rex, but I could tell it was hard for him to let Eve out of his sights.

"I believe our prodigal witchling is trying to heal you." Killian's tone was wry as he glared back down at Eve's crimson curls, like he could peek beneath her skull and learn all her secrets if he only stared hard enough.

My head cocked aside as I studied her, half confused, half in awe. "Aren't you too young to have affinity powers?"

"Don't you start." She huffed with a smirk. "I'm older than I look. Plus, I'm a hybrid."

"Huh. Well, by all means." I waved a hand at Rex's chest, trying to pry myself from his grip so she could get close enough to work her magic.

Healers were rare, the affinity highly prized amongst the mage community. Even with her demon heritage, how she'd ended up as an outcast in Rex's kingdom was beyond me. Unless she'd been born in hell rather than the human realm.

The sound of claws scrabbling against concrete stabbed tension through the room. Everyone stilled, bracing for an attack.

Except me.

I staggered towards the doorway as the bond in my chest thrummed hard.

Alpha bounded inside, barking and swinging his colossal head from side to side. "What happened? Where are the hunters?"

Relief flooded me at seeing him, even though I knew he was unhurt from the lack of pain ghosting through our shared bond. He felt as tired as the rest of us, but he'd battled through with only a few minor scrapes. The bullet wound to his side must have already healed.

I reached out, scratching behind his purple ear. "You're late—" A series of yips cut me off as a flurry of black blurs raced in behind him.

I gaped at the terrifying hell-mutts, bounding around playfully like puppies. One even nipped at Alpha's tail. The hellhound spun with an easy growl, casually swatting at the smaller creature.

From the corner of my eye, I spied several bewildered demons cringing back from the animals, but thankfully, nobody moved to attack.

"I managed to talk sense into some of my offspring." Alpha woofed, tail wagging happily behind him. "They've decided to join us."

I blinked, struggling to process his meaning even though it was magically translated straight through my thick skull. "Um. Your pups?"

He bared his fangs in a feral snarl, growling low. "Yes. Part of the reason they kept me alive."

My fingers clenched in the scruff of fur at the back of his long neck. My heart ached, but I could feel a warmth through the bond. Maybe being reunited with his offspring was a silver lining to an otherwise dark cloud.

"In that case, we're going to need a bigger hotel room." I stroked a hand along his head as I stared into the purple flames burning in his eyes, trying to radiate love and support through our connection.

"Done!" Eve declared just as a subtle magic on the air faded.

Rex grunted, ruffling her blood-red curls with a smirk. "Thanks, kid."

Relief hit me as I inspected the narrowed wounds on his chest. Only three small holes that appeared to have stopped bleeding.

"I'm a fully grown demoness." Eve scowled, slapping his hand away. "And next time, I'm going to turn you into a chubby bull-frog."

Rex snorted. "You youngsters have no respect for your elders. Your *king* no less."

"Pfft, you're an irritating uncle." She gave her hair a sassy flip over one shoulder, the ends brushing Killian's bare chest as he loomed over her. "At best."

Rex and Eve grinned manically at each other. My heart warmed at the wholesome sight.

"Boss, we need to head back. Eve's stopped the bleeding, but that big oaf needs rest to heal properly," Killian drawled, jerking his chin at Grell, but his lazy tone couldn't cover for the constant subtle looks he kept shooting towards a certain demon-witch. He hovered even closer to her, if that was possible. A muscled wall of tension and tattoos.

"I'm fine," Grell huffed from the corner of the room, even though he was clutching his side as he leaned heavily on Coran. Merlot blood splashed across his ruby-red skin, and I prayed most of it wasn't his.

I bit my lip. "You guys go ahead. There's something I need to do first."

"You're not leaving my sight." Rex's eyes narrowed on me before he turned to Killian with a knowing look. "Take everyone back and offer assistance to all the freed captives. Both demons and mages are welcome in the Hybrid Kingdom, should they choose to join us. I'll meet you in a few days. Please make sure my kingdom hasn't fallen apart in my royal absence."

Killian shook his head with a smirk. "Your kingdom practically runs itself, boss, but I'm sure your niece will keep us all in line."

Everyone filed out pretty quickly, Coran and Briar supporting a protesting Grell between them. I led Rex and Alpha on a search of the rest of the building, with Alpha's new family trailing haphazardly in our wake.

Several of the rooms we searched looked like budget labs, with glass and equipment everywhere. One even had a bloodied operating table and stained cuffs that had me shuddering in revulsion.

Just what kind of sick experiments had they been running here?

Luckily, one of the first rooms along the corridor held exactly what I'd been searching for. I had enough nightmare fodder as it was.

My throat tightened as I shouldered open the broken door, entering the small room beyond, barely a glorified cupboard. A series of basic metal shelves lined three walls, laden with smooth glass pebbles, each several inches long.

"Tracker stones," I breathed.

In the centre of the room, a glass basin rested on a pedestal. Filled with water, the bowl revealed a thick paper plastered along the bottom. It was a crude map well, used to locate the signature bearers through their trackers.

I skirted the basin, hurrying to the nearest wall.

The top two shelves on the left held glass stones in a deep ruby shade, seeming to vibrate with power. Most of the other trackers were lifeless ovals of hollow glass, clear as day. I hoped they were keeping the stones ready for future use, but I knew at least some of them would represent mages caught and killed, their replica signatures dying out alongside them.

On the second shelf down, a ruby pebble called to me, like a high-pitched note ringing through the fog in my mind.

Heart in my throat, I lifted the coloured glass up to the buzzing artificial light. It vibrated between my thumb and forefinger like a tuning fork, racing through my digits and along my arm to infiltrate my chest.

My face scrunched in discomfort, but I couldn't put it down.

"That's what they've been using to hunt you?" Rex asked, voice a husky rasp. He might have been healed by Eve, but I could tell he was just as exhausted as I was.

A tired exhale escaped my lips. "Yes. Such a small thing for something that's caused me so much trouble, huh?"

Rex narrowed his gaze on the tracker stone I held aloft.

Alpha growled. "How do we destroy it?"

"We break it." I glanced around the shelves filled with hundreds of tracker stones. "All of them."

I raised my hand high and threw the stone down with all the force I could muster. It smashed into the concrete and ruptured open, releasing a smoky red wisp, quickly dissipating as the shards turned clear.

Glass shattered, and it sounded like freedom.

But there was one more thing I needed to do before I could finally put my past to rest and embrace my future.

And for that, I had to go back to where it all started.

Chapter 49

"Not that you need my help, but I'll be right there with you." Rex's low voice rolled across me in a soothing wave, but anxiety still squirmed through my gut. "Nobody will hurt you, little mouse."

I flashed him a grateful smile, taking a single moment to admire his stunning features: from his proud double horns rising from a fiery halo to his burning eyes, so eye-catching amid his smooth grey skin and the surrounding greenery.

Alpha woofed at my side in agreement, warming my heart even more.

Behind us, ten of his hell-mutt pups frolicked beneath the leafy canopy of oaks and birches. The beasts ranged in size from an almost-cute Scottish terrier up to an intimidating Irish wolfhound. Alpha shot them a stern look and a low growl. They paused their play, stilling briefly. With a loud chuffing, they fell all over one another once more, tails wagging as they doggy-laughed at their sire.

Alpha barked, sterner this time. "Behave."

They ignored him completely.

How had these hounds gone from chasing me down, ready to tear me apart, to bouncing around like overgrown puppies?

But even their terrifying yet cute antics couldn't distract me.

Last night, we'd spoken with the remaining captives from the warehouse. Those who hadn't wanted to journey to Rex's kingdom, or needed to rest before making the long trip, had ended up checking into the same hotel as us. Rex, Alpha, and his pups had all filed into my room and I'd briefly cleaned myself up before climbing into bed. The need to talk over everything that had happened, and what was coming next, had been a nagging worry, but I was asleep before my head had even hit the pillow.

I'd woken up with Rex curled around me, his muscular body protecting mine even in sleep.

Alpha and his hell-mutt family had formed a huge puppy pile in front of the door, creating a sea of black fur, accented with the occasional splash of purples, blues, and reds. Some of which was probably blood.

I'd slept right through to the afternoon. We'd got takeout delivered and devoured our body weight in noodles while I'd steeled myself for what needed to be done.

I felt as energised as one could be the day after participating in a full-scale assault. Which was not much at all.

I took a deep breath, letting my burning need for vengeance fortify me. Since Fenton's confession, it had taken root in my heart, and it wasn't going to be so easily satisfied. Fenton may have been the reason I was kicked out of Quartz, but their leader—Elder Murray—was the monster responsible for it all.

If what Fenton had said was true, his father had arranged for my family to be tortured and killed by our sworn enemies. He'd kicked me out at the first opportunity and set the hunters after me again. But it wasn't just my family he'd betrayed.

This morning, I'd had time to look back at things in a new light. Along with Gregor, the mage I'd recognised in the warehouse, others had also disappeared not long after joining the coven. Most of us had assumed they'd left of their own accord. That their connection to the communal magic had severed because they'd died in some unknown way. Elder Murray had claimed to have found a few of them and removed their anchor marks, letting them move on to find new covens.

Now I knew the truth was likely far more sinister.

And I wasn't going to let the evil fucker orchestrating it all continue.

I pushed up my sleeves, revealing the poisonous, thorny plants wrapping my forearms. Diving into my magic, I sent it outwards, reaching for the surrounding trees. A connection thrummed to life, resonating deep in my chest with a strength that took my breath away. Their essence fuelled me, like they knew I needed their strength and were already agreeing to my unspoken cry for help.

I fought back the tears that threatened to gather. Was this how my father had felt when he'd connected to his cherished plants?

"Thank you," I whispered, drawing their energy into myself with an instinctual pull. It wasn't enough to harm them, but skimming from the collective forest was enough to stagger me under the mounting energy coursing through my body.

The power built higher and higher until I felt like I'd burst from channelling so much wild energy.

Alpha added his support, the bond between us helping filter some of the excess.

"Now." Alpha barked.

Trusting my familiar, I thrust my hands forwards, unleashing my flames. Lilac swallowed the air in front of me, glinting with edges of black. Haunting fire collided with the invisible ward and bit clean through it.

A sense of victory thrilled through me as I pulled back on my power.

"We're through!" I yelled, just loud enough to be heard over the crackling flames dying out in my palms.

Rex shot me a smug look. "Told you it would work. Now let's go see a mage about a murder." He bared his fangs in a feral grin, matching the vicious retribution swirling through me.

The three of us raced through the gap, trampling Lyndsey's wild herb garden as we ran towards the small settlement, blending with the distant trees. Grass gave way to packed dirt as we passed between rustic cabins. Almost identical, they had a two-storey square shape and angled roofs, interspersed amongst towering oaks. Within minutes, we hit an inner ring of commercial buildings, bustling with mages trading and working, going about their day.

"Demon!" a woman screeched as we entered the main square. Yolanda waved her arms, gesturing at some mages nearby. "We're under attack! Get help!"

Panicked voices joined the fray, gasping and yelling as mages rushed around in a disorganised mess.

Rex waved at the terrified mages like a pageant queen. I rolled my eyes with a snort.

We slid to a halt in front of a decorative pond in the centre, an ancient willow sipping from its edge.

The senior witch tried to call on her water affinity, but the pond merely stirred in her panic, churning and bubbling like a kraken thrashed below the surface.

"Wait!" I snarled as more mages poured from the nearby streets, hands outstretched. "Where's Murray?"

"Zo?" A familiar voice had my breath stuttering. I tried to stem the flow of emotions as Lyndsey hurried through the small crowd, tucking a mossy curl behind her ear with a frown. "What are you doing here?" Her eyes widened as she took in the bristling demon and snarling hellhound flanking me.

I raised my voice over the din of anxious mages. "You've been lied to for years. Elder Murray sold out my family to the hunters."

Shocked gasps detonated from the wary onlookers, followed by immediate denials.

"Why in the name of the goddesses would I do such a thing?" A booming voice preceded the serpent himself.

The coven leader stepped out from behind a nearby cabin. He was almost the spitting image of his golden son but with greying temples, a few wrinkles, and a darker complexion. He strode confidently towards me despite the threats loaded on either side of me.

His gaze raked my exposed arms, lip curling at the sight of my ink. I'd always known how much he despised tattoos. It was one of the reasons I'd covered them up so religiously. But no more.

Bone-deep rage blazed through me at the sight of him. I sneered, "For power and greed, I imagine."

Deathly neutral, he merely raised an unimpressed brow. "Is that so? And what evidence do you have of this ludicrous accusation? Might I remind you that your last one landed you in quite a bit of trouble."

The way he talked down to me only riled me up further. I could feel the thrum of the surrounding trees lending me their strength even after all they'd already gifted me.

The urge to just burn him to a crisp was strong. But I wanted the coven to *know* how blind they'd been. Nobody should mourn the evil that had twisted their lives.

I called on the grand willow rising beside the water, thickening the bond between us as I summoned its aid. Dark roots burst up from the earth, wrapping around the arrogant leader's ankles like snakes.

A few cries of protest sounded from the crowd, but Elder Murray merely sneered at the woodsy shackles trapping him, feigning a confidence he would regret.

"Your son confessed it," I hissed.

Uncertainty tripped across his features in a brief blip before he settled on a scowl. "Don't be ridiculous, you spoiled little girl."

"You've seen Fenton?" Lyndsey asked from the front of the gathered mages, borderline desperate. "Where is he?"

I ignored her in favour of the puppet master. "You and him have been selling out new mages that join Quartz, giving them up to the hunters for a healthy pay cheque." I turned my attention to the crowd. "Why have there not been any new mages that stayed? Are you really so wretched to newcomers that they all leave within weeks?"

Murmurs rippled through the crowd, a seed of doubt taking root.

Now for my trump card.

"Gregor? Please join us," I said, raising my voice over the din.

Surrounded by Alpha's rowdy offspring, the battered animal mage inched past the cabins, entering the square. Cuts and bruises littered every visible inch of him, but he already looked better after a night of rest and spending time with the hell-mutts. Oddly gentle-natured, the hounds had offered him snippets of their energy to help him heal despite all they'd gone through at human hands.

Everyone fell silent as the mage came to stand skittishly behind Alpha. He cleared his throat. "It's true." His vocal cords were raspier than before, damaged from weeks of screaming. The reminder knifed through my chest, threatening to draw tears. "I was picked up after Elder Murray sent me on an errand into the city."

"Lies!" Elder Murray hissed, trying to yank his foot from the bindings, but I held him fast. "Look at them, cavorting with evil! They cannot be trusted."

"You murdered my family." Flames swallowed my arms as I unleashed the rage inside me. "They trusted you. We all did."

Pain slammed into my skull as lethal magic clamped around my brain. I screamed, thrusting out my hands. A torrent of purple fire raced across the pond towards the monster, fuelled by grief and rage, and the power of the trees connected to my soul. Alpha leaped, colliding with the twisted male. Bone snapped at the impact, and a high-pitched wail rent the air.

Rex turned and punched someone in the face, roaring at the crowd to stay back as he kicked someone else down.

Elder Murray screamed again, trying to smack at the hellhound as Alpha ravaged the mage's thigh. Flames devoured the corrupt leader, passing across Alpha without harm.

In seconds, it was over.

My head throbbed. Liquid dripped down my nose. I swiped away the blood, trying to focus through the pain. The trees soothed away some of the ache, and I thanked them before ending our connection. The willow's roots released what remained of Quartz's elder.

Shocked silence echoed through the clearing, accented by the sickening, oily stench of burned flesh.

"Goddesses...," Lyndsey choked. "Zoella, help! Please!"

I turned to find her trembling in Rex's hold. He gripped the traitorous witch around her throat. Small hands, glowing an anaemic green, scrabbled at the grey hand holding her in place.

"This one tried to attack you while your back was turned," Rex growled, eyes black with his need for violence. "Want me to snap her tiny bird neck?"

Lyndsey whimpered, the magic at her hands fizzling out. Wide eyes pleaded with me. "No! Please, Zo. I-I never meant to hurt you. We're family, remember?"

I stiffened, old hurts rearing their ugly heads. "You're as bad as him." I gestured to the burned remains on the opposite side of the pond. "You knew Fenton was selling *people* to the hunters. And you did nothing. You betrayed us all. And for what?"

Exhaustion hit me as all my rage drained in a rush. I stared blankly into her teary moss-coloured eyes.

"I never knew they were selling mages from our own coven!" she protested, trying in vain to loosen Rex's hold.

The demon quirked an unimpressed brow down at his prey. The other mages just watched on, imprisoned in silence.

Her words slid right off me. I felt oddly hollow. Maybe I should have had some kind of emotional response, but only a soul-deep weariness remained. That and the mother of all headaches, despite the infusion from nature.

What did her words matter now, anyway? Lyndsey had already shown what a monster she truly was.

"Leave her. She's not worth it."

Rex released her with a shove. Lyndsey tumbled into the shallow pond with a splash.

He bared his fangs in a wicked grin. "Whoops."

My lips twitched at his demonic antics. The prissy witch spluttered as she resurfaced, wet hair sticking to her face like seaweed. With a wary glance at Rex, she remained sprawled in the water, stilling like a frightened rabbit.

Yolanda stepped forwards, holding her palm to her mouth as she stared at Gregor, a picture of horror. "Goddesses... I... I had no idea. *Gregor*." Anguish twisted her strong features. She turned to me. "For what it's worth, Zoella, I'm sorry. We were blind to the evil within our own ranks, and you suffered for it. If you want, we can finish the induction and initiate you fully. Come home. Let us protect you as we should have from the start."

The sincerity in her tone, along with the pained nods and murmurs of agreement from others in the crowd, helped heal a little of the damage inside me. But this wasn't the future I wanted.

"Remove the anchor. This was never my home."

She nodded, understanding softening the faint lines of her face. "Then all I can do is thank you for your courage, in coming back here and ridding us of the corruption in our midst." Her hand glowed a stunning aqua shade, and the mark etched into the centre of my chest stung like a thousand tiny ants nipped at my skin. Muttering low, she clenched her fingers into a fist as she tore her palm away.

It felt like she'd ripped a tree out of my chest by its roots. I grimaced, hissing at the sharp burn.

Warm fingers threaded with mine. I looked up at my dark demon, concern swimming in his fiery gaze.

I'd severed the final tie to the past. This place, these people, had no hold over me now.

A wicked grin stretched my lips, and he matched it perfectly. Already, I felt strangely lighter.

Revenge wouldn't bring back my family, but I hoped I could find peace in knowing that the man responsible couldn't tear apart any more innocent lives.

"My fierce mate," Rex murmured, burning eyes filled with devotion. "Let's go build a new home. Together."

Epilogue

One month later...

Tonight was the night.

Finally.

Ebony-like trees swayed around me, cheering me on as their auburn leaves rustled in the light breeze. The scents of nutmeg and something fresh I couldn't name filled the air, giving everything a light spice. Playful currents tugged at the loose wisps of my hair like lilac ribbons floating around me. Fading rays of sunlight kissed my skin as dusk settled over the Bloodwood. Despite nearing Autumn, the air was mild, though rather unsurprisingly, hell was hotter than England.

A smile tugged at my lips.

My connection to nature buzzed inside my chest. The foreign sensation of the surrounding trees only added to the nerves already making me jittery. I twisted my hands in the thick material of my gown. The soft fabric was unlike anything I'd ever owned, a silky ivory accented with delicate lace.

The sleeveless dress bared my ink for all to see.

Alpha barked, padding along beside me on silent paws as we wound through the unearthly woods. "Quit worrying. You've been through the Bloodwood many times before."

The dangers of the forest weren't what had me on edge, and he knew it. Alpha wasn't wrong though. At this point, I was spending more time in the Hybrid Kingdom, on the edge of the deadly forest where Rex had been abandoned as a child, than I was in Riverside.

I'd been nervous as a chicken in a pie factory, but Rex had taken my hand and led me through a swirling portal not long after we'd confronted—well, *murdered*—my old coven leader. We'd had to fight our way through a squadron of demons from the neighbouring kingdom, guarding the portal, before making it safely into Rex's territory.

Since then, Rex had brokered an uneasy truce with the kingdom next door, regularly trading some of the rare poisons that grew within the Bloodwood for free use of the portal. Nowadays, it was only time we lost, rather than blood, to cross between the realms.

Ultimately, Rex had been right all those months ago. The hunters couldn't reach me here.

Who knew hell would be the best place for a covenless witch?

But it was more than that. Hell was a world full of charm and wonder. Sure, it had dangerous beasts, and even more dangerous demons, but I'd loved every moment Rex had spent showing me his home.

I grinned at my familiar, reaching up to smooth a palm between his triangular ears. Alpha being bigger than some horses I'd seen, his flaming purple eyes reached almost to my chin. He peered up at me with what I'd come to recognise as his stern look.

"How did I get so lucky to be blessed with such a loyal familiar?" I scratched behind his purple ear, cooing to my noble beast.

He bared his fangs in a canine grin. "Loyal and fierce."

I snorted, a small giggle filling the woods as I ruffled his fur. "Not to mention humble."

The hellhound uttered a rumbled series of barks. "One of my many supreme talents." He lifted his nose in a snooty fashion with a yip. "You're welcome."

I shook my head at his antics. Over the past month, we'd gone a long way to making up for time lost, spending most days together, helping each other heal.

If anything, today wasn't just about me. It was about him too. I wanted him to be safe and happy in his homeland. I wanted him to be free. To enjoy all the things he'd missed out on during his decade of captivity.

My heart squeezed every time I thought of it, but I didn't want the past to ruin today's celebration.

Not to mention his hell-mutt pups had been uncontrollably excited as soon as they'd stepped their massive paws through the portal here. They'd quickly formed their own pack in Rex's territory within the Bloodwood. With Alpha as their leader, of course.

Excitement hastened my steps as I neared the glowing fairy lights strung through the low branches up ahead.

I twisted my mother's silver ring on my index finger to steady me. The belladonna flower was a symbol of love from my father. I wished more than anything that my parents, my brother, could be here with me today, but I knew they would be proud of me, of the decisions I'd made. They'd have loved Rex too. Especially my fierce mother. I folded away my longing, letting thoughts of my family give me strength rather than anguish.

A buzzing crowd appeared through the trees. Colourful demons in all shades of the rainbow, with horns, tails, wings, spines, scales, tentacles. The list was endless. They were a beautiful mismatch of features that would stand out even amongst most of demonkind.

All Rex's generals were there, fierce grins on their faces. Grell was back to full health and as irritating as ever.

Eve gave me a huge smile and an enthusiastic wave that had her crimson curls bouncing as I neared. I'd loved getting to know Rex's mischievous niece over the past month, bonding over shared lessons where I taught her new spells and she taught me about demonkind. We'd even started our own grimoire together. Almost all her wounds had healed now. At least, those on the outside.

My gaze finally zeroed in on my favourite hybrid. The formidable monster waited at the front of the gathered demons. Like most days, Rex was bare-chested. Three round scars over his heart, where Fenton had shot him with magic poisoned bullets, were the only interruption to his smooth slate skin. The scars were a reminder of how much Rex had been willing to sacrifice to save me. I traced them every night so I'd never forget—when he told me forever, he meant it.

Today, a stiffer, tailored version replaced his usual black trousers. A necklace of fangs and claws rested over his collarbones, only adding to his feral visage. His arrowhead tail swayed from side to side, peeking above his broad shoulders. His horns shone glossier than usual, like a dark crown upon his fiery hair.

As soon as he caught sight of me, he stilled. His eyes darkened from glowing coals to a black night as he took me in from head to toe. His full lips parted, giving me a peek at his fangs.

A self-conscious blush stole across my cheeks, but I squared my shoulders, continuing my steady pace towards him.

The demons, his subjects, made space for the two of us in the middle of the clearing.

An elderly female, with stunning silver hair tied up in flowing braids, eased from the crowd, standing at the wooden altar behind Rex. It reminded me of the one my old coven had used, an ancient tree stump worn by nature and time. Unlike Quartz's blackened one, this altar was a healthy, rich bark, the surface gleaming with dried sap like polish.

"Today we celebrate the mating bond between our king and his chosen, Zoella, our fierce Witch Queen," the priestess began, her melodic voice perfectly matching her waifish elegance.

The crowd roared, and I squeaked in alarm, almost stumbling a step before Alpha pressed into my side. I flashed Rex a sheepish grin that he returned with a broad baring of fangs. Of course he'd seen me startle, like the mouse he'd accused me of being all those months ago.

The demons stomped their feet, causing the ground to shake with the force.

Before, it might have intimidated me, but now I had my future waiting before me, and nothing was going to get in my way. From today, Alpha and I were officially moving in with Rex, here in hell. I wasn't yet sure what I was going to do with my life—besides loosely act as a "queen," which, to my relief, I'd been told was more of a ceremonial title. Thanks to the handsome devil before me, though, I finally had the freedom to choose. To figure out what I wanted, without what my magical affinity would dictate for me or the constant fight for survival.

Rex hadn't stopped staring, his gaze a heated caress as I strode towards him.

As we drew close, Alpha yipped and nosed my shoulder. "You've got this." His flaming purple eyes seemed a little too shiny before he joined the front of the crowd, beside a gaggle of hell-mutts panting happily and wagging their tails.

Who knew hellhounds could be so emotional?

I blew out a nervous breath, coming to stand before Rex. His black-as-sin gaze filled with silvery glints like shooting stars as he captured my hands in his warmth. His strong fingers threaded through mine, giving me a reassuring squeeze.

"King Rexar, do you vow to bind yourself to your chosen mate, Zoella, from now until your flesh returns to the land?" the priestess asked, breaking me from Rex's spell. "Do you vow to protect and cherish her? To breed her and keep her?"

I blinked at the wording, but Rex had warned me that the demon mating ceremonies were a little different from the human-style marriages mages favoured.

He grinned, an expression of joy suffusing his handsome features as he held my gaze, unblinking. "I vow it."

The crowd roared their approval, their voices deafening for a heartbeat before the priestess raised her palm. Silence descended.

"And you, Zoella, do you vow to bind yourself to your chosen mate, King Rexar, from now until your flesh returns to the land? Do you vow to protect and cherish him? To breed him and keep him?"

A smirk twitched my lips. A part of me had worried the wording for my part would be different. Demons were many things—violent, bloodthirsty, sometimes monstrous or cruel—but they weren't usually sexist.

Rex seemed to hold his breath. All that powerful muscle tensed as he embraced my small hands in his, frozen before me.

How could he doubt what my answer would be?

"I vow it."

A grin broke across his features, his expression brighter than the moon. He pulled something from his pocket, holding it up between us.

"For you," he murmured, low tone rolling out over the hushed crowd.

A ring glinted between his clawed fingertips, tiny and delicate in his grasp. Stunning flowers adorned the silver band, their arrow-shaped petals reminding me of Rex's tail. The antique style was an exact replica of my mother's belladonna ring.

"Beastbane," he whispered, eyes burning with intensity. "Our deadliest flower here in the Bloodwood, yet the most beautiful."

I blinked rapidly, eyes swimming with moisture. That Rex would honour my family like this meant more than I could express with words. I swallowed back the urge to sob at his thoughtfulness. "It's perfect, Rex. They'd have loved it. They'd have loved you."

I lifted my hand, and he slid the precious metal onto my ring finger with a heart-stopping grin. He threaded our fingers and raised our joined hands, proudly displaying his gift. The crowd roared in response.

"Then let us bear witness to the most auspicious of bondings, our great King to his beloved, Queen Zoella the Fierce!" the priestess boomed, her gentle voice turning ferocious enough to carry over the whooping demons gathered in the clearing.

Rex hooked his tail around my waist, yanking my body firmly against his front. His lips descended, stealing my breath as he kissed me until I was dizzy, drunk on the very essence of him. The world ceased to exist as he conquered my mouth with his sweet dominance.

I gasped for air as he released me, gazing down at me with such adoration, such love, that tears threatened to overflow. I'd never felt so much joy as I did in this moment, gazing up at the man I loved.

We were bonded as one. Mated. Forever.

Happiness swelled through me until I thought I'd burst, radiating from me like I was the sun. The same joy reflected in the dark gaze of my monster.

My mate leaned down, spanning the inhuman size difference to hover his lips inches from mine once more. "You know… There is one demonic custom I haven't mentioned…" A devious glint filled his black eyes.

I quirked a brow, waiting for whatever delicious madness he was about to indulge in. I'd learned so much about him in the past weeks, everything from how his favourite colour was apparently the lilac of my eyes, he had a slight allergy to groundnuts, and demons didn't even have last names.

I'd seen first hand how he ran his kingdom here in hell with an open welcome for all hybrids, creating a safe space for those abandoned by the rest of their kind. Really, he was just *very* good at seeing the value in outcasts like me.

He licked his full lips, like he was preparing to devour me. "At a mating ceremony, one mate usually chases the other down and takes them beneath the stars."

I swallowed hard, too many primal fantasies running through my brain to latch onto any single one.

"How very demonic of you," I whispered against his sweet lips. "But you'd never catch me."

His eyes flashed. "Run, little mouse."

I pressed my lips to his, a forceful kiss of my own making. "Go to hell."

With a wink, I turned and fled, laughing as I raced through the crowd of cheering demons, gown swishing around my legs.

Rex's smoky chuckle chased after me. "I'll always catch you, Zoella!"

I'd be one lucky witch.

Afterword

I'd just like to take a moment to thank you for reading this saucy tale!

If you want more of Rex and Zo, then sign up to my newsletter at <u>sakurablackbooks.com/subscribe</u> for the exclusive bonus epilogue – Cherries and Blueberries – which features Rex chasing down his witch queen after their mating ceremony. Warning: it's pretty steamy!

As an indie author, it would mean so much to me if you could please leave a review. This helps other readers to find my wild stories and take a chance on me so I can keep on writing and working towards my dream of becoming an author full-time (my day job is way too sensible for me!).

The next instalment of the Playing with Demons series will feature Sin and his hunter. Capturing Sin is a sizzling, captive enemies-to-lovers standalone romance.

Acknowledgements

A huge thank you to my editor, Lyss, for her brilliant suggestions and all of her help.

I'd also like to thank my awesome beta readers – Mandy, Summer, Christy, Amber and Chauncey. Not only was your input invaluable, but having you guys tell me you enjoyed it (despite all the tweaks needed) was the morale boost I needed during the marathon that was getting my first full novel over the finish line.

My ARC team has been amazing, and I'd like to thank them for their support in getting this book in front of more great readers like yourself.

And finally, I'd like to thank coffee – you were always there when I needed you.

Also By Sakura Black

Fae Mate Hunt Series *(complete)***:** A spicy reverse harem monster romance novella series

0.5 – <u>The Nymph's Dark Pleasure</u>

1 – <u>Selected for the Shifters</u>

2 – <u>Hunted by the Minotaur</u>

3 – <u>Burning for the Fire Nymphs</u>

4 – <u>Fleeing the Feline King</u>

5 – <u>Their Concubine Queen</u>

1-5 – <u>Fae Mate Hunt: Complete Series Collection</u>

Monster Mate Hunt Series: A spicy reverse harem monster romance novella series

1 – <u>Rattled</u>

2 – <u>Get Foxed</u>

3 – <u>The Stones for It</u>

4 – <u>Reeled In</u>

5 – <u>Their Crown Jewels</u>

Playing with Demons Series: A spicy demon romance connected standalone series

1 – <u>Take Me to Hell</u>
2 – <u>Capturing Sin</u>
3 – <u>Hellish Witch</u>

For all the latest book release information, subscribe to Sakura's newsletter at <u>sakurablackbooks.com</u> and for a limited time, get a FREE bonus short story – The Nymph's Dark Pleasure – the prequel to Selected for the Shifters, all about Newbury's hot night with a dark stranger. Warning: it's a steamy one!

About the Author

Sakura Black is a writer of steamy fantasy and paranormal romance, often dreaming up wild stories about frightfully sweet monsters and the women they're lucky enough to fall horns over tail for.

For more saucy action head to sakurablackbooks.com

You can also find Sakura's Author Page on <u>Amazon</u> or reach out on <u>Instagram</u> / <u>Facebook</u> / <u>TikTok</u> @sakurablackbooks - she loves hearing from readers (but is crap at social media so the best place to find her is her <u>Newsletter</u>)!

www.ingramcontent.com/pod-product-compliance
Lightning Source LLC
Chambersburg PA
CBHW050112120726
47904CB00004B/1314